WAS

P9-CKS-010

3 1235 03732 3909

**Praise for *New York Times* bestselling author
Jill Shalvis**

"Riveting suspense laced with humor and heart
is her hallmark and Jill Shalvis always delivers."
—*USA TODAY* bestselling author
Donna Kauffman

"Romance does not get better than a Jill Shalvis
story."
—*Romance Junkies*

"Shalvis firmly establishes herself as a writer
of fast-paced, edgy but realistic romantic
suspense, with believable and likable supporting
characters and fiercely evocative descriptive
passages."
—*Booklist*

"For those of you who haven't read Jill Shalvis,
you are really missing out."
—*In the Library Reviews*

"Danger, adrenaline and firefighting heat up
the mix in Jill Shalvis's blistering new novel."
—*RT Book Reviews* on *White Heat*

"Jill Shalvis displays the soul of a poet with her
deft pen, creating a powerful atmosphere."
—*WordWeaving*

Damaged Noted

Stain on
edge 5/16/15
WOLS read SP?

New York Times and *USA TODAY* bestselling author **Jill Shalvis** is the award-winning author of over four dozen romance novels. Among her awards are a National Readers' Choice Award and a prestigious RITA® Award. Visit jillshalvis.com for a complete book list and a daily blog chronicling her *I Love Lucy* attempts at having it all—the writing, the kids, a life…

New York Times Bestselling Author

Jill Shalvis

FIREFIGHTERS

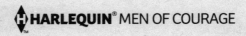

If you purchased this book without a cover you should be aware that this book is stolen property. It was reported as "unsold and destroyed" to the publisher, and neither the author nor the publisher has received any payment for this "stripped book."

Recycling programs
for this product may
not exist in your area.

ISBN-13: 978-0-373-60975-8

Firefighters

Copyright © 2014 by Harlequin Books S.A.

The publisher acknowledges the copyright holder
of the individual works as follows:

Flashpoint
Copyright © 2008 by Jill Shalvis

Flashback
Copyright © 2008 by Jill Shalvis

All rights reserved. Except for use in any review, the reproduction or utilization of this work in whole or in part in any form by any electronic, mechanical or other means, now known or hereinafter invented, including xerography, photocopying and recording, or in any information storage or retrieval system, is forbidden without the written permission of the publisher, Harlequin Enterprises Limited, 225 Duncan Mill Road, Don Mills, Ontario, Canada, M3B 3K9.

This is a work of fiction. Names, characters, places and incidents are either the product of the author's imagination or are used fictitiously, and any resemblance to actual persons, living or dead, business establishments, events or locales is entirely coincidental.

This edition published by arrangement with Harlequin Books S.A.

For questions and comments about the quality of this book, please contact us at CustomerService@Harlequin.com.

® and TM are trademarks of the publisher. Trademarks indicated with ® are registered in the United States Patent and Trademark Office, the Canadian Intellectual Property Office and in other countries.

Printed in U.S.A.

CONTENTS

FLASHPOINT

To the readers of my daily blog.
Having you there with me on my *I Love Lucy*
adventures makes my day, every day.
This firefighter's for you.

PROLOGUE

"Now's your shot with me, Zach. I say we get naked."

Exhausted, filthy, Zach Thomas still managed to lift his head and stare at Cristina. "What?"

Just as filthy, she arched a come-hither brow streaked with soot, which made it difficult to take her seriously. So did the mustache of grime. "You and me," she said. "Naked. What do you think?"

He couldn't help it; he laughed. He thought that she was crazy. They both wore their fire gear and were dragging their asses after several hours of intense firefighting. All around them, the stench of smoke and devastation still swirled in thick gray clouds, penetrating their outfits, their skin. Nothing about it felt sexy.

"Hey, nobody laughs at my offer of sex and lives," she told him. "Not even you, Officer Hottie."

When he grimaced at the nickname, she laughed. "You doing me tonight or not?"

Sex as a relaxant worked—generally speaking, sex as anything worked—but Zach was so close to comatose he couldn't have summoned the energy to pull her close, much less do anything about it once he got her that way. "I can't."

"Now we both know that's a lie."

Firefighting left some people exhilarated and pumped with adrenaline. Cristina was one of them.

Normally he was, too, but they'd just lost a civilian—an innocent young kid—and he couldn't get that out of his head. "I can't," he repeated.

Cristina sighed. She was in her midtwenties, blond, and so pretty she could have passed for an actress playing a firefighter, but she was the real deal, as good as any guy on the squad. She was also tough-skinned, cynical and possessed a tongue that could lash a person dead without trying.

He should know; he'd been on the wrong end of it plenty of times. So he braced himself, but she just sighed again. As sardonic and caustic as she could be, they really were friends. Twice they'd been friends with benefits, but it had been a while. She let it go, rolling her eyes at him, but moving off, leaving him alone.

He stood there a moment more, surrounded by chaos, his gear weighing seventy-five pounds but feeling like three hundred as the radio on his hip squawked. Allan Stone, their new chief, was ordering everyone off the scene except the mop-up crew, who would stay through what was left of the night to make sure there were no flare-ups. Tommy Ramirez, the fire inspector, was already on scene, his job just beginning.

Zach's crew was slowly making their way to their respective rigs. He needed to move, as well, but his gut was screaming on this one—someone had set this blaze intentionally. Unfortunately, it wasn't the first time he'd suspected arson when no one else had. Even more unfortunately, the last two times he'd thought so, he'd been reprimanded by Tommy for having an "authority" issue.

He didn't.

Okay, maybe he had a *slight* authority issue, sometimes, but not tonight.

He could ask Aidan what he thought but Zach knew what his firefighting partner and best friend would say. *Grab a beer, a woman and a bed, in any order.* And if Zach called Cristina back, he could knock out two of the three. Yeah, that was what he should do.

So why he headed toward the burned-out shell of a house instead, he had no idea, except that he trusted himself enough to know something was off here.

Something big.

And he couldn't just walk away from it.

He never could.

CHAPTER ONE

BROOKE WAS A VIRGIN. Not in the classic sense of the word—that status had changed on her seventeenth Halloween night when she'd dressed as an evil, slutty witch and given in to a very naughty knight in shining armor—but that was another story.

She was a *California* virgin, but as she drove up the coast for the first time and into the small town of Santa Rey, she lost that cherry, as well.

Santa Rey was a classic West Coast beach town, mixing the best elements of Mexico and Mediterranean architecture, all within steps of the beach shimmering brilliantly on her left. There were outdoor cafés, shops and art galleries, skateboarders and old ladies vying for the sidewalks with surfers and snotty tourists, and if she hadn't been so nervous, she might have taken the time to enjoy it all more.

She took a last glance at her quickly scrawled directions, following them to Firehouse 34. Parking, she peered through her windshield at the place, nerves wriggling like pole dancers in her belly.

A new job as a temp EMT—emergency medical technician.

One would think that after all the moves and all the fresh starts she'd made in her lifetime that *new* would be old hat to her by now, but truthfully she'd never quite gotten the hang of it.

The Pacific Ocean pounded the surf behind her as she got out of her car. The hot, salty June air brushed across her face as her nerves continued to dance. What was it her mother had said every time she'd uprooted them to follow yet another get-rich-quick scheme or new boyfriend or some other ridiculous notion?

It will be okay. You'll see.

And though her mother had been wrong about so many things, somehow it really had always been okay. Today would be no different. The azure sky held a single white puffy cloud hanging high over a dreamy sea dotted with whitecaps and a handful of sailboats. Three-foot waves hit the sand, splashing the pelicans fishing for their morning meal. Nice…if she had to make yet another new start, this didn't seem like such a bad way to go.

Hitching her bag up on her shoulder, Brooke started toward the station, a two-story brick-red structure with white trim and a yard filled with grass and wildflowers swaying in the breeze.

In the huge opened garage sat three fire trucks and an ambulance. One wall was lined with equipment such as hoses and ladders.

Surfboards leaned against the outside of the building. Oak trees dotted the edge of the property, and between the two largest, near the path to the front door, a man swung on a large hammock.

A man with broad shoulders, long legs and the unmistakable build of an athlete. His boots lay on the grass beneath him, as well as a discarded button-down shirt, leaving him in blue uniform pants slid just low enough on his hips to reveal a strip of black BVDs. His white T-shirt invited the general public to bite him. He had his hands clasped behind his head, and a large straw hat covered his face. His stillness suggested he was deeply asleep.

She slowed to a tiptoe, trying not to stare but failing. She was petite, and therefore constantly had to prove to people how strong she could be, but she'd bet he'd never had to prove anything; even from his prone position, he radiated strength and confidence. Of course that long, tough body didn't hurt, with all that aesthetically pleasing sinew defined even as he snoozed.

She envied the nap. She couldn't remember the last time she'd taken one. Or the last time she'd taken a moment to just lie on a hammock and soak up the sun.

Or even just to breathe, for that matter.

A lot of that came from being raised by a wild child of a mother, with little to no stability or security. And though Brooke had been on her own since high school, things hadn't changed much. She'd followed suit, living how she knew, moving around, bouncing from junior college to undergrad to working as an EMT, all in different cities. Hell, different states. Some habits died hard.

But she'd never landed in California before. She'd come to deal with her grandmother's estate, which included a great big old house and no cash to take care of the mortgage. Wasn't that just like an O'Brien.

It left Brooke with no choice but to sell the place off before it dragged her down in debt. Except she had to pack up some sixty-plus years of living first. And hell, maybe while the house was on the market, she could learn more about the grandma she'd never known.

In the meantime, she needed money for the immediates—like, say, eating—and the temp EMT position was for six weeks.

Perfect.

At least on the outside looking in, which was pretty much how she lived her life. Someday she'd like to change that. Someday she'd like to find her niche.

Find where she really belonged…

But for now, or at least the next six weeks, she belonged here. As she moved past the dozing firefighter, the sea breeze stirred her hair and tickled her nose. Then another gust of wind hit, knocking her back a step, and still the occupant of the hammock didn't move, breathing slow and deep, his chest rising and falling in rhythm. She kept tiptoeing past him, then pretty much undid all her careful stealth by sneezing. And not a dainty-girl sneeze, either.

The long body stirred, and so did something deep within her, which was so odd as to be almost unrecognizable.

Lust?

Huh. It'd been a while since she'd felt such instant heat for a guy, especially one whose face she hadn't even seen yet.

His hand reached up to tip off his hat, revealing short, sun-streaked brown hair. When he turned his head in her direction, she caught a quick flash of a face that definitely matched the body, and more of that stirring occurred. He'd been blessed by the gene-pool angels, and freezing on the spot, Brooke watched as two light green eyes focused, then offered a lazy smile. "Bless you," he said.

He had a voice to go with the rest of him—low, deep

and melodic. Uh-oh. Lots more stirring and a rise of in-stantaneous heat, because, good Lord, if she'd thought him virile with his eyes closed, she needed a respirator to look at him now. "Sorry to wake you."

"No worries. I'm used to it. Besides, you're a much prettier sight than anything I was dreaming about."

They were just words but they brought a little zing to her good spots. Good spots she'd nearly let rust. *Whew.* Suddenly, she was actually beginning to sweat. If some-one had asked her before this moment if she believed in lust at first sight, she'd have laughed. No, she needed more than hot sexiness in a guy, always had.

But she wasn't laughing now.

Wanting to hear him talk some more, she asked, "What were you dreaming about?"

"We responded to a fire last night and lost a kid."

Some of that overwhelming lust relegated itself to the background of her brain, replaced by something far more real to her than mere physical attraction. *Empathy.* She'd lost people, too, and it never stopped hurting. "I'm so sorry."

"Yeah. Me, too." Shifting his muscular, athletic body in the hammock so that he lay on his side facing her, he propped his head on his hand. "So let me guess. You're the latest EMT."

"Yes. Brooke O'Brien."

"Zach Thomas."

"Hi, Zach Thomas."

His eyes warmed to a simmer, and a matching heat came from deep in her belly. Holy smokes, could he see the steam escaping from her pores? It was so strange, her immediate reaction to him. Strange and unsettling. "What do you mean latest?"

"They've sent us six EMTs so far." He smiled without much mirth. "No, seven. Yeah, you're the seventh."

Okay, that didn't sound promising. "What's wrong with the job?"

"Besides crazy twelve-hour shifts for the glory of low pay and little or no recognition?" He let out a low laugh, and she found that the butterflies in her belly were dancing to a new tune now. Not nerves, but something far earthier.

"No one mentioned that I'm the seventh temp, or that they'd had any problem filling the position."

"Did I scare you off?"

"Did you want to?"

He lifted a shoulder, not breaking eye contact. "If you scare easily, then it'd be nice to know now."

A challenge, and more of that shocking, undeniable sexual zing.

Did he feel it? "I don't scare at all."

At that, something new came into his gaze. Approval, which she didn't need, to go along with that undeniable awareness of her as a woman.

She didn't need that, either, but damn, it was good to know she wasn't alone in this. Whatever this was. Since she wasn't ready to put a finger on it, she forced herself to stop looking at him. "I don't actually officially start until tomorrow, but the chief suggested that I come by, check the place out." And, she supposed, meet the crew, who, it sounded like, were tired of meeting people who didn't stick.

But she'd stick. At least for the six weeks she'd been hired for, because if she was anything, it was reliable.

"Would you like the tour?"

Yes, please, of your body. "No, don't get up," she

said quickly when he started to do just that. "Really. I'll manage."

"Door's unlocked," he said, watching her, gaze steady.

"Great. I'll just…" *Try to stop staring at you.* Jeez, it'd been too long since she'd had sex. *Waaaay* too long. "Nice meeting you."

"How about I say the same if you're at work tomorrow?"

"I'll be here." She might be nearly drunk with lust but she knew that much. She would be there.

"Hope so." His light eyes held hers for another beat, and more uncomfortable little zings of heat ping-ponged through her.

Whew. Any more of this and she was going to need another application of deodorant this morning. "I will," she insisted. "I always follow through." She just didn't always grow roots. Okay, she never grew roots. Turning away, she let out a long breath and, hopefully, some of the sexual tension with it, and headed toward the door, which stood ajar. "Hello?"

Utter silence, broken only by a gurgling sound. The front room looked like a grown-up version of a frat house, not quite as neat and organized as the garage, but clean. There were two long comfy-looking sofas and several cushy chairs in beach colors that were well lived in. Shelves lined one wall, piled and stacked with a wide assortment of books, magazines and DVDs. On the floor sat a huge basket filled with flip-flops and bottles of suntan lotion. Another wall was lined with hooks, from which hung individual firefighter gear bags.

She could see the kitchen off to the right and a hallway to the left, but still no sign of life, which was odd—

they couldn't all be off on calls, not with the rigs still out front. *"Hello?"*

Still nothing.

With a shrug, she headed toward the gurgling sound, which took her into the kitchen, and a coffeemaker, making away. "Who'd want coffee on a hot day?" she asked herself.

"A crew who's been up all night."

Turning around, she faced sexy firefighter Zach Thomas, and as potent as he'd been lying down, his hotness factor shot up exponentially now that he was standing, even with bed-head—or hammock-head—which was good news for him…and bad news for her.

Letting out a huge yawn, he covered his mouth, then grimaced. "Sorry."

He looked good even when yawning. She was so screwed. "Don't be."

He set down his boots and shirt and stretched. His T-shirt rose, giving her a quick peek at a set of lickable abs. He ran a hand over his hair, which only encouraged the short strands to riot in an effortlessly sexy way that might have been amusing if she hadn't been in danger of drooling.

She'd never been one to lose it for a guy in uniform, so she had no idea why now was any different, but *oh my*.

"We had seven calls last night," he explained. "Fires, an explosion in the sugar factory, a toxic-waste spill at the gas station on Fifth. You name it, we were at it, all night. None of us got more than an hour." Again he ran his hand over his already-standing-on-end hair. "We're wiped. Everyone's sleeping."

Beneath all that gorgeousness, true exhaustion lined

his face, and suddenly Brooke saw him as a flesh-and-blood man. "I'm sorry I woke you. Especially after such a rough night."

He lifted another shoulder, not anywhere close to how irritated and frustrated she'd be if she'd had only an hour of sleep. "That's the way this job works. You wanted to meet the crew?"

"I'll come back."

"You want coffee first?"

She opened her mouth to say no thanks, but then she saw it in his gaze. His guard coming up. Here he was, overworked, the place obviously short-staffed, and in his eyes, she was just one in a long line of people that had flaked. That would flake. "You know, coffee would be great."

He turned to the cupboards while she took in the kitchen. The table was huge, with at least twelve chairs scattered around it. On the counter ran a line of mugs the length of the tile. "How many of you are stationed here?"

"We're on three rotating shifts, with only six fire-fighters and two EMTs each, which makes us…twenty-four? Down from thirty, thanks to some nasty cutbacks."

A medium-size station, then, but huge compared to the private ambulance company she'd last worked for, where there'd been only four on at all times.

She'd have to be far more social here than she was used to. The firefighters worked twenty-four-hour shifts to the EMTs' twelve, but it was still a lot of time together. She told herself that was a bonus, but really it just drove home that, once again, she was the new kid in class.

Zach eased over to the coffeepot. "Black, or jacked up?"

"Jacked up, please."

He reached for the sugar. Without her permission, her eyes took themselves on a little tour, starting with those wide shoulders, that long, rangy torso, and a set of buns that—

He turned and, oh perfect, caught her staring.

At his butt.

Arching a brow, he leaned back against the counter while she did her best imitation of a ceiling tile. When she couldn't stand the silence and finally took a peek at him, he was handing her the mug of coffee, his eyes amused.

"Thanks," she managed.

"You're not from around here." He poured another mug for himself.

All her life she hadn't been "from around here," so that was nothing new. Getting caught staring at a guy's ass? That was new. New and very uncomfortable. "Is that a requirement?"

"Ah, and a little defensive," he said easily. "You look new to Santa Rey, that's all."

"And you know that because...?"

"Because of your skin." Reaching out, he stroked a finger over her cheek, and instantly she felt as if all her happy spots sparked to life. She sucked in a breath.

So did he.

After a pause, he pulled his finger back. "Huh."

Yeah, huh.

"You're pale," he said. "That's what I meant. You're obviously not from a beach town."

Okay, so they weren't going to discuss it. "I'm just careful, is all."

Zach nodded slowly. "I didn't mean to ruffle you."

Even though he was clearly ruffled, too. He slid his feet into his boots, leaving them unlaced as he set down his coffee and shrugged into his uniform shirt.

Maybe he hadn't meant to ruffle her, but that's exactly what he'd done, was still doing just by breathing. "I'm a big fan of sunscreen."

With a nod, he came close again, his gaze touching over her features. "It was a compliment. You have gorgeous skin, all creamy smooth." Again, he stroked a finger over her cheek, and like before, she felt the touch in a whole bunch of places that had no business feeling anything.

He was ruffling her again. Big-time ruffling going on, from her brain cells to all her erogenous zones, of which she had far more than she remembered.

"Back East?" he guessed.

"Massachusetts." Brooke was trying not to react to the fact that he was in her personal bubble, or that she was enjoying the invasion. "You, uh…" She wagged her finger toward his shirt, still partially opened over the invitation to bite him, which she suddenly wanted to do. "Didn't finish buttoning."

"You distracted me."

Yeah. A mutual problem, apparently. This close, he seemed even taller and broader, and now his surfer good looks were only exaggerated by the firefighter uniform. "Are the surfboards outside yours?"

"Why?" He flashed a smile that must have slayed female hearts across the land. It certainly slayed hers. "Because I look like a surfer?"

"Yes."

"Do you surf?"

"I've never tried," she admitted. "I'm not sure it'd be a good idea."

"Why?"

"I'm…" She paused, not exactly relishing telling this gorgeous specimen of a man her faults.

"A little uptight?" he guessed, then looked her over. "Maybe even a little bit of a perfectionist?"

"Are you suggesting I'm anal? Because I'm not."

He just kept looking at her, a little amused, and she caved like a cheap suitcase. "Okay, I am. What gave me away?"

"The hair."

Which she had in a neat braid. "Keeps it out of my way."

"Smart. And the ironed cargoes?"

She slid her hands into her pockets. "So I hate wrinkles."

A smile tugged at the corners of his mouth. "Yeah, wrinkles are a bitch."

Damn it. He was gorgeous *and* perceptive. "Fine. I'm a lot anal."

He let out another slow and easy grin.

And something within her began a slow and easy burn.

Oh, this wasn't good. It was the opposite of good. "Maybe I should just come back—"

But before she could finish that thought, a loud bell clanged, and in the blink of an eye the surfer firefighter went from laid-back and easygoing to tense and alert.

"Units two and three, respond to 3640 Rebecca Avenue," said a disembodied voice from the loudspeaker.

"That's me." Zach set down his mug as movement came from down the hall.

People began filing into the front room in various stages of readiness, most of them guys—really hot guys, Brooke couldn't help but notice—half of them pulling on clothes, some shoving on shoes, others giving orders to others. All looked exhausted, and somewhat out of sorts. Having been up all night, they couldn't be thrilled at having to move out now, but she still expected someone to ask about her, or even acknowledge her, but no one did.

"Mary's temp is here," Zach said into the general chaos. "Brooke O'Brien, everyone."

People gave a quick wave, one or two even quicker smiles, and kept moving. Zach squeezed her shoulder as he headed to the door, once again a simple touch from him giving her a jolt. "See you around, New Hire Number Seven." And just like that, he was gone.

They were all gone.

Yeah. Definitely still the new kid.

CHAPTER TWO

BROOKE SPENT THAT night walking through the three-story Victorian her grandmother had so unexpectedly left her, marveling that it was in her name now. She'd never met Lucille O'Brien, who'd been estranged from her only child, Brooke's mother, Karen, so it'd been a shock to everyone when Brooke had been contacted by an attorney and given the details of Lucille's will.

As she'd been warned by the attorney, every room was indeed filled to the brim with...stuff. For Brooke, for whom everything she owned could fit into her car, this accumulation of stuff boggled the mind. All of it would have to go in order to sell the house, but she didn't know where to start. Her mother had been no help, wanting nothing to do with any of it, not even willing to come West to look.

But Brooke was glad she'd come. If nothing else, being in Santa Rey, experiencing that inexplicably over-the-top attraction to Zach, staying here in the only place her family had any history at all, gave her a sense that she might actually have a shot at things she'd never dared dream about before.

She finally decided to go top to bottom and headed to the attic. There she went to the first pile she came to and found a stack of photo boxes that unexpectedly snagged her by the throat. The way she'd grown up hadn't allowed for much sentimentality. None of her few belongings included keepsakes like photos. She'd told herself over the years that it didn't matter. She *liked* to be sentiment light.

But flipping through boxes and boxes of pictures, she realized that was only because she hadn't known any different. Karen and Lucy hadn't spoken in years, since back when Brooke had been a baby, so she hadn't known her grandmother, or how the woman felt about her. But some of the pictures were from the early 1900s and continued through her grandmother's entire life, enthralling Brooke in a way she hadn't expected.

She had a past, and flipping through it made her feel good, and also sad for all she didn't know. She and her mother weren't close. In fact, Karen lived in Ohio at the moment, with an artist and wasn't in touch often, but now Brooke wished she could just pick up a phone and share this experience.

That she had anyone to pick up a phone and call...

She fell asleep just like that, surrounded by her past, only to wake with a jerk, the sun slanting in the small window high above her. She had two pictures stuck to one cheek, drool on the other. She'd been dreaming about the big house, filled with memories of her own making.

Was that what she secretly wished for? For this house to represent her roots?

Was that what she needed to feed her own happiness?

She glanced at her watch and then panicked. Tossing off the dream and the photos, she raced through her morning routine, barely getting a shower before rushing out the door, desperate not to be late on her first day at work.

The hammock by the firehouse was empty, and she ignored the little twinge of disappointment at not getting to gawk at Zach again. Not that she was going to gawk. Nope, she was going to be one hundred percent professional. And with that, she stepped inside.

"Well, look at you. You really came back."

Danger, danger…sexy firefighter alert. Slowly she turned and looked at him, thinking, *Please don't be as hot as I remember, please don't be as hot as I remember—*

Shit.

He was as hot as she remembered. He didn't look tired this morning. Instead, the corners of his mouth were turned up, and his eyes—cheerful and wide-awake—slid over her, making her very aware of the fact that while she might have a little crush going, it was most definitely, absolutely, a two-way thing.

Which didn't help at all.

"Guys," he called out over his shoulder. "She's here."

"Number Seven showed?" This from a tall, dark and extremely drool-worthy firefighter in the doorway to the kitchen.

"Meet Aidan," Zach said to Brooke. "He dated New Hire Number Two and she never came back, so he has orders to stay clear."

"Hey, I didn't plan on the shellfish giving her food poisoning," Aidan said in his own defense. "But just in case…" He flashed a smile at Brooke, a killer smile that rivaled Zach's. "We'd better not go out for shellfish."

Several more men crowded into the hallway to take a look. Yeah, they really did make them good-looking here. Must be the fresh sea air. "Hi," she said, waving. "Brooke O'Brien."

The bell rang, and everyone groaned, their greeting getting lost as they headed for their gear.

"Aidan and I roll together," Zach said, stepping into his boots. "With Cristina and Blake." He gestured to two additional firefighters, the first a tough-looking beautiful blond woman who smiled, the other, male, tall and lanky, not smiling.

Zach shook his head. "Or, as we call Blake, Eeyore."

Okay. Brooke wasn't smiling, either, so she put one on now, but it was too late; they'd turned away.

"You're with Dustin," Zach called back.

Dustin, who looked like Harry Potter The Grown-Up Years, complete with glasses, raised his hand. "We're the two EMTs on this shift. Nice to meet you. Hope you orientate fast."

She hoped so, too.

Dustin gestured to the door, nodding to the two fire-fighters not moving. "This is Sam and Eddie. Their rig wasn't called, so they get to stay here and watch *Oprah* and eat bonbons."

They took the ribbing with a collective flip of their middle fingers, then vanished back down the hall.

"Actually, they're scheduled to go to the middle school on Ninth this morning and give a fire safety and prevention speech to the kids," Dustin told her with a grin. "They'll eat their bonbons later. Let's hit it, New Hire Seven. It's a Code Calico."

"Code Calico?"

But he was already moving to the door that led directly to the garage and the rigs.

Cristina brushed past Brooke and set her mug in the sink. "Good luck."

"Am I going to need it?"

"With Dustin, our resident McDweeb? Oh, yeah, you're going to need it."

"What's a Code Calico?"

Cristina merely laughed, which did nothing to ease Brooke's nerves.

Blake poked his head back in the door. He'd pulled on his outer fire gear, which looked slightly too big on his very lean form. "Hey, New Hire. Hit it means hit it."

So she did what was expected of her—she hit it. Dustin drove, while she took the shotgun position. "So really, what's a Code Calico?"

Dustin navigated the streets with a familiar sort of ease that told her he knew what he was doing, not even glancing at the GPS system. "Want to take it?"

"Take it?"

"Be point on the call." He glanced at her. "The one in charge."

She sensed it was a test. She aced tests, always had. That was the analness in her, she supposed. "Sure."

He pushed up his glasses and nodded, but she'd have sworn his lips twitched.

Huh. Definitely missing something.

When they pulled onto a wide, affluent, oak-lined street, she hopped out and opened the back doors of the rig.

"Gurney's not necessary on this one," Dustin told her.

Behind the ambulance came the fire truck. Zach and the others appeared, smiling.

Why were they all smiling?

Before she could dwell on that, from between the two trucks came an old woman, yelling and waving her cane. "Hurry! Hurry before Cecile falls!"

The panic in her voice was real, and Brooke's heart raced just as Dustin nudged her forward, whispering in her ear, "All yours."

This was the job, and suddenly in her element, her nerves took a backseat. Here, she could help; here, she could run the show. "It's okay, ma'am. We're here now."

"Well, then, get to it! Get my Cecile!"

"Where is she? In the house?"

"No!" She looked very shaky and not a little off her rocker, so Brooke tried to steer her to the curb to sit down, but she wasn't having it.

"I'm not sitting anywhere! Not until you get Cecile!"

"Okay, just tell me where she is and I'll—"

"Oh, good Lord!" The woman blinked through her thick-rimmed glasses, taking a quick look at the others, who stood back, watching. "She's another new hire, isn't she?"

"Yes," Brooke said. "But—"

"What number are you?"

Brooke sighed. "Seven."

"Well, get a move on, New Hire Number Seven! Save my Cecile!"

"I'm trying, ma'am. What's your name?"

"Phyllis, but Cecile—"

"Right. Needs my help. Where is she?"

"That's what I'm trying to tell you!" The woman jerked her cane upward, to a huge tree in front of them. Waaaay up in that tree, on a branch stretched out over their heads, perched a cat.

A big, fat cat, plaintively wailing away.

Brooke turned and eyeballed Dustin, who seemed to be fascinated by his own feet, and that's when she got it. She was going through some ridiculously juvenile rite of passage. "I'm beginning to see how they got to number seven." Good thing she was used to being the newbie, because she hadn't been kidding Zach yesterday. Little scared her, and certainly not a damn cat in a damn tree.

"Hurry up!" Phyllis demanded. "Before she falls!"

"I'll get her." Zach had separated from the others and walked toward the tree.

Oh, no.

Hell, no.

They'd wanted to see her do this, they were absolutely going to see her do this.

"Brooke—"

"No." She kept her eyes on Phyllis. "Cecile is a cat," she clarified, because there was no sense in making a total and complete fool of herself if it wasn't absolutely necessary.

"Yes," Phyllis verified.

Okay, it was going to be absolutely necessary. Damn, she hated that.

By now, Barbie Firefighter Cristina was out-and-out grinning. Cutie Firefighter Aidan was smiling. Harry Potter look-alike Dustin was, too. Not Eeyore, though. Nope, Blake was far more serious than the others, she could already tell, though she'd have sworn there was some amusement shining in his gaze.

Zach was either wiser, or maybe he simply had more control, but his lips weren't curved as he watched her. Quiet. Aware. Speculative.

Sexy as hell, damn him. Fine. Seemed she had a lot to prove to everyone. Well, she was good at that, too, and she stepped toward the tree.

"Brooke—"

She put a finger in his face, signaling Don't You Dare, and something flashed in his eyes.

Respect? Yeah, but something else, too, something much more base, which would have most definitely set off one of their trademark chain reactions of sparks along her central nervous system, if she hadn't been about to climb a damn tree. "I can do this," she said.

His eyes approved, and even though she didn't want it to, that approval washed through her.

So did that sizzling heat they had going on.

Oh, he was good. With that charisma oozing from his every pore, he could no doubt charm the panties off just about any woman.

But though it had been a while since anyone had charmed Brooke's panties off, she wasn't just any woman.

Reminding herself of that, she stepped toward the tree.

CHAPTER THREE

ZACH WATCHED HOW Brooke handled herself and something inside him reacted. He didn't know her, not yet, not really, other than that they had some serious almost chemical-like attraction going, but she was crew, and as such, she was family.

Except he felt decidedly un-family-like toward her. Nope, nothing in him looking at her felt brotherly.

Not one little bit.

The gang was being hard on her, there was no doubt of that, but he'd seen many new hires hazed over the years—six in the past few weeks—and it had never bothered him.

Until now. This bothered him. *She* bothered him, in a surprising way. A man-to-woman way, though that wasn't the surprise. It was that he felt it here, at work.

People came in and out of his life on a daily basis. It was the nature of the beast, that beast being fire. Every day he dealt with the destruction it caused, and what it did to people's existence. Hell, he'd even experienced it in the most personal way one could, when he'd lost his own parents to a tragic fire. He coped by knowing he made a difference, that he helped keep that beast back when he could.

What also helped were the constants in his life, and since the loss of his mom and dad at age ten, those constants were his crew. Aidan, his partner and brother of his heart. Eddie and Sam, fellow surfers. Dustin, resident clown, a guy who gave one hundred percent of himself, always, which usually landed him in Heartbreak City. Blake, whom he'd gone to high school with and who'd lost his firefighting partner Lynn in a tragic fire last year, a guy who'd give a perfect stranger the heavy yellow jacket off his back. Even Cristina, a woman in a man's world, who was willing to kick anyone's ass to show she belonged in it. All of them held a piece of Zach's heart.

For better, for worse, through thick and thin, they were each other's one true, solid foundation. They meant everything to him.

But the emergency community they lived in was a lot like the cozy little town of Santa Rey itself—small and quirky, no secrets need apply. Everyone knew that the constant gossip and ribbing between the crew members acted as stress relief from a job that had an element of danger every time they went out. Zach had always considered it harmless. But looking at it from Brooke's perspective, that ribbing must feel like mockery.

She dropped her bag to the ground and walked to the tree.

She was going to climb it for the cat. And hell if that didn't do something for him. He didn't interfere— she was Dustin's partner, not his—but he wanted to. The chief would have a coronary, of course, but the chief wasn't there throwing the rule book around as he liked to do. Zach wasn't much for rules or restrictions, himself, or for drawing lines in the sand—which hadn't helped his career any. Nor did he make a habit of stretching his emotional wings and adding personal ties to his life. How many women had told him over the years that he wouldn't know a real relationship if it bit him on the ass?

Too many to count.

And yet he felt an emotional tie now, watching Brooke simply do her job. It shouldn't have been sexy, but it was. *She* was sexy, even in the regulation EMT uniform of dark blue trousers and a white button-down shirt, with a Santa Rey EMT vest over the top, the outfit made complete by the required steel-toed boots.

She made him hot. He thought maybe it was the perfectly folded-back sleeves and careful hair twist that got him. Her hair was gorgeous, a shiny strawberry blond, her coloring as fair as her hair dictated. He knew after any time in the sun—and in Santa Rey, sun was the only weather they got—she'd probably freckle across that nose she liked to tip up to nosebleed heights. She was petite, small-boned, even fragile-looking, and yet he'd bet his last dollar she was strong as hell, strong enough for that tree.

She looked up at the lowest branch, utter concentration on her face. A face that showed her emotions, probably whether she wanted it to or not. It was those wide, expressive baby-blue eyes, he knew. They completely slayed him.

She put her hands on the trunk of the tree and gave it a shake, testing it. Nodding to herself, still eyeing the cat as if she'd rather be facing a victim who was bleeding out than the howling feline on the branch twenty feet above her, she drew a deep breath.

Unbelievable. She was slightly anal, slightly obsessive and more than slightly adorable.

And she had guts. He liked that. He liked her. She

was taking his mind off his frustration over the Hill Street fire and Tommy's investigation. But while his career was shaky at the moment, hers was not, and she was going to climb that damn tree if no one stopped her. "Dustin."

Cristina shushed him. Blake, the one of them who couldn't stand to see anything suffer, even before losing Lynn last year, shot her an annoyed look. Zach leaned toward Dustin. "Stop her."

"On it." The EMT stepped forward and put his hand on Brooke's shoulder, saying something that Zach couldn't quite catch, though he had no problem reading her expression.

Relief that she didn't really have to climb the tree.

Embarrassment that she'd let them all fool her.

And a flash of a temper that made him smile. Good. She might be reserved, but she wasn't a doormat.

Aidan grabbed the ladder. Zach helped him. As he passed a brooding Brooke, their eyes met before he climbed the ladder to reach Cecile.

Yeah, quiet and reserved, maybe, but also a little pissed. So was Cecile, but she was one female he could soothe, at least, and when he brought the cat to Phyllis, he had to smile.

Brooke had the older woman sitting on the curb and was attempting to check her vitals, which Phyllis didn't appear to appreciate.

"Ma'am," Brooke said, "you have an elevated blood pressure."

"Well, of course I do. I'm eighty-eight."

Brooke lifted her stethoscope, but Phyllis pushed it away. "I don't need—Cecile! Give me my baby, Zachie!"

Blowing a loose strand of hair from her face, Brooke gave Zach a look. *"Zachie?"*

"Small town." With a half-embarrassed shrug, he handed the cat to Phyllis.

"I used to change his diapers," Phyllis told her, and patted Zach's cheek with fingers gnarled by arthritis. "You're a good boy. Your mother would be so proud of you."

He'd found it best not to respond to these types of statements from Phyllis, because if he did, she'd keep him talking about his family forever, and he didn't like to talk about them. He thought about them every day, and that was enough. "I thought we decided you were going to keep Cecile inside."

"No, *you* decided, but she hates being cooped up." She nuzzled the cat. "So how's all your ladies, Zachie? Still falling at your feet?"

Brooke arched a brow but Zach just smiled. "You're my number-one lady, Phyllis, you know that." Her color wasn't great, plus her breathing was off, which worried him. She'd probably forgotten to pick up her meds again. He crouched at her side and took her hand. "You're taking your pills, right?"

She bent her head to Cecile's, her blue hair bouncing in the breeze. "Oh, well. You know."

With a sigh, he reached for Brooke's blood pressure cuff. "May I?"

Their fingers brushed as she put it in his hand, and again he felt that electric current zing him, but as hot as that little zap was, he didn't take his gaze off Phyllis. "You know the drill," he said, gently wrapping the cuff around her arm as above him he heard Brooke say to Dustin, "So did I pass the test?"

"Yep. Nice job, New Hire Seven."

"You've got to keep the cat inside," Zach said to Phyllis, handing back the blood pressure cuff to Brooke, making sure to touch her, testing their connection. Yep, still there. "Cecile's not safe out here, Phyllis."

"She's safe now."

"Yes." With effort, he shifted his mind off Brooke and focused on Phyllis. "We have a new chief."

"Yes, of course. Allan Stone. Santa Rey born and raised, back from Chicago to do good in his hometown. I read all about him in the paper."

Everything was in the Santa Rey paper. Not that Zach needed to read it. Not when he and the chief were becoming intimately familiar with each other; every time Zach put his nose into Tommy's business regarding the arsons, he got some personal one-on-one time in the chief's office. "After all he saw in Chicago, he's not going to think this qualifies as an emergency."

"But it was an emergency."

"I'm sorry, Phyllis."

"Yes." The older woman sighed. "I know. I'm old, not senile. I get it." She lovingly stroked the cat, who sprawled in her lap, purring loudly enough to wake the dead. "It's just that Cecile loves the great outdoors. And you always come—"

Seemed his heart was going to get tugged on plenty today. "That's my point. We can't always come. If we're here when there's an emergency, then someone else might go without our help. I know you don't want that to happen."

"No, of course not." She hugged the cat hard. "You're right. I'm sorry."

"No apologies necessary." He scratched the cat behind her ornery ears and rose to leave.

Brooke blocked his path. She still held her stethoscope and blood pressure cuff, looking sweetly professional while she tried to maintain her composure, but her annoyance at being played was clear.

"I'd like to talk to you," she said primly.

He enjoyed that, too, the way she sounded so prissy while looking so damn hot. So put together, so on top of everything, which perversely made him want to rumple her up. Preferably the naked, hot and sweaty kind of rumpled. "Talk? Or bite my head off?"

"I don't bite."

"Shame." Passing her, he headed back to his rig to help Aidan put away the ladder. But she wasn't done with him yet, and followed.

"I nearly climbed that tree, Zach. Without the benefit of the ladder, I might add."

Aidan shot Zach a look that said Good Luck, Buddy and moved out of their way. Zach turned to face a fuming Brooke. "No one was going to let you climb that tree."

"Really? Because I think that the crew thinks I was sent here to amuse them."

"You have to understand, you're the seventh EMT—"

"To walk out, yeah yeah, got it. But I'm not going to walk out. I'm not."

"I believe you."

"You do?"

He smiled at her surprise. "I do. And I was never going to let you climb that tree, Brooke. Never."

She stared at him for a long, silent beat. "Is your word supposed to mean something?"

He was a lot of things, but a liar was not one of them. Not that she could possibly know that about him yet. "Hopefully it will come to mean something."

She continued to look at him for another long moment, then turned and walked away with a quiet sense of dignity that made him feel like an ass even though, technically, he'd done nothing wrong.

OVER THE NEXT few days the calls came nonstop, accompanying a heat wave that had everyone at the firehouse on edge, Zach included. If they'd had the staff that they used to, things would have been okay, but they didn't. So they ran their asses off in oppressive temperatures with no downtime, while the higher-ups got to sit in air-conditioned offices.

By the end of the week, they were all exhausted.

"Crazy," Cristina muttered on the third straight day of record-high temperatures *and* calls. "It's like with the heat wave came a stupid wave."

They were all in the kitchen, gulping down icy drinks and standing in front of the opened freezer, vying for space and ice cubes. Cristina rubbed an ice cube across her chest, then gave poor Dustin the evil eye for staring at her damp breasts.

Zach didn't blame Dustin for looking; the view was mighty nice. He did worry about the dreamy look in the EMT's eyes. Dustin tended to put his heart on the line for every single woman he met, which left him open to plenty of heartbreak. If Cristina caught that puppy-dog look, she'd chew him up and spit him out. Instead, she elbowed everyone back and took the front-and-center spot for herself.

"You forgot to take your pill this morning," Blake

told her, not looking at her chest like everyone else but nudging her out of the way so he could get in closer.

"I'm not on the pill," Cristina said.

"Not that pill. Your nice pill."

Dustin snorted and Cristina glared at him, zapping the smile off his face.

Zach cleared some space for Brooke to get in closer, and she sent him a smile that zapped him as sure as Cristina had zapped Dustin, but in another area entirely.

He wished she was rubbing an ice cube on her chest. He maneuvered himself right next to her. Their arms bumped, their legs brushed and every nerve ending went on high alert.

The bell rang, and with a collective groan, they all scattered. It was exhausting, and *he* was seasoned, as was the crew. He could only imagine how Brooke felt. If he'd had time to breathe, he'd have asked her.

As it was, they couldn't do much more than glance at each other, because between the multitude of calls, they still had the maintaining and keeping up of the station and vehicles, not to mention their required physical training.

But he did glance at her.

Plenty.

And she glanced back. She appeared to hold up under pressure extremely well; even when everyone else looked hot, sweaty and irritated, she never did. Look sweaty and irritated, that is.

Hot? That she most definitely looked.

It'd been a long time since he'd flirted so slowly with a woman like this, over days, mostly without words. A very long time, and he'd forgotten how arousing it could be. He figured if they had to pass each other one

more time without taking it to the next step—and he
had plenty of ideas on what that next step should be, all
involving touching and stripping and nakedness, lots of
nakedness—they'd both go up in flames.

One late afternoon a week and a half into Brooke's
employment, he headed toward her to see about that
whole thing, but of course, the bell rang.

It was a kitchen fire, with a man down. Zach and
Aidan were first on scene, with Dustin and Brooke pulling in right behind them in front of a small house that
sat on a high bluff overlooking the ocean. By the time
they got inside, the fire had been extinguished by the
supposedly downed man himself, who was breathing
like a lunatic and looked to be in the throes of a panic attack. Zach and Aidan checked to make sure the doused
fire couldn't flare up and then began mop-up while
Dustin tried to get the guy to sit, but he wasn't having it.

"No." Chest heaving, covered in soot, he pointed at
Brooke. "I want her. The chick paramedic."

Everyone looked at Brooke. For some reason, she
looked at Zach. He wanted to think it was because
they'd been looking at each other silently for days,
building an odd sense of anticipation for…something,
but probably it was simply that he'd been the first person she'd met here.

"I'm an EMT," she told the victim. "Not a paramedic."

"I don't care." The guy was gasping for air, clutch-
ing at his chest. "It's you or nothing."

HER OR NOTHING. Brooke could honestly say that she'd
never heard that sentence before, at least directed at
her. She looked at the crew around her, all of whom

were looking at her, perfectly willing and accepting of her taking over.

And in that moment, she knew. They might tease her and call her New Hire, but the truth was, they treated her as a part of their team, a capable, smart part of their team, and she appreciated that. "What's your name?"

"Carl."

"Okay, Carl. Let's sit."

"I'm better standing. Listen, I was just cooking eggs, but then the pan caught fire."

"It's okay," Brooke assured him. "The fire's out now. Let's worry about you."

"I have a problem."

Yes, he did. He was pale, clammy and sweating profusely. "Let's work on that problem."

"It's, uh, a big one. It won't go away." Still breathing heavy, the guy looked down at his fly. "If you know what I mean."

Everyone stopped working on the kitchen mop-up and looked at the guy's zipper, and Brooke did the same.

He was erect.

She glanced at the guys. Dustin pushed up his glasses. Aidan busied himself with the cleanup. Zach rubbed his jaw and met Brooke's gaze, his own saying that he'd seen it all, but not this.

Carl shoved his fingers through his hair, still trying to catch his breath. "See, I was supposed to have this hot date last night, but Mr. Winky wasn't working. So I took a vitamin V."

"Vitamin V?" Brooke pulled out a chair and firmly but gently pressed him into it. "What's vitamin V?"

"Viagra."

Brooke processed that information while Carl stared

down at his lap with a mixture of pride and bafflement. "It worked, too. A little too well."

"Okay." Brooke opened her bag and began to check his vitals, carefully not looking at the guy's zipper again.

"So…can you fix this? I've never had a twelve-hour case of blue balls before. Could it…kill me?"

"No one's dying today." Behind her, Dustin was checking in with the hospital, as was protocol. From the victim she took the basics: name, age, weight, etc. Dustin set down his radio and turned to her. "We have a few questions."

"Not you," Carl said, shaking his head. *"Her."*

"Right." Dustin wrote something down and pushed the piece of paper toward Brooke. It was the questions the E.R. doctor wanted answered. She paused, tucking a nonexistent stray piece of hair behind her ear while she tried to figure out how to do this and keep Carl's dignity, not to mention her own. "Carl? How many Viagras did you take?"

"Oh. Um." He looked away, catching Aidan's and Zach's eye. "Just the one."

Brooke gave him a long look. She was not a pushover, not even close. "One?"

"Okay, two."

"Are you sure?"

Mr. Vitamin V caved. "Four. Okay? I took four. I really wanted to do this." Still breathing unsteadily, he put his hand on his heart. "Am I going to have a heart attack? Because I feel like I'm having a heart attack."

Brooke was waiting on Dustin, who was talking to the E.R. about the four pills. "Just hang tight for a second."

"Hanging tight. Or at least my boys are." He smiled feebly at his joke. "Do I have to go to the hospital?"

"Finding that out now." She did her best not to squirm, extremely aware of all the eyes on her, especially Zach's, as Dustin gave her another piece of paper, which she read. *Oh, boy.* "Carl, when did you last have sex?"

Carl blinked. "When did I last have sex? Are you kidding me? That's why I took the pills in the first place!"

Again Brooke accidentally met Zach's gaze. He was cool, calm, and not showing a thing, but she felt her own face heat. If she had to answer this question, she'd have to admit that she couldn't even remember. "We need to know when you last ejaculated."

"Oh." Carl let out a long breath. "Jesus. Yesterday. In the shower."

Nodding, she made the note.

"Twice."

Brooke dropped her pen.

"That's normal, right?" He looked at Aidan, Dustin and then Zach for affirmation. "Back me up here, guys. It's just what we do, right?"

Aidan got really busy, fast.

Dustin scribbled on his notepad.

Zach just raised a brow.

"Damn it!" Carl slapped his hands on the table. "Don't you guys leave me out here hanging alone! Tell her."

Dustin sighed, then after a hesitation, nodded.

Aidan, too.

Brooke looked at Zach, who met her gaze evenly, not looking away, neither embarrassed nor self-conscious as he nodded, as well.

Carl was waiting for her next question, but she couldn't stop staring at Zach, couldn't stop picturing him—

Oh, perfect. And here came the blush.

Dustin nudged her and she jumped, jerking her gaze off Zach.

"Really, it's what guys do," Carl was still saying.

It was what guys did.

Drive her crazy.

They made the decision to transport, and while loading the patient in the small kitchen, Brooke bumped into Zach. She looked into his face, feeling hers heat, watching him smile as if he knew what she was thinking.

It's what guys do...

She moved past him but their arms touched, and damn if she didn't feel her stomach quiver. Because their arms touched. How ridiculous was that? If he ever touched her in a sexual way, she'd probably come before he even got her clothes off.

"You okay?" he murmured. "You're looking at me funny."

"Me?" Her voice was as high as Mickey Mouse. "No. Not at all." *I was looking at you like I wanted to gobble you up for my next meal, that's all.*

He cocked his head and studied her a moment. "Sure?"

"Sure." Liar, liar...

CHAPTER FOUR

"HEY, NEW HIRE SEVEN," Cristina said several days later, the next time she saw Brooke. "Any more Viagra calls?"

Brooke looked over as Firefighter Barbie entered the fire station living room grinning from ear to ear. "Brooke. My name is Brooke."

"So. You ever have a patient with a perma-boner before?"

"No. That was a new one," Brooke admitted.

"At least you didn't have to climb a tree to get to him, huh?"

"At least he was human."

Cristina laughed and walked past Blake, who was on the computer, and affectionately rumpled his hair. "You get the message that your sister called?"

"Yep, thanks."

"Kenzie sounds good. I saw her on *Entertainment Tonight* last night, she was being interviewed about being nominated for a daytime Emmy for her soap."

"I taped it."

"We still all having dinner tonight, right?"

"Yep."

Brooke knew that they did that a lot, got together. All of them. They'd asked her to join them weeks ago, on her first night, but she had been anxious to get started packing up her grandma's house. Now that she'd been doing that for two weeks, she'd love to be included, but didn't know how to ask.

A lifelong problem—not knowing how to belong. But for the first time in her life, she wanted to. She didn't know if it was her grandmother's house with all that family history, or the way she yearned and burned for Zach at night, or just wanting more for herself from life, but she wanted to be a part of this team. A part of their family. At least for the month she had left. Then, when she did go, she'd have these memories. She'd have her own history to look back on and remember.

Cristina leaned over Blake's shoulder. "Got anything good today, Eeyore?"

Blake pulled open a drawer and held out a candy bar. "Careful," he warned. "I rigged it. The person who eats that is going to turn sweet."

"Not a chance."

With a sigh, Blake went back to the computer.

Brooke headed into the garage to restock their rig as end-of-shift protocol dictated. And then, blessedly, she was off the clock. Stepping outside, she was immediately hit by a sucker punch to the low belly area—not by the hot, salty summer air, but by good old-fashioned lust.

Zach stood on the bumper of the truck, hose in hand, leaning over his rig, squirting down the windows. Stripped to the waist, his skin glistened with a light sweat. She broke into a sweat, too, just from looking at him.

His back was sleek, smooth and sinewy, and improving the already fantastic view was the fact that his pants had slid low enough to once again reveal a strip of BVDs, blue today. His every muscle bunched and unbunched as he moved, hypnotizing her, fusing her to the spot. She didn't mean to keep staring, she really didn't, but was unable to help herself as she eyed his sun-streaked hair, his rock-solid and ready-for-action body, all corded bulk honed to a fine edge, topped with so much testosterone she could hardly breathe. He looked like the perennial surfer boy all grown up—and it hit her.

This might be more than a crush.

"If you come help, you can get a better view."

Oh, for God's sake. She jerked her gaze off him and pretended to search her purse for her keys while silently berating herself. "I'm sorry, I—"

"Are you kidding? A pretty woman looks at me, and she's sorry?"

"I wasn't looking—"

Tossing aside his hose, he lithely hopped down from the rig and came closer, letting out that damn slow, sexy smile of his. "Anal, uptight *and* a liar?"

"Okay, so I was looking." She crossed her arms and tried not to look at his chest but it was right in front of her, drawing her eyes. "But I didn't *want* to be looking."

With a soft laugh, he turned the tables, letting his gaze slowly run over her, from her hair to her toes and then back up again, stopping at a few spots that happily leaped to hopeful attention.

"Stop it." God, was that her voice, all cartoony-light and breathless? "What are you doing?"

"Looking," he murmured, mocking her. "And I wanted to."

"Okay, you know what? You need a damn shirt. And I'm going now."

Leaning back against the rig, he smiled, and damn

if it didn't short-circuit her wires. "Have anything special planned for your days off?" he asked. "Visiting friends, family?"

No. Fantasizing about you...

Unacceptable answer. She'd be working on the house. The house that she was beginning to wish was hers in more than name, because being there reminded her of exactly how rootlessly she'd lived her life, and how much she'd like to change that. Going through decades of family history had brought it home for her. It was exhausting, almost gut-wrenching, but also exhilarating.

And honestly? Flirting with Zach was the same.

But no matter what the house represented to her, no matter what someone like Zach could represent to her, she still didn't know how to get there.

How to belong. "I don't have either friends or family here."

"Everyone back East?"

She hated this part. Telling people about herself, getting unwanted sympathy. "My mother's in Ohio. I'm an only child. And I haven't made any friends here yet."

He didn't dwell or give her any sympathy. "I thought we were friends."

She gave him a look.

"Aren't we?"

"I don't know."

"Let's do something, then, and you can decide."

"I can't. I'm closing up my grandmother's house before it sells, and I've only got a month left in town."

"You think you'll be able to leave Santa Rey without falling in love with it? Or the people?"

She looked into his eyes, wishing for a witty response. But the truth was, she fell a little bit more for her grandma's house every single night she slept there. "I don't know."

"Do you know how you feel about surfing?"

"I'm pretty uncoordinated."

"I'm a good teacher."

Uh-huh. She bet he was.

"Come on, say yes. I'm betting you don't take enough downtime."

"I take lots."

He arched a brow, and she let out a breath. "Okay, so I don't."

"Is that because you like to be so busy your head spins, or because you don't know how to relax?"

"Is there an option number three?"

"You work a stressful job."

"So?"

"So…" He smiled. "Maybe you should let that hair down and just be wild and free once in a while."

"Wild and free. Is that what you do?"

"When I can."

She hadn't expected him to admit it, and she ran out of words, especially because he was still standing there with no shirt on.

"Not your thing, I take it," he said. "Letting loose."

"I've never thought about it." Okay, she'd thought about it. "I'm not sure how to…let loose," she admitted, going to tuck her hair behind her ears. But he shifted closer and caught her fingers in his.

That electric current hummed between them. He looked at their joined hands and then into her eyes. "Maybe it's time to think about it," he said silkily and stroked a finger over the tip of her ear, causing a long set of shivers to race down her spine. Then, with a look that singed her skin, he walked off.

She managed, barely, not to let her knees give and sit right there on the ground. He wanted her to relax? Ha! So not likely, and not just because he wound her up in ways she hadn't anticipated. Relaxing, getting wild and free, those were all alien concepts for her. No matter what her secret desires were, she had responsibilities, always had. She didn't have time for letting loose.

But, as he'd suggested, she thought about it. Thought about it as she drove home—yes, she'd begun to think of her grandmother's house as home—and she thought about it as she finished the attic. She thought about it, dreamed about it, fantasized about it…

Ironically enough, in the pictures that chronicled her grandma's life, she saw plenty of evidence that her grandma had known how to relax, and be wild and free.

How was it her grandmother had never insisted on getting to see her only grandchild?

It made her sad. It made her feel alone. She had missed out on something, something she needed badly.

Affection.

A sense of belonging.

Love.

Damn, enough with the self-pity. Having finished the attic, she moved down a floor to box up her grandmother's bedroom. There she made an even bigger find than pictures—her grandmother's diaries. Brooke stared down at one dated ten years back, the year she'd graduated from high school.

I tried calling my daughter today but she's changed her number. Probably long gone again on another of her moves. Of course she didn't think to let me know the new number, or where she's going.

She's still mad at me.

I really thought I was doing the right thing, telling her what I thought of her bohemian lifestyle and the shocking way she drags that child across the world for her own pleasure. I thought she needed to hear my opinion.

For years I thought that.

Now I know different. I know it's her life to live as she wants, and if I'd only arrived at this wisdom sooner, I wouldn't be alone now, with no one to belong to and no one to belong to me.

Brooke remembered that year. Her mother had gone after some guy to Alaska, and she'd entered junior college in Florida, feeling extremely…alone. Hugging the diary to her chest, she stared blindly out the window, wondering how different her life might have been if stubbornness hadn't been the number one trait in her grandmother's personality…

Or her mother's.

Or hers…

IF ANYONE HAD ASKED, Zach would have said he spent his days off surfing with Eddie and Sam, and replacing the brakes and transmission on his truck.

What he wouldn't have mentioned was how much time he spent thinking about Brooke. They most definitely had some sort of an attraction going on, one he wanted to explore. He wished she'd taken him up on spending some of their days off together. His weekend might have turned out differently if she had.

But with too much time to think, he'd gone over and over the Hill Street fire, the one he was so sure had been arson.

Tommy wouldn't give him any info. He and Tommy went way back to when Tommy had sat on the hiring board that had plucked Zach out of the academy, but the inspector wasn't playing favorites. Sharp as hell and a first-rate investigator, he was as overworked as the rest of them and frustrated at Zach's pressing the issue. All week his response had remained the same: "I'm working on it."

Still, Zach found himself driving to the site, where he'd gotten an unhappy shock. Back on the night of the fire he'd only had three minutes before the chief had ordered everyone out, just long enough for him to catch sight of *two* points of origin. One in the kitchen beneath the sink, the other in the kid's bedroom inside a wire-mesh trash can.

But now the kid's bedroom had been cleaned, and there was no sight of the wire-mesh trash can or flash point marring the wall.

And no sign of an ongoing fire investigation.

What *didn't* shock Zach was finding Tommy waiting for him at the start of his next shift.

Tommy was a five-foot-three Latin man with a God complex compounded by short-man syndrome. Added to this, ever since his doctor had made him give up caffeine, he'd been wearing a permanent surly frown; now was no exception as he stalked up to Zach as he got out of his truck. "We need to talk."

Zach shut his door without locking it. No one ever locked their doors in Santa Rey. "Still off caffeine, huh?"

"The Hill Street fire."

Zach sighed. "What about it?"

"I just left the scene."

"Okay." Zach nodded and grabbed his gear bag out of the back of his truck. "So maybe you can tell me what happened to the second point of origin, the one I saw in the kid's bedroom the night of the fire."

Tommy's jaw bunched. "The fire is out. Your job is done."

Zach turned to look at him, and it was Tommy's turn to sigh. "We found the point of origin in the kitchen. Beneath the sink. There were rags near the cleaning chemicals, which ignited. The fire alarm was faulty and didn't go off. It wasn't called in by anyone in the house, but by an anonymous tip reporting smoke."

"There was a metal trash can in the kid's room—"

"Zach, stop." Tommy's voice was quiet but his eyes were intense. "The chief's signing off on the report today. Accidental ignition."

"He can't sign off. It's arson."

"I'm not having this conversation." Tommy turned and started to walk away. "Not with you."

"Are you kidding me?"

Tommy looked back, regret creeping into his expression. "Look, you're not the most credible of witnesses right now, okay? There were those two other fires earlier in the season that you cried arson—"

"*Cried arson?* What am I, the boy who cried wolf?"

"Just leave the case to those who are trained, Zach. I've got a helluva workload right now and I don't need you—"

"I don't care about your workload. We're *all* overworked. What I care about is making sure that whoever killed that kid pays his due."

"*My* job, Zach. My job."

"But you don't believe it was arson."

Tommy gave him one hard, long stare. "I never said that."

"What the hell does that mean?"

"Look, I get that after what happened to your parents, that you'd see arson in every fire, but—"

No. Oh, hell, no. "We dealt with that in my interview, remember? That fire was years ago and has nothing to do with this."

"Are you saying that what happened to them when you were a kid has nothing to do with you being a firefighter?"

"I'm saying that I know what I saw on that Hill Street fire."

"No, you don't." Tommy scrubbed a weary hand over his face. "Listen, you should have several strikes on your permanent record by now, but I've always stepped in for you. I trusted you, and now I'm asking you to trust me."

"To do what?"

"To not go over my head with this. The chief is getting pissed off, Zach. And when he's pissed, he reacts. You know that by now. So do this, for me." He paused. *"Please."* And with that, he walked away.

Zach watched him leave in frustrated disbelief before turning to go inside, coming face-to-face with Brooke.

"Hey," she said softly.

"Hey." Before he could ask how much she'd overheard, she put her hand on his arm and literally gave him a physical jolt. Gave her one, too, by the way she pulled her hand back. Jesus, when they finally touched each other sexually—and they would—he was convinced they'd spontaneously combust.

"You okay?"

Better now, he thought. "Yeah." He took her hand in his, and felt the jolt all the way to his toes. "Quite a zap."

"Yeah."

Something about her made him forget his troubles. Well, not forget, but be able to ignore them, anyway. Her eyes were soft and also somehow sweet. After nearly three weeks, Number Seven had finally let her guard down, and damn, but it looked good on her. He wondered if she wanted to put that concern to good use, because he had several ideas—

"Are you sure you're okay?"

Soft, sweet, sexy, and too perceptive. "I'm fine."

"Because it's understandable if you're not. I'm here if you wanted to—"

Oh yeah. He wanted to. He wanted to in his bed, in hers, with her panting out his name as she came all over him.

"—talk."

He blinked the sexy vision away. "No. Not talk."

She blushed but didn't go there. "I'm sorry about your parents."

So she'd heard everything. "It was a long time ago."

"And it doesn't change what you saw at that Hill Street fire."

He stared at her, a little stunned. "No, it doesn't." He felt his heart engage, hard. "You're different, Brooke O'Brien."

"I've heard that before."

"Different good. Different great."

She didn't believe him, that was all over her face. "If you'd gone surfing with me," he said, "I could have shown you, proven it to you."

"Maybe another time."

Now that, he could get behind. "I'll count on it."

With an unsure but endearing nod, she walked away.

CHAPTER FIVE

IF BROOKE HAD talked with Zach for even another minute, she'd probably have thrown herself at him. She wouldn't have been able to help herself. He'd been standing there, looking fiercely unhappy, and her ears had been ringing with all she'd heard Tommy say to him—about his parents, about that kid dying, about how Zach needed to stay out of it. God, she'd wanted to grab him and hug him and kiss away that look on his face.

Even now she wanted to, hours later, sitting by herself in the house.

Good thing she was off duty for two days. Two days in which to get herself together and find some semblance of control. Because there were other ways to offer comfort than sex, for God's sake. She could buy a Hallmark card, for instance. Or make cookies.

But neither appealed. No, she wanted to offer a different kind of comfort all together.

A physical comfort.

A grip. She needed one. So she buried herself in packing. By the time her weekend was over, she'd gotten to the halfway point, setting aside a shocking amount of boxes to keep.

Keep.

Odd, how she wished she could keep even more, but she'd talked herself out of that, going only for the photos and diaries, still surprised at the sentimental impulse. What was she going to do with it all and no house to keep it in? Oh sure, her name was on the deed of this one, but that was temporary.

Like everything in her life.

The answers didn't come, not then, and not when she drove to work for her next scheduled shift. As she got out of her car, her eyes automatically strayed to the hammock, empty of one übersexy firefighter. Not there.

And not washing his rig, half-naked. His rig was parked, though, so she knew he was here, somewhere. Pulse quickening for no good reason other than she was thinking about him, she stepped inside her new home away from home and found a big poster had gone up in the front room, announcing the chief's upcoming big birthday beach bash.

A party.

She wasn't great at those. Turning to head into the kitchen, she ran smack into a warm, solid chest.

Zach's T-shirt didn't say Bite Me today. It didn't say anything. No, this one was plain black, half-tucked into loosely fitted Levi's that looked like beloved old friends, faded in all the stress points. He had his firefighter duffel bag over his shoulder and was clearly just getting here for his shift, same as her.

"Hey." It was the low, rough voice that had thrilled her in waaaay too many of her dreams lately. "You showed."

At the old refrain said after all these weeks only to make her smile, she found herself doing just that even as her body came to quick, searing life. She had it bad for him, and it was as hot and uncontrollable as a flash fire. "I told you, I finish everything I start."

He smiled a bad-boy smile, and touched her, a hand to hers, that was all—and the whole of her melted. "Everything?" he murmured.

Oh, boy. She recognized the heat in his gaze, and felt a matching heat in her belly.

And her nipples.

And between her legs.

A kiss. She wanted just one kiss. Was that so bad?

"Because I think we've started something very interesting here. Something we should finish. What do you think?"

"I...uh..."

"I'm all ears," he murmured and shifted just a little closer. So close that she had to tip her head up to see into his eyes, giving her an up-front and personal view of the scar that slashed his right eyebrow in half.

Her gaze dropped from that scarred brow to his mouth. *Way* too dangerous. Also too sexy-looking for his own good, for *hers*—his smile too easy on the eyes, his *everything* too easy on the eyes.

"Brooke?"

"Don't I hear a fire bell?" she managed.

He chuckled softly. "No, but nice try." He shifted to let her move past him, but somehow they ended up bumping against each other, softness to hardness. For a brief breath she closed her eyes and allowed herself to absorb it—his scent, his proximity, the feel of him brushing up against her.

She'd had no idea how much she'd craved this nearness, a physical touch; that it was *him,* the object of her secret nighttime fantasies, only intensified the sensation.

He put his hands on her arms, sensuously slid them

up and down, and she forgot they were in the firehouse, forgot that they should really make at least an attempt to be discreet. Hell, she forgot to breathe. "Zach." She tore her gaze from his and looked at his mouth.

A mouth that let out a low, rough sound of hunger, and then, blessedly, *finally,* was on hers, and then she was kissing him with *her* mouth, with her entire body, and most likely her heart and soul, because, good Lord, the man could kiss. He gave her everything—his hands, his body, his tongue—and when they broke apart for air, he stared down at her in astonishment. "Damn."

"What?"

"Just damn." Eyes a little dazed, he took a step back, looking off his axis enough to send a surge of lust and power skittering through her, but she managed to control herself. Controlled and composed. Yeah, that was her, one hundred percent put together.

With hard nipples.

And a telling dampness between her thighs.

"You ever feel anything like that before?" he asked.

"Truthfully? It's been so long, I can't remember."

His soft but not necessarily amused laugh ruffled the hair at her temple and ran down her spine. "Love your honesty."

She didn't. And she didn't love the idea that anyone could have seen that wild kiss they'd just shared. What was the matter with her? She turned away, but he caught her, a hand curving around her shoulder. "Don't go."

She needed to. *So* needed to. "Listen, maybe we could forget about this, at least until I figure out what it is."

His hand slid down her arm, settling on her waist, where his thumb lazily stroked one of her ribs. The motion liquefied her bones and altered her breath. "For-get it? I don't think that's possible. Did you feel that?"

"I felt…something." Which she was fighting. She wasn't sure why, when she'd wanted that kiss more than her next breath—but that hadn't been just any kiss. No. And being with him wouldn't be just sex, either, and she knew herself enough to know that she wasn't quite equipped to walk away. Not from that.

And she *was* walking away. In a matter of weeks. Her job would be over, her grandmother's home on the market… "It's natural that we'd feel…" She watched him arch a curious brow. "This. Natural. I'm a woman, you're a man." A really, *really* hot man, but still. "Nat-ural," she repeated again, and tried to mean it. "We've been working hard, and not relaxing, and…"

His head dipped to hers, his eyes a lethal combo of heat and good humor. "So you'd feel this with every-one, then? Say, Dustin? Or Blake?"

"Okay, no. But—"

Triumph surged in his eyes to go with that heart-stopping heat. "Maybe we should do something about it."

Yes, cried her body. Oh please, yes.

A bell sounded, thank God, and before she could form a response, the call went out for all the firefight-ers, no EMTs required.

Aidan popped his head in for Zach, who nodded, then looked down into her face. "We can finish this when I get back."

"No need," she said quickly.

"Oh, there's a need."

And then he was gone.

BROOKE SPENT MOST of the day out on transport calls with Dustin, and though she gave her all to what she was doing, her mind wandered. Not to the house she needed to sell, or how it was going to make her feel to leave a place she was slowly, reluctantly, started to think of as hers, but to a man and his kiss, and to the fact that he was making her yearn and burn when she never yearned and burned.

"Where are you today, New Hire? Disneyland?" Dustin shot her an exasperated look after having to ask her the same question three times in a row.

"I'm sorry. I'm preoccupied."

He pushed up his glasses. "It's because you guys haven't knocked it out yet. That's very preoccupying."

She stared at him. *"What?"*

"Come on. Are you going to tell me that you don't want to be with Zach?"

"Yes," she said quickly. "I'm going to tell you that. I don't want to be with…"

He waited patiently, but the lie wouldn't come off her damn tongue. Frustrated, she turned to look out the window, watching the town go by. Farmers' market. An art gallery. An outdoor café. "It's personal."

"Hey, don't worry. Your secret's safe with me. Hell, I've got the same problem."

"You want to have sex with Zach?"

He pushed up his glasses again, grinned, and pulled into the station. "Not quite." He hopped out and walked away whistling, getting inside before she could ask him *who* he had the same problem with.

Zach and Aidan's rig was in the garage, and her heart skipped a beat. The kiss, the kiss, the kiss…it was all she could think about. That, and getting another. And then she stepped into the kitchen and found Zach just standing there, looking ten kinds of wow.

He was in his gear, a little dusty, a little sooty and a whole lot sexy. He was still practically shimmering with adrenaline from the fire he'd just fought, looking far too edgy to be the laid-back, easygoing surfer guy she knew him to be.

And far too much for her to handle, no matter how much her body sent up a plea to let it do just that. He was too experienced for her, too...everything.

She'd spent too much time in her life trying to get somewhere, trying to find herself, to let a man like this in. Unfortunately, right now, at this very second, she wasn't thinking about finding herself. She was thinking about seeing him naked. "Hey. You okay?"

"Yeah."

But that was a lie, and that haze of lust he always created faded a little as she stepped closer. "Did anyone get hurt?" Or God forbid, like in the Hill Street fire that she knew haunted him, die.

"No."

But the memory of something bad was etched in the drawn, exhausted lines of his face. He took his losses hard, very hard, and that fact only deepened how she felt about him.

"I'm just tired," he said. "And needed a moment alone."

"Oh. I'm sorry." And she went to leave, because she understood that, but then he added, "I don't want to be alone from you."

She turned to look at him, but he'd moved closer and she bumped right into him. Her chest to his, his thighs to hers, and she actually let out a shuddering sigh that might have been a moan.

"What was that?"

Oh, just her brain cells blowing fuses left and right. "Nothing."

Snagging her hand, he held her close, peering into her face. "You let out a...sound."

"Yes. It's called breathing."

His hand slid to her waist and gently squeezed. "It sounded like more."

How about a sexually charged, needy whimper? Did it sound like that? "No."

His gaze searched hers for a moment. "Maybe we should talk about the kiss."

Kisses. Plural. "Probably we shouldn't. It might lead to..."

More.

He was waiting for her to speak.

"I think I heard the fire alarm."

"Huh," he said, sounding curious.

"What?"

"You're not as honest as I thought."

"Yes, I am."

"Really?" His hand slid to the small of her back and stroked lightly. "Then what are you thinking right now?"

That he'd look mighty fine naked. "That I'm hungry."

Not a lie. She *was* hungry. For his yummy body.

"Brooke..."

"Yeah. Listen." She let out a breath. "I'm trying to resist you here, okay? I'm failing miserably, but I'm trying."

"Why?"

Wasn't that the question of the year. "Because this is unlike me, this thing we have going on. I don't flirt, and I certainly don't do…whatever it is *you're* thinking right now."

"Never?"

"No, not—not in a long time."

"That's just not right, Brooke."

Just the image of what they were talking about gave her an odd shiver and changed her breathing, and she realized he wasn't breathing all that steadily, either. "Not helping, Zach."

He laughed—at himself, at her, she had no idea really, but she found herself staring up at him, torn between marveling at the ease with which he showed his emotions and laughing back because the sound of his genuine amusement was contagious. "Happy to amuse you."

"I'm sorry." Still smiling, he sighed. "Ah, hell, that felt good. Laughing."

"Laughing at me felt good."

"Oh, no." Gently, he tugged on her ponytail. "Definitely laughing with you, I promise. And I should be resisting, too. But I can't seem to do that."

His words caused more of those interesting shivers down her spine, and to other places, as well, secret places that wanted reactivating. Standing there in the hallway, way too close to this sexy man, a smile wanting to split her face, laughter spilling in her gut, she realized something.

Whether she'd meant to or not, she'd made roots here, temporary ones, but roots she would treasure and remember always. And now she wanted to strip naked and let him do things to her, lots of things, things that would create more lasting memories that she could take with her. "So how often, when you give that look to a woman, when you talk to her in that low, sexy voice, when you touch her, do her clothes just fall off?"

When he opened his mouth, she shook her head. "No, you know what? I'm sorry. Don't answer that. Because I was on board for that. The clothes-falling-off thing. But…"

"But…?"

"But I'm not mixing business and pleasure, no matter how sexy you are. I can't, much as I want to. I just can't, not for anything less than a meaningful, lasting relationship, a real connection."

Her own words shocked her but she found she meant them. To the bone. Being in her grandmother's house had obviously sent that yearning within her rising to the surface, and she couldn't help it. "I mean it. I'm sorry if I let you think otherwise, but I really do."

Looking torn between bafflement and disappointment, he nodded. "Okay."

"I'm sorry if I led you on. If it helps, I led myself on, too. I hope we're still friends." All that was left to do was walk away gracefully, when in her heart of hearts she didn't want to walk away at all. She started with one step, a baby step, and then another. "I also hope that the rest of your shift goes well," she managed.

"Thank you. That's…friendly of you."

Was he was mocking her? "Well," she said primly, backing to the door. "Just because we're not going to…"

"Mix business and pleasure," he supplied helpfully.

"Yes." Because obviously he was not looking for a deep or meaningful relationship, or he'd have said so. "It doesn't mean that we can't get along."

"I think," he said slowly, in a tone she couldn't quite place, "that we're not going to have a problem in that department."

No. No, they weren't.

She nodded, and managed to turn and leave, but in the hallway, alone, she leaned back against a wall and let out a long breath. There. That hadn't been hard or awkward.

Ah, hell. It'd been plenty of both.

But she'd done the right thing. Now she wouldn't fall for him and mourn him after she left. Yep, definitely the right thing.

Damn it. Why couldn't she have gotten all self-protective after she'd gotten to see him naked? Brooke turned around to look at the closed kitchen door, nearly going back in, but she restrained herself.

The right thing.

CHAPTER SIX

SEVERAL SHIFTS LATER, Brooke was sitting outside the fire station on a rare break, laptop open, flipping through a national job database to see where she might go after the house sold and this job ended in a few weeks.

The warm sun beat down on her, the waves across the street providing the perfect white noise. It should have been incredibly peaceful. Instead, she was thinking about Zach. About the kissing. About her opening her mouth and saying that she wasn't going to mix pleasure and business.

She'd meant it, but she *really* regretted saying it.

Cristina came outside. She wore her blue uniform trousers, a pair of kick-ass boots and a tiny white tank top, which emphasized a figure that a Playboy model would envy. Chomping into a red apple, she glanced at Brooke. "Are you actually relaxing, New Hire?"

"Brooke. My name's Brooke." This was now a three-week-old refrain between the two of them.

Hard to believe she'd been in California for so long already, but it was a fact. And as she always did, Cristina shrugged. "Hey, I called Number Four Skid Mark, so consider yourself lucky."

She would. Cristina might be sarcastic and caustic but she was brutally honest, emphasis on brutally, and loyal to a fault. In short, if you were on her good side, you had a friend to the death. Brooke knew the two of them weren't there, not even close, but at least she didn't have a nickname she couldn't live with.

"There's no point in remembering your name when you all eventually quit," Cristina continued.

"I'm not leaving until my six weeks are up. I'm just past halfway."

Leaning back against a tree, Cristina studied Brooke with interest. "People who aren't from around here rarely stick."

"Gee, really? Even with your sweet and welcoming attitude?"

Cristina smiled. "It's too bad you're not sticking. You could grow on me."

"I *am* sticking. Until the job is over."

"Speaking of sticking, I hear you were sticking to Officer Hottie's lips. That true?"

Oh, boy. "Officer Hottie?"

"Yeah. So were you?"

"That's…" She settled for the same line she'd given Dustin. "Personal."

"How personal?"

Wasn't that the question. She and Zach had only kissed, but it seemed like more, and there'd been lots of close encounters since… All she knew was that the wild sexual tension seemed unrelenting.

And overwhelming.

She really wanted to face that tension, and release it. Let loose.

Assuming Zach still wanted to.

"I know my faults," Cristina said into her silence. "I'm sarcastic, mean and I don't like many people. But

Zach? I like him. A whole lot. He's going through a tough time, and he's vulnerable."

The thought of big, rough-and-tumble Zach being vulnerable might have been funny only a week ago but Brooke knew Cristina was right. "The arson thing?"

"The chief's riding Tommy's ass, and Tommy's riding Zach's. Zach could just shut up and walk away from it all, but it's not in his blood to walk away, not when he knows he's right. I care about him, we all care about him, and he needs to stay focused."

"How do I threaten that?"

"You're messing with his head. *I'm* the only one who does that."

As warnings went, it wasn't exactly subtle. "I didn't realize you two were dating."

"Oh, I wouldn't call it dating," Cristina said with a smile.

Okaaaaay. "What would you call it?"

Cristina just looked smug, then, standing up, grabbed hold of a tree branch above her. "Any new interesting calls lately?"

"Hard to top Viagra Man, but I'm sure there's something just around the corner. What are you doing?"

"Pull-ups." She did five in a row, and still managed to talk normally. "Cats and hard-ons. Interesting job, you have to admit."

"True."

"So where are you going when this is over?"

"Don't worry. It'll be far, far away." Brooke just wished she knew where. She always knew—but this time nothing was coming to her.

Looking pleased, Cristina executed ten more pull-ups, then dropped to the ground to do push-ups.

Brooke went back to her laptop. Cristina didn't seem to mind being ignored, and Brooke tried for some peace and quiet. When another set of footsteps came up the walk, she didn't even bother to look up. She was busy, very busy, thank you very much, and needed no more distractions.

"Didn't anyone ever tell you that all work and no play will make you a very dull girl?"

Everything within her went still at the sound of Zach's low, husky voice. He wore his uniform, looking just hot enough that she felt little flickers of flame burst to life inside her. "Maybe I like dull."

"Nobody likes dull."

"I don't know." This from Cristina, now doing sit-ups on the grass like a machine. "I can believe she likes dull."

With an irritated sigh, Brooke closed her laptop yet again and stood. She'd find another place to study. Some place where the not-so-subtle barbs couldn't pierce her skin. Some place where there were no gorgeous, sexy firefighters making her yearn for things she shouldn't, like a connection, a real connection. And letting loose... She made it to the door before a big, warm hand hooked her elbow and pulled her around.

For a guy who only moved when he needed to, she was surprised at how fast he'd caught her. "I'm busy," she said with unmistakable irritation. She used that tone when she needed someone to back off, and it'd never failed her.

But it failed her now. Utterly.

"Yes, I can see that you're very busy."

Cristina, apparently finished torturing her body, walked past them with a smirk.

But Zach just studied Brooke's face. "You're always busy. You like it that way."

So damn true. But they weren't going there. "Where were you?"

"A meeting with the chief."

He was no longer amused, and she read between the lines. "How did it go?"

"Terrific."

"Really?"

"Sure. All I have to do is learn to respect authority, and everything will be just terrific. So were you and Cristina bonding?"

Nice subject change, she thought, but she saw misery in his eyes, and she didn't want to poke at it. "Yeah. We're like this." She held up two entwined fingers.

He smiled.

"Officer Hottie?" she asked. "Really?"

He had the good grace to wince. "If it helps, I don't answer to it." It was just the two of them in the yard now, with no company except the light breeze and waves. Perfect time to tell him she wanted to mix business and pleasure, just once. He stood close enough that she could see flecks of dark jade swimming in that sea of pale green. He hadn't shaved this morning, and maybe not yesterday morning, either, and she could feel the heat radiating off his body and seeping into hers. She could smell him, too, some delicious, intoxicating scent of pure male that had her nostrils twitching.

Bad nostrils. *Tell him...*

"Cristina doesn't mean to be rude," Zach said.

It made her laugh. "Yes, she does."

"Okay, yeah. She does."

"You're all a very tight unit. I get that loud and clear."

"We are. It's what makes us so good. But there's room for more. There's room for you. You could fit in, if you wanted to."

Her greatest fantasy… "*If* I wanted to?"

"Yeah, well, you have a tendency to stand on the outside looking in."

"No, I don't."

He just looked at her, all patient and quietly amused, and she sighed. "Okay, I do."

"But you don't want to be on the outside looking in."

How was it that he knew her? "We both know I don't really fit in."

"You could."

"Uh-huh. Cristina's waiting with open arms."

His expression was serious now. "She's had it rough and is a little distrustful, that's all. It has nothing to do with you."

She had a feeling it wasn't only Cristina who'd had it rough. "You're sleeping with her."

Brooke hadn't meant for that to escape from her lips. She wanted to pretend it hadn't, but Zach's brows had shot up so far on his forehead they vanished into his hair.

"Not that it matters," she said quickly, trying like hell to backtrack. "Because it doesn't."

"It doesn't?"

She shook her head. "It doesn't. It really doesn't. It really, really, *really* doesn't—"

He set a finger on her lips and she shut up.

"Cristina and I are friends," he said quietly. "We have been for a very long time."

She wrapped her fingers around his wrist and pulled

it away. "And more than friends? Have you been more than friends for a very long time, as well?"

"Twice. A very long time ago."

She didn't want to acknowledge the relief that flooded through her at that. "You might want to remind her of that part the next time she's going around marking her territory."

"She has no territory to mark. Or I never would have kissed you like I did." He ran a finger over her jaw.

A simple touch.

But there was nothing simple about the way her body reacted, starting with the breath backing up in her throat and her nipples tightening as they hoped for some attention, too. So much for not mixing business and pleasure, because there was pleasure when she was with him. Lots of it. "Oh boy."

His gaze met hers. "Oh boy bad, or oh boy good?"

"We're friends."

"Yes."

"Th-that touch felt like...more."

"Did it?" He smiled innocently. "Then *you're* the one mixing the business with the pleasure, aren't you?"

She stared at him, but he only smiled, touched her again, then walked off, leaving her to talk to herself. "Am not," she whispered.

But she was.

She *so* was.

THE NEXT DAY, Brooke and Dustin hit the ground running and never slowed. They delivered a baby at a grocery store, transported a set of conjoined twins, stood by at a bank robbery and helped locate two fingers belonging to a construction worker, who'd lost them in a pile of sawdust thanks to the blade of his handsaw. It was early evening before they finally made their way back to the station, where a delicious smell had Brooke's nose twitching.

"Ohmigod," Dustin moaned. "Smell that?"

"Tell me it's for us."

"If there's a God."

Following the scent into the kitchen, they found the crew grabbing plates and helping themselves to a huge pan of lasagna. Zach was already seated at the table, his uniform trousers and a gray T-shirt spread taut over that hard body.

Brooke's gaze locked on his. They hadn't spoken since yesterday, where she'd done that whole mixing-business-with-pleasure thing, confusing their issues.

Her issues.

The memory of their kiss—that deep, hot long kiss—was *still* burned in her mind. In spite of herself, she wanted another one, and she had a feeling it was all over her face.

"Ah, man," Aidan moaned loudly from the table, mouth full—which didn't stop him from loading more in. "This lasagna is better than sex."

Cristina snorted. "Then you're doing it wrong." She took a bite, then also moaned. "But, oh yeah, baby, this is a close second. Nicely done, Officer Hottie."

Zach rolled his eyes. "Thanks. I think."

Brooke stared at him as she sat. "You cooked?"

"Well, we tried letting Cristina cook," Aidan said. "Remember, Eeyore?" He nudged Blake with his elbow. "For your birthday?"

"Disaster," Blake confirmed with a dour nod.

Aidan nodded, winking at Brooke as he successfully

ruffled Cristina's feathers. "Cristina here burns water with spectacular flare."

"Hey, I've got other talents," Cristina said.

Aidan grinned. "Sure you do."

Cristina waved her fork in his face. "Don't make me kick your ass."

"You cooked," Brooke repeated, looking at Zach.

"Why are you so surprised?"

"Because—" Because it was a hidden talent, and now she was wondering at his other hidden talents. "I'm just impressed, that's all."

"Well, welcome to the twenty-first century," Cristina muttered, still glaring at Aidan. "Where men cook. And in case you haven't heard, us women can vote now, too."

Everyone laughed, and Brooke rolled her eyes, but when she looked around, she realized they weren't laughing *at* her at all. She was included in the joke.

Zach was gazing at her, his mouth curved, looking relaxed and easygoing and, damn it, gorgeous, and something came to her in that moment.

She belonged.

Aidan and Cristina were still bickering, Blake and Dustin were thumb wrestling for the last serving of lasagna, Sam and Eddie were shoveling in their food and laughing over something...they were all as dysfunctional as they could be, and they were a family.

And she was a part of it.

Sam took the last of the lasagna and everyone protested. "Hey, there's two kinds of people in here—the fast and the hungry. I'm the fast, that's all."

Zach smiled at Brooke with a genuine affection that stole her breath.

And replaced it with heat.

Oh boy, a lot of heat.

"Hey," Sam said. "Don't forget, I need everyone to sign up for party duty. The chief's b-day bash isn't going to throw itself."

"Yeah, and why are we doing this again?" Blake asked, classic Eeyore.

"To have an excuse to have a party," Eddie explained.

"To kiss up, you mean," Blake said, sounding disgusted with all of them. "Don't forget the kissing-up part."

"Well, maybe if Zach spent some time kissing up—" Sam accompanied this with kiss-kiss noises "—he wouldn't be called to the principal's office to get spanked every other day."

Zach sighed.

Cristina reached across the table and squeezed his hand. "I'd rather be spanked than hold my tongue."

"Me, too," Aidan said, in between mouthfuls of food. "Me, too."

"Yes, but…" Blake sent Zach a frustrated look. "It wouldn't hurt to lay low, let the chief get distracted by someone else's ass once in a while."

Zach shook his head.

No can do on the lying low thing, apparently.

"I can tell on Sam," Eddie suggested. "For leaving porn in the bathroom. Maybe that would take some of the heat off Zach."

"Hey, what did porn ever do to you?" Sam protested.

They all laughed, and Zach smiled, but Brooke could see that it didn't reach his eyes.

Later, she sought him out in the kitchen. He opened the refrigerator for a bottle of water, then leaned back against the counter, taking a long drink. He was behaving himself. Not mixing business and pleasure.

He was also quiet. Hurting.

Telling herself she was crazy, she walked toward him and took the water from his hand.

He just looked at her.

"That friend thing…" she started.

"Yeah?" He gripped the edges of the counter by his sides, and she wondered if that was to ensure he didn't touch her. She wished he could have put those hands on her, but she'd seen to it that he wouldn't try.

For her own good.

Damn, she was tired of for her own good. "If we're friends," she said softly, "then I should be able to do this."

"What?"

She set her hands on his chest, then let them glide up around his neck, bringing her body flush to his as she hugged him.

For one beat he held himself rigid, then with a low, rough breath, let his hands drop from the counter and come around her, hard.

She didn't look into his face, knowing if she did, she'd kiss him again, and this was just a hug, comfort.

Friendship.

So she pressed her face into his throat and held on.

"Brooke," he murmured, and the hand he had fisted in her shirt low on her back opened, pressing her even closer as he buried his face in her hair and just breathed her in. "Brooke—"

The kitchen door opened, and Eddie looked at them, brows raised. "If I cook tomorrow," he asked, "can I have the same thank-you?"

MUCH LATER THAT night, back at her grandmother's house, Brooke thought about the evening. About the hug and her reaction to it. Partially, because her body was still revved from what should have been an innocent touch, but there was more to it.

According to Sam, she could be the fast, or the hungry. But when it came to her life, she'd always been the fast, never slowing down, never relaxing, always doing, going, running. And for what? To always end up alone, wondering what she was missing? She'd come here out of duty, but she'd also wanted to find herself. Maybe... maybe she couldn't do that at the speed of light, maybe she had to slow down. Maybe *that's* what was missing.

She needed to give herself time to catch her breath, time to relax.

Needed to do that whole let-loose thing.

Moving through the kitchen with a mug of tea, she looked out the window at the dark night and thought about it, thought about Zach. As she did, a now-familiar tingle began low in her belly and spread. And suddenly, she had a feeling she knew exactly how she should be letting loose. And it included mixing business and pleasure.

A *lot* of mixing.

CHAPTER SEVEN

ZACH RAN IN the mornings. It woke him up, kept him in shape and gave him time to think. Typically, he thought about work or, more recently, Brooke. He really liked thinking about Brooke.

But this morning, after having a dream about the arson fire, it wasn't Brooke on his mind, and he changed his routine, running past Hill Street. When he reached the fire site, he thought maybe he was still dreaming.

The place had been demolished, razed.

He stared at it in disbelief. On a hunch, he ran back to his house, got into his truck and drove to the site of a different fire, the one from a few months previous, a fire he'd also "cried" arson to Tommy about and had gotten his wrist slapped for.

That property was also demolished.

And the one before that? Yeah. Demolished. Standing at the edge of the third lot, where nothing remained but dirt, he pulled out his cell phone, but didn't hit any numbers as his last meeting with the chief ran through his head. He'd been asked, and not very nicely, to do his own job and no one else's.

Somehow he doubted stalking the fire sites would be considered doing his own job.

Shit.

Tommy Ramirez had told him to be on his best behavior, but that was proving damn hard to do. Driving home, he called Aidan, but had to leave a message. While waiting for a return call, he tried to distract himself with a Lakers game but his mind kept wandering to the arson.

He couldn't let it go. Driven to do something, Zach pulled out his laptop. He'd already typed up all his thoughts and notes on the fires. Now he needed to talk it out with someone, and oddly enough, the person that kept coming to mind wasn't Aidan, but someone with sweet baby blues and a smile that pretty much destroyed him.

Brooke. He was driven by her, too, because, damn, she was something. She was something, and…and she wanted a relationship.

Driven as he was, he didn't do relationships. Relationships always came to an end, and he hated endings. He didn't need a shrink to attribute that to losing his parents so young, to growing apart from the brother he had nothing in common with except grief and, in a way, losing him, too.

No, he didn't like endings, and therefore, avoided beginnings.

Still, Brooke drew him. She was a little buttoned-up, a little rigid, and—and hell. She had a smile that could melt him from across town, and a way of looking at him that suggested she could see right through to all his flaws, and she didn't mind those flaws.

Jesus. He went back to his laptop, burying himself. He had property deeds, architectural plans, records of sales, and looked it all over for the hundredth time to see if there were any obvious connections.

When his doorbell rang, he figured it was Aidan.

When he opened the door, it turned out to be a beautiful redhead.

Nope, not Aidan, but his neighbor Jenny with a pizza in one hand, a six-pack dangling from her other, and a fuck-me smile firmly in place.

"Hi, neighbor." She lifted the pizza. "Interested?"

She was a high school librarian, but nothing about her was a stereotypical keeper of books. She hosted a weekly poker party, enjoyed car racing, and brewed her own beer. They were friends, and so far, *just* friends, but she'd made it clear that she was ready for that to change. Now here she was, flirting. Normally he'd flirt right back, but he didn't. Stress, he decided. Stress and frustration. "I'm sorry, Jenny. It's not a good time—"

"Don't even try to tell me you're not hungry. I'll have to take your temperature." She pushed her way in, carrying the food, swinging the beer. "Everyone has to eat."

True. And she'd obviously decided the way to his heart was by way of his stomach, maybe with a side trip past other certain body parts. Up until a few weeks ago, he might have been happy to take that side trip, but he no longer wanted to. Not with another woman on his mind.

Jenny turned to face him, and her smile slowly faded. "What's the matter?"

"I'm not sure." Yes. Yes, he was. He wanted a blue-eyed, sweet, sexy EMT with a smile that slayed him.

And only her.

"Zach?" Jenny waved a hand in front of his face. "You look like you were just hit by a train."

Uh-huh. The Brooke train. At some point, probably

during the wild kiss, he'd decided no one else would do. *Holy shit.*

Jenny set down the food and popped the top off two of the beers, handing him one. "Here. You look like you could use this now."

"Thanks." He took a long pull.

"So who is she?"

"I didn't even know there was a she until two seconds ago. How did you know?"

"It's all over your face."

He scrubbed a hand over his face, images of Brooke coming to him. That very first day when she'd woken him, or when she'd so fiercely approached Code Calico, and then Viagra Man...or the way she'd looked at him with her heart and soul in her eyes when she'd said she wanted a relationship.

"Damn," Jenny said softly, still staring at him. "She's...special, isn't she?"

"I—yeah." He managed to meet her gaze. "I'm sorry."

"Not as sorry as I am." With another sigh, she stepped toward him, and in a show of how stunned he was, managed to nudge him down to the couch with a single finger. Then she plopped next to him and clinked her bottle to his in a commiserating toast. "You're good and screwed, you know that, right?"

He leaned back and shook his head. "You have no idea."

ON THE DRIVE to work, Brooke took in the high morning surf on her left, and the joggers, walkers and bikers on her right. She'd lost track of how many times she'd moved in her life, but all of those places had been big cities. She had to admit small-town living appealed. Little to no traffic, good parking spots...

But she was almost four weeks down, and only two to go. Past halfway. Soon enough she'd be gone, far away from here, starting over yet again. She'd found jobs available in both Seattle and L.A., and had filled out applications, telling herself there was just something about the West Coast.

But actually, there was just something about Santa Rey, and it had little to do with the great weather and everything to do with the fact that in spite of herself, she was making ties here.

Blake was on his laptop when she entered the firehouse, and at the sight of her, he jumped guiltily, quickly slapping the computer shut.

"Don't worry," she quipped. "Your porn is safe with me."

Instead of laughing, he grabbed his laptop and left the room.

Cristina was on one of the couches reading a *Cosmo*. She flipped a page. "Hey, New Hire. Maybe you should read this when I'm done. There's an article here on how not to scare off men."

Brooke shot her an exasperated look. "One of these days you're going to call me Brooke."

"I doubt it. Oh, and don't forget to read this article. 'How Not To Be Annoying At The Work Place.'"

Giving up, Brooke went into the kitchen. Her eyes automatically strayed to the counter—the scene of her two indiscretions: one a heart-stopping kiss, the other the best hug she'd ever had. Letting out a breath, she poured herself some iced tea and was adding sugar when the door opened behind her.

"Hey."

At just the one word, uttered in that easygoing, low, husky voice, she dropped her spoon. "Damn it." She crouched down, and so did Zach, handing her the spoon, smiling at her. He was in uniform, filling it out with that mouthwatering body, but there was something... quiet about him today. Something quiet and, frankly, also outrageously sexy.

He helped her up. "You've been getting sun." He touched the tip of her nose. "And a few freckles." He stroked his finger over her cheek, her jaw.

Her body was so pathetically charged her toes curled at his touch. That's what happened when she spent her spare time dreaming about seeing him naked.

"You're looking at me funny again. Do I have something in my teeth?"

"No."

"Do I smell bad?"

That tugged a laugh out of her. He smelled delicious, and she suspected he knew it. "No."

"Then what?"

"I dreamed about you," she admitted.

"Ah. Were we mixing business and pleasure?"

She opened her mouth to say yes, oh most definitely yes, but then shut it again. No need to give him more power.

He just laughed softly. "We were, weren't we?"

She felt the blush creep up her cheeks.

"Yeah." Another low laugh and a naughty grin. "We were."

"Zach—"

"Was it good?"

She bit her lower lip but it must have been all over

her face because his eyes went all sexy and sleepy. "Off the charts, huh?"

She closed her eyes. Oh yeah, off the charts.

Tell him you want to do the mixing in person. She was still trying to find the words when he said with a smile, "So, exactly how off the charts were we?"

"Zach!" yelled Dustin from the other room. "Phone!"

Zach sighed. "I'll be back. Don't move."

When he was gone, she let out a breath and fanned her face, saying the words she'd meant to say in front of him. "I was wrong. I *want* to mix business and pleasure. Just once." She smacked her own forehead. "How hard is *that* to say?"

Behind her, someone cleared his throat.

Oh, God. Wincing, she turned around. Blake had come in the back door in his silent way and stood there. "Sorry."

She just closed her eyes.

"No, it's okay. I didn't hear anything."

"Nothing?"

"Nothing," he said.

"Really?"

"Nothing except you want to jump his bones."

"I didn't say that!"

"Then I didn't hear it." He strode to the refrigerator, where he scrounged around and pulled out a soda, raising a brow when he realized she was still staring at him. "What? I won't tell anyone."

"Everyone tells everyone everything around here."

He acknowledged that with a shrug of his shoulders.

"Okay, you know what? I'm going to need a secret of yours."

He choked on his soda. "What?"

"That way I can guarantee that neither of us will talk."

Blake looked at her, then turned away. "I don't think that's a good idea."

"Are you kidding? It's a great idea."

His narrow shoulders were tense now. "But my secret is really someone else's."

"What do you mean?"

"Nothing. Never mind." Abruptly, he set his soda on the counter and walked out.

"Blake?"

But he was gone, carrying her very revealing secret. And then the fire bell went off and she put it out of her mind.

LATER THAT DAY, Brooke and Dustin were in the kitchen devouring a box of cookies between them while standing in front of the opened refrigerator trying to cool off.

"We're having a poker game Friday night at Cristina's," Dustin said. "You should join us."

"Did you ask Cristina?"

"Don't worry about her. She'll be happy to see you."

"Happy? Really? Cristina?"

"Okay," he said with a fond smile. "So she can be aloof, but it's just a facade. She's really just a toasted marshmallow."

"What did you call me?" Cristina came into the kitchen. She was in the bottom half of her fire gear, with a snug T-shirt on top. Her hair was pulled back and she looked hot, grumpy and irritated as she grabbed a handful of cookies.

"A *toasted* marshmallow." Dustin grinned at her,

leaning back against the counter. "Crispy on the out-side, soft and gushy on the inside."

Cristina hopped up on the counter next to him and set her head back against the upper cabinets, arms and legs spread in the aggressive sprawl of an alpha female who knew her place in the world. "Dustin?"

"Yeah?"

"The next time you call me a marshmallow, I'm going to pound you into the ground." She uttered this threat with her eyes closed, without moving a single muscle. "Next time."

Dustin winked at Brooke. "Definitely crispy on the outside."

"I can be a marshmallow sometimes, too," Brooke said.

A sound escaped Cristina, who still didn't move or open her eyes. "You don't know crispy. Dustin? Get me a water?"

"Ah, but I didn't hear the magic word."

"Get me a water. *Please.*"

"See?" Dustin grinned as he reached for a glass. "Soft and mushy."

"I'll have you know there's not a single inch of soft and mushy on me anywhere," Cristina muttered with-out her usual heat, making Brooke take a closer look at her. The female firefighter looked pale and just a little clammy, alerting her to the fact that maybe Cristina wasn't just being her usual pissy self, but might actu-ally be in pain. "Hey, are you okay?"

"Migraine." Dustin filled the glass, which he gently nudged into Cristina's hands. Then he lay a cold, wet compress over her forehead.

"Thanks." Cristina let out a sigh. "Christ, this sucks.

I'm going to the chief's party tonight. No matter what, I'm going."

"You should go home and sleep this off," Dustin said.

"I know. But first…" She sat up and groaned. "I've got to clean out my unit from that last call. Blake's doing something for the chief, so—"

Dustin set his hand to the middle of her chest and held her down. "If you're going to get rid of that headache, you need to sit real still and you know it."

The bell rang, and Cristina moaned, covering her ears as dispatch called for her and Blake's unit.

Dustin headed for the door. "I'll tell them you can't. They can get a different unit."

"Dustin—"

"Save it." He left the room.

Brooke looked at Cristina, so carefully still, pale and clearly miserable. "Can I get you anything?"

"Got a spare head?"

"Why don't you go home and go to bed?"

"I can't go anywhere until the rig is cleaned. We've got an inspection today."

"I know. We're all in the same boat."

"Oh, really? Are you on probation for falling asleep and not hearing a call?"

"Uh, no."

"Do you have a recent traffic violation?"

"Well, no, but—"

"Then get the hell out of my boat." Cristina sighed and straightened, looking positively green now. "Okay, I'm getting up. Watch your shoes."

"Stay." Brooke didn't quite dare put her hands on Cristina as Dustin had done, but she held them up. "I'll clean out your rig for you."

Cristina pulled the cold pack from her head and stared at Brooke. "Why? What do you want?"

Brooke let out a little laugh. "I'm offering to do something nice for you, even though you're not all that nice to me, and you're questioning it?"

"I'm less than 'not all that nice' to you, I'm downright bitchy. So the question stands, New Hire. Why would you do my job for me?"

Brooke shrugged. "Why not?"

Cristina just stared at her, the pain evident in her eyes but not hiding her cynicism. "The question isn't why not, but *why?*"

"Maybe I like to help people."

"We all do. Hence our jobs."

"Maybe I just do it nicer than you."

A ghost of a smile crossed Cristina's lips at that, then she very carefully covered her eyes with the compress again and leaned back. "Everyone does everything nicer than me."

"True," Dustin agreed, coming back into the room. "You're officially off duty, Cris."

Cristina peeked out from the cold pack to shoot him a look.

"You're sick. Take the break."

Cristina sighed. "Go away. Both of you just go away and let me die in peace."

Dustin lifted her off the counter.

"Hey!"

"If you won't put yourself to bed, I'll do it for you."

"Oh, sure, wait until I'm debilitated before you finally make a move on me."

He stared down at her, clearly shocked, his glasses

slipping down his nose. "You want me to make a move on you?"

She didn't answer.

"Cristina?"

"There's a very real possibility I'm going to throw up on you. So if you could stop talking, that would help."

"And if you could stop trying to tell me what to do when you're as green as a leaf, that would help."

She laughed very very softly. "Assertive, too. Who knew? Hey, New Hire?"

Already heading for the door to go clean Cristina's rig, Brooke glanced over. "Yeah?"

"Thanks."

"A PARTY," BROOKE muttered to herself. She'd showered and was now standing in the center of the bedroom she'd made hers, the first bedroom in her life that she loved without reason.

She had no idea if that was because her grandmother had put silly white-lace curtains over the window, which ruffled prettily in the wind, or if it was the dark cherry antique furniture. Or maybe it was because she'd come here looking for an exterior change of pace and had found an interior change of pace instead.

Because deep inside, she'd settled here. Her heart had engaged, for this town, this house.

For a man...

She stared into the closet. She had only one thing appropriate for a party on the beach, and that was a pretty little halter sundress she'd bought on a whim and had never worn.

With a sigh, she pulled it on, then didn't look at herself in the mirror. She did not want to change her mind.

In that vein, she slipped into a pair of flip-flops and headed directly toward her car before she could come up with a million and one reasons not to go, starting with needing to work on the house and ending with because she was nervous.

Being nervous was not an option.

Not only was she going to go to this party, she was going to go and relax.

Let loose.

She needed to remember the concept. She needed to live the concept. She was going to smile and laugh. She was going to let go. And maybe even manage to do so with one wildly sexy Zach Thomas.

If he was still interested.

Please let him still be interested.

She drove to the beach, parked and got out of her car, the salty air brushing at her hair, the waves pounding the surf sounding all soft and romantic. Then she glanced over at the man getting out of the truck right next to her and her heart knocked hard into her ribs.

Zach wore board shorts and a T-shirt, his body looking at ease and beach ready. His eyes, though...not so relaxed. Nope. As she watched them lock on her, they were filled with the same hunger and frustration she felt, and she knew.

He was most definitely still interested.

CHAPTER EIGHT

IT HAD BEEN a shitty day all around, Zach thought as he got out of his truck. He'd had another unpleasant phone call with Tommy, who refused to tell him what was happening with the arsons. Then he'd covered for Cristina on three calls and as a result, hadn't been ready for their monthly inspection, and the chief had chewed him out.

Zach had almost not come tonight.

But now, looking into Brooke's eyes, he was suddenly glad he had. Very glad. Just taking her in, he felt a visceral reaction clear to his toes. For the first time since he'd met her, she wasn't dressed for the practicality of their work. No uniform trousers and matching shirt, no steel-toed work boots, no carefully controlled hairdo that said, *Back off. The rest of me is wound as tight as my hair.*

Not that *that* look didn't have some hotness to it.

But tonight she was in a pale blue sundress of some lightweight material that hugged toned limbs and a body that reminded him she was in shape.

Great shape.

She'd left her hair down, the strawberry blond strands falling in soft waves just past her shoulders, lit softly by the moonlight. A few long bangs were swept to one side, curving along her cheek and jaw, emphasizing her face.

A beautiful face.

Looking at him.

Smiling at him, with just a hint of nerves.

And he stood there, a little stunned, because when she smiled for real it lit up her face and her eyes, revealing humor and a sharp intelligence, and…and a sexual awareness that sparked his.

Hell, his had been sparked from the moment he'd first set eyes on her, but once he'd realized she wasn't going to play, he'd tried like hell to redirect.

She wasn't going to play. Playing wasn't her thing. He needed to remember that. He really did. Turning, he headed down the beach. Not to the party, not yet. He needed a moment—

"Zach?"

Alone. He'd needed a moment alone, away from her, to clear his head, where he couldn't see her looking at him, so sweet and sexy, smiling that smile—

A little breathless, she ran around to the front of him, one hand stopping her loose hair from sliding into her face, the other spread on her dress as if to keep it from blowing up in the wind.

Torn between hoping for a gale-force wind or running away, he stood there instead, rooted to the spot. "You look…"

"Silly, right?" She smoothed down the fabric but the breeze continued to tease the flimsy material, lifting it, revealing her lovely thighs for one all-too-brief, tantalizing glimpse. "I know. I should have stuck with something more practical—"

"Amazing," he managed. Even the sound of her voice lifted his spirits. Somehow she made him feel better by just being. "I was going to say you look amazing."

"Oh." She flashed another kill-him-slowly smile. "It's just a dress."

"I like it. I like the lip gloss, too." It smelled like peaches, and he wondered, if he leaned in right now, would she let him have another taste of her?

Just one.

Who was he kidding? One taste wouldn't cover it. Neither would two. Nope, nothing less than an entire night of tasting would be good enough.

Tipping back his head, he stared up at the star-littered sky, taking a moment to draw in the salty air, to listen to the waves.

But that moment didn't give him the peace he needed. Not when she was still looking at him, her gaze word-lessly telling him that she wanted him, too. "You should head on over to the party." He gestured with a hitch of his chin to the bonfires already going about a hundred yards down the beach, and the growing crowd.

In spite of what Zach thought of him, the new chief was extremely popular.

"Can we walk first?" Brooke gestured in the oppo-site direction. "Just us?"

Walking alone with her on a moonlit night along the beach? A fantastically bad idea.

"Please?"

No. Absolutely not.

She held out her hand. "Sure," his mouth said with-out permission from his brain, and taking her hand, he led her down the path to the water. There they kicked off their flip-flops and walked with the surf gently hit-ting the shore on their right, the cliffs on their left and the moonlight touching their faces.

Pretty damn romantic, which didn't help.

A wave splashed over their bare feet and legs, and the bottom of Brooke's dress got wet, clinging like plastic wrap.

Perfect. Just what he needed. Brooke all wet.

Letting out a low laugh, she gathered the material in her hands, pulling it up above her knees as she backed farther up on the sand.

He thought she'd turn and head toward the party, but she didn't. She kept going.

And like a puppy on a leash, he followed.

"It's beautiful, isn't it?" she asked.

He took in her profile, the small smile on her glossed lips, the few freckles across her upturned nose, her hair flying around her face. "Yes," he agreed. "Beautiful."

Her gaze flew to his. "I was talking about the scenery."

"I know."

"But you weren't looking at it."

"No."

"I…" She let out what sounded like a helpless sigh. "You were saying that I'm beautiful?"

"Yes."

"See, that's the thing."

"There's a thing?"

"Well, you make me feel a thing." She looked away. "A few things, actually."

Uh-huh. And that made two of them.

The breeze continued to toy with the wet hem of her dress and his mind at the same time. He took in the empty beach, the myriad alcoves and cliffs lining the shore, forming lots of private little spots where they could escape to without being seen.

Where he could slowly glide that dress up her legs and—

"Ouch." She hopped on one foot, then bent to pick something up. "A shell."

He traced his finger over it in the palm of her hand. "I used to have jars and jars of these when I was little."

"You grew up here?"

"Yep. Santa Rey born and bred. My parents were surfers. I think my first words were surf's up."

She laughed, but then the sound faded. "You miss them. Your parents."

Lifting his eyes from the shell, his gaze collided with hers. "It was a long time ago, but yeah. I miss them."

"I lost my dad before I was even born, and I still miss him."

"What happened?"

"He died in a car wreck. My mom…she didn't really recover. She never settled in one place again, or with one man."

"That must have been rough on you."

"Not as rough as losing both parents." She squeezed his hand.

Yeah, it'd been rough. He and his parents had lived in an old apartment building on the beach. It'd been run-down, but it had fed their surf habit. He'd remembered every second of the night their building had caught fire. Every second of hearing his mother scream in horror at being stuck in the kitchen, surrounded by flames. Every second of watching his father battle those flames to try to get to her. The fire department had been volunteer at the time. They'd done the best they could, but their best hadn't been enough to save his parents.

Their rescue effort had been a recovery effort pretty much from the start.

"Your older brother raised you?"

"He did."

"Does he live here, too?"

"No, Caleb's a high-powered attorney in L.A. Driven and ambitious...we're very different." He smiled. "He's still after me to do something with my life."

"Firefighting isn't doing something?"

He shrugged. "Well, it's not going to get me fame and fortune, or into a cushy old-age home."

"You don't care about any of that."

"No."

She nodded, looked down at her fingers, then back into his eyes. "We're very different, too. You and I."

"I know."

"Are you okay with that?"

Zach felt a smile tug at his mouth. "I happen to like the differences between a man and a woman."

She let out a soft laugh. "I meant that you're laid-back and easygoing, and I'm...not."

"I don't judge my friends."

"Yeah, about that." Her gaze dropped to his mouth. "I have a question."

He hoped like hell it was something like, *Can I kiss you again?*

She hesitated, then shook her head. "I need to walk some more."

"Okay." But he was saying this to her back because she'd already started walking, not along the water this time, but up the sand toward the bluffs, where they could move over rocks the size of houses. She did just that, climbing one, reminding him that she was a capable, strong woman who spent her days lifting heavy gurneys.

He followed behind her, enjoying the way her dress bared her back, her arms, how it kept catching between her legs.

With a huff of frustration, she finally hiked the dress to midthigh so she could move easier, a sight he greatly enjoyed from his lower vantage point.

Her panties matched her dress.

Then she vanished from view. "Brooke?"

"Up here."

He found her on a ledge the size of his pickup truck, sitting with her arms wrapped around her knees, her face turned out to the ocean, the waves tipped in silver from the moonlight. "Isn't it amazing?" she whispered.

Yeah. Yeah, it was, but she was even more so. He sat next to her so that their shoulders touched, and for a long moment neither of them spoke.

"The waves are mesmerizing." She sighed. "I could watch them all night."

"You should see them beneath a full moon."

"I've rarely taken the time to just sit and watch waves. Actually, that's not true. I've *never* taken the time to just sit and watch waves." She let out a long breath and looked at him.

"You had a question," he reminded her.

A ghost of a smile crossed her lips. "I was thinking maybe I'm too rigid. For instance, I shut down this thing between us without giving it full consideration. I said I wanted a relationship, but the truth is, I'm leaving in a matter of weeks. I couldn't really have a relationship, anyway. Plus, you were right about me not relax-

ing enough. Letting loose. I need to try some of that."
She paused and looked at him for a reaction.

"Okay," he said carefully. "So..."

"It's just that I'm not exactly sure how to start." She
flashed an insecure smile. "I've always been in school,
or working. It's not really left a lot of time for anything
else. I mean, I've had feelings for guys before, of course,
but...but not in a while. A long while, actually." She
paused again. "Do you understand?"

He was trying.

With a sigh, she took his hand. "I'm attempting to
come on to you." She brought his hand up to her chest,
over the warm, creamy skin bared by her halter dress
to her heart.

He looked down at his long, tanned fingers spread
over her, feeling the curve of her breast beneath his
palm, and the way her heart beat wildly, and then stared
into her eyes.

"Just once," she said very softly, "I want to be wild
and crazy without worrying about anything. No meaning, no strings, no falling for anyone, just...let loose."

"I want to be very clear," he said, just as softly.
"You're looking to—"

"Have sex."

"Have sex." She wanted to have sex. Just once. Had
she been dropped here by the fantasy gods? How the
hell had a shit-spectacular day turned so perfect?

"Zach? Am I doing this wrong?"

He let out a low laugh—it was for real. "You're not
doing anything wrong, believe me. But..." He looked
around them, at the rock. "Now?"

"Yes, please."

Again, he laughed. *Laughed.* "Here?"

"Here."

His entire body reacted to the thought, so apparently he was on board with the here and now.

"Just the once," she clarified.

"To be wild and crazy."

She smiled. "That's right. And no falling. No messy emotions. Promise me."

"No falling. No messy emotions." He was so ready, his board shorts had gotten restricting, but he hesitated. "Brooke. What if that doesn't work?"

"Well, of course it'll work. We'll take our clothes off and lie on them, and then—"

He interrupted with a smile. "Trust me, I know how to do *that* part. I meant, what if once isn't enough? What if we still go up in flames when we look at each other at work? What if afterward, someone gets hurt?"

"Won't happen," she said so firmly that he was momentarily stymied by the fact that she was so sure she wouldn't want him again. "You just promised me no falling," she said. "I promise it right back. I'll be leaving town before I can start worrying about any sort of meaningful relationship."

True, all true, but...

"Besides, I'm not exactly the type to ignite any sort of wild passion, so—"

"Whoa." He was still reeling from her certainty that she would get him out of her system so easily. *"What?"*

She lifted a shoulder. "I'm awfully buttoned-up, Zach. Ask anyone."

"I'm asking you."

"It's years ingrained. Far too long a story to tell you now, but—"

"Give me the CliffsNotes version, then." This he

had to hear. Not the type to ignite wild passion? Was she serious?

"I just put the prospect of sex on the table," she said. "And you want to talk? See? Proof right there that I don't ignite passion."

"Oh, don't worry. We're going to have sex on the table. Or on the rock." He smiled when just the words brought a blush to her cheeks. "But first I want to hear the long Brooke story."

"Really?"

She sounded so surprised that it squeezed his heart. Had no one ever bothered to try to get beneath her skin? "Really."

"Well...you already know I came here from back East."

"Boston. And before that, Florida."

"You remembered."

"I'm a good listener."

"And a good cook. And a surfer. And—"

"This is about you," he reminded her.

"But see, that's my point, Zach. I'm not good at a bunch of things like you are. I've never had the time to be. Before college, I lived in South Carolina. Before that, New York. Before that, Virginia. Before that... so many other places I can't even remember them all."

"Because your mom liked to move around a lot after your father died."

"Yeah."

So Brooke had been dragged around like a rag doll, with no say in her life until she'd been on her own. No wonder she liked her careful control. "Sounds tough."

"It doesn't matter—this isn't a poor-me story. My point is, I got my uptight analness from my childhood, or lack thereof, but I could be worse, and yes, I realize you're thinking that'd be quite a feat, but it's true. In any case, I've led a sort of wanderlust life."

"When all you really wanted was stability. Comfort."

Again, she revealed surprise that he got her. "Yes. And then my grandmother died and shocked everyone by leaving me her great big old house, chock-full of sixty-plus years of stuff, even though she didn't know me. I shouldn't have cared, but I did. I couldn't just let strangers box it up and get rid of it."

"Of course not."

She looked around, at the rock, the ocean, gesturing wide. "So here I am."

"So here you are. In a house. A home, actually. That's probably new to you."

"Very." She lifted a shoulder. "At least for another few weeks, until the job's over, and the house sells. It's going on the market this weekend." She met his gaze, and in hers the truth was laid bare. No matter what happened, despite the danger of caring too much, or falling a little too hard, she didn't want to miss out on this.

Neither did he. The wind kicked, stirring the warm evening. Her bare arm bumped his, a strand of her hair slid along his jaw as he slowly pulled her closer.

She tipped her head up to his, eyes luminous as her hand came up to his chest. She waited until their mouths nearly touched before she held him off. "I'm going to let loose tonight, Zach." Her fingers dug in, just a little. "Consider yourself warned."

His pulse leaped. So did other parts of his anatomy. "I think I can handle it."

"Sure?"

"Very," he murmured, stroking a hand down her hair,

her back, cupping her sweet ass and scooting her a little closer, closing his eyes when her mouth brushed over his jaw, then met his.

Oh, yeah. He ran his hands down her body, half braced for her to come to her senses and stop him.

Any moment now...

Instead, she kissed him just the way he liked to be kissed, long and deep and wet, and raw, helpless pleasure flooded him.

And instead of her coming to her senses, he lost his.

CHAPTER NINE

AT ZACH'S RESPONSE to her kiss—a thrillingly low, rough sound from deep in his throat—Brooke melted and kissed him again, and then again...

"Brooke."

Lifting her head, she looked into his eyes.

His breathing had gone uneven, and against her body she could feel his, solid and warm and...hard.

Very hard.

She put her hand to his chest and felt the solid thudding of his heart. "Don't change your mind."

"No." Eyes hot, a low laugh escaped Zach. "No. But we could go to my place, or—"

"No." She wanted another kiss. She loved the way he tasted, the way he smelled, so innately male she could hardly stand it. How long since she'd felt this way? Too long, that's all she knew. "Right here. It'll help me relax, Zach. I really need to relax."

Laughing silkily, he slid his hands to her waist, squeezed, then let them glide up her ribs, stopping just before her breasts. Her aching breasts. "Anything to help," he murmured, leaning in to kiss her again.

That worked. So worked. He wanted her. She could feel it in the tension in his broad shoulders, in the taut muscles of his back. Knowing it gave her a heady rush of power, and she demanded more, pressing closer.

His hands slid down her back, pulling her onto his lap, making her momentarily lose concentration as she tried to remember—did she have on pretty panties?—but then she couldn't think at all because his hands were skimming beneath her dress and were on those panties, and he let out another of those sexy rough sounds...

Oh yeah, letting loose worked. She should have tried it a long time ago. Already it was beating back the in-explicable loneliness she hadn't been able to put a name to. With Zach, she never felt alone; it was part of his appeal. He fascinated her. He had from the start. He was such a presence, so virile, so physical—especially right this minute.

"Brooke?"

He wore his intense firefighter face, or maybe that was just his intensity, period, but mixed in with it was need and desire, stark, glorious desire—for her. "Yes?"

His eyes were on hers as his hands continued to mess with her mind. "What are you wearing beneath this dress?"

"Not much."

The sound he made gave her another heady rush, and she gripped the hem of his T-shirt. Helping her, he tugged it over his head, then pulled her back in. The full physical contact made her hum, and then his fingers played with the tie at the back of her neck, the only thing holding up her dress, and the breath evapo-rated in her lungs.

"Your skin is so soft." He was touching as much of it as he could, running his hands up and down her sides, her arms, her back, under her dress, pressing his face to her throat. "And you smell so damn good..."

He smelled good, too. So good she leaned in and put

her mouth to his shoulder, opening it on him because she needed a taste, just a little teeny tiny taste—

He sucked in a breath when she bit him.

"Sorry," she managed behind a horrified laugh when he lifted his head. "I'm sorry. I couldn't help it, I just had to—"

The words backed up in her throat as the front of her dress slipped to her waist. He immediately filled his hands with her breasts. "Sorry," he murmured, repeating her words. "I couldn't help it, I just had to."

She would have laughed again but his thumbs slowly rasped over her nipples, and any laughter vanished. Unbelievable. She was closer to an orgasm than she'd been during the last time she'd actually had sex. "Zach..."

"Relaxing yet?" His voice was low, silky.

"T-trying."

"Good. You keep trying." Bending her back over his arm, he dragged hot, wet, openmouthed kisses down her throat and across a breast, and sucked her into his mouth.

At the feel of his tongue stroking her nipple, she gasped, and then again when he settled her so that his erection pressed against the core of her.

He felt hard, very hard. And big. She looked into his glittering eyes, gulping as his hands slid down her thighs, then up the backs of them to play with the edging of her panties.

Oh, God. This was happening. They were doing this. She untied his board shorts.

He hooked his thumbs in the sides of her panties.

She tugged his shorts down, freeing the essentials.

He repeated the favor with her panties and slipped

his hardness between her legs, using the rough pad of one finger to stroke her.

She quivered. "Zach—"

He did it again, adding a second finger, and she tightened her legs on his hand so he couldn't stop, because if he did she was going to die.

"I won't stop," he promised, reading her mind, playing in the slippery heat he'd generated, a heat she'd forgotten existed.

"Condom," she managed.

He went utterly still, then pressed his forehead to hers. "Christ. I don't—Brooke. I didn't think about—"

"I have one."

His gaze, so steamy hot it singed everything it touched, met hers.

"In my purse. It's been there for a while..." She fumbled for the zippered compartment. "I wish I had two—"

His laugh was soft and sexy as he took it from her fingers. "This'll work for now."

Biting her lower lip, she nodded, touching his chest, his flat abs, and then lower still, where his shorts were opened.

He stopped breathing.

So did she.

Bold in a way she hardly recognized, she wrapped her fingers around him. Loving the way that made him let out a rough oath, she slowly stroked. Swearing again, he slid the skirt of her dress up to her waist, baring her to the night and his searing gaze.

"Um..."

"Relaxed yet?"

"Not quite, no." Her dress was now bunched across

her belly, leaving her hanging out in the wind. Literally. Relaxed? Try wound up tighter than a coil.

"Lie back, Brooke."

Doing so would pretty much spread her out like a feast. "Yeah, but—"

He merely laid her back himself. Towering over her, he slid a leg between hers and glided his hands down her arms to join his fingers with hers. "How about now? Relaxed now?" he murmured, pulling their entwined hands up, over her head.

Was he kidding? She was so far from relaxed she couldn't even remember the meaning of the word. He was holding her down in the dark, only the moonlight slashing across his face, making him look like a complete stranger. But instead of the logical response of panic, she arched up against him, wanting more.

He gave it to her. Lowering his mouth to within a fraction of hers, he nipped at her lower lip, then danced his tongue to hers, long and sure and deep, and she gave back everything she got.

She was a different woman with him, someone who let herself live and love. And she wanted to be loved, more than she'd imagined. Closing her eyes, she rocked into him, moving impatiently against him, her fingers digging into the muscles of his back. "Zach, please."

"I plan to. I plan to please you until you—"

"Relax?"

"Come." He slid down her body, kissing her stomach, her ribs. "And then again." Making himself at home between her thighs, he smiled wickedly. "And again."

Oh, God. If he kept at it, she was going to go off in approximately two minutes—

He gave a slow, sure stroke of his tongue and she

revised her estimation to two *seconds*. His hands skimmed up her legs to her inner thighs, holding her right where he wanted her, and then he added a finger to the mix and she couldn't have stopped from exploding to save her life. It hit her like a freight train, and he made her ride it out to the very end, slowly bringing her down...

After a moment, or maybe a year, she came back to her senses and realized she lay there on the rock, staring up at the stars, her hands fisted in Zach's hair, holding him to her in a way that would have horrified her if she'd been capable of rational thought, which she wasn't. Not quite yet.

He pressed his lips to one inner thigh, then the other, then crawled up her body, his mouth trailing hot and wet kisses along her skin as he went. She ran her hands up and over his back, his shoulders, and he let out a quiet sound of pleasure.

Taking her face in his hands, his mouth came back on hers as he pushed inside her, filling her so that she thought she might burst, holding her there on the very edge with fierce thrusts that sent pleasure spiraling through her, so far beyond anything she could have imagined. They never stopped kissing, not until the end when she fell apart for him again, and when he did the same for her, his head thrown back, her name on his lips.

When it was over, he rolled to his back so that they lay there on the rock side by side, breathing like lunatics, staring up at the stars, listening to the ocean crashing onto the sand just below them.

"That was..." She let out a half laugh. Words failed.

"Yeah." His voice was husky, rough. "That was."

Turning her head, she looked at him and felt her heart catch at the sight of him, all long, defined grace, lit only by the silvery moon, which was a good color for him. Hell, any color would be good for him with that mouthwatering body.

Shifting to his side, he smiled as he reached for her and pulled her against him.

A cuddle.

Damn it, he really knew the moves, didn't he. Hard to keep her distance with him, that was for sure. But she was letting loose, so what the hell. Brooke scooted in as tight as she could get, loving the steady thud of his heart beneath her ear, loving the warm strength of his body all around hers, loving the feel of his hands skimming over her. "Maybe we should get up before we forget we only had the one condom."

His answer was a soft laugh, and he pressed his mouth to her ear. "There are plenty of ways around that."

She stared into his naughty, bad-boy smile, a smile that assured her that whatever *ways* he had in mind, she was going to like them. Her body was already halfway to another orgasm at just the thought. "The party."

"Yeah." He let out a breath. "Right."

"I mean, we should go, right? Blake said you need the kiss-up points with the chief." She sat up, looking for her panties, which were behind them, lying on top of his shorts. It was silly, given what they'd just done, but it looked so intimate. Too intimate. Snatching them both, she tossed him his shorts, and watched him pull them on that body she could happily look at unclothed for hours.

Days.

Weeks.

Oh, God. So much for keeping her head.

She spent the next few awkward seconds trying to right her dress, and not having much luck until he turned her away from him and tied her halter himself. "Brooke?"

Just the sound of his voice did her in. Closing her eyes, she swallowed hard. "Yeah?"

Zach stroked a finger down the back of her neck, evoking a shiver and a yearning that weakened her knees again. "I loved watching you let loose."

"Twice."

He grinned as he pulled on his shirt. "I still think we should try for a perfect hat trick."

"Party," she said weakly, tempted to do just that. "We're going to the party."

THEY WALKED DOWN the beach toward the party together, Brooke's mind working overtime. The hot, sexy guy walking alongside her had seen her naked.

Touched her naked.

Kissed her naked—

"Well, well. What do we have here?"

Brooke jerked her thoughts to the present and looked at Cristina, who stood in front of them on the sand in a tiny bikini top and a pair of board shorts riding low on her trim hips. "You two look quite...*flushed* this evening."

Just behind her, the chief's birthday bash appeared to be in full swing. There was a big bonfire and several barbecues going. Music blared out of a set of speakers, and people were sitting on the sand, standing around the fire or dancing. Aidan was swaying like peanut butter on jelly with a pretty brunette. Dustin and Sam were happily flipping burgers. Blake was adding logs to the fire.

There were a bunch of other people, as well, from different shifts and different firehouses. In the center, enjoying the attention, stood Chief Allan Stone himself. A tall man in his fifties, he had the air of an army general and commanded respect—even fear—on the job. But tonight he was smiling and looking more comfortable than Brooke had ever seen him.

But mostly all she could see was the cynical twist to Cristina's lips as the female firefighter took the time to scrutinize Brooke from head to toe.

Brooke could only imagine what she looked like, and shifting uncomfortably, glanced down at herself. Yep, her dress was a wrinkled mess, not a surprise given that ten minutes ago it'd been rucked up to her waist.

Zach reached out and pulled something from her hair. A piece of dried seaweed. Perfect.

"I'd call the cute police," Cristina said dryly, "but they wouldn't know who to arrest first." And with that, she turned and walked back to the fire.

"She knows," Brooke whispered.

Well, she wouldn't go back and change it even if she could. She'd be remembering tonight for many, many nights to come, and would undoubtedly get all hot and bothered all over again at the remembering, and maybe even ache over what might have been, but she wouldn't take it back.

"Ready?" he asked.

She nodded, and they joined the crowd. Zach was immediately pulled away and put on barbecue duty, leaving her standing on the outskirts, a little bit anxious.

Which was ridiculous. She'd just been bare-ass naked on a rock, she sure as hell could handle this.

Dustin came up to her and offered a plate of food. He waited until she'd taken a big bite of the burger. "Hungry, huh?"

She slid him a glance. "Yes."

He nodded and said nothing else. Just stared a little glumly at the dance floor where Cristina was dirty dancing with someone Brooke had never seen before. "Why don't you ask her to dance?" she asked.

"Because she'd think it was funny."

"Funny that you have a crush on her?"

"I don't have a crush on her." He sighed. "Okay, I do. *Shit*."

Sam and Eddie brought Brooke a drink. "To replenish the fluids," Sam explained. Both men looked at her expectantly.

"What?"

"You tell us," Eddie said.

Instead, she took another large bite of her burger.

"Don't you have anything you want to share?" Sam looked hopeful. "With your two best friends?"

"We're best friends?"

They both nodded eagerly. "So if something was on your chest," Sam said. "And you just needed to, you know, get it off—"

"In detail," Eddie added. "We're all ears."

Her burger congealed in her gut. "You know?"

"Oh, we know all."

She looked at Dustin, who grimaced, then nodded. She handed him back the plate, and Eddie the drink, and then walked off. She stopped at the water's edge.

"Stop sulking, will you?"

Brooke turned and faced Cristina. "I'm not sulking."

"Pouting, then. Look, this is a fire station. We're all walking God complexes who put our lives on the line every day, and yet socially? Immature as high school kids. Come on—" she snorted when Brooke scoffed "—we love to talk. You've given us something new to talk about. Deal with it."

Brooke sighed. "How long will it last?"

"Until it's over."

"It is over."

"Please."

"It is. It was a one-time-only thing."

"Okay, now I *know* you're crazy."

"Why?"

"Why would you sleep with that man only once? That's just a waste of all that hotness."

"I'm leaving in a few weeks. We agreed it was just a letting-loose thing."

Cristina stared at her, then laughed. "And let me guess. You're already regretting that stupid decision."

Brooke looked away, into the bonfire. "No." *Yes.*

Cristina just shook her head. "Well, lucky for me, your shortsightedness is another woman's gain." And she walked away in her sexy little top and shorts, heading directly toward Zach, stopping to hug Blake.

Zach stood at one of the barbecues, holding a long spatula, flipping burgers and laughing at something Aidan was saying to him. Just looking at him, something happened inside Brooke. A clutch. A quiver.

What would it be like if she wasn't leaving? she wondered.

But she always left.

Always.

Besides, she'd said no strings. She'd insisted. She'd come here tonight, just wanting to let go, to live and, oh boy, had she. She just hadn't realized that in doing those things, something else would happen.

In spite of her promise, she'd begun to fall for Zach.

She watched as Cristina took the plate out of his hands and handed it to Aidan before drawing Zach over to where people were dancing, proceeding to grind up against him in tune to the music.

"Here."

Brooke stared down at the proffered beer, then into Blake's face.

"You looked like you could use it," the tall, thin firefighter said gently.

"I…"

"Drink. Then we'll dance. If it makes you feel better, you can rub all over me like she is with Zach. I'm a good friend like that."

"I'm not jealous or anything."

"Okay."

"I'm not."

He just nodded.

And she drank the beer, then took him up on his offer to dance.

CHAPTER TEN

AFTER DANCING WITH CRISTINA, Zach moved to the coolers to get a drink. He pulled out a soda, then stood there with the waves at his back, looking for Brooke.

She'd been dancing with Blake, but now was with Sam, who was making the most of his time with her. Twice the firefighter's hands slipped to her ass, and twice Brooke lifted them to her waist.

Sam grinned in a can't-blame-a-guy-for-trying way, and Zach considered going over there and tossing him into the ocean, but he didn't.

An hour ago, Brooke had been in *his* arms, panting his name as she came all over him. She'd let loose now. Washed him right out of her system and that was fine. Hell, that was great. He'd just move on, too, and—

"You holding up?" Tommy asked, stopping next to Zach, sipping a beer.

"Why wouldn't I be?"

"Haven't heard from you in a few hours. Couldn't figure out if I should be worried, or if it was because you were finally trusting me to do my job."

Zach let out a long breath. "And how is that going? Your job?"

Tommy just took a drink.

"Shit. Don't tell me it's not going."

"I'm not saying that. I'm not saying anything."

"Well, then, say something."

"You're just going to have to trust me a little bit longer."

Unfortunately, he really had no choice. Tommy walked away, and Zach watched Brooke dance some more. Her cheeks were flushed, her hair a little wild. She'd definitely loosened up tonight, and he couldn't tear his gaze off her. Forcing himself to, he moved to stand by Blake, who was back at the bonfire.

The other firefighter tossed a log into the flames, watched it catch. "You could just ask her to dance."

"Who?"

Blake shook his head in disgust, then tossed another log into the fire before swiping a forearm over his sweaty brow. He didn't look so good, and Zach frowned. "You okay?"

"Yeah."

"Why don't you take a break, let me relieve you for a few?"

"I've got it."

Blake had been quiet and down all year since Lynn had died. Of all of them, Zach thought maybe he at least knew a little of what he was feeling. "Blake—"

"I said I'm good."

Great. They were both good.

And they were both liars.

FOR ZACH, THE next few days whirled by, a blurry, crazy merge of calls. He didn't sleep well, and finally gave up even trying, ending up at the firehouse kitchen table with his laptop, going through all his gathered arson information to distract himself from daydreaming about the feel of Brooke's curves, the taste of her skin...

And then the object of his fantasies walked into the room.

She was early for her shift, looking a little sleepy and a whole lot sexy as she headed directly toward the coffeepot on the counter.

They hadn't had a chance to speak alone since she'd worn that pretty dress with her hair down, her body soft and giving and sweet.

So goddamn sweet.

Her mouth was still soft and sweet now, but she was back in the uniform, complete with her hair all carefully pulled back.

Buttoned-up.

It didn't matter. He remembered what she looked like with her hair down, not to mention without her clothes, and he wanted to undo her all over again.

He wanted that. *He,* the one who'd not wanted a relationship.

Jesus. He really needed more sleep.

Brooke doctored herself some coffee, then looked at him. "What are you doing?"

Since the answer to that was, "something I shouldn't be," he shut the laptop.

"You and Blake. I caught him looking at porn, too."

"Excuse me, but I was *not* looking at porn."

Over her mug, she raised a brow. "What was it Viagra Man said? Guys will be guys?"

"For God's sake." He opened the laptop back up. "Come here and look for yourself."

"Oh no, thank you." She was laughing now, and lifted her free hand. "What you do in your own spare time—"

Reaching out, he grabbed her hand and tugged her

over, letting go just before she fell right into his lap, where he really wanted her.

She sat in the chair next to him and looked at him for a long beat; he looked back.

"Hi," she whispered.

He smiled. "Hi."

Turning her head, she stared at the screen, at the list of property deeds and the records of ownership he'd been studying, and her smile faded.

"The fires," she said quietly. "The arsons."

"Yeah. Doing some research." Which was getting him nowhere. Nothing matched. None of the current owners, none of the past owners, none of the three properties were related to each other in any way. After all these weeks, he was at an impasse, and was afraid Tommy was, too.

"You're trying to link them together."

He wasn't supposed to be doing any such thing. He certainly shouldn't be discussing it.

"What about the way the fires were started?" she asked.

They'd all been started in a wire-mesh trash can, with a second point of origin as bait for the investigator to find and be misdirected, but he was afraid he was the only one who knew that. "Similar," he admitted.

"Suspects?"

He stared at her. She wasn't lecturing him on how stupid it was to risk his job digging into this. She wasn't telling him all the reasons why these fires hadn't been arson. She was sitting here, believing him, believing *in* him. "Most arson is committed by the owners. But the owners of these properties aren't connected in any way that I can see."

"New structures? Or old?"

"Newer."

"What about contractors, then?"

"All different."

"Okay, then. Back to location." Standing up, Brooke paced the length of the kitchen and back again. Leaning in over his shoulder, she typed on the keys of the laptop. "If we compare their footprints..."

He couldn't stop staring at her, bowled over by her analytical mind, her quick thinking. "I already did."

"And?"

And her scent was extremely distracting. As was the way her breast gently pressed into his arm. "They were all different square footage," he told her. "Different building types. Different everything."

"Show me."

He brought up the map he'd created. Her arm was resting on his shoulder. Her skin looked so damned silky, and he knew from experience that she tasted amazing.

Everywhere.

"There's got to be a connection." She was studying the screen, her brow furrowed, her mouth grim. "Somewhere."

She believed in him. The knowledge was staggering. "Brooke."

"Somebody is connected in some way. An employee, a relative, someone..." She was thinking, chewing on her lower lip, eyes still glued to the screen, and he couldn't take his off her.

"Maybe—"

"Brooke."

Her gaze cut to his questioningly.

And he lost his breath. Instead of talking, he tugged on her hand, so that she was forced to lean in closer until she lost her balance.

He caught her.

And then he kissed her.

With a soft murmur, she wrapped her arms around his neck and kissed him back. Oh yeah, *this* was what he'd needed for days—hell, maybe his entire life—and he kissed her until they had to break apart to breathe.

They were still staring at each other when the kitchen door opened and Aidan walked in. "Hey."

Brooke leaped back to her chair like a Mexican jumping bean.

"Anyone got food?" Aidan asked.

"Uh…" Brooke put her hands to her cheeks. "I have cookies on the top shelf."

"Score." Aidan helped himself while Brooke rose to her feet.

"Gotta clock in," she said and, with a last glance at Zach, left the room.

Zach thunked his head to the table.

"What?" Aidan took two fistfuls of cookies and plopped himself down next to Zach, peering at the laptop. "Trying to link them." He nodded. "Hey, maybe if you—"

"Aidan."

"Huh?"

He had to laugh. "I was sort of in the middle of something with Brooke."

Aidan blinked. "Oh. You mean…" He pointed a finger at himself. "You wanted me to leave you two alone?"

"Man, you are quick."

"I thought you two already knocked it out."

Zach winced, and Aidan sat back. "Wow."

"What?"

"Nothing."

"Oh, it's something."

"Okay. You're falling for her."

The door burst open again and Brooke stood there looking more than a little ruffled.

Aidan got to his feet. "Apparently I'm supposed to leave you two alone."

Zach rolled his eyes.

Brooke just kept staring at him until Aidan was gone. "Did you know everybody is talking about us? Why is everyone talking about us? It feels like we're twelve and in middle school."

"Since there's sex involved, let's call it high school. Ignore it. It'll blow over."

She glared at him. He couldn't help it; he laughed. "It will."

"You're not bothered at all?" she asked.

"I'm just saying it's what they do. Seriously, it'll all fade away if you just—"

"Yeah, yeah. Let it go. But maybe I'm not like you, all cool and calm and so laid-back that I have to be checked for a pulse."

Before he could say anything to that, she sighed and rubbed her eyes. "I'm sorry. That wasn't fair. I guess I'm still having bad new-kid flashbacks."

He moved toward her and lowered her hands from her face. "We're adults, and we made a decision. A decision that turned out to be the best night of my entire summer. Don't regret it, Brooke. Please don't."

As she looked at him, her eyes softened. Her body softened, too, and she nodded. "It *was* nice, wasn't it?"

"Nice?" He shook his head. "Nice is a walk in the park. Nice is a sweet goodbye kiss. Nice is a lot of things, Brooke, but it doesn't come even close to covering what we did on that rock."

"Okay, so maybe nice isn't quite the right word. How about good? Do you like that word better?"

He looked into her eyes. Beyond the irritation was a light that said she was playing with him now, but he'd show her good. Backing her to the refrigerator, Zach covered her mouth with his, swallowing her little gasp of surprise, a gasp that quickly turned into the hottest murmur of undeniable need and hunger he'd ever heard when his tongue swept alongside hers.

And though he'd meant only to show her up, he ended up showing himself something. That she fit against him as if she'd been made for the spot. That her scent filling his head, and the feel of her hands fisting in his shirt fueled his hunger as she sighed into his mouth, until it became so damn arousing he couldn't bear it. Pulling back, he stroked a hand down her body and felt her knees buckle.

His own weren't so steady, either, but a fierce sense of satisfaction went through him. Still holding her between the refrigerator and his own hard, aching body, he looked down into her face. "Tell me again that that was merely *good*. I dare you."

"Okay." She licked her lips, an action that didn't help calm him down any. "Does shockingly incredible work for you, Officer Hottie?"

He rolled his eyes but could admit that yeah, shockingly incredible worked far better. "So what now?"

"The million-dollar question, Zach? From you? Really?"

He found himself staring at her. Holy shit, had he actually asked, "What now?"

"Yeah," she said into the charged silence. "That's what I thought. There's *nothing* now. Both of us know it. We just have to remember it."

LATER THAT DAY, after having been out for hours on a series of nonemergency transport calls, Dustin and Brooke were directed to a familiar address for another Code Calico.

"How about you take it this time," Brooke said to Dustin.

He looked amused. "You catch on quick."

"I try."

"You're trying a lot of things lately. Or people. What?" he said innocently when she sent him a long look. "Just wondering about the status."

"I'm not asking you the status of *your* love life."

"Ha!" He grinned victoriously. "So you admit there *is* a love life."

They arrived on scene, mercifully saving Brooke from having to answer, since she didn't know the answer. The truth was, she no longer knew anything at all about what she and Zach were doing. Stepping out onto the sidewalk, she craned her neck, searching the three large trees out in front of Phyllis's place for the cat.

No Cecile in sight.

"Dustin," she said, watching as Aidan and Zach pulled up, moving with steady purpose toward the house, not the yard. "What's going on?"

Dustin put the radio mic back in its place, his expression suddenly serious. "It's not Cecile after all. Grab your bag."

For a split second, she stared at his back as he headed to the front door, then grabbed her bag and ran after him.

Inside the house, the shades were drawn, but she could still see well enough. As her grandmother's place had been, the house was filled to the brim with furniture from another era, upon which knickknacks covered every inch. But there wasn't a speck of dust anywhere, even the wood floors had been shined.

"In here!"

She and Dustin followed Zach's voice down a hallway, its walls hidden by photographs from at least five decades, to a bedroom filled completely with lace. In the center, on the floor, lay Phyllis. Far too still at her feet sat Cecile, gaze glued to her mistress, tail twitching.

Zach was kneeling at Phyllis's side, holding her hand, saying something to her.

Phyllis, eyes closed, responded with a nod. "Yes, Zachie, I can hear you. Tell Cecile I'm okay. She's worried."

"Phyllis, about your meds." Zach spoke calmly, evenly, any personal concern well tucked away, but Brooke could see it in his eyes. "Did you forget to take them?"

"No, I took my damn pills. You hound me enough about it, I don't forget."

"Okay, good." Zach squeezed her hand. "That's good."

Dustin moved in and crouched at her other side, and began taking vitals. Brooke recorded everything, all the while watching Zach be so sweet and gentle and kind.

Why she was surprised, she had no idea. She'd seen

him in action before, with many victims by now, and he was always sweet and gentle and kind.

He'd been nothing but those things with her, as well.

And once, on a rock beneath a star littered sky, he'd been much, much more...

When it was determined that Phyllis had to be transported to the hospital, Zach helped get her on a gurney, where the older woman began to panic. "I can't leave. What about Cecile?" Reaching out, she gripped Zach's shirt with an iron fist. "I don't want to go!"

"Phyllis." Zach took both her hands in his. "Your doctor wants you to meet him at the hospital. He wants to stabilize your condition—"

"Condition shmondition. I don't have time for him. I'm fine. Completely fine, I'm telling you."

But she wasn't. Her color was off, her breathing coming too shallow and too fast, and, given the grimace on her face, she knew it, too. "Damn it," she said, sagging back. "Damn it. I'm not going." But she said this much weaker than before. "I'm not. You can't make me."

"Phyllis." Zach stroked back her gray hair as he leaned on the gurney to look into her eyes. "You do this for me and I'll take care of Cecile. Okay?"

"You'll take care of her?"

"I promise."

Phyllis covered her mouth with a shaking hand and nodded. "Your mother would be so proud of you. I hope you know that."

He squeezed her hand. "Just get better." He gestured to Dustin and Aidan, and they carried her out of the bedroom, navigating down the tight, cramped hallway.

Zach looked around Phyllis's room with an unreadable expression. Then, with a sigh, he grabbed the unhappy cat and tucked her into the crook of his arm. Turning to leave, he found Brooke watching him.

As it had since the beginning, their odd connection caused a spark to pinball off her insides, from one erotic zone to another, and all the ones in between—but this wasn't about their crazy physical attraction. Standing there, looking at him, she suddenly knew. It didn't matter that she'd told herself she wouldn't get her heart involved.

It already was.

"You okay?" she whispered.

"Yeah. It's just that she—" Shutting his mouth, he shook his head. Brooke moved closer and put her hand on his arm.

Something went between them at the touch. Not the usual heat but something much, much more.

Yeah, her heart was involved. Big-time.

PHYLLIS RESISTED GETTING into the ambulance. She wanted to stay home, she wanted her cat, she wanted everyone to get the hell away from her. She even tried a diversion technique.

"There was a man in my yard," she claimed suddenly as they loaded her inside the rig. "Did you see him? He was holding something."

"Phyllis," Dustin said gently. "You're going to the hospital. If not for me and Brooke, then for yourself."

"I recognize his face, I just can't quite place him…"

"It's going to be okay." Brooke sat with her and held her hand. "You're going to be okay. We're just going to the hospital so your doctor can check on you—"

Phyllis shook her head, her eyes cloudy as she struggled to get up. "You people are idiots."

Brooke sighed. "You promised Zach you'd do this, remember?"

The old lady closed her eyes. "Zachie."

"Yes. He gave you his word that he'd take care of Cecile. And you gave him yours that you'd go get checked out."

Phyllis's mouth tightened, but she stopped fighting at least. Zach's name had calmed her down.

Brooke had a feeling Zach had that control over every woman in his life, whether he realized it or not.

"There really was a man in my yard with a blowtorch, or something like one," Phyllis grumbled, sounding more like her old self.

In the back of the unit as she was, Brooke couldn't see out. She met Dustin's eyes in the rearview mirror and he shook his head. He didn't see a man.

Brooke squeezed Phyllis's hand.

The older woman held on with surprising strength as she looked into Brooke's eyes, her own filled with grief and fear. "I really want to stay home."

"You'll go back soon."

"Promise?"

She was so scared. Brooke's throat tightened, burned. If there was one thing she never quite got used to, it was the helplessness she felt over the things she couldn't make better. "Yes," she whispered. "I promise."

AFTER DROPPING PHYLLIS off in the ambulance bay of the E.R., Brooke and Dustin were called to another transport. The minute they were free again, Brooke tracked down a nurse to find out what she could about Phyllis's condition.

The nurse pulled her chart. "She's in renal and heart failure."

Brooke's brain refused to process that. "What?"

"Yes, the doctor was just with her."

"Oh my God."

"It's been happening for quite a while. Apparently the patient has actually known for months. She'll be staying a while this time."

"But—I promised her she'd be back home soon."

The nurse frowned at her over the chart. "It's not your job to make promises of any kind."

"I…" Brooke knew that, so she had no idea why she'd done so. "I didn't know about her condition."

"Of course not, because you're not her doctor." The nurse looked down her nose at Brooke, reigning supreme. "Do yourself and your future patients a favor and don't make rash promises. Don't make any promises." Spinning on her heels, she walked away.

Brooke staggered to a chair and let her weak legs sink until she was sitting. Renal and heart failure…

"Rough day?"

She looked up at Zach, in full firefighter gear and looking a little worse for wear himself. "Yeah. Rough day." Damn it, she could barely speak past the huge lump in her throat. "But not as rough as Phyllis's."

"So you know."

When she nodded miserably, he sighed and crouched in front of her. He was in her space but in a very lovely way, his big body sort of curled around her protectively, his eyes easy and calm and full of something she hadn't known was missing in her life.

Simple and true affection.

"I've got Cecile at the firehouse," he said. "Happily scratching the furniture and terrorizing the crew."

He'd made a promise and had followed through. For some reason, that got to her. "Zach. I screwed up."

"We all do."

"I promised Phyllis she could go home soon. But—" Her voice cracked and she stopped talking. Had to stop talking because she couldn't stand the thought of breaking a promise. Her past was a virtual wasteland of promises broken by her mother, and she'd made it a rule to never, ever do the same thing.

Zach let out a long breath, then reached for her hand.

"Now's probably not a good time to be nice to me," she managed. Damn it, she hated this. Hated that she'd failed, much less failed a woman she cared about. "When I'm near a breakdown and someone's nice, I tend to lose it."

"You should know I'm not so good with tears."

She pulled her hand free and closed her eyes. "Well, then, you're not going to like what's coming next." Eyes still shut, she felt him shift his weight. When he didn't speak, she figured that he'd left her by herself, which was definitely for the best. With a sigh, she opened her eyes, prepared to be alone.

As she always had been.

But to Brooke's shock, he'd never left her side.

CHAPTER ELEVEN

Zach watched Brooke's expression register surprise on top of the pain already there. She'd really believed that he'd walked away. Tears or no tears, he wouldn't have left a perfect stranger, but she'd actually expected him to abandon her. He knew that wasn't a reflection on him, but on her own experiences. People didn't stick in her life.

Odd how he wanted to. "Phyllis wouldn't want you to lose it over her."

"I told her everything would be okay. I *promised* her. But everything isn't going to be okay."

He knew that, too. Heart heavy, calling himself every kind of fool, he sank into the chair next to her and leaned his tired head back to the wall and studied the ceiling.

It didn't matter that he wasn't looking at her. He could still see her; she'd been imprinted on his brain. A body made for his. A mouth that fueled his fantasies. Eyes that destroyed him with every glance. "Promises are a bad idea all the way around."

Especially the one he'd made to her. Not to fall for her. Man, that one was going to haunt him.

"I know."

Brooke still sounded way too close to tears for his comfort. Turning his head, he found her watching him, eyes still thankfully dry. "Don't be too hard on your-self. We all break promises."

"Some of us do it more spectacularly than others."

"I don't know about that."

She stared at him for a long moment. "Zach...I've not handled any of this well."

"This."

"The new job. Making friends at the new job." She lowered her voice. "You."

"What about me?"

"Sleeping with you and thinking I could just walk away. It was supposed to be letting loose, but you should know I'm having some trouble with that whole walking-away portion of the plan. I have no idea how people do the one-night thing, I really don't."

"There was no sleeping involved."

"What?"

"Our night. We didn't sleep. It's an important clari-fication, because sleeping implies intimacy."

"What we did felt pretty damn intimate," she said.

"Temporarily intimate. There's a difference. Now, if we'd been getting naked every night since...that would be true intimacy." He looked at her, wanting a reaction, but hell if he knew what kind of reaction he wanted, or why he was even going there.

"You agreed readily enough," she reminded him. "And it's what you do, anyway. Light stuff only."

She was watching him carefully, and sitting there in the hospital chair, surrounded by strangers, the scent of antiseptic and people's suffering all around them, she was clearly waiting for him to deny it. And given how he kept baiting her about it, it made sense that she was confused.

But what he wanted didn't really matter. Not when she was out of here in less than two weeks. But apparently his mouth didn't get the message from his brain because it opened and said, "Whatever this is, clearly we're going to drive each other nuts for the next two weeks, so we might as well take it as far as we can."

She blinked. "You mean..."

"Yeah."

At his hip, his pager beeped. Hell. Rising to his feet, he looked down into her still surprised face. "Think about it."

"I...will."

ZACH'S CALL WAS to an all-too-familiar address for a house fire.

Phyllis's.

When they pulled down her street, his stomach hit his toes. The house was lit up like a Fourth of July fireworks display. The flames were hot, fast and, as it turned out, unbeatable. Even with Sam and Eddie's engine already there, and two others from neighboring firehouses, in less than twenty minutes they'd lost the entire structure.

Afterward, with the crew all cleaning up, Zach slipped inside the burned-out shell. He moved through the clingy, choking smoke, down the blackened hallway where Phyllis's pictures were nothing but a memory. Inside her bedroom, he took in the soot, water and ashes.

And a wire-mesh trash can, tipped on its side.

On the wall above it, black markings flared out, indicating a flash burn. Probably aided by an accelerant.

Just like the Hill Street fire.

And the two before that.

Jaw tight, Zach stared at the evidence, pulling his cell phone out of his pocket to take a picture, which he e-mailed to both Tommy and himself. This time, whatever happened, he was going to have his own damn evidence, because no way had Phyllis had a wire-mesh trash can in here, not in the lacy, frilly, girly room.

His cell phone rang, and when he saw Brooke's name on the I.D., he experienced a little jolt. *I've thought about it,* he imagined her saying. *Do me, Zach...*

"I just heard about the fire," she said instead, sounding tight and grim. "Zach, when we were taking Phyllis out of the house, she tried to tell us that someone was standing on the edge of her property, watching us. A man with a blowtorch."

His fantasy abruptly vanished. *"What?"*

"She was fighting us, trying to stall, saying whatever she could to get us to let her go back into the house. We didn't listen to her. And now..."

"And now you just might have helped catch a serial arsonist," he said firmly. "If you were here, I'd kiss you again."

She let out a breath. "But what if—"

"Don't kill yourself with the what-ifs," he said. "I've been there. They don't help."

"Old heating element," Tommy told him the next morning when he found Zach waiting at his office. "Shoddy, unreliable, and as we saw firsthand, dangerous. Thank God Phyllis was still in the hospital and not at home."

Zach just shook his head. "This was no more accidental than the Hill Street fire. The trash can—"

"Zach—"

"Look, Phyllis said she saw a guy standing on the edge of her property with a blowtorch."

Tommy sighed and retrieved two Red Bulls from a small refrigerator on his credenza. "I can't discuss the investigation."

Zach declined the caffeine-rich drink. "Thought you were off caffeine."

"Sue me." Tommy drank deep and sighed again. "Just don't tell my wife."

"Tommy—"

"Look, I talked to Phyllis myself this morning. She's incoherent and in and out of consciousness. She doesn't remember a damn thing about yesterday. Not a guy with a blowtorch, or if she had a wire-mesh trash can or not."

"That's the drugs talking."

"That's all we have. The fire was put out, Zach. It was a job well done on our part. No injuries, no fatalities."

And that was the bottom line. Zach got that. He just didn't happen to agree. "It was also arson."

"Goddamn it."

"I suppose your next line is for me to leave this one alone, too."

"Yes," Tommy said very quietly. "It is."

"You got the picture I sent."

"I got the picture."

"You'd better be on this, Tommy."

"You need to go now, Zach."

Yeah. Yeah, he did, before he did something he might deeply regret. Like lose his job.

When he finally got to the fire station and went to the kitchen for something to put in his empty, gnawing gut, Brooke was there. He'd hoped to see her last night at his place. In his bed. But clearly she'd thought a little too much. He tried to move past her, but she grabbed his arm.

"Brooke, don't." He felt raw. Exposed. If he let her touch him right now, it might make him all the more vulnerable. Pulling free, he backed up a step and came up against the damn refrigerator.

She merely stepped in against him, trapping him there. He could have shoved past her, but he didn't. Her warm, curvy body pressed to his, her eyes wide and open, reflecting her sorrow, her sympathy.

"The house is completely gone?" she asked.

"Yes."

"Was she right about the guy she saw? Was it arson?"

"I believe so."

"Tommy—"

"Told me again to stay out of this."

"Oh, damn. Zach, I'm sorry." She slid her hands up his chest to cup his jaw. "I'm so sorry."

But not sorry enough to have come to him last night. Knowing that, he might have been able to resist what she did next, except he didn't. She pressed her mouth to his cheek, and then to the corner of his mouth, and then, because he'd apparently lost his mind, he turned his head and hungrily met her lips with his.

Reason went out the window. Everything went out the window as he did his best to inhale her whole. She had her arms wound around his neck, her hands fisted in his hair. He had a hand up the front of her shirt cupping her breast over her bra, the other down the back of her pants, when he vaguely heard someone clear his throat behind them.

Shit.

Lifting his head, he locked eyes with Blake over Brooke's head.

"Bad time?" Blake asked drolly.

Brooke squeaked and hid her head against Zach's chest.

"Very bad," Zach said.

Blake gestured to the refrigerator at Zach's back. "But I'm hungry."

With a choked sound, Brooke stepped away from Zach. Without a word, she walked out of the kitchen.

Blake just arched a brow, gesturing to the fridge.

"Jesus." Zach pushed away from the refrigerator and let Blake at it.

THE NEXT NIGHT, off duty and at home, Zach sat at his own kitchen table with all the evidence he had on the arson fires so far spread out on a board laid in front of him. He was trying to connect the dots instead of thinking about Brooke when the doorbell rang.

It was pizza delivery by Aidan. His partner handed off the extra-large, loaded pie and pushed past him to get inside.

"Well, gee," Zach said dryly. "Come on in."

"We've got to talk." Aidan moved into the kitchen and helped himself to a beer in the refrigerator. He twisted off the top, drank deeply, then gave Zach a long look.

"It's not good," Zach guessed.

"It's you. And what you're doing."

"Look, we're both adults. If we decide to go at this until she leaves, it's our business."

Aidan looked confused. "Huh?"

"You're not talking about Brooke?"

"No." Aidan cocked his head. "Although, I did hear some interesting rumors today, which I ignored. Erroneously so, apparently."

"It's no big deal."

"Okay."

"It's just casual."

"Okay."

"But Jesus, the way everyone's going on about it, I might as well marry her."

Aidan's eyes nearly bugged out of his head. "Whoa. The M word? Out of *your* mouth?"

"It's just a word."

Aidan was still eyeing him like a bug on a slide. "Why are you harping on this?"

"Because you are."

"I said okay about twenty minutes ago, dude. It's all you."

Zach opened the pizza box, pulled out the biggest piece and stuffed a bite in his mouth. "Jenny brought me pizza a while back. Hers was better."

"That's because hers came with a hot bod. You boinking her, too?"

"No."

"Then can I boink her?"

Zach sighed. "Why are you here again?"

"To yell at you. But not for the women. I only wish I had half your woman problems."

"Hey, you've had your problems."

"Name one."

"Okay, how about you doing Blake's soap-star-diva sister and not telling him about it."

Aidan winced. "Hey, she wasn't a soap-star diva at

the time. And besides, I was really young and really stupid back then."

"Uh-huh."

"You're unusually testy. You're either PMSing, or those new rumors are definitely true."

"Which are what exactly?"

"That you and Brooke nearly did it up against the refrigerator. Which, by the way, if it's true? *Nice.*"

"Do you ever think of anything besides sex?"

"Alas, rarely." Aidan grabbed his own huge piece of pizza.

"Fine. But I don't want to talk about Brooke."

Aidan shot him an amused look. That rankled. "Okay."

"I don't."

"Fine. Let's talk about a little thing called arson. You told Tommy you thought Phyllis's house fire was deliberately set."

"Yes."

"Are you crazy?"

"It *was* arson."

"Okay, but Tommy is the best investigator this town has ever had and you know it, which means he's on it."

Zach opened his mouth to speak, but Aidan stopped him. "And you also know he has the biggest mouth this town has ever seen. Everyone is talking about you."

"So what?"

"So what? You love this fucking job, that's what. You work your ass off. You're one of the best in the whole damn city, and there's a lieutenant position coming up that you're going to take yourself right out of the running for because you won't leave this alone."

"I can't leave it alone."

Aidan sighed. "You're that damn sure?"

Zach pointed to the material he'd been working on.

Twisting one of the kitchen chairs around, Aidan straddled it, steepling his hands over the back and setting his chin on them as he studied the board on the table. After a long moment, he let out a breath. "Mysterious points of origin. Metal trash cans. And now, maybe a blowtorch." He shook his head. "So what now?"

Zach sat heavily and for the first time put words to the terrible thoughts in his head. "I'm not sure. But look at this." He tossed down the photos he'd taken of the razed properties.

Aidan shifted through the pictures. "Who ordered the demolitions?"

"I'm working on that."

Aidan finished his beer, silent.

"I know. I'm crazy." Zach shoved his fingers through his hair. "I feel crazy."

"No." Aidan shook his head. "Someone is systematically destroying evidence. Tommy either knows this, or..."

They stared at each other at the unspoken implication that Tommy could be behind any of it.

"You're not crazy," Aidan said. "And you need to get to Phyllis before someone convinces her to destroy any more evidence we can use."

"We?"

"Partners," Aidan said. "For better or worse."

LONG AFTER AIDAN had left, Zach stood on his back deck, staring out at the night, his mind whirling.

Arson.

Brooke.

Restlessness…

He was surrounded by the life he'd chosen, a life both exhilarating and challenging. He loved it. And yet there was no denying he'd shut himself off from the very thing that people would say mattered most.

Love.

Had he really done that because of losing his family so long ago? Or had it just been an excuse, a handy reason not to let himself get hurt? If so, that had backfired, because he'd gotten hurt, anyway. Whether he was ever with Brooke again almost didn't matter—his emotions were involved.

She hadn't come to him tonight, either. That left him two choices: be alone, or go to her.

Easy enough choice. He went inside and grabbed his keys, and then whipped open the door—to find Brooke standing there, hand raised to knock.

CHAPTER TWELVE

BROOKE STOOD ON Zach's front steps, having gotten his address courtesy of Dustin. One minute she'd been at her grandmother's, absorbing the sensation of feeling at home inside a house for the first time in…well, ever, and the next, she hadn't been able to stop her mind from wandering to Zach. She had no reason for being here. None.

Okay, that was a lie. She knew. And her body's reaction to the sight of him, all big, bad and slightly attitude-ridden, cemented it.

She was here to, what had he said? Take it as far as they could.

He wore a T-shirt and jeans, no shoes, no socks. Simple clothes.

Not such a simple man. "Hi," she said.

"Hi." He let out a breath and hooked his hand around her elbow, pulling her up the last step and closer to him. In the dim light he was all lean lines and angles and hard muscle as he jangled his keys in his other hand. "I was just coming to see you."

Her heart skipped a beat or two. "You were?"

"Yeah. I got tired of waiting for you to finish thinking." He moved aside so she could come in, but she hesitated.

"Give me a second," she murmured.

"Okay. For what?"

"For my brain to catch up with the rest of me." She smiled nervously. "It's my body that brought me here, you see. For some of that letting loose we're so good at."

He smiled, and her body began to tingle.

"Maybe you should let your body lead on this one," he suggested in a very naughty, silky tone.

"You think?"

"Oh, yeah."

"Just sort of let my brain take a rest?"

"Exactly." Gently crowding her in the doorway, he put his hands on her hips and his mouth to her ear. "So, are you going to come inside?"

"That was going to be my question to you."

His soft laugh stirred the hair at her temple and all her good spots. Then he slid his arms around her and gave her a hug, and along with the lust came such a rush of affection that her heart hurt. She buried her face in his throat and held on tight. "Okay," she said. "Maybe I'll come in for a little while."

"Great idea. We could—"

"Let loose?"

"Anything you want," he murmured, pulling back to look into her eyes. "I wanted to see you tonight."

Her breath caught. "You're seeing me."

"Yeah. I am. I see you, Brooke. The real you."

"With lines like that, you're awfully hard to resist."

"I'm trying to be." Pushing the door shut, Zach kissed her and, turning them both, backed her to the door. This freed up his hands, which he used to cup her face, a touch that turned her on more than any other. "I needed this connection tonight."

"With me?"

"Only with you." He kissed her again, his mouth making its way over her jaw to her throat.

"Zach?"

"Mmm-hmm."

"Zach."

"Right here." His hands slipped beneath her shirt and her eyes crossed with lust.

"I don't have a condom this time. I forgot to put a new one in my purse."

He shoved his hand in his pocket and pulled out...

"Three." Her knees wobbled as she let out a shaky laugh. "Think we can use them all in one night?"

"I have more in my nightstand."

"Oh," she breathed, staring at him.

At her expression, he let out a shaky laugh. "God, Brooke. I don't know what the hell it is about you, but you always make me..."

"What?" She needed to know. "I make you what?"

"Well, it's a bit of a problem." He pressed against her, and she could feel that he did have a problem. A big one. "Oh my. I see."

"Do you?" His voice was a rough whisper against her ear. "Any ideas?"

"Uh, well, I do have a few. You know, all in the name of assisting a friend in need."

Against her skin, he grinned. "Is that what you're going to do, give me some assistance?"

"I'm a giver, Zach."

He was still laughing when he kissed her this time, and so was she, but his tongue sliding against hers had all that good humor fading away. Pulling up his shirt, Brooke put her hands on his chest, his hard, warm chest, while he lifted her, sandwiching her between his body and the door, rocking into her, and at the sensation, she thunked her head back against the wood, a needy moan escaping her lips as his mouth latched on her neck.

"Love that sound."

So she repeated it, and with a groan, he peeled off her shirt. Beneath she wore only a camisole. He slid the straps off her shoulders, then tugged it to her belly, exposing her breasts. "Look at you," he whispered in awe, leaning in, running his tongue over a nipple then sucking it into his mouth.

She found her fingers in his hair, and tightened her grip, arching up into his mouth. "Now, Zach. Please, now."

Now must have worked for him. He went directly to the button on her shorts while she yanked at his jeans. Somehow, he managed to tear open one of the condoms, and then with their clothes still half on and half off, he slid into her.

Time slowed.

Or stopped.

Or something.

It just felt so right, having him inside her, filling her. It was the only thing that made sense in her unsettled life, the only thing…and she didn't want it to end.

"Brooke." That was all, just her name, as if he felt everything she did. Then he was kissing her, moving within her. Her vision burst into a kaleidoscope of colors, and her blood rushed through her head, roared in her ears. She barely heard herself cry out as she came, or the answering low, strained groan from him as he followed her over.

Lifting his head, he slapped a hand on the door to

keep them from hitting the floor. His eyes were dark and sexily sleepy as he looked into her face.

"How was that for some letting go?" she asked, still breathless.

His eyes were still scorching. "If I were to say it wasn't quite enough...?"

"I'd have no choice but to make use of those two other condoms you're carrying."

"Because you're a giver."

"That's right."

They made it to his shower, where Zach smiled down at her in a way that said he was rough and ready, all tough sinew wrapped around enough testosterone to leave her weak in the knees.

His hands were all over her, up and down her back, smoothing her wet hair from her face, skimming her breasts, her hips, her bottom, her thighs, between them...making her groan softly in his mouth, because yeah, his fingers knew her, knew exactly what to do to make her gasp. "Zach—"

"God, you're wet."

She managed a laugh, though it backed up in her throat when he slid a finger into her. "That's because I'm in the shower."

He played that finger inside her, in and then out. "This isn't from the shower."

Before she could respond, he dropped to his knees, pressed her back against the tiled wall and slid his hands up her thighs. "This is from me. You're wet from me." Using his fingers to part her, exposing exactly what he wanted, he leaned in and kissed her, then groaned in pleasure at her taste.

"Me," he repeated thickly, with unmistakable satisfaction.

He was right. Even now, after knowing him in a way she knew few men, he could merely look at her and turn her on.

And his touch...

He wasn't done with her, not even close. "Oh, God," she gasped as he, with gentle, heart-stopping precision, used his tongue, his teeth, his fingers, driving her right to the very edge and holding her there until she gripped his wet hair in her hands, silently begging him to finish her off.

Which he did, and she came again. Exploded, actually. Maybe imploded. She couldn't tell because she departed from her own mind for a few minutes, and when she'd have slipped to the tile in a boneless, orgasmic heap, he caught her. Caught her and surged to his feet, once again pressing her back to the wall, bending his dark, wet head to rasp his tongue over a nipple.

"Wrap your legs around me," he commanded, his voice a low, husky whisper as he lifted his head and impaled her with that dark, direct gaze. "There—God, yeah. There..."

Her breath caught again when he rocked his hips to hers, entering her. He pushed again, going deeper this time, and her entire body welcomed him.

"Don't," he growled when she arched into him. "Don't move, not yet—"

But she couldn't help it, and he swore again as he moved, a slow thrust of those hips, gliding against her sensitized flesh, wrenching a horrifyingly needy whimper out of her as her head thunked back against the wall.

He had his arms low around her hips. One slid up her

back, his fingers slipping into her hair, cushioning her head, protecting it from the tile. "God, you feel amazing." He let out a slow, rough sound of sheer pleasure. "You're so beautiful, so goddamned beautiful…" He thrust into her, wrenching low moans from both of their throats, which comingled in the fogged-up shower as he moved within her…

She'd already come, but she was there again, right there, primed and ready to go, his rhythm knocking her right off her axis. "Zach—"

"I know." Again he bent his head, this time to watch the sight of himself sliding in and out of her body, the pull and tug of their glistening flesh, hers so soft and pliant and wet, his wet, too, but hard, hard everywhere—his chest, his abs, his thighs, between them—

That was it, that was all she took in before her mind went white with blinding pleasure. Vaguely, she felt him follow her over, but she was gone, simply gone.

WHEN SHE COULD breathe once more, Brooke looked into Zach's eyes, which were still dazed enough to stir her up again. She'd wanted to let loose and, oh boy, had she. She'd wanted a change—well, being naked with a man was a huge change. She'd wanted to belong, and she'd found that, too.

She tightened her grip on him so he couldn't move, couldn't break free, not yet, and he pressed his hips to hers as if he didn't want to let go, either.

But then she realized how ridiculous that was. She didn't cling, ever, and she was sure he didn't, so she forced herself to relax her hold, to free him.

But he remained right where he was, muscles still quaking, eyes still a bit glazed over, just holding her, and something happened to her in that moment, something ripped deep in the region of her chest.

Oh, no. No, no, no...

She was not going to fall in love.

At least not any further than she already had...

Only she wasn't stupid, or slow-witted. She knew the truth. Knew it was far too late. Needing to lighten the mood, she lifted her head and smiled. "Two condoms down..."

He let out a half laugh, half groan.

"Hey, if you're too tired for that third one, I understand."

Eyes glittering at that challenge, Zach bit her lower lip. He then proceeded to teach her a whole new kind of appreciation for her handheld showerhead—and she risked her knees to return the gesture.

By the time they hit his bed and tore open the third condom, she'd "let loose" multiple times and she was one quivering, sensitized nerve ending who could do nothing *but* feel.

And she felt plenty.

So damn plenty.

"Jesus," Zach breathed shakily in her ear some time later. "That third time was..."

"Yeah."

Turning his head, he softly kissed her throat, then her lips, coming up on an elbow to look into her face. "If we don't have the words for it, I say we keep going."

There were many, *many* reasons why she should get up and go home, but there was only one reason why she turned into his arms.

CHAPTER THIRTEEN

ZACH WOKE UP with a hard-on and a smile, both of which vanished when he realized he was alone.

Great. Terrific. Brooke wasn't clingy, and he'd always liked that in a woman. Unable to pinpoint the basis for his sudden irritability, he took a shower, and just looking at the showerhead, remembering its use last night, had him smiling again.

He dressed and stopped to visit Phyllis at the hospital on the way to work. She wasn't awake but he left her flowers and a Polaroid of Cecile sprawled on the firehouse couch, looking like the Queen of Sheba.

The picture reminded Zach that Tommy hadn't called him regarding the photo he'd sent, and something niggled at him, just in the back of his brain, a connection that he couldn't quite put together. It bugged the hell out of him.

At the station, he headed directly for the kitchen and caffeine. He found Cristina raiding someone's lunch and Cecile meowing at her feet for handouts.

Cristina looked at Zach, then did a double take.

"What?" he asked, looking himself over to see if he'd put his pants on backward.

"Hey," Dustin said, coming into the room, gesturing to the sandwich in Cristina's hand. "That's mine."

Cristina took a bite, still staring at Zach. "You know what."

"Not a clue," Zach told her.

"*My* sandwich," Dustin said again.

With a shrug, Zach headed for the coffee, but Cristina muttered something beneath her breath and, frustrated, he turned back to her. "Spit it out then."

She put her hands on her hips. "You're flaunting your just-gotten-laid airs."

"Hello," Dustin said to the room. "Am I invisible? That's my sandwich."

Cristina sighed and handed it over.

Brooke came in but stopped short when she saw them all. A smile slipped out of her at the sight of Zach, one that had *we had great shower sex last night* all over it, and it was adorable.

Cristina saw it and rolled her eyes as Brooke headed to the coffeepot. "Jesus. You two did it *again?* You know it's a dry summer when even the New Hire is getting more than me."

At that, Brooke spilled coffee over the edge of her mug and onto her fingers. *"Ouch."*

"Karma," Cristina told her.

"Hey, Cranky Pants." Dustin tossed Cristina back the sandwich. "Maybe I should go bring you some Wheaties instead."

"I'd rather get lucky."

"You could get lucky," Dustin responded. "Anytime."

"No, I can't." She opened the Baggie and took another bite, still frowning. "My vibrator broke."

Dustin's jaw fell open.

Zach handed him a mug of coffee and gently tapped his chin until his mouth closed. "Easy there, big D."

"Seriously, look at this face," Cristina demanded of Dustin, waving the sandwich around. "Does it say I've gotten any good action lately? Does it say freshly laid? Does it say orgasm central? No, it does not."

Zach glanced at Brooke, who was desperately trying not to look at any of them. He didn't want to brag, but he was pretty damn sure she'd visited orgasm central just last night, compliments of *him*.

Dustin cleared his throat. "You could try a man," he said to Cristina. "You know, instead of a vibrator."

"A *live* penis? Gee, why didn't I think of that?" Cristina poured a pound of sugar into her coffee, stirring so hard some of it splashed out.

Zach leaned in. "A little less anger, you might scare away the penises. Or is it peni?"

She pointed at him. "You, of the Recently Had Sex Club, shut up. You don't get to give me advice."

Brooke went even more red.

"How about me?" Dustin asked. "Can I give you advice?"

"*Hell,* no."

"Why not?"

"I don't take advice from a man who throws his heart into every relationship, only to get it crushed."

"If you don't put yourself out there, then why bother?"

Cristina stared at him as if she'd never seen him before. "You're hopeless. A hopeless romantic."

"You say that like it's a bad thing."

"It's…it's…" But for the first time in, well, history, Cristina seemed to run out of words.

THEIR FIRST CALL of the day came in for a large fire in a warehouse across from the wharf, and all units responded.

By the time Zach and Aidan pulled up, black smoke stretched hundreds of feet into the blue sky like a vicious storm cloud, and the chief was setting up the ICS—Incident Command System. The street was a chaotic mess, making it difficult to get close, but the police were working on directing the civilians out and the fire units in.

Word had come through that there were several people trapped in the warehouse, and Zach eyed the inferno critically. "Not good."

"Going to be tricky," Aidan agreed as they pulled out their equipment.

The chief sent a group of them to the south side of the building, where the missing people had last been seen. Sam, Eddie, Cristina and Blake manned the hoses, while Aidan and Zach prepared to enter the building.

"Now," Blake yelled from the rig, gesturing them in as the gang beat back the flames.

Aidan and Zach went in together, immediately choking on the thick, unrelenting smoke in spite of their protective masks. Visibility was ten feet at first. But only a few yards in, that was cut in half.

"You see red?" Aidan yelled.

"No, but I hear popping like Rice Krispies, so it's coming." In fact, it was earsplitting.

They had no idea where their victims were so Aidan gestured for Zach to go left, and he'd go right. About twenty feet down the dark, smoky hall, Zach heard a woman screaming. "Got one," he said via radio to Aidan, pounding on the doors as he went, stopping at the one from behind which came the screaming.

The wood was hot to the touch.

A door opened behind Zach, and as he turned, a man stumbled right into his surprised arms.

"Claire," the man gasped, and fought to get past Zach. "I hear her, I have to get to Claire!"

The guy was half-unconscious, and the size of a linebacker, an overweight linebacker. Zach gripped him tight, completely supporting his weight. Clearly the guy couldn't go after anyone in his condition. Hell, he couldn't even walk on his own. "You're not going anywhere—"

"I've got to get to Claire! Claire, it's me, Bob! I'm coming!"

"I'll get her."

"No, I—" That's all Bob got out before his eyes rolled up in the back of his head and he slumped to the floor, a dead weight.

Zach hunkered down to sling him over his shoulder, but Bob suddenly came to life, and with what seemed like superhuman strength, grabbed his ankle and tugged.

Zach hit the floor hard.

"Claire!" Bellowing, Bob crawled over him toward the office door.

Zach rolled and managed to hold him down. "You can't go in there. You don't have a mask. I'm taking you out—"

Good old Bob slugged Zach in the gut.

Zach absorbed the blow, using precious oxygen as he got the guy in a choke hold just as the ceiling began crashing down in flaming chunks, one narrowly missing the man's head, and only because Zach yanked him out of the way. "You're wasting time! Wait here—"

"No!" Bob charged for the door, but on the way there,

a huge piece of burning tile fell, hitting him hard enough to slam him to the ground, where he finally was still.

Great. Now Zach had to get Bob out and to medical help before he could go for Claire, whose screams were already fading.

Calm but furious, Zach hoisted the man up in the classic fireman's hold and made his way back down the hallway. Luckily, Aidan met him halfway. "Take him," Zach directed. "I'm going back for the woman."

"We've got orders to get out now. The roof's unstable."

No shit. "I can get to her quick." Hands free, Zach turned back. The smoke was even thicker now, pouring in through the walls, making it seem like night. He couldn't see his hand in front of his face.

But worse, Claire was no longer screaming.

Then Eddie and Sam showed up, their lights barely cutting through the darkness. "Zach! Out of here!"

"I know—hold on!" He opened the office door. Behind him he heard Eddie and Sam yelling into their radios for lines of water to come through the office windows and the roof. They were going to get their asses kicked for breaking protocol, but Zach had never been so happy to see them in his life. "Claire!" he yelled as flames roared out the door, right at them, attracted by the new source of oxygen.

From outside, the hoses beat the flames back enough for them to move in; they found Claire crumpled on the floor beneath a desk. Zach dropped down and pulled her toward him. With Eddie flanking one side and Sam the other, he carried her into the hallway, where they were shoved back by flames coming from both directions now.

"Go back the way you came!" came the chief's voice via radio. "Out the way you came!"

They wouldn't make it. They needed a faster way—the office windows. But they couldn't get to them without hoses.

"Do it," Blake shouted into their radio. "I'm on the roof, I'll cover you."

Shocked, they all looked up, and through the burning ceiling, they could see an arc of water coming through.

Blake.

"Hurry!" he yelled down to them. "Move it!"

Eddie went out the window first, straddling the ledge, reaching back for Claire. Sam went next. Waiting until the ladder cleared, Zach took one last look over his shoulder at the flames rushing them, but Blake still had his back.

"Go," Blake shouted as the ceiling started to cave.

"Jesus, Blake!" Zach's heart stopped. *"Get back!"*

"I will when you're out—"

But a thundering shudder silenced them both. Zach made to leap for the ladder, but the ceiling crashed down. As he yelled Blake's name, everything went black.

"Two firefighters are down," Dustin said grimly, setting down the radio.

Brooke's heart stopped. "Oh my God. *Who?"*

Dustin didn't meet her eyes.

She grabbed his sleeve. *"Who?"*

"Blake and Zach." He grimaced, but tried to sound reassuring. "Don't worry, they'll get them out."

"Ohmigod, they're trapped?"

The male victim Aidan had carried out was sitting

on the curb holding an ice pack to his head, and at this news, he moaned. "It's my fault. I freaked out. And now Claire's trapped in there, too."

"She's out," Dustin told him. "She's in the ambulance, where you should be."

"Oh, thank God." The man surged to his feet, grabbing Brooke's hand, his eyes wet. "I'm sorry. I'm so sorry—"

She shook her head. "You need to sit down—"

"No, I'm fine. I'm just so damn sorry—"

Dustin brought him to Claire, while Brooke stared up at the building, which was a virtual inferno.

Zach was in there.

She took a step toward it but Dustin was back, blocking her path. *"What are you doing?"*

"I need to get closer."

"You're not a firefighter. And we're hospital-bound, Brooke. Two vics, remember? It's our job."

Damn it, he was right. The job. The job always came first. It was what she'd signed on for, and she'd never before minded it taking over her life. Not once.

Unfortunately, she'd given herself a taste of *real* life here in Santa Rey, and she liked it. Hell, loved it.

But now the person who'd given her that taste of life was in danger of losing his.

BROOKE AND DUSTIN were still unloading their patients at the E.R. when word came from the fire scene that they had the flames eighty percent contained, and the injured firefighters had been evacuated safely.

Alive.

And on the way to the hospital.

Brooke took her first deep breath since she'd heard

the words *firefighters* and *down* in the same sentence. She and Dustin tried to wait but an emergency call came in for them—a woman with chest pains needed assistance.

While Dustin drove, Brooke called Aidan.

"Blake's in surgery," Aidan said, sounding tense and stressed. "Badly broken leg."

Ohmigod. "Zach?"

"A concussion, broken wrist and a few second-degree burns. I know that sounds bad, but he's going to be okay, Brooke."

Relief hit her like a tidal wave, but she couldn't lose it because they'd arrived at their call, where she and Dustin found a three-hundred-and-fifty-pound woman stuck in her bed, needing assistance to the bathroom.

"You said you had chest pains," Dustin said.

"Right. I do. But I think it's heartburn."

"Are the pains gone now?" Brooke asked.

"Yes. Completely."

"Ma'am, we still need to bring you in to be checked—"

"Okay, so I never had chest pains. I called because you people won't come out unless it's serious."

They were speechless.

"Would you hand me my TV remote?" she asked them. "Oh, and that box of doughnuts?"

Brooke stared at her. She'd missed being at Zach's side for this, for a woman who couldn't reach her damn remote so she'd called 911? She handed over the remote but not the doughnuts. "Ma'am, the 911 system is for *real* emergencies—"

"It was a real emergency."

Dustin still couldn't speak.

"Hey, I'm sorry, but *Grey's Anatomy* is repeating and I missed it the first time around."

"*Medical* emergencies," Brooke said tightly.

The woman finally had the grace to look a little abashed. "I know, but who else am I going to call?"

"You could do it yourself." No longer speechless, Dustin was clearly furious. "Consider it your daily exercise."

They left there in silence, and it was several long moments before either could speak.

"That didn't just happen," Dustin finally said.

But unfortunately it had, and they had another call, and then another, and it was several hours before Brooke could get another status check on Zach. By that time he'd been released from the hospital and was at his house, supposedly resting.

She wanted to get over there, needed to get a good look at him herself and make sure he was okay, but the chief put their rig on overtime; neither she nor Dustin was going anywhere.

It killed her.

She'd always given her heart and soul to her job, and that had always fulfilled her. But she could see that was no longer the case. Zach's accident had driven home to her that work was *not* enough.

Here in Santa Rey, she'd found more.

CHAPTER FOURTEEN

WHEN THE DOORBELL rang late that night, Zach was in bed, nicely doped up, flying high on whatever the doctor had given him. Aidan had already brought him dinner and had stayed for a movie, but was gone now. Jenny had brought another movie and a few of her pole-dancing pals by, but they'd left, too.

And now someone else was ringing… He sat up very carefully, and then stayed there, head spinning. He'd never been injured on the job before and wasn't quite sure how it had happened. He remembered nearly getting outside the burning building, but that was all until he'd woken up to a headache from hell and Aidan pulling his sorry ass out of the fire just before it ate them both alive.

He knew the dangers of his job. Hell, he knew the dangers of life, but that reality hadn't hit him since his parents had died.

It hit him now. He could have died.

Morbid thought, but he was a realist. If he'd died, life would go on. People would mourn, sure, but no one's basic existence would change with his passing, and that meant facing something uncomfortable—he hadn't made much of a dent.

After his parents' death, he'd just gone along, minding his business, working hard, playing even harder, and that had always been enough for him, because why go for more when life was so damn short? He'd always looked at his colleagues, the ones who'd tied themselves down with marriages and kids, and had been thankful it wasn't him.

But now he couldn't help but wonder if he'd missed out on something that he'd never fathomed.

The doorbell rang again.

"Coming!" he called out, then instantly regretted it because that hurt. Note to self: *don't yell.* Getting out of bed wasn't too much of a problem, but remaining upright proved to be. It turned out his head didn't feel quite attached, and he brought up his uncasted wrist to hold it in place as he made his way to the door like someone on a three-day drunk. He managed to unlock it, then sagged back against the wall, weary to his bones of the jackhammer going off inside his skull. Everything hurt—his wrist, the burns on his left shoulder, arm and chest...

The door creaked open. "Zach?"

Ah, he knew that voice. He knew what it sounded like when she was in the throes of an orgasm, panting, sobbing for breath. He knew what it sounded like when she was slowly drifting back to him, and his name rolled off her tongue as if maybe, just maybe, he were the best she'd ever had.

At the sight of him, she let out a little gasp. "Zach, you shouldn't be up."

"You rang."

"Oh, God. I'm sorry." And then her hands were on his waist, gently pulling him away from the wall so she could slip her shoulder beneath his good one and wrap an arm around him, supporting his weight. "Okay?" she asked.

He slung his arm around her and smiled into her face. "Okay." She was wearing a tank top and capris, looking as if she was learning to fit into the beach world after all. Her hair had been pulled back as usual, neat and tidy as could be, so he tugged on her ponytail, just enough to have some strands slipping free. "There," he said. "A little messy. I like you that way best."

"Bed," she said firmly.

"I thought you'd never ask."

She gave him a look. "What do they have you on?"

"Good stuff."

"Sounds like it." One arm was firmly around him, the other hand low on his abs. He wouldn't have thought it possible, but she was actually completely supporting him, even though he was a foot taller and probably had seventy pounds on her.

As he'd always known, the little city girl was a helluva lot tougher than she looked.

At the top of the stairs, she kept moving to his bedroom. He was just dizzy and shaken enough to let her put him to bed, although he did attempt to pull her down with him. "You need liquids," she said. "Water? Tea?"

"A kiss."

"Both," she decided, and vanished.

Uptight, stubborn as a mule, know-it-all, anal woman.

When she came back and set a tray on his nightstand, he struggled to open his eyes, surprised to find even that took effort. "I'm cold," he said. "Possibly hypothermic."

"I'll get you a blanket."

"You're supposed to offer to strip down and press

your heated body to mine. It's in all the movies. The girl always strips."

"Zach." With her hands on her hips, and her hair suitably messed up thanks to his doing, Brooke looked so pretty and sexy he couldn't think straight.

And she had no idea. No idea at all that she messed with his head just by being. "You really should be out by now," he said, bemused.

"I'm not leaving you alone."

"I meant out of my head." He closed his eyes. "I can't get you out of my damn head."

What if *she'd* gotten hurt today? What if *she'd* died? At the thought, his throat closed up. Just refused to suck air into his lungs, because apparently he'd screwed up and let himself care. If something ever happened to her...

He'd never put words to his biggest fear before, but he was doing so now. And he didn't like it. Not at all.

"Zach." Softly, gently, she cupped his face. "You're in my head, too. *Way* too much."

He hadn't planned to go there—had, in fact, never planned to go there again. His parents dying had nearly been the end of him. "It's the drugs for me." He closed his eyes. "What's your excuse?"

She was quiet a moment. "Maybe you've proven irresistible."

He tried to laugh, but that hurt, so he sobered up quickly. "If it'd been you..."

"But it wasn't. I'm fine." She stretched out next to him on his bed and gently pressed her body to his aching one, easing his pain with no effort at all.

With a sigh, he pulled her closer, holding her tight, tucking her head beneath his chin, wondering how it was that suddenly, with her here in his arms, everything felt all right.

"Are you really okay?" she whispered. Pulling back, she looked up into his face. Her eyes were bright, and warm, and so open Zach could see into her soul.

Was he okay? He didn't feel it. Things had gotten a little crazy in that fire—maybe it was just residual adrenaline making him need her so. "If I said I'm not okay, what would you do?"

Her fingers drifted over his chest in a touch he knew she meant to be soothing, but was actually having an entirely different effect. "I'd do everything in my power to make you comfortable."

"Then, no." He went to shake his head, but the pain stopped him cold. "Definitely not okay."

"Tell me what hurts."

He looked deep into her eyes and saw so much. So much that he had to close his own.

Coward. Yeah, despite the tough-guy image his job gave him, he was a coward. At least he knew it, knew his limitations, knew that loving her, loving anyone, was something he couldn't do. "What hurts?" He stayed very still. "Everything hurts like hell."

Leaning over him, she very carefully kissed his jaw beneath a bruise. "Does that help?"

"Yeah," he decided. "Yeah, definitely."

"How about here…" She kissed him again, closer to his ear this time, making his breath catch.

"Uh-huh."

"Maybe I should kiss all your hurts."

"Okay."

"Tell me where," she murmured.

"Here." He pointed to his throat.

Nodding somberly but with a hint of humor in her beautiful eyes, she obediently kissed his throat, slowly, hotly, with a touch of tongue that shot all the blood in his head to his groin in zero point four.

"Where else?" she asked against his skin, her hand slipping down his side, then back up again, lifting his T-shirt as she went. "Here?" She kissed him over the bandage on his left shoulder and part of his chest, and then the other side, where there were no bandages, just skin, and he felt his heart leap. "Zach?"

"Yeah, there—" He broke off on a shaky breath when she licked his nipple and then began a trail of hot, wet, openmouthed kisses down his torso, southbound.

"Maybe here, too?" She was at his abs now, her fingers toying with the string tie of his sweats. She stopped to glance up at him with an expression that said there was nowhere on earth she'd rather be than right here licking him.

He could come from just looking at her. "Everywhere," he said hoarsely, and felt her yank on the tie and slip her hand inside, beneath the material, wrapping those magic fingers around him. "God, Brooke."

"Shh." She worked his sweats down. "I'm healing you here." Her lips hovered over him and he held his breath, which came out in a rush when she kissed him.

And then drew him gently into her mouth. He lost himself for a while after that, but managed to tug her up before he exploded. "Skin to skin," he whispered, and with an eager smile, she pulled off her clothes, and then with such slow care that he was aching by the end of it, she removed the rest of his, as well, before raiding his nightstand for a condom. Shaking with need, he pulled her down over the tip of him and kissed her as she spread her legs, straddling his, and brought him home.

Sensations swamped him, but then she began to move so that he slid in and out of her, in and out, and he lost his breath again. Time drifted away, his entire world shrinking down to the feel of her surrounding him, milking him, and he had to fight the inclination of his own body to let go and fly.

"Are you hurting?" she murmured, her mouth on his jaw, her hands—just her hands had him letting out a groan of agonized pleasure. "Zach?" She stilled. "Am I hurting you?"

"*Killing* me." He swept his one good hand down her back to grip her sweet, sweet ass, loving the way she panted his name softly in his ear. Slipping his fingers in her silky wet heat, he stroked and teased, doing his damnedest to bring her up to speed to where he was, which was standing on the edge, teetering, so desperate for the plunge he shook with it.

"Zach—"

Unable to help it, he thrust up into her. She was letting out soft whimpers with every breath, assuring him she was as turned on as he.

"Zach, I'm going to—"

"Do it. Come," he murmured against her mouth. "I want to feel you."

And she did. She came completely undone for him, on him, her unbound hair in his face, her fingers tightening painfully in his hair. She was breathless, crying out, and he was gasping as her tightening thighs and the slow grind of her hips set off his own climax. He followed her over, swamped with a tidal wave of unnamed emotion as he poured himself into her.

A WHISPER, THEN a low male laugh broke through Brooke's subconscious, and then it all came back to her. Going to Zach's house, him answering the door, her taking in all that rumpled, surfer-boy glory.

Taking him to bed, taking him *on* the bed, seeing the look in his eyes that told her he was way more invested in her than he wanted to believe or admit…

She opened her eyes. Yep, still in bed with Zach. Actually, she was wrapped around him like a pretzel, thankfully with the covers up to their chin, because at the foot of the bed stood Aidan, Sam, Cristina and Dustin.

"Definitely, he's doing better than Blake," Dustin said. "Blake didn't have a woman with him in his hospital bed."

They were holding fast-food bags, and, as Sam so cheerfully held up to reveal, porn. "To cheer you up."

"But apparently Brooke had other ideas on how to cheer him up," Cristina said.

Dustin shushed her.

"Well, she did." Cristina gave him a little shove. "And as I told *you* before you turned me down, sex is really good for cheering people up."

Everyone looked at Dustin, who shifted uncomfortably. "Maybe I don't like casual cheer-up sex," he said in self-defense.

"Everyone likes casual cheer-up sex," Cristina scoffed. "*Normal* people like casual cheer-up sex."

"Maybe I like it to mean something." Dustin looked into her eyes. "Maybe I want to know it's going to happen again."

She jabbed him in the pec with a finger. "I told you, I don't make plans."

Dustin lifted a shoulder, wordlessly admitting they were at an impasse.

Cristina glared at him, then at the others. "And what are you all looking at?"

In unison, eyes swiveled away from the train wreck waiting to happen, to the other train wreck that had already happened.

Brooke, in Zach's arms.

In his bed.

Surrounded by goggling eyes.

"Get out," Zach said to them all. "And Aidan, I want my key back."

"You gave it to me for emergencies."

"Is there an emergency?"

"Well, I thought junk food and porn constituted one, but I can see I was mistaken."

"Brooke's hair is down," Sam noted. "That's new."

"Out." Zach pointed at the bedroom door with his injured arm. *"Now."*

When they'd filed out, Brooke covered her face. "This is bad. I fell asleep—"

"It's okay."

"They thought it was funny!"

"It is funny," he said. "A little."

Slipping out of the bed, she hurriedly reached for her clothes. Hearing the guys in the kitchen, digging into the food, she felt naked.

Very, very naked. "I've got to go."

"At least stay and eat."

She couldn't stay. Not right now. Not when she'd just realized that in her heart, she was like Dustin, and not cut out for this lightweight sex thing. In spite of herself and her promise on that night on that rock, her damn heart had opened to Zach.

How stupid was that? She'd fallen all the way, leaving herself vulnerable to pain. And there would be pain. She was okay with that, but she needed a moment, a few moments, before she could smile and mean it.

"Hey. *Hey,*" he said when she turned away, snagging her hand, pulling her back. "Brooke? What is it?" The bruise on his jaw had darkened, the white bandage wrapped around his left shoulder stark against his tanned skin. He had bed-head again, and tired eyes that said he was hurting like hell.

He didn't need this, the burden of her feelings. "I need to go home for clothes before work," she said, faking a smile. "That's all."

He was quiet while she pulled on her shirt, so quiet that she finally glanced over to find him looking at her. And in his eyes was a wariness because he felt things for her, too, she knew he did, feelings he kept inside because he didn't intend to let them go anywhere—but what was worse was the comprehension she found there.

Oh, God. Despite her best effort, he could see what she was feeling. "Yeah, I really, *really* have to go."

With a wince, he sat up in bed. "Brooke—"

"No." She shook her head. "Please don't say anything."

"I'm sorry."

Oh, God. "Don't be silly. You have nothing to be sorry for."

"Yes, I do. I'm sorry that I can't give you what you want."

Casually as she could, she slipped into her shoes

and attempted to wrangle her hair. "And what is it you think I want?"

Reaching out, he grabbed her hand again, stilling her frenetic movements, waiting until she looked at him. "Love," he said quietly.

She managed a light laugh. She realized she might be pathetically needy when it came to that particular emotion, but love hadn't exactly been prominent in her life. She'd come here to Santa Rey a little bit in limbo, but the one thing she'd known was she'd wanted that to change. But she'd made Zach a promise *not* to get attached, *not* to have messy emotions.

She'd failed on both counts.

"Brooke." He stroked a strand of hair from her face, all the while holding her gaze with his so that she couldn't look away to save her life. In these eyes were affection, heat…and a brutal honesty. "I don't want to hurt you. I never wanted to hurt you, but—"

"It's not your fault—"

"I wanted a physical relationship with you, you know that. And now I'm holding back, you know that, too. It's just that if you're going to add love into the mix—" He grinned ruefully. "Well, you can't. I don't seem to have the parts required to do love. So you can't fall, not for me."

Her throat tight, she nodded. "I know."

Only she also knew it was too damn late.

CHAPTER FIFTEEN

ZACH SLEPT ON and off for two days. Or rather he tossed and turned for two days. He spent his third night at home surrounded by the guys, grateful not to still be in the hospital like Blake, who'd suffered a more serious head trauma, his leg broken in four places, and two cracked ribs, and was by all accounts cranky as all hell.

Zach was glad for the company. Sort of. But mostly he kept thinking about the fact that Brooke hadn't come back, and that this was her last week in town, and that he was an idiot.

"Why are you moping around like you lost your puppy?" Sam asked.

"I'm not."

The guys all exchanged a careful-with-the-deluded-patient look, and he sighed.

Yeah. He was moping.

Because he'd sent away the best thing that had ever happened to him.

"You've got pizza, beer and us," Eddie joked. "What else could you need?"

"Brooke." This from Aidan, his mouth full of pizza and a knowing look in his eyes. "He wants Brooke."

"No." Sam shook his head. "Our Zach's not much of a repeater."

Zach opened his mouth, but in lieu of absolutely nothing to say in his defense, shut it again.

"If I had Brooke looking at me the way she looks at you, I'd become a repeater," Dustin said as he reached for more pizza.

Yeah, but Zach was a moron. Brooke wouldn't be looking at him like that again. He'd made sure of that.

"You're only saying so because you got laid by the woman of your dreams," Sam pointed out. "Cristina."

"Cristina?" Zach blinked. This was news. "Since when?"

"Since last night," Sam informed him. "Dustin fixed her car and then she slept with him."

Not one to kiss and tell, Dustin tried to hold back his stupid grin and failed.

"Cristina's not going to settle down," Aidan warned Dustin. "She's not the type."

"She might, for the right guy," Dustin said, pushing up his glasses. "It could happen."

"You're asking to be crushed," Aidan told him. "Like a grape. *Again.*"

"Actually," Zach said quietly, "you never know."

"Then why aren't you seeing Brooke?" Aidan asked. "With only one week in town left, that makes her the perfect woman in my eyes."

"So why don't *you* date her?" Eddie jeered.

"Maybe I will."

Suddenly the pizza Zach had consumed sat like a lead weight in his gut. He tried to picture Brooke moving on and dating any one of these guys. His friends.

Then he had to admit it wasn't the pizza weighing his gut down. "No."

Aidan raised a brow. "What?"

"Nothing." Zach tossed his pizza aside. "She can date whoever she wants."

"Really?" Aidan said dryly. "So you wouldn't care if I ask her out?"

Zach opened his mouth, shut it, scrubbed a hand over his eyes and sighed. "We've been friends for a long time."

"Years."

"Yeah. And I've always said you should go out with whoever floats your boat, but…"

"But?"

"But if you go out with Brooke, I'll have to hurt you."

Dustin laughed and clamped him on the shoulder in commiseration.

Aidan just arched a brow that said, *You're in deep*.

Didn't he know it.

LATER THAT DAY, the bad news came from Zach's doctor—he wasn't cleared to go back to work until his cast came off, which was a minimum of three weeks away.

Three more weeks without work just might kill him, not that the doctor seemed to care, and not that the chief seemed to, either, when he called to check on Zach.

"Enjoy the time off. We'll be waiting for you."

"I want to come in," Zach said. "I could handle light duty—"

"No. We want you back, Zach, but sound."

Sound. What the hell did that mean?

But as the mind-numbing boredom set in, Zach had to admit he didn't feel so *sound*. He sat on his couch with the remote, but nothing on daytime TV interested him. Nothing on his bookshelf interested him. Hell, even the porn didn't interest him. He couldn't go surfing because of the cast and bandages. He couldn't work.

All he could do, unfortunately, was think. *Way* too much thinking going on. About Brooke, about… Brooke.

It was another whole day before he remembered.

The arson fires. He'd actually come close to figuring something out…something really important. He called Aidan. "Where was I with the arson stuff?"

"Close to screwing up your career."

"Come on. We've fought hundreds of fires, and out of all of those, I'm only talking about four—"

"Five."

"—So how in the hell is that screwing up my career—"

"Five fires."

"What?"

Aidan sighed. "Let's get real crazy, okay? I think that the warehouse fire was arson."

"Why?"

"Gut feeling. Too many things went wrong. And guess what Tommy told me when I mentioned it?"

"I'll go out on a limb here and say, 'Mind your own fucking business?'"

"Bingo."

"Did you look around afterward?" Zach asked. "Get sight of the point of origin?"

"No, I was sitting by your side in the hospital after saving your sorry ass."

"Damn it."

"You're welcome."

After they hung up, Zach went out onto his deck and stared off into the night. Maybe it was exhaustion, maybe it was pain, maybe it was simply that he didn't want to face the fact that his chest hurt, and so did his heart.

Or that he missed Brooke.

Over the years, he'd slept with enough women to lose count, and that had never bothered him any, but now he wondered what it would be like to stay with the *same* woman instead of moving on each time? To have some familiarity? A real relationship with depth instead of just heat?

He bet there was comfort in that, which he'd never had any use for before. But now, honestly, he could use a little TLC.

Zach hadn't taken his pain meds in two days, so showering was a bitch, but he got through it, dressed and walked out to his truck. He stopped short at the sight of Brooke getting out of her car.

She was carrying a bag from the local sandwich shop and wore an expression that said she wasn't too sure of her welcome, an expression that changed to disbelief when she saw the keys in his hand. "What are you doing?"

"I was going to ask you the same thing."

"I'm bringing you something more substantial than pizza or McDonald's." Her eyes met his. "Now you."

"I was coming to see you."

She let out a breath. "Okay, you have no idea how I both love and hate that. You shouldn't be driving. How are you feeling?"

Like I missed the hell out of you. "Great."

She arched a brow.

"Good."

"Zach."

"Okay, like shit. I feel like complete shit."

With a sigh, she stepped close, and did something he hadn't expected, given how things had gone the last time he'd seen her.

She hugged him.

For a moment, just a heartbeat, really, he stood still, shocked, because normally when he pushed someone away, they willingly went. After all, he was a master pusher when it came right down to it. And he'd all but thrown her feelings for him back in her face.

But Brooke, petite, sweet-but-steely-willed Brooke, hadn't just held her ground with him, she was pushing back.

If that didn't grab him by the throat.

Unable to resist, he slid his arms around her, pulling her in tight. Bending his head, he buried his face in her hair, breathing her in.

Keep it light, keep it casual...

But then she was pressing her mouth to his cheek and he was turning his head to meet her mouth, and as he deepened the kiss he knew the truth.

He didn't want to push her away anymore. He really didn't. So he hoped like hell someone threw him a line, because he was going down.

"You need to get back inside," she murmured. "You're pale."

Pale, and apparently stupid, because he kissed her again.

Deep.

Wet.

He was in the middle of working on the long part, but she pulled back. "Careful, I'll hurt you—"

Shaking his head, he kissed her again, then dropped

his forehead to hers. "No." Drawing a deep breath, he straightened and pulled free. "I'll hurt you."

"Oh." She stared up at him, then took a step back and nodded. "Right."

They were still just staring at each other when Aidan pulled up, followed by all the guys.

Incredible timing, as always.

"Okay," Brooke said. "I'm going to go."

"No, don't."

"No, really. It's okay. I just wanted—" She thrust the bag of food in his hands. "Here."

"Wait—"

"Listen, I know I wear my heart on my sleeve and feel too much, but I'm not slow. I really did hear you the other day, what you were trying to say. You don't want me to get invested, and I get it. I'm leaving and all that, and this was never about that kind of thing. I just want you to know that I understand, and there's no hard feelings."

Damn, she killed him. "Brooke—"

"Don't." She shook her head. "Don't go there. Not now."

"Fine. Later, then. Just please stay until I get rid of these guys?"

She glanced at them all getting out of their cars. "Okay, but Zach? That kiss…"

He couldn't help looking at her lips again. He could still taste her. "Yeah?"

"That didn't feel like a hey-how-are-you kiss. Or even a one-night-stand kiss." She moved in and whispered for his ears only. "It felt like a helluva lot more."

Yeah. It had.

"So you might want to think about that next time you tell yourself I'm the only one going to get hurt here."

EVERYONE ENTERED ZACH'S HOUSE, carrying food and news of their day. Brooke joined them because Zach had asked, but mostly because she wanted to. She wanted to be with them.

With Zach.

He sat sprawled on the couch, and if it hadn't been for the cast, the bandages and the slight paleness of his face, she'd never have guessed that he'd nearly died.

Her heart tightened at that, but she'd always licked her wounds in private, so stressing about what could have happened, as she had been doing since the fire, would have to wait.

Sam tossed her a soda.

Dustin handed her a plate.

Aidan kicked a chair her way.

She sat in the chair, holding the soda and plate, staring at the group talking and laughing amongst themselves, a huge lump forming in her throat.

She really was part of them. She belonged. And hadn't that been what she'd been looking for at the beginning of the summer? A place to belong?

Zach sipped his soda, his eyes hooded as he watched her over his drink.

She watched him back.

Around them, the laughter and noise went up a notch, but Zach didn't join in. Probably because he was hurting far more than he'd let on. She could see it in the grim set of his mouth and the lines of exhaustion on his face. He eyed the pizza on the coffee table in front of him but didn't take a piece.

He loved pizza.

"You okay?" Aidan leaned in to ask her quietly.

"Not me I'm worried about."

They both eyed Zach. "Let's try this." Aidan tossed two slices of pieces on a plate, then handed it to Zach. "Hey. The annual picnic is in one week."

"So?"

"So we need an anchor for the tug-of-war against Firehouse 32."

"I repeat. So?"

"So no pansy-asses need apply. Eat up."

"Not hungry."

"Really? You like being home all day, watching *Oprah,* eating bonbons?"

Zach opened his mouth, probably to tell Aidan where to go, but the doorbell rang again, and in came Cristina, carrying a tray of cupcakes.

Everyone looked at Dustin. Everyone except Cristina, that is, alerting Brooke to the fact that something was going on. Happy not to be at the center of the gossip mill for once, she watched with fascination as the blonde shuffled around without her usual cockiness.

"The grocery store had a small fire in their bakery." She set the tray down and grabbed a cupcake in each hand before looking at the gang, carefully avoiding Dustin's eyes. "So, what's up?"

"Nothing," everyone but Dustin said.

Cristina sighed and faced the silent and clearly brooding Dustin. "Okay, fine. I'm sorry." She offered him a cupcake. "Very sorry."

Dustin stared down at the double chocolate fudge cupcake, eyes shadowed, mouth unaccustomedly tight. He didn't take it. "What's this?"

"It's called dessert. It's what people do when they're sorry. They bring people treats."

"Why are you sorry?"

"You know why."

"Say I don't."

Cristina sighed. "I'm sorry I got mad when you wouldn't have sex with me again."

Dustin raised a brow in tune to the juvenile catcalls from the guys.

"I *am* sorry, all right?" Cristina ignored everyone else. "Jesus! Would you just eat a damn cupcake?"

"I don't think so."

"Oh my God." Cristina sighed again, looking at the others, all of whom got real busy with their cupcakes. "Look, I really needed to get laid, okay? It'd been too long and you might have noticed that I was a little on edge."

"Was?"

She rolled her eyes.

"Maybe you're on edge for other reasons," Dustin said. "Ever think of that?"

"No." She waggled the cupcake in front of his nose. "Are you going to take this or not?"

Dustin took it, then licked the frosting while studying Cristina thoughtfully.

The room was unusually quiet now. Brooke was especially so, mostly because she really felt for Dustin. He'd put himself out there and was now hurting.

She knew the feeling.

"I'm sorry, too," Dustin said, mouth full of frosting.

Cristina went still. "For?"

"For not having more meaningless sex with you."

Sam let out a choked laugh and, without taking her eyes off Dustin, Cristina pointed at him.

Sam shut up.

"Does that mean you want to?" Cristina asked Dustin. "Have more meaningless sex?"

"No."

Cristina looked deeply disappointed, but tried to hide it. "Okay."

"*I'll* have meaningless sex with you," Eddie said. When Cristina rounded on him, Aidan helpfully stuffed a cupcake into Eddie's mouth to keep him quiet.

"Or you could try it my way," Dustin suggested to Cristina.

Cristina turned back to Dustin and blinked.

Dustin didn't.

Zach sighed, and with some struggle, stood up, gesturing the others to follow him, clearly not wanting to stay and witness the bloodshed.

This time, Cristina pointed at Zach. "Don't move. Did you put him up to this?"

"Give me some credit," Dustin answered for him. "I've had it bad for you since day one. There's no way you haven't noticed."

"Whoa." Cristina staggered back a step and collided with a wall. "What? What the hell did you just say?"

"I gave you an offer for sex," Dustin said calmly. "As I believe you were lamenting about your continued lack of."

"After that," she whispered.

"I said give me some credit. Of course Zach didn't put me up to this."

"No, after that." She swallowed hard. *"What the hell did you say after that?"*

"The part where I said I've wanted you since day one?"

"Yeah. Hang on." And she sat, right there on the floor. "That."

With a sigh, Dustin got up and crouched in front of her. "It's not a death sentence, Cristina."

"Ohmigod."

He sighed again. "I was hoping for a more articulate response than that."

"Articulate?" She looked bowled over, but he just waited, and she swallowed hard. "Okay, articulate. How about…" She shook her head as if at a loss. "Thank you?"

He arched a brow. "Thank you?"

"Look, I'm trying to be polite here, but I really need to throw up. Are you crazy? You've got a thing for me? You don't even know all my faults."

"I think I know a lot of them," he said dryly.

"Ohmigod."

"You're starting to repeat yourself. Let's go for a walk."

"A walk."

"Yes. On the beach."

"Are you trying to romance me?"

"Uh-huh. Is it working?"

"I don't know. Maybe. No more talk about…wanting me. Promise?"

"Take my hand, Cristina."

She stared at his proffered hand, and then took it. "You should know I'm not putting out on the first date."

"Maybe on our second, then."

That shook a laugh out of her and, shocking Brooke

and probably everyone else, Cristina allowed Dustin to pull her out the door.

Brooke watched them go, something deep inside her aching. Then she realized Zach was looking right at her. What she'd give to know that he was aching, too, but whatever he was thinking, he kept it to himself.

A LITTLE WHILE LATER, Zach managed to escape to the kitchen, where he leaned on the sink and stared out the window. He could still hear his friends talking and laughing in the other room. He was grateful for them, but he wished they'd all go away and leave him alone with Brooke.

The door opened and he turned hopefully, but it was Tommy.

"How are you feeling?" the inspector asked.

"I'd be better if you'd convince the chief to let me go back to work."

"No can do."

"Tommy—"

He held up a hand. "I agree with you about those fires," he said quietly. "Okay? You're right. They're arson, all of them. I've always believed you." He let that sink in. "But believing you wasn't the problem. My investigation was—is—undercover."

Zach stared at him. "Because...you suspected me."

Tommy's expression was apologetic but firm. "Past tense."

Zach let out a breath. "Jesus, Tommy."

"I know you want to come back to work, but I'm advising you to wait."

"You don't think—"

"What I think is that you're in danger."

"What the hell does that mean?"

"You've been a damn thorn for me, Zach, and we're on the same side. Imagine how the bad guy feels about you."

"I don't understand."

"You're getting close. Close enough for the arsonist to try to hurt you. He burned Phyllis's house because you care about her. Then at the warehouse fire, you were hit."

"By a burning piece of ceiling."

"By a chunk of debris, yes, but I've been at the site. I think it was thrown at you."

Zach staggered to a chair and sat.

"I've combed every inch of that site," Tommy said. "You went back in where you weren't supposed to, and I believe you almost caught the arsonist red-handed."

"But the only people inside at that point, besides the victims, were firefighters."

Tommy just looked at him, and that's when he finally got it. They weren't looking for some nameless criminal.

It was someone they all knew.

CHAPTER SIXTEEN

AFTER EVERYONE HAD GONE, Brooke grabbed a trash bag and started to clean up.

"Leave it," Zach told her, weary to the bone. "I can do it."

She put her hands on her hips. "You're going to do it?"

"Yes."

"Even though you've barely moved all night?"

He lifted a shoulder, which pulled at his burns and had pain shooting through him. He didn't make a sound, he very carefully didn't make a sound, but she was at his side in a heartbeat.

"Damn stubborn man," she murmured, helping him up.

Suddenly, all he could think about was how her hands felt on him. "What are you doing?"

"Putting you to bed."

Just the words had his body leaping to attention. Even in pain and pissed off at the world, he could still get it up for her. "Sorry, but I'm bound to disappoint you tonight."

"Shut up, Zach."

Upstairs in his room, she got him onto the bed. He looked up into her face. Her beautiful face. She was worried sick, and, he realized with some shame, that he was not the only one hurting. "I talked to Tommy tonight. He said he believed me."

"What?" Brooke went still. "Oh, Zach," she breathed. "I'm so glad! Does he know who the arsonist is?"

This was the hard part. "He suspects an inside job."

"Inside…" Her mind worked fast, and she gasped. "No."

"The warehouse fire wasn't an accident." He went to reach for her and gritted his teeth at the pain.

"I'm going to get your meds and water. Don't move."

When she was gone, he tried to pull off his shoes, but the cast on his arm felt heavy. Plus, moving hurt. Not feeling up to taking off his own damn shirt, much less his pants, he lay back on the bed, out of breath and frustrated.

"Why don't you get undressed?" she asked, coming back into the room with a glass of water and a pill.

He closed his eyes. "Yeah. Good idea."

"Need help?"

"No. I can do this. Seriously."

"Seriously? Get real, Zach." He felt her hands pulling off his shoes, heard them hit the floor one at a time. "Because, seriously? You are full of shit." Carefully, with a surprisingly gentle touch considering the sarcasm in her voice, she helped him out of his shirt. "So what else did Tommy say?"

"That I've pissed off the arsonist."

She went still. "You're in danger?"

"I'm safe here."

Her eyes searched his as her hands slid over his bare chest.

Instead of the pain he'd felt for days, all he felt was the touch of her warm hands. She was better than Vicodin. Then she trailed those hands down and reached for the buttons on his Levi's. "You still need my help, right?"

Oh, yeah. He nodded, and pop went the first button. And then the second, and suddenly Zach was breathing as if he'd been running.

She wasn't breathing too steadily, either.

"Okay, maybe I'd better do this." His hands were shaking as he pulled open the rest of the buttons, but shoving the denim down his legs required grating his teeth and lifting his hips. By the time he got them down a mere inch, he was beginning to sweat.

"Here." She got on the bed for leverage, straddling his lower legs, and pulled his jeans down to his thighs, revealing the fact that he'd gone commando that morning.

Which left the part of him that was the happiest to see her bouncing free.

Her eyes widened.

"I told you I should do this."

"I'm sorry." She was still staring.

"Not helping."

At that, Brooke actually snickered, but he could hear the breathlessness in the sound.

And the wanting.

"Yeah," he managed. "Still not helping."

"Right." She scrambled off his legs.

Good. Great. She was going away. But then she pulled his jeans the rest of the way off, tossing them to the floor. Leaving him buck naked.

"You…need a blanket."

Which was beneath him. He rolled toward her just

as she leaned in to try to pull it out from under him, and they bumped into each other.

"Sorry," she gasped, but in countering her own movement, she bumped into him again.

They went utterly still.

He had his hands on her arms. She had hers braced on his chest, and she was still staring at the part of him boring a hold in her belly.

"Zach?" she whispered.

"Yeah?"

"You seem to need some…" Her gaze met his. "Letting loose."

He laughed, which hurt like a son of a bitch.

"Yeah?"

"Oh, yeah. It's just what I need." *You*… And with that, he tugged her overtop of him.

AT THE FULL body contact with Zach, what happened within Brooke was what happened every time—a shockingly intense, insatiable hunger arose. "Zach—"

"I know. Condom."

She leaned over and grabbed one from his nightstand, while he tugged at her zipper, but his fingers were shaking. "Why are you wearing so many clothes?"

"I have no idea—" Before she got the words out, Zach had her capris down and pushed open her legs. Pretty damn talented for a man with one arm. Then he lifted her up and thrust into her.

Their twin groans of pleasure mingled in the air.

Her hands were braced on either side of his face, her head bent low to his. Staring into his eyes, she was startled at how easily she lost herself in him.

Every.

Single.

Time.

Brooke had no idea how she could want him this way, as if she would die if she didn't have him. The hunger filled her so that she could think of nothing else, and she rocked her hips, a movement that wrested a grunt from him. His good hand gripped her, holding her still. "Don't move." His voice was like sandpaper. "God, don't move, or this'll be over—"

She moved. She couldn't help it; she had to. She rocked her hips again, absorbing the low, rough sound torn from deep in his throat. Leaning over him, she went to bury her face in the crook of his neck but he caught her, cupped her jaw and held it so that she could do nothing but look right into his eyes as he met her thrust for thrust, until she began to tremble, then burst. He was right with her, pulsing inside her even as she shattered around him.

"Yeah." He breathed a shaky sigh as she sagged over top of him, a boneless puddle of raw nerve endings. "Just what the doctor ordered." She felt his mouth press to the side of her throat and closed her eyes, letting the drowsiness take her—which was infinitely preferable to facing the fact that she had no idea how she was going to walk away from this man.

BROOKE AWOKE TO the sun pouring in through the window and splashing all over her face with startling cheer.

But she always shut her shades, so...

She jerked upright. Yep, she wasn't in her bed, she was in Zach's. Legs entwined, arms entwined, no covers in sight because their body heat had been enough.

Once again she'd slept the entire night wrapped around him as if...

As if she belonged here.

Zach stirred, opened an eye. He had two days' growth on his jaw, and some serious bed-head, and he looked so hot she wanted to gobble him up.

Again.

"Overslept," she said, and tried to free herself. "Going to be late—" She broke off when he merely tightened his grip on her. "What?"

"Just wondering if it worked. If I'm suitably relaxed or if maybe we should kept working on it."

She stared into his gorgeous, sleepy face and remembered his warning not to fall in love with him. "You're fine." She scrambled up, glanced at the clock again on the off chance it had miraculously changed in her favor. "Where the hell are my panties?"

Zach came up on an elbow and surveyed the room. "There."

On his lamp. Perfect. Her bra was draped over a bedpost like a trophy. Snatching it up, she glared at him, just lying there looking like sin on a stick. "I'm late," she said more to herself. Very late. Late for the rest of her life, which was right around the corner. In fact, she was meeting the real estate agent today to discuss an offer she'd received on the house yesterday. With a sigh, she headed toward the door.

"Brooke?"

She turned back. "Yes?"

"Be careful out there."

"I always am."

"I know. But..."

But now one of them was a possible arsonist and had

hurt Zach. Anyone could get hurt. She got that. "I can take care of myself."

"But—"

"And after next week, I'll be on my own." Because that brought a lump to her throat, she had to swallow hard to continue. "I realize that last night was mostly my doing, but you should know, I got an offer on the house. Three more shifts, and I'm gone."

He closed his eyes, but not before she saw a flash of emotion much deeper than affection. "I know."

"Goodbye, Zach."

Now he opened those eyes again, and let her see his sadness. "Is that it? Goodbye, the end?"

"What else is there?"

When he opened his mouth and then shut it, she shook her head. "Exactly. Goodbye, Zach."

WELL, WHAT HAD she expected, a marriage proposal? She'd only met him five and a half weeks ago, and he wasn't exactly known for being a commitment king. Brooke drove to work, not acknowledging the burning in her eyes, doing her damnedest not to think about the fact that he'd let her walk away.

He'd let her say goodbye.

She pulled into the parking lot. With Zach and Blake both still out, plus several others hit by a flu bug, she was on the B shift for the first time, with a whole new gang, and she found herself working with an EMT named Isobel. Adding to her stress, Brooke was the scheduled driver for the day, which began the moment she got out of her car and the bell rang.

"Watch your speed," was Isobel's most common refrain, uttered every two seconds on every one of their many, *many* calls. Isobel had a cap of dark hair and darker eyes, both her expression and demeanor screaming, *I know I'm a woman in a man's world, but hear me roar.* "Watch that turn—"

"I'm watching."

"Watch—"

"I'll keep watching," Brooke said evenly, each and every time, though by the afternoon, she didn't feel so even. She missed Dustin. "Believe it or not, I've actually driven once or twice before."

"You can never be too careful is all." Isobel eyed the speedometer. "Watch—"

"Okay." Brooke took a deep breath. "Still watching."

"Sorry." Isobel flashed a small, conciliatory smile. "I know I'm a pain. I'm just overly cautious."

Nothing wrong with that. If only Brooke had watched over her own broken heart as cautiously...

Isobel was blessedly quiet until they turned on Third Street, heading toward their call, an outdoor beach café with a kitchen fire, where one of the cooks had passed out from the smoke and hit his head. A hundred yards ahead, the light turned red.

Isobel pointed. "Watch—" Then she caught herself, and cleared her throat. "Nothing."

Brooke pulled up behind two fire trucks. They had the fire contained, but the flames were still impressive, leaping fifty feet into the sky. She and Isobel got out of their rig and immediately one of the firefighters came up to them. "The vic vanished on us. We're still looking for him."

Isobel went back to the radio to report the information. As Brooke took in the fire, she was shocked to see Blake there, standing just off to the side. He was supposed to still be recuperating in the hospital. She'd visited him the day before, and he'd been in no shape to be up. Worried, she moved to his side. "Blake?"

A low, raw sound escaped him and she took a closer look. He wasn't in his gear. He couldn't have been, not with the cast on his leg. His jeans were cut over the cast, and he wore a sweatshirt that looked odd, given it was at least eighty-five degrees outside. He leaned his weight on a crutch, but what caused Brooke concern was how pale he looked, and the fact that he was sweating profusely. "Blake?"

He didn't respond. Eyes locked on the flames, face tight, he seemed miles away.

When she set her hand on his arm, he nearly leaped out of his skin. "Hey, just me." She sent him a smile he didn't return. "You all right?"

"Yes."

"You don't look it. You're in pain."

"Nah. I've got enough pain meds in me to change my name to Anna Nicole Smith."

With a low laugh, she turned back to the rig and saw Isobel had located their vic. He was shaking his head, pushing her hands away before walking off. He didn't seem to want treatment. "Looks like we don't have a transport after all. Can we give you a ride?"

When Blake didn't answer, she looked at him—he was limping away with shocking speed. Running after him, Brooke caught up just as he got as close as he could to the flames without igniting. "Blake, what are you doing?"

At the sound of her voice, he jerked. "Brooke?" He blinked, as if surprised to see her, as if he didn't remember seeing her only two seconds ago.

"Okay, you know what? You're not okay." She put her hand on his arm. "Let's go sit down."

"What are you doing here?"

"I'm working. On you. Why are you out of the hospital?"

"I don't know." He closed his eyes. "I'm sorry. I just...I'm sorry. For everything."

"Come on. Let's get you back." Away from the fire and the pain she suspected he was suffering. "We're in the way here."

He looked around and blanched. "God, I'm sorry."

"For what, Blake?"

"I can't..." He shoved his fingers through his hair and turned away from her, but not before she saw a suspicious sheen to his eyes. "I'm so damned sorry. I should have handled this better. I should have stopped it sooner."

"Blake? Stopped what sooner?"

Staring at the flames, he appeared transfixed. "I don't want to lose another partner. Or a friend."

"What do you mean? Blake, done *what* sooner?"

"Lots of things, actually." He walked off, but again she stopped him.

"I don't think being alone is what you need, Blake."

"Please." He jerked free, his face tortured. "Just leave me alone. There's nothing you can do to stop it from happening."

"What do you mean?" But she was afraid she knew, or at least was starting to know. "Blake—"

"It's not what you think."

But she was suddenly sure it was *exactly* what she thought. The arsonist was someone from within their own ranks. Possibly, terrifyingly, the someone standing right here in front of her. "Okay, let's go over to the ambulance, and—"

"Isobel needs you."

Brooke turned back to the rig and saw Isobel waving at her frantically.

"We have a call!" she was yelling.

Brooke turned back to Blake. "I have to go but I want you to come with me—"

But she was talking to herself. *"Blake?"*

He'd vanished.

CHAPTER SEVENTEEN

BROOKE RAN BACK to the rig. Hopping into the driver's seat, she pulled out her cell phone.

"No talking on the phone while you're driving," Isobel said.

"I'm not driving yet." She punched in Zach's cell phone number.

"We have a call. Eighth and Beach."

"I know, but this is an emergency, too." She got Zach's voice mail. Damn it. "Zach," she said, very aware of Isobel listening to every word. "I need to talk to you. ASAP." She shut the phone and tried to order her racing thoughts. "We need to get someone else to take this call. Blake—"

"There is no one else. We need to go, now."

"Fine." She handed her cell over to Isobel. "Call the station, have someone come to get Blake. Then call Tommy Ramirez. Tell him—" What? What the hell could she say? All she had were suspicions. "Tell him I need to talk to him. That it's urgent. Ask him to meet us at the hospital after we pick up our vic."

But Tommy didn't meet her. So after Brooke and Isobel had turned their patient over to the E.R., she tried the chief, and shock of all shocks, got him.

"This better be important, O'Brien," he said in his sharply authoritative voice. "I'm in a meeting."

"It's about Blake."

The chief was silent for a single, long beat. "What about him?"

Brooke moved away from Isobel so that she could speak frankly. "He was at the scene of the Third Street fire today, and he didn't look right. And..." Oh, God, how to say this? "And I think he was trying to confess to arson."

"You *think?* What the hell does that mean? And what arson?"

"He wasn't coherent. He—" She frowned at the static in her ear. "Sir? Hello, Chief?" She'd lost him. *"Shit."*

"You're not supposed to swear while in uniform," Isobel said.

Brooke contained the urge to wrap her fingers around Isobel's neck and drove them back to the station.

The chief was there, waiting for her. "Blake isn't at the hospital or at the fire."

"What's going on?" Cristina stood in the doorway, looking unnerved. "What's the matter with Blake? Eddie went to go get him but he couldn't find him."

"He's missing," the chief said. "And he's not answering his cell."

"He was at the Third Street fire," Brooke told Cristina. "He was walking with a crutch, definitely disoriented—*oh my God.*"

The chief turned on her. "What?"

"What if he went *into* the fire?"

"Why would he do that?" Panic raised Cristina's voice. "He wasn't suited up, he wasn't working—"

"But he wasn't himself," Brooke said slowly, reviewing their conversation. "He was rambling, not making much sense, and just staring at the flames."

"Rambling about what?" Cristina cried.

"He kept saying sorry about the fires, like he was trying to confess."

Cristina gasped and covered her mouth. "He didn't—he wouldn't—"

"He didn't look good, and then we got a call. He'd vanished."

The chief headed for his truck with long strides while Cristina dragged Brooke inside, where she sank to the couch in the living room.

"That building is gone," Brooke said. "Completely gone. I should have stopped him. I should have—"

"You couldn't have stopped him," Sam said, coming in behind them. "And he's not that stupid."

Cristina let out a low sound of grief.

"Look, he hasn't been the same since Lynn died," Sam told her. "We've all tried to talk to him about it, but you know how he is. He's Eeyore. He's stubborn. But not stupid," he repeated. "No way did he go into that fire."

"He was hurting," Cristina whispered. "He lost his partner."

"And *he's* dealing with it." Dustin said this very gently, coming in from the kitchen. "You can't do it for him."

Covering her face, she sank to the couch next to Brooke. "This. *This* is why I like to alienate people. Goddamn it, you made me forget to alienate him and now I care!"

"Cristina." When she didn't answer, Dustin crouched at her side. *"Cristina."*

"Caring sucks," she whispered through her fingers.

He pulled them from her face. "Not always."

She just stared at him.

"Not always," he repeated softly. "What I feel for you doesn't suck. And what I'm hoping you feel for me doesn't suck."

"Damn it." She closed her eyes. "It doesn't. It only scares the living hell out of me. You should brace yourself now." She opened her eyes. "Because I'm maybe falling in love, too. And it's all your fault."

Dustin looked staggered as he drew a shaky breath.

"Don't you have anything to say?"

"Thank you?"

She stared at him, then with a shocked laugh at having her own words tossed back at her, she lunged up and hugged him tight.

Desperate to take her mind off Blake, Brooke tried to be happy for her partner. Putting himself out there had paid off for Dustin, in a big way. It was right then that she realized she hadn't put herself out there for Zach at all. Instead, she'd done the opposite, hiding behind her six-week time limit. She'd even said goodbye already.

"You okay?"

She opened her eyes to Aidan. Was she okay? She was leaving a job she loved in less than a week. Her grandmother's house was all but sold in spite of the fact that beneath all the clutter, she'd discovered a gorgeous, well-tended home that seemed to say *Don't sell me* every time she walked in the door.

The truth was, this decision to move yet again wasn't being dictated by family or school or anything but her own fear.

Funny, really.

And damned ironic.

All her life she'd been racing from one spot to an-

other, and now she was free to do as she chose, go anywhere she wanted, and…and all she wanted was to stay.

With Zach.

"Brooke?"

She looked at Aidan. "It's nothing. I'm fine."

"Even if that was true, if you're fine, how's Zach?"

"When I left there, he was in a little pain but—"

"Not what I meant."

"Yeah." She sighed. "He was…good."

"He's the master at good. Look, I love the guy, but—"

"I'm sure you two will be very happy together."

"You're funny." He shook his head. "Look, neither
Zach nor I have ever really needed a woman in our life."

"I know. I get it."

"No, see that's the thing. Zach looks at you differently. He has from the beginning. If you leave, it'll be
like losing his parents all over again. Or his brother."

"He lost his brother?"

"Caleb moved to L.A. the day Zach turned eighteen,
pretty much deserting him. Can't blame the guy. He
hadn't signed on to be a parent, but still, it was rough
on Zach. He's not good with opening up. He's afraid."

She tried to picture the big, laid-back, easygoing
Zach Thomas afraid of anything. After all, the man
faced danger every single day on the job without so
much as a flinch.

But that wasn't the same.

In a way, work was much easier because it was pure
testosterone and adrenaline. Putting himself on the line
probably made Zach feel better about his losses, almost
as if he were offering himself up to fate, as well. And
as a bonus, he never had to open up emotionally, except
with these guys, the brothers of his heart.

She got that; she'd done the same with her chosen career.

But Cristina and Dustin had managed to find something real, and Brooke wanted that. It was time, *past* time, to get it for herself, because if she'd learned anything today, it was that life was too damn short not to go for it. She stood up.

"What are you going to do?"

"It's...complicated."

"The best things are." Aidan hugged her. "I hope it's good complicated."

"I hope so, too."

"I TRIED CALLING YOU, Zachie."

Zach sat at the side of Phyllis's hospital bed. "I'm sorry. I can't find my cell phone. I think I lost it in the warehouse fire."

"Don't worry." Her voice sounded shaky. "You asked me not to demolish the house if someone asks, and I won't. I was just telling Blake the same thing."

"Blake came here to see you?"

"Yes. He wanted to talk about my house fire."

"Why?"

Phyllis had a razor-sharp memory, but she'd been too doped up on meds for anyone to take advantage of that. Until now, apparently. "Because he was there. Yes," she said at his surprise. "It finally came to me. It was Blake I saw standing on the perimeter of my property, holding a blowtorch."

The air deflated from Zach's lungs. Blake at the scene just before the fire, with an ignition device... "Phyllis, are you sure?"

"Well, when I brought it up, he said no, my memory

was all twisted from the trauma, but..." She shook her head. "But I don't believe it. I remember."

Blake was the missing link? Blake connected all the fires?

Blake was the arsonist?

It made no sense, and yet...and yet in a crazy way it made *perfect* sense—Blake's ongoing obsession with fire, any fire, and his need to be near it, even the bonfire from the chief's birthday party. "Phyllis, listen to me. I need you to trust me, okay? I have to go but I'll be back."

"Will you bring Cecile?"

"I'll bring you more pictures of her, I promise."

When he got to the parking lot and into his truck, he remembered—no cell phone. Running back inside the hospital, he went straight to a pay phone and called Tommy.

Tommy listened to every word and then said, "Go home. You hear me? Get home and keep your ass right there or I'll get it fired."

"You can't do that."

"Trust me, I'll find a way."

Frustration beat at Zach as he drove home, feeling useless and helpless—two emotions he couldn't resent more. God, Blake... *Could it be true?*

And yet the evidence was there, at least circumstantially. The blowtorch at Phyllis's was huge. And he'd been quiet and withdrawn and secretive for months, pushing all of them from his life.

Zach had to go see him, had to look into Blake's eyes and judge for himself.

But Blake wasn't home, so Zach went back to his

place and paced a groove into his living room floor, which did nothing for his adrenaline level.

At the knock on his door, he opened it to the one person he'd have given everything to see.

Brooke, still wearing her uniform, eyes shadowed, mouth grim, looking like the best thing he'd seen all damn day.

"Damn, are you a sight for sore eyes," he said.

"I'm not supposed to be here," she said. "I forgot to clock out at work."

"Good. Because I'm not here, either. I'm on my way to find Blake's ass and probably get mine fired."

"You know where he is?"

"No."

They both stood there and stared at each other, unsure what to say next.

"I'm really not here," she finally said again, "telling you that I take back my goodbye."

"Then I'm not really doing this." Hauling her to him, he covered her mouth with his.

She sighed in pleasure and sagged against him, fisting her hands in his shirt to keep him close.

As if that was necessary.

"Zach," she murmured. "We need to talk."

"Yeah."

But then she nipped at his lower lip, making him groan. He stroked his tongue to hers, his hands running down her body, filling them with her glorious curves. "We'll talk," he promised her. "In a minute. Maybe ten." He needed to lose himself in her before he faced the unthinkable—that one of their own was an arsonist.

Not going there, not yet. He kicked the door shut, tugging her upstairs to his bedroom.

She stared at his bed. "First I really need to tell you what I came for—"

"You haven't come yet." He nudged her onto the bed and followed her down. "But you're going to."

CHAPTER EIGHTEEN

ZACH'S WORDS SENT a shiver of desire skittering down Brooke's spine. In his eyes was a fierce intensity—for her, which she loved, but also the same grief she'd seen in Cristina's.

He knew about Blake.

He kissed her, hard. She knew he was hurting and destroyed over Blake's betrayal, that he was trying to lose himself in her. She understood. She wanted to get lost in him, too.

He pulled off her shirt, and she did the same for his, sliding her hands up his heated skin, feeling the hard planes beneath quiver for more. "Are we letting loose again?"

"No." His mouth slid over her neck, her shoulder, making its way toward a breast. "This time it's more, damn it." He curled his tongue around her nipple.

Sinking her fingers into his hair, she arched up into his mouth. "More?"

"Everything's all fucked up." His voice was low, raw, as he slid a hand into her panties.

His physical pain matched the mental anguish in his eyes, and both broke her heart. "I know."

"Except this, with you." He tugged her panties down to her thighs to give him better access. "I don't usually do this."

"Pull a woman's pants down?"

"No, smart-ass. Get into a relationship."

When his gaze caught hers, she couldn't look away. "Is that what we're doing?"

"I thought you were safe. You're leaving, for Christ's sake. You're outta here. Can't get much safer than that."

Moved by his pain and frustration, she pressed her forehead to his. "Zach."

"I mean, I wasn't going to fall for a woman with one foot already out the door. It was never going to happen."

She closed her eyes.

"But goddamn it, it did."

Before she could open her mouth, he covered it with his. Reality had no place then, no place at all. Until she smelled smoke. "Zach—"

"I know. We're both idiots."

"No." She coughed. *"Smoke."*

"Uh-huh. I think I'm on fire."

"No, I mean *real* smoke." Just as she said this, his smoke alarm went off.

"What the—" Eyes hot, body hard, his face was a mask of frustration as he lifted his head and sniffed the air. "Shit, it *is* smoke." He pulled free and leaped off the bed, staring at the wisps curling beneath the bedroom door.

"Zach!"

"I see it." He tossed her his phone from the nightstand. "Call it in!" He ran into the bathroom, coming out with towels, which he shoved under the door to block the smoke while she called 911.

Coughing, choking, Brooke dashed to the window and then gasped. Zach peered over her shoulder and swore.

Down on the grass far below stood Blake. He was propped up on one crutch, face gray, holding a blow-torch as he looked right at them.

Zach threw Brooke her clothes and shoved his feet into his jeans. Then he reached under his bed and pulled out a portable rope ladder. "My house is on fire. My damn house is on fire. I'm going to kill him."

But Brooke was still staring at Blake, who had tears running down his face as he limped toward the door, vanishing inside.

"He's in—" Brooke gasped, still coughing. "Zach, Blake's inside." The smoke tightened in her lungs so that she couldn't talk.

Zach covered her mouth with a towel. "Breathe into that." He tossed the ladder out the window. Straddling the ledge, he reached for her. "Come on. You're going down and out. Quickly." He pulled her out the window and onto the rope. "Don't stop until your feet touch the ground. Got that?"

Right. Don't stop. Except she wanted to stop. She wanted to stop time and go back to a few minutes ago, when he'd been about to bury himself deep inside her, telling her he'd fallen. "I'm not leaving you."

"Go!" His voice was already hoarse, his eyes flashing fear and anger. "I'm getting Blake, then I'll be right behind you—"

"Zach—"

"Brooke, listen to me." He gave her a little shake. "You have to be out of here for me to do this."

"But—"

"No, I mean it. I can't lose you. I can't." He set his forehead to hers. "I can't do this with you still in here, in danger."

He meant he couldn't lose another person who meant so much to him. Brooke's heart swelled until it felt too big for her body.

"Please go," he said, hugging her hard. "Because if something happens to you—"

"It won't, it won't. I'm going." She squeezed him tight, breathing through the towel and still coughing. "But you should know something. I love you, Zach."

He looked staggered. "Brooke."

"I do. I love you." It'd probably sound better if she could talk more clearly, but she could tell he understood. "And I swear to God if you die in here, I'll come find you and kill you again."

He choked out a laugh. Off in the distance they could finally hear sirens. *"Go."*

"Going." And down the ladder she went, leaving him to face Blake alone.

BROOKE SAT ON the curb, staring up at the flames. Dustin kept trying to put the oxygen mask over her face, while dabbing at a nasty cut on her arm that she'd managed to get from the rain gutter on her way down the ladder. She kept slapping the mask away, not taking her eyes off the house.

Where was he? Sam, Eddie and Aidan had all gone in after Zach and Blake. Why weren't they—

Finally the door burst open and Sam and Aidan appeared, with Zach between them, Eddie just behind.

No Blake.

Shoving the blanket off her shoulders, Brooke went running toward them.

"Brooke," Zach was saying to Isobel. "Where the hell's Brooke?"

"Here," she managed.

At the sound of her voice he whipped around. He still wore only his Levi's. Dirt and ash were smeared over his chest and torso, blackening the bandages from the last fire he'd been in. He was bleeding from several cuts, as well, and couldn't stop coughing. His eyes were wild, though they calmed at the sight of her as he hauled her into his arms.

"Blake?" she whispered.

Eyes revealing his misery, he shook his head. "We found the blowtorch, and his hard hat. Nothing else."

Heart heavy, she hugged him tight, but she didn't get to hold on to him for long. The scene was chaotic as all hell. Tommy appeared, and the chief, not to mention every rig out of their firehouse, plus too many police units to count.

Zach was pulled aside. "For questioning," Aidan told her.

"He didn't do anything wrong—"

"They know that," he quickly assured her. "But with Blake gone—"

"Gone?"

"They didn't find a body, but—" His voice broke, and he cleared his throat. "But they expect to. There's going to be an internal investigation. Zach wants me to take you to the hospital for stitches—"

"I've got her, you stay with Zach." Dustin flanked her on one side, and Cristina was on the other, looking devastated over the news about her partner.

They took her to the hospital, where she received eight stitches and a tetanus shot. Exhausted and woozy, she let Dustin take her home, where she had a message waiting from her Realtor about the offer on the house.

Was she taking it?

Good question. She'd gotten her asking price. Didn't that just put a nice neat bow on her life. The end of yet another era...

Dustin called in for an update. The fire was out; Blake was presumed dead. Cristina showed up with Thai takeout and a brown bag. The three of them sat around Brooke's table, grimy and filthy, stuffing their faces.

"I still can't believe it was Blake," Cristina said very quietly. "That he—" She broke off, her voice choked. "He was a pyromaniac. In some ways we all are, or we wouldn't do this, but he was mentally ill. Tommy said that looking back, you could see he started unraveling when the chief came from Chicago, right about the time that Lynn died." She closed her eyes. "He needed help."

Dustin squeezed her hand. They ate in silence, an emotional but companionable sort of silence until Cristina looked at the stack of boxes filled with the stuff Brooke hadn't been able to make herself get rid of—the photos, the diaries—all things that had helped Brooke find the missing parts of herself. "Looks like you've been busy, Brooke."

She raised a brow. "Did you just call me Brooke?"

"That is your name, right?"

"I thought it was New Hire to you."

Cristina shrugged. "You stuck."

Her throat tightened. "Yes, but the job's nearly over."

"You could apply for a permanent position."

She'd never done anything permanent. But this, with the people she now thought of as her friends, felt very permanent. And wasn't that part of what she'd been searching for? "I'm ready for the booze now."

Cristina lifted a brow.

"The brown bag you brought. It's alcohol, right?"

Cristina pulled out a bottle of bubble bath and Dustin laughed.

"What?" Cristina demanded.

"You're so damn cute."

"Oh, shut up." Cristina squirmed, looking uncomfortable. "I'm new at this girl-pal stuff, okay? I thought she might want to just soak, and God, I know, it's stupid."

"No." Brooke hugged her. "It's perfect."

They stayed for ice cream, and two more calls for info, of which they got very little except that Zach was still at the fire site.

After Dustin and Cristina left, Brooke drew herself a bubble bath and lay back, soaking.

Thinking...

A knock at her front door stopped that and her heart. It wasn't Zach, it couldn't be Zach. He was no doubt still with the chief and Tommy. It was probably the real estate agent, whom she'd not yet called back. Wasn't ready to call back, not when she felt as if she'd found all her answers right here in this house—answers about her life, and how she wanted to live it. Which was pretty much the opposite of her grandmother and mother.

Brooke didn't want her memories stuck in boxes in some attic. She wanted to share them with real people. She wanted to create new ones every day.

The knock came again. Wrapping herself in a towel, she went to the door. "Who's there?"

"Me."

Oh, God. She whipped open the door.

Zach stood there in his jeans and someone's fire-fighter jacket, opened so that she could see he was still as grimy as she'd been only a few moments ago. It didn't matter. One minute she was holding on to the door and the next moment she was holding on to him.

"Brooke," he murmured, his hand fisting in the towel at her back.

She pulled away to look into his face. "Are you all right?"

"Yeah."

"Your house?"

"Not so much."

"Oh, Zach."

"Aidan's putting me up at his place, but I needed to see you."

"I needed to see you, too. Are you sure you're okay?"

"I am now."

"I feel sick about Blake."

"Yeah." Zach blew out a breath. "They found a stack of wire-mesh trash cans in his garage. The chief is saying he was always a pyromaniac, that this job was just a cover to be near fires, that his illness got too much for him so he started setting fires to put them out. Then I started stirring it all up, which made it worse, and he went crazy." He shook his head. "He was one of us, Brooke. How the hell did this happen to one of us?" He turned in a slow circle. "And there's something else bugging the hell out of me. How did Blake manage to order the properties demolished? He didn't have that kind of pull. It doesn't make sense to me."

She just shook her head and hugged him again, closing her eyes to breathe him in. "You're safe. That's all that matters right now. The rest of the questions will get their answers later."

His eyes cut to the stack of boxes. "You've been busy. Did you take the offer on the house?"

"Not yet."

"Where will you go?"

"I—I'm not quite sure."

"You probably have lots of choices," he said quietly, still looking at the boxes.

"I don't know. I like this coast, a lot."

He turned back to her. "Yeah?"

"Yeah." She swallowed past a lump of emotion the size of a basketball. "There's lots of coastal cities hiring EMTs right now."

"Including Santa Rey."

"I know." Brooke ran her hand over his sooty chest. "I have a tub filled with hot, bubbling water. Interested?"

"As long as you're in it."

"That could be arranged."

They ended up draining the tub so he could shower the grime off him first, then filling it back up. Then they climbed in together, her back to his chest, his legs alongside of hers, his arms surrounding her, cast carefully out of the water. For a long moment he just pressed his jaw to hers. "Rationally, I knew you weren't going to die today," he murmured. "But I've found I'm not always rational when it comes to you."

"Ditto." She was grateful that he couldn't see her face, or the tears that suddenly filled her eyes. *Rational* had gone out the window weeks ago, somewhere around that night on a rock overlooking the ocean.

"Brooke?"

She shook her head and forced herself to laugh. "What does rational have to do with us anyway? We just clicked, that's all."

He ran a finger up her wet arm, leaving a trail of bubbles and goose bumps. "We could keep clicking. If you weren't leaving."

Craning her neck, she looked into his face.

There was no humor in his gaze, not a single drop. "I realized something that first day with you," he said quietly.

"What, that I was going to be a pain in your ass to dump?"

"That my lifestyle, the one I've reveled in for so long, had finally caught up with me and bit me on the ass. Because for the first time since losing my parents, something was going to matter. You were going to matter, Brooke."

She stared at him. "Is that why you wanted to keep this light?"

"That, and because it was what I thought you wanted."

"You told me I shouldn't fall in love with you. Remember?"

"Yeah, that's because I'm insanely stubborn. I've always thought I was so damn brave. I mean I put myself on the line every single day on the job." He laughed, and it was not in amusement. "But not my heart. Never my heart. And that doesn't make me brave at all. It makes me a coward."

His gaze held hers. "Until I met you. I met you and something happened. The walls crumbled. I put my damn heart on the line for the first time in years, with absolutely no backup, no safety net. And it worked. It felt right," he said, sounding staggered. "Hell, it felt amazing." Zach shook his head. "I want to be with you, Brooke."

"For tonight."

"For tonight," he agreed. "And tomorrow night, too."

She looked into his eyes, feeling a little kernel of hope and love, so much love she couldn't draw a breath.

"And the night after that. I want all your nights. I love you, Brooke. But there's something even more shocking."

She managed to breathe. "Are you sure? Because that's...that's pretty shocking."

He finally smiled and, oh baby, was it worth the wait. "Turns out I wasn't out there without a backup at all."

"No?" she whispered.

"No." He cupped her face, stroked his thumbs over her jaw. "You're my backup. You're my safety net. You're all that I need."

"So..."

"So stay. Stay here in Santa Rey with me. Or go. But take me with you."

Now Brooke was the one staggered. "You'd leave here?"

"My home is wherever you are."

Twisting all the way around, she propped herself up on his wet chest. "I don't want to go anywhere."

"You don't?"

"Nope. I know you planned to stay at Aidan's house, but I have this big place all to myself, and I don't really want to leave it, or my job. I think New Hire has a certain ring to it, don't you?"

Laughing softly, Zach pulled her close. "How does New Hire *Thomas* sound?"

Her breath caught. She could hardly speak. "Like everything I ever wanted."

* * * * *

FLASHBACK

CHAPTER ONE

THE FIRE BELL rang for the fourth time since midnight, interrupting Aidan Donnelly in the middle of a great dream in which he was having some fairly creative, acrobatic sex with a gorgeous blonde. The last thing he wanted was to be shaken awake, but apparently sex, imaginary or otherwise, wasn't on his card for the evening.

He was on the last few hours of a double shift from hell. The loudspeaker mounted in one corner of the bunk room was going off, telling him and his crew that they would not be going home in one short hour after all, but back into the field on yet another emergency call.

Putting the blonde back where she belonged, in the file in his brain labeled Hot Erotic Fantasy, Aidan got up to the tune of a bunch of moans and groans from his crew.

So close. He'd been so close to three desperately needed days off....

Across the room Eddie kicked aside the latest issue of *Time,* which had an entire company of firefighters on the cover. "A lot of good being the sexiest occupation does us," the firefighter grumbled, "when we're too exhausted to take advantage of it."

"Some of us don't need beauty sleep." This from

Sam, Eddie's partner. "Like, say, Mr. 2008 here." He slid a look Aidan's way, but Aidan found himself too tired to rise to the bait.

Through no fault of his own, he'd been named Santa Rey's hottest firefighter for 2008. This dubious honor came along with another—being put on the cover of Santa Rey's annual firefighter's calendar. "I told you, I didn't submit my name."

Eddie grinned in the middle of dressing. "No, we did, Mr. 2008."

Aidan gave him a shove, and Eddie fell back to the mattress, snorting out a laugh as he staggered upright again and grabbed his boots. "Yeah, like being that pretty is a hindrance."

"I am not pretty."

No one answered him in words as they pulled on their gear, but several made kissy noises as they headed toward their rigs. Still groggy, and definitely out of sorts, Aidan took the shotgun position next to Ty, his temporary partner, on loan from a neighboring fire-house, since his usual partner Zach was still off on medical leave.

Eddie and Sam grabbed their seats, as well as Cristina and Aaron, another on-loan firefighter, and they were all off into the dark night—or more accurately, the dark predawn morning—following the ambulance, which had pulled out first. The air was thick with dew, and salty from the ocean only one block over. For now the temperature was cool enough, but by midday the California August heat would be in full bloom, and they'd all be dying. Aidan got on the radio to talk to dispatch. "It's an explosion," he told the others grimly.

"Where?" Ty asked.

"The docks." Which could be anywhere from the shipping area, to the houseboats filled with year-round residents. "Only one boat's on fire, but several others are threatened by the flames, with no word on what caused the explosion."

Behind him, Eddie swore softly, and Aidan's thoughts echoed the sentiment. Explosions were trickier than a regular fire, and far more unpredictable.

"Are they calling for backup?" Sam asked.

They needed it. Firehouse Thirty-Four was sorely overworked and dangerously exhausted going into the high fire season. They'd had a rough month. Aidan's partner and best friend Zach had been injured after digging into the mysterious arsons that had plagued Santa Rey. Mysterious arsons that were now linked to one of their own.

Blake Stafford.

Just the thought brought a stab of fresh pain to Aidan's chest. Now Zach was off duty and Blake was dead, leaving them all devastated.

Cristina was especially devastated, and with good reason. She'd been Blake's partner, and the closest to him. She'd suffered like hell over his loss, and also over the arsons he'd been accused of committing.

She blamed herself, Aidan knew, which was ridiculous. She couldn't have stopped Blake.

As it turned out, none of them could have stopped him.

Aidan considered himself pretty damn tough and just about one-hundred-percent impenetrable, but losing Blake had been heart-wrenching. He missed him, and hated what he'd been accused of. He didn't want to believe Blake was dead, and he sure as hell didn't want to believe Blake guilty of arson, and the resulting death of a small boy—none of them did, but the evidence was there. He could hardly even stand thinking about it— classic denial, Aidan knew, but it was working for him. "Dispatch's sending rigs from Stations Thirty-Three and Thirty-Five."

No one said anything to this, but they were all thinking the same thing—it'd take those stations at least ten extra minutes to get on scene from their locations— and the sense of dread only increased as they pulled up to the docks.

Turned out that the fire wasn't at the shipping docks, but where the smaller, privately owned boats were moored at four long docks, each with ten bays. Possibly forty boats in total, many of them occupied.

Chaos reined in the predawn. Their senior officer was usually first on scene, setting up a command center, but he was coming from another fire and was five minutes behind them. The sky was still dark, with no moon, and the visibility wasn't helped by the thick plumes of black smoke choking the air out of their lungs. Flames leaped fifty feet into the air, coming from a boat halfway down the second of the four docks. Aidan took a quick count, and his stomach tightened with fear. There were boats on either side of the flaming vessel, and more on the opposite side of the dock.

Not good.

As they accessed their equipment and laid out lines, three police squad cars tore into the lot, followed by the command squad, all of whom leaped to work evacuating the surrounding docks. Aidan and company needed to contain the flames, but the explosion burned outrageously hot. He could feel that mind-numbing heat from a hundred feet back. With the chief now on scene, barking orders through their radios, Aidan and the others moved with their hoses, their objective to keep the flames from spreading to any of the other boats. They were halfway there when it came.

A sharp, terrified scream.

The sound raised the hair on the back of Aidan's neck, and he dropped everything to run toward the burning boat, Ty right behind him.

The scream came again, clearly female, and Aidan sped up. No one knew better than a firefighter what it was like to be surrounded by flames, to have them lick at you, toy with you. It was sheer, horrifying terror.

They had to get to her first.

Behind them came Sam, Eddie, Cristina and Aaron, directing water on the flames to clear Aidan and Ty's path down the dock toward the boat. Twenty feet, then ten, and that's when he saw her. A woman standing on the deck of the burning boat, wobbling, the flames at her back.

"Jump!" he yelled, wondering why she didn't just make the short leap to the dock—she could have made a run for safety. "*Jump*—"

Another explosion rocked them all. Aidan skidded to a halt, spinning away and crouching down as debris flew up into the air to match the intensifying flames. The chief was shouting into the radio, demanding a head count. Aidan lifted his head and checked in as he took in the sights. The boat was still there. With his heart in his throat, he searched for a visual on the woman—

There. In the same spot she'd been before, still on the deck but on the floor now, holding her head. *God-*

dammit. He got to his feet, took a few running steps, and dove onto the boat.

She nearly jumped out of her skin when he landed next to her. "It's okay." He dropped to his knees at her side to try to get a good look and see how badly she was injured, but the smoke had choked out any light from the docks and she was nothing but a slight shadow. A slight shadow who was hunched over and coughing uncontrollably.

"The boat," she managed. "It k-keeps b-blowing up—"

"Can you stand?"

"Yes. I—" She let out a sound that tugged at his memory, but he pushed that aside when she nodded. She got up with his help, twisting away from him to stare up at the flames shooting up the mast and sails. "Ohmigod…"

He pulled her closer to his side, intending to jump with her to the dock and the hell off this inferno, but several things hit him at once.

The name of the boat painted across the outside of the cabin, flickering in and out of view between the flames.

Blake's Girl.

No. It couldn't be. Then came something of far more immediate concern—the rumbling and shuddering of the deck beneath their feet. "We have to move."

"No. No, please," she gasped. "You have to save the boat."

"Us first." He couldn't have put together a more coherent sentence because of all that was going through his head. *Blake's Girl…*

Blake's boat. God, he'd all but forgotten that Blake had owned a boat.

Then there was the woman in his arms, facing away from him, but invoking that niggling sense of familiarity. There was something about her wild blond curls, about the sound of her voice—

The warning signals in his brain peaked at once. In just the past thirty seconds, the flames had doubled in strength and heat. The deck beneath their feet trembled and quivered with latent simmering violence.

They were going to blow sky high. Whipping toward the dock he got another nasty surprise—the flames had covered their safe exit.

On the other side of those monstrous flames stood Ty, Eddie and Sam, hoses in hand, battling the fire from their angle, which wasn't going to help Aidan and his victim in time. Cristina was there, too, with Aaron, and even in the dark he sensed their urgency, their utter determination to keep him safe.

They'd so recently lost one of their own; there was no way they were going to let it happen again.

"Ohmigod," the woman at his side gasped, staring, as if mesmerized, at the sight of the flames closing in on them.

She wasn't the only one suddenly mesmerized, and for one startling heartbeat, Aidan went utterly still, as for the first time he caught a full glimpse of her.

He knew that profile.

He knew her. *"Kenzie?"*

At the sound of her name on his lips, uttered in a low, hoarse, surprised voice, her head whipped toward his, eyes wide. Her wavy blond hair framed a pale face streaked with dirt and some blood, but was still beautiful, hauntingly so.

She was Mackenzie Stafford, Blake's sister. Kenzie to those who knew and loved her, Sissy Hope to the millions of viewers who watched her on the soap opera *Hope's Passion.*

She was not a stranger to Aidan, but not because of her television stardom. He knew her personally.

Very personally. "Kenzie."

"I can't—I can't hear you."

People never expected fire to be noisy, but it was. The flames crackled and roared at near ear-splitting decibels as they devoured everything in their path.

Including them if they didn't move, a knowledge that was enough to pull his head out of his ass and get with the program. Old lover or not, he still had to get her out of there alive. But she was looking at him through Blake's eyes, and his heart and gut wrenched hard. There was maybe twenty feet of water between *Blake's Girl* and the next boat, which was starting to smoke as well, and would undoubtedly catch on fire any second. It didn't matter. They had no choice. "Kenzie, when I say so, I want you to hold your breath."

"D—do I know you?"

He wore a helmet and all his equipment, and in the dark, not to mention the complete and utter chaos around them, there was no way she could see him clearly. Still, he had to admit it stung. "It's me, Aidan. Hold your breath now, on my count."

"Aidan, my God."

"Ready?"

"The boat's going to go, every inch of it, isn't it?"

Yep, including the few square inches they were

standing on. In fact, it was going to go much more quickly than he'd have liked. Since they couldn't get to the dock, it was into the ocean for them, where they'd wait for rescue.

"No," she said, shaking her head. "There's got to be another way."

Unfortunately there wasn't, and he quickly stripped out of his jacket and gear because the protection they offered wouldn't be worth the seventy-five pounds of extra weight while treading water and holding up Kenzie to boot. At least she was conscious. She didn't appear to have on any shoes, or anything particularly heavy on her person, all of which were points in her favor. "On three, okay? Remember to hold your breath."

"I don't think—"

"Perfect. Go with that. One—" He nudged her in front of him, pushing her to the railing.

"Aidan—"

"Two—"

"Are you crazy?"

"Three."

"Hell, no. I'm not going into the—"

He dropped her into the water, and she screamed all the way down.

CHAPTER TWO

KENZIE HIT THE icy ocean, and as she took in a huge mouthful of water, she realized she'd forgotten to hold her breath, a thought that was completely eradicated when *Blake's Girl* exploded into the early dawn.

In the brilliant kaleidoscope, she barely registered the splash next to her, or the two strong arms that came around her, supporting her as flying pieces of burning debris hit the water all around them.

Aidan. My God, Aidan... That it was him boggled her mind. She tried to remind him that she could swim on her own, but the shock of the cold water sapped both her voice and the air in her lungs, and also hampered the working of her brain.

She'd never experienced anything like it. Never in her life had she been so hot and so frozen at the same time. The heat came from the flames, so high above them now that she was in the water, but no less terrifying. And yet, an icy cold had taken over her limbs, making movement all but impossible, weighing her down, sitting on her chest, sucking the last of the precious air from her overtaxed lungs.

Someone was screaming, and Kenzie envied their ability to draw air into their lungs because her own felt as constricted as if she had a boa slowly squeezing the life out of her.

The scream came again.

Huh?

It sounded sort of like her.

And then she realized, as if from a great distance, that it *was* her screaming, which meant that somehow she was breathing. Okay, that was good. So was the man holding her in the water, tucking her head against him, shielding her from the pieces falling out of the sky at his own risk. Without him, she'd have gone down like a heavy stone and she knew it.

"Shh," he was murmuring. "I've got you. It's okay, Kenzie, it's going to be okay...."

She was hurt, but not so hurt as to stop the memories bombarding her at the sound of his voice. How could she not have *instantly* recognized him?

He was the first man who'd ever broken her heart.

He'd ditched his helmet and she could see his face now. He didn't look happy to see her, and honestly, on that point, if he hadn't been saving her sorry ass, they'd have been perfectly in sync. "Aidan." She could see the fire reflected in his eyes. *Blake's Girl* was really blazing now. "My God, we almost—"

"I know." His short, dark hair was plastered to his head. Water ran in rivulets down his face, which was starkly pale. His long, inky-black eyelashes were spiky, and he had a cut above one eyebrow that was oozing blood. In spite of all of that, she had the most ridiculous thought: *wow,* he looked good all fierce and intense and wet.

Aidan Donnelly, first real boyfriend. First...everything.... She could hardly believe it, certainly couldn't process it, so she craned her neck, staring at the boat that looked like one big firecracker. "It just blew, and I—"

"Kenzie—"

"—I mean one minute I'm sitting there missing my brother, and the next…"

He looked into her eyes, his cool and composed. "It's going to be okay, but I need you to—"

"And it blew. I was just sitting there, surrounded by his things, missing him, and then *boom*. My Choos are probably halfway to China by now. I really liked those Choos."

"Kenzie," he said in a tone of authoritative calm. "I need you to listen to me now. Can you do that?"

She could take a gulp of air. But listening? The jury was still out on that one. Her ears were ringing. And the water was so damn cold. In fact, she was shaking and hadn't even realized it, shudders that wracked her entire body and rattled her teeth.

"Hold onto me, Kenzie. That's all you have to do, okay? Just hold onto me."

Right. Hold onto him. She'd grown up here in Santa Rey, and once upon a time she'd held onto him plenty. She'd held onto him, laughed with him, slept with him…

Actually, there'd never been much sleeping involved between them, a thought which brought an avalanche of others. Him fresh out of the firefighters' academy and possessing a body that had made her drool, not to mention the knowledge of how to use that body to make hers go wild…

But that had been what, six years ago? Hell, she could barely think, much else handle any math at the moment, so she couldn't be sure.

He was towing her out, away from the boat and any danger of falling debris, while shouting something to two firefighters on the other side of the burning vessel, both of whom had hoses on the fire.

She'd been in a fire before. On the set of her soap opera, *Hope's Passion,* before it'd been cancelled. But that was under carefully controlled circumstances. This wasn't a TV show with lines for her to follow. This was the real thing, with no makeup department standing by to color in pretend injuries, dammit.

She'd have loved a script right about now, with a happy ending, please.

At least she was still breathing.

Hard to beat that.

Blake's Girl hadn't gotten so lucky.

Neither had Blake. Oh, yeah, *there* was the familiar rush of pain, slicing right through the numbness from the cold water, lancing her heart—the pain that had been with her since she'd learned Blake was dead. Making it worse, adding confusion and anger to her grief was the fact that he'd been accused of being an arsonist and murderer.

God, Blake...

Another chunk of burning debris fell from the still flaming boat, and she imagined it was something of Blake's, something she'd never see again. Or maybe it was her own suitcase, or her laptop, which wasn't a big loss in the scheme of things, but it held the scripts she'd been writing...

At least if she died, she would no longer be a freshly unemployed soap star.

It was so damn ironic—she'd never been able to come home when Blake had been alive because she'd been too busy working. Then days after he'd died, her soap had been cancelled. Now she could drive up all she wanted, and he was gone.... Her first trip home in forever and it had been to see after his things, things that were now smoldering in the water around her.

"Don't give up on me," Aidan said. His eyes focused ahead on where he was swimming to, some point invisible to her. It was too dark to see their color clearly but she knew them to be a light brown with flecks of green that danced when he laughed.

He wasn't laughing now.

Nope.

He glanced at her, then resumed swimming straight and sure, moving them away from the flames, which also meant away from any warmth, while she did as he'd asked and just held on. She could do nothing but. Like old times...

Why did it have to be *him,* the guy who'd crushed her heart, stomped on her pride and then walked away from her without a backward glance?

Did *he* hurt over the loss of Blake?

Did *he* believe the lies?

Because that thought, and all the others that came with it, came close to defrosting her, she shoved them aside. The blessed numbness was working for her. She hadn't come to Santa Rey in the past six years, but Blake had visited her in L.A. on the set, whenever he could, and on top of his visits, they'd been in frequent contact by email, texting and phone calls, and had remained close despite their physical distance. He was the only family she'd had.

And now he was gone.

Forever gone.

"Kenzie? You still with me?" Aidan's lean jaw was

tight with tension and was scruffy, as if he hadn't had time to shave in a day or two. Or four.

"Unfortunately." She'd like to be anywhere but "with" him. She could feel his longer, stronger legs moving, bumping into hers, and it made her irrationally mad. She didn't want help, not from him, but when she wriggled free to prove herself fine, she went down like a stone. Straight beneath the surface of the icy water, where she promptly did the stupid thing of opening her mouth to breathe and got a lungful of extremely cold salt water for her efforts.

Thankfully, she was immediately hauled back up again and pulled against a hard chest, one hand fisted in the back of her shirt, the other arm across the backs of her thighs in a grip that could have rivaled Superman's.

Firefighter to victim.

Not ex-boyfriend to ex-girlfriend.

And wasn't that just the problem? Once upon a time he *really* had had her, only he'd been the one to let go. He'd done it, he'd said, because of their respective careers and because he didn't like hiding their relationship from his friend Blake, but she knew the truth. It was because he'd decided she'd been falling in love with him and he hadn't been ready for love, so he'd shooed her away and had moved on.

She'd hated him for that for a good long time, for not giving himself a chance to feel what she'd felt, and, yeah, he'd been right—she *had* been more than halfway in love with him. It'd taken a while, but eventually her anger had drained, and she'd acknowledged that he'd been right to break it off with her before she'd gotten even more hurt.... But that hadn't eased her pain at the time.

Maybe she should consider herself lucky they were doing this reintroduction in an official capacity—him on the job, and her being just one in a blur of people he rescued. Less personal.

"Stop fighting me." His voice cut through the shocking noise of the night: the sirens, the shouting of the other firefighters and personnel, the ever-present, horrifying crackling of the flames, the small waves smacking into each other, waves that would be cresting over her head if it wasn't for Aidan's holding her with what appeared to be little to no effort. "I've got you."

"I don't want you to have me."

"Okay, roger that. But at the moment you don't have a choice."

"Of all the firefighters in this damn town…"

She thought she caught a flash of a grim smile. So he was no more thrilled than she was. He wasn't even looking directly at her, his attention instead focused on the boat behind her, and the dock behind that, reminding her that not only was he saving her hide, he was simultaneously looking for other people who needed help.

"I was alone on the boat," she told him.

"What were you doing?"

"Saying goodbye to Blake."

Sorrow, regret, and anguish all briefly flashed in his eyes. "Kenzie—"

"He didn't do those things you're all accusing him of, Aidan."

She had his attention now, all of it, and she'd forgotten the potency of having Aidan Donnelly giving her one-hundred-percent of his focus. *"He didn't."*

"Did he say something, anything to you at all, before he died?"

Died... Hearing the words from his mouth made Blake's death all the more real, as did being back here in her hometown, and it hit her hard. Throat so tight that she couldn't speak, she shook her head. No, Blake hadn't said anything at all, which made her feel even worse. "It wasn't him who set those fires. I know it."

"Kenzie," he said very gently, but she didn't want to hear it, didn't want to hear anything he said, so she shook her head again and closed her eyes, which brought an unexpected and horrifying sense of vertigo, making her clutch at him.

"I want out."

"I know. They're coming for us right now."

That was good. Because something was definitely wrong. Her vision was getting fuzzy. Her brain was getting fuzzier. Scared and a little overwhelmed, she pressed her face into the crook of his neck, her nose to his throat, the position hauntingly familiar and at once flooding her with memories.

She'd been here before.

Okay, not here, not in the water, freezing, scared, but she'd been held by him, had pressed her face against his warm flesh and inhaled him in, absorbing the way he held her close, as if he'd never let anything happen to her.

He smelled the same, a scent she'd never quite managed to forget, and it was messing with her brain in spite of the fact that she'd just survived an explosion, a nighttime swim in the freezing ocean, and an uncomfortable reunion with the one and only guy she'd ever let break her heart.

Dammit. She blamed Blake. *Blake...*

"Kenzie." Aidan gave her a little shake. "Stay with me now."

No, thanks...

"Open your eyes," he demanded. "Come on, Kenzie. Stay awake, stay with me."

As opposed to giving in to the delicious lethargy slowly taking over? *Nah...* "Too tired."

"I know, but you can do this. You can do anything, remember?"

She nearly smiled at the reminder of her own personal motto, but then remembered who was talking. Yeah, she'd once believed that she could do anything, with him at her side.

He'd proved her wrong.

Oh, boy. Her eyes *were* closing. It'd be so easy to let them, to just drift off and not feel the cold anymore, but even in her fuzziness, she knew that was bad, so with great effort, she pried her eyes open.

And her gaze landed on him. The last time she'd seen him, she'd been so young. *They'd* been so young. She'd just turned twenty-two, been signed by a Los Angeles agent, and had landed her first small walk-on role. He'd been two years older, fit and gorgeous, and on top of his world as a young firefighter.

Plastered against him, her hands clenched on his biceps, her legs entwined with his, her chest up against him the way it was, she could feel that he was still fit.

Very fit.

And thanks to the flames and also the spotlights from the guys on the dock keeping track of them, she also knew that he was still gorgeous. If he hadn't cut her loose without a backward glance, she'd be happy to see him.

Very happy.

A group of firefighters had made their way through the flames to the end of the neighboring dock, and had secured it with criss-crossing lines of water. One of them leaped into the ocean, and with long, sure strokes swam toward them.

"Here," he called out to Aidan, holding out an arm for Kenzie.

"I've got her," Aidan said.

But Kenzie had had enough, of Aidan and his capable, strong arms, of his scent and especially of the memories. So she reached out for the second firefighter, going into his arms without looking back, arms that had never held her before, arms that didn't know her, arms that didn't evoke the past.

Even though she wanted to, she wouldn't look back.

CHAPTER THREE

BY THE TIME Aidan hauled himself out of the water, Ty had handed Kenzie off to the EMTs. Dustin and Brooke took her away from the flames and straight to their ambulance.

Good.

Chilled, drenched to the skin, Aidan made his way through the organized mayhem to his rig, where he stripped down and pulled on dry gear, the questions coming hard and fast in his head.

What the hell had Kenzie been doing there? Odd timing, given that in all these years, she'd not shown up in Santa Rey, not once. At least that he was aware of. Blake had never mentioned any visits, but then again, why would he? He'd had no idea that Aidan had dated his baby sister, and then walked away rather than engage his heart. They'd never told him, knowing he wouldn't have liked it.

Nope, Kenzie hadn't been back, not even for Blake's memorial service, and yet suddenly here she was, on Blake's boat, a boat that just happened to blow sky high once she'd set foot on it.

Odd coincidence.

During the time the two of them had been in the water together, the sky had lightened. Dawn had arrived. The chief had put an explosives team in place, and had a plan to contain the fire. Aidan needed to get back into the thick of it, but first he had to see Kenzie and make sure for himself that she was okay. She'd had a head laceration and multiple cuts and wounds, and that had been before he'd tossed her into the water.

He looked through the horde of people working the flames—Eddie and Sam, Aaron, Ty and Cristina, plus the guys from Thirty-Three, all on hoses and past the explosives experts surveying the still burning shell of *Blake's Girl* to where the ambulance was parked.

Kenzie was seated at the back of the opened rig between Dustin and Brooke. She was dripping everywhere, her clothes revealing what he already knew, that she was petite and in possession of a set of mouthwatering curves that had gotten only more mouth-watering in the past few years. She wore layered tees, the top one pink, ribbed and long-sleeved, unbuttoned to her waist, the one beneath white with pink polka-dots, opened to just between her breasts, both soaked through and suctioned to her body enough to expose her bra, which was also pink, lace and quite sheer.

He'd been a firefighter for years and he'd rescued countless victims, many female, some of whom had been as wet as Kenzie, and never, not one single goddamn time, had he ever stopped in the middle of a job to notice their breasts.

It was his first clue that he was in trouble, deep trouble—but when it came to Kenzie, that was nothing new. He chose to ignore his observation for now, for as long as he possibly could. His gaze dropped past her shirt with shocking difficulty, to a pair of button-fly jeans low on her hips, also dangerous territory because he'd always loved her legs, especially how bendy they could get....

Don't go there.

She shoved her hair out of her face, which still looked far too pale, even a little green, although that didn't take away from her beauty. Once upon a time she'd been a gorgeous study of sexy, frou-frou feminine mystery to him.

Some things never changed.

As if she felt his gaze, she looked up, and from fifty feet, between which were other firefighters, equipment and general chaos, she found him.

Between them the air seemed to snap, crackle, pop.

Six years ago, the thought of a long-distance relationship had been as alien to him as a close-distance relationship, and he'd told himself he had no choice but to break things off, even though that had really just been an excuse.

He'd broken things off because she'd scared him, she'd scared him deep. And apparently, given the hard kick his heart gave his ribs, she still did.

She'd been able to get inside him, make him feel things that hadn't been welcome, and, yeah, he'd run like a little girl.

He felt like running now.

But this time it was Kenzie who turned away. Dustin unfolded a blanket and wrapped it around her shoulders, while Brooke checked her pupils, then dabbed at the various cuts on her face.

Kenzie sat still, eyes closed now, looking starkly pale but alive.

Alive was good.

She huddled beneath the blanket, cradling a wrist,

nodding to something Brooke asked her. Aidan knew that Brooke and Dustin, both close friends, would take good care of her. They took good care of everyone, which meant that Kenzie was in the very best hands.

Still in the thick of the organized chaos around him, Aidan took a second to let his gaze sweep over her. She really did seem as okay as he could hope for, and he told himself to turn away.

He was good at that. After all, he'd learned to do so at a young age from his own family, who'd shuffled him around more than a deck of cards on poker night. Yeah, he was good at walking away. Or at least good at pretending he didn't care when others walked away from him.

And after all, he'd done the same to her.

God, he'd been cruel to her all those years ago. Not that he'd meant to be. Going through the academy had been a life lesson for him. He *could* belong to a "family." He *could* make long-lasting friends. He *could* love someone with all his heart.

But loving his fellow firefighters like the brothers they'd become was one thing.

Loving Kenzie had been another entirely.

Since she'd left, he'd seen her only on TV. As a rule, he didn't watch soaps. He didn't watch much TV at all, actually. If he wasn't working, he was renovating the fixer-upper house he'd bought last year, emphasis on *fixer-upper.* If he wasn't doing that, he was playing basketball, or something else that didn't cost any money because the fixer-upper had eaten his savings.

But there'd been the occasional night where he'd sat himself in front of a game and caught a promo for Kenzie's soap. There'd also been the few times at the station where one of the guys had flipped on the TV during her show.

Three times exactly—and yeah, he remembered each and every one. The first had been five years ago, and she'd been wearing the teeniest, tiniest, blackest, stringiest bikini in the history of teeny-tiny black string bikinis, her hair piled haphazardly on top of her head with a few wild curls escaping, looking outrageously sexy as she'd seduced her on-screen lover. It'd taken him a few attempts to get the channel changed, and even then it hadn't mattered. That bikini had stuck with him for a good long while.

The second time had been a few Christmases back. She'd been wearing a siren-red, slinky evening dress designed to drive men absolutely wild. She'd been standing beneath some mistletoe, looking up at some "stud of the month." Aidan hadn't been any quicker with the remote that time, and had watched the entire, agonizing kiss.

The third time had been for the daytime Emmys. She'd accepted her award, thanking Blake for always believing in her, and then had thanked some guy named Chad.

Chad.

What kind of a name was Chad?

And where was Chad now, huh? Certainly not hauling her off a burning boat and saving her cute little ass. Guys named Chad probably only swam when playing water polo.

In the ambulance, Dustin said something to Kenzie, and she opened her eyes, flashing a very brief smile, but it was enough.

She was okay.

Aidan forced himself to move, to get back to the job at hand, and it was a big one. The explosions had caught the boats on either side of *Blake's Girl,* escalating the danger and damages. They had the dock evacuated, and as the sun streaked the sky, they were working past containment, working to get the flames one-hundred-percent out.

With one last look at Kenzie, Aidan entered the fray.

IT TOOK HOURS.

Aidan and his crew piled into their rigs just as the lunch crowd began to clutter the streets of Santa Rey. If he closed his eyes, he could still feel the imprint of Kenzie in his arms. He'd held onto her for what, three minutes tops? And yet she'd filled his head and his senses, and for those one-hundred-and-eighty seconds, time had slipped away, making him feel like that twenty-four-year-old punk he'd once been.

He'd been with Kenzie for one glorious summer, and she'd wanted to stay with him, which should have been flattering. She'd wanted to wear his ring and have a house and a white picket fence.

And his children.

But it hadn't been flattering at all. It'd been terrifying.

So he'd acted like a stupid, shortsighted guy. There was no prettying that up, or changing the memory. Fact was fact. He'd gotten a great job, and he'd had the world at his feet, including, he'd discovered, lots of women who found his chosen profession incredibly sexy.

He'd not been mature enough to realize what he already had; he'd been a first-class asshole. He'd sent Kenzie away, pretended not to look back and had filled his life with firefighting, women, basketball, wood-working, more women…

A hand clasped his shoulder. "Hey, Mr. 2008. Home sweet home."

"Shut up." They'd pulled into the station. He hopped out of the rig and went straight to Dustin, who was cleaning out the ambulance. "The victim? How is she?"

Cristina poked her head out from the station kitchen. "Hey, guys, there's food—" At the sight of Dustin, who she'd gone out with several times before unceremoniously discarding him without explanation, she broke off. "Oh. *You're* here."

Dustin looked at her drily. "What, is the food only for the staff that you *haven't* slept with and dumped?"

Aidan winced at the awkward silence, and if he wasn't in such a desperate hurry to hear about Kenzie, he might have refereed for the two of them, because if anyone needed refereeing, it was these two. "The vic," he said again to Dustin.

"Sorry," Dustin said, turning back to him. "She's not bad, thanks to your quick thinking. A few second-degree burns, possible broken wrist, some lacerations."

"Her head trauma—"

"No concussion."

"Stitches?" he demanded, causing Dustin to take a quick glance at Cristina, who raised an eyebrow.

Aidan knew he was bad off when the two of them could share a worried look over him.

"No stitches," Dustin said. "You okay?"

"Yeah." Aidan took his first deep breath in hours, which prompted another long look between Dustin and Cristina.

"You sure?" Cristina asked.

Jesus. "Yes." Leaving them alone to work through their issues, he headed inside the station. After he'd showered, cleaned up and clocked out, he got into his truck and debated with himself.

Home and oblivion were attractive choices.

Or he could go to the hospital, see Kenzie and get a question or two answered.

Not quite as attractive, because nothing about sitting with Kenzie and looking into her soulful eyes was going to be simple. Nope, that was a guaranteed trip to Heartbreak City.

Home, then, where he wouldn't have to do anything but fall facedown into his bed. Yeah, sounded good. He put his truck in gear.

And drove to the hospital.

KENZIE OPENED HER eyes and stared at a white ceiling. She was on a cot in the emergency room, her cuts and burns all cleaned and bandaged, her wrist wrapped, her head stitched back on—okay, so it'd only needed butterfly bandages. Now she was being "observed," although for what, she had no idea.

At least she was warm again, or getting there. She had three blankets piled on top of her, which helped, and a hospital gown, which didn't.

She'd just seen the fire investigator, Mr. Tommy Ramirez. Tommy was short, dark, and quite to the point. The point being that he'd found it extremely odd that she'd been on Blake's boat at the time of its explosion.

She did, too, considering she'd only gotten to town that night. Closing her eyes, she frowned. She also found it odd that he was wasting his time questioning her instead of investigating the real perpetrator of the arsons, because her brother was *innocent*. No way had Blake set all those awful fires they were trying to pin on him. Blake, sweet, quiet, loving Blake, the brother who'd been there for her when their parents had died fifteen years ago, when they'd gone through foster care, when she'd wanted to go off to Hollywood. He'd never have hurt a fly much less purposely hurt another human being. And endanger a child?

Never.

God, she hated hospitals. They smelled like fear and pain and helplessness, and all of them combined reminded her of her own uncertain childhood. She wished she was back on the L.A. set of *Hope's Passion,* acting the part of the victim instead of really being one. Comfort food would help. Maybe a box of donuts—

From the other side of her cubicle curtain came a rustling, and then the hair at the back of her neck suddenly stood up, as if she was being watched. Opening her eyes, she blinked the room into focus. Everything was white and...*blurry.* But not so much so that she missed the back of a guy's head as he ran off and out of sight. "Hey!"

He hadn't been wearing scrubs but a red T-shirt, so he couldn't have been hospital staff. Who'd come to see her and then leave without a word? She struggled to think but she was so tired, and a little woozy still, and when she let her eyes drift shut, she ended up dozing off...

"NOT THE SAME type of point of origin as the other fires."

Kenzie opened her eyes and turned her head, taking in the curtain, now pulled all the way closed around her cot. She was a woman who liked change, who in fact thrived on it, but she had to say, she didn't like this change. Not at all.

How much time had passed?

"So you're saying what, Tommy, that the chief has you on a gag order?"

Oh, boy. She didn't need to peek around the curtain to know *that* voice. That voice had once been the stuff of her daydreams, of her greatest fantasies. That voice had used to melt her bones away and rev her engines.

Aidan.

"I'm not saying anything," Tommy said. "Except what I told Zach weeks ago. I'm on this. It's a kid glove case. So you need to back off."

"I want to see Kenzie when she wakes up."

He'd been the one who'd looked in on her? She didn't know how she felt about that. Had he seen her sleeping? Had she been snoring?

Why hadn't he come back when she called out?

"Tell me this much at least," Aidan said, presumably still to Tommy. "Did either you or the chief even know Blake had a boat?"

"No, but I was waiting on a full investigative report from the county, and it would have shown up on there."

"And then you would've what, seized the property as evidence?"

"Yes, of course. To search it, just like we've done with his house. All the current evidence regarding the case points to Blake being in on the arson."

In on the arson. Kenzie absorbed the odd choice of words. Did he mean that he thought there could be more than one arsonist?

"So who beat you to the boat, Tommy? Who wanted

to make sure there was no chance of extracting any evidence from it?"

The answer actually gave Kenzie hope—because it meant that someone *else* could possibly be proven to be responsible for the arsons, maybe even someone who'd framed Blake.

"There's been at least seven highly destructive fires," Tommy said. "Adding up to millions of dollars in damages. The chief's ass is on the line, and so is mine. If Blake was still alive, he'd be behind bars. That he's not doesn't change anything. The investigation is ongoing."

"But it's possible he was working with someone," came Aidan's voice. "Is that what you're saying?"

"No comment."

"Do you know who?"

"No comment."

"You know something's off, Tommy, or you wouldn't be here."

"Yes," the investigator agreed tightly. "Something is off, and…"

Their voices lowered to a whisper. She leaned toward the curtain, but they were talking so quietly now she couldn't hear anything but…her name. Definitely, she'd heard her name.

Why were they talking about her?

She scooted even closer to the edge of the cot and cocked an ear, but still couldn't hear anything. *Dammit!* Blake couldn't have done any of those things they'd accused him of. She knew it, and she was going to prove it herself if necessary, starting with eavesdropping on this conversation. Tommy said something Kenzie couldn't quite catch, so she leaned even further, and—

Fell off the cot to the floor. *"Ouch."*

At the commotion, the curtain whipped open. She tried to push herself upright but with one wrist useless and the other pinned beneath her, she was pretty much a beached fish. A nearly naked beached fish, with her butt facing a crowd of three: Tommy, the nurse and, oh, perfect—Aidan. She could see the tabloids now: Ex-Soap Star Mackenzie Caught Panty-less. "Ouch," she said again and rolled to her back, gasping when the cold linoleum hit her bare backside. She sighed just as someone dropped to his knees at her side, and then Aidan's face swam into her vision.

"Are you okay?" he demanded.

Sure. Sure, she was okay. If she didn't think about the fact that she'd just mooned him.

"Here." After helping him get her back on the cot, the nurse fussed a moment, checking all of Kenzie's various injuries. Luckily, Tommy had backed out of the room, vanishing, for now at least.

"What the hell were you doing?" Aidan demanded when the nurse left them alone, too.

"Oh, a little of this, a little of that—" Realizing her gown was twisted very high up on her thighs—which, of course, was nothing to what he'd just seen—she grabbed her blanket and tried to cover herself up. A little like closing the barn door after the horse had escaped, she knew, but she was mortified. Except the movement made her want to throw up, and she reached up, holding her head tightly.

"Here." He took over the task of covering her, quickly extricating his hands when he was done, not quite meeting her gaze as he sat at her side.

Awkward moment... "So," she said. "What are you doing here?"

"Looking in on you."

Yep. And he'd gotten to look in on far more than he'd probably intended.

"Are you all right?" he asked.

"Depends on your definition of *all right*."

At that, his eyes cut to hers and he sighed, scrubbing a hand over his face, his fingers rasping over the growth there. He looked and sounded exhausted. "I'm sorry, Kenzie."

"For what? That I just mooned you, or that I'm here at all?"

Aidan got to his feet, pulling the curtain shut again to give them privacy, privacy that she wasn't sure she wanted.

He'd changed his clothes. He wore a pair of jeans now, loose on his long legs, low on his hips, with a long-sleeved shirt unbuttoned over a gray T-shirt that seemed to emphasize his broad shoulders and tough, athletic build. "Your shirt isn't red," she said slowly.

"What?"

"Before, somebody in a red shirt was looking at me."

"When?"

"I don't know." She rubbed her temples. "I'm out of it."

"It was a tough night."

"Yeah." But *he* didn't look like he'd just worked his ass off and managed to save her life to boot; he looked casual, relaxed.

Cool as a cucumber.

And so hauntingly familiar, not to mention gorgeous, that she couldn't keep her eyes on him. How unfair was it that he'd gotten even better-looking with age?

"Thanks for stopping by, Aidan, but you can see I'm fine. You can go."

He looked doubtful.

"Seriously. I'm really okay."

She almost had him, she could tell, but then she ruined it by shivering.

Without a word, he grabbed another blanket and settled it over her. She appreciated his sense of duty, but what she would appreciate even more would be his vanishing.

Or her.

Yeah, that might be better. If she could just vanish on the spot. *Poof.* "Okay, now I'm good, thanks. Really."

"Really?"

"Yes. I mean you can't even look at me, so—"

Lifting his head, he met her eyes, his hot enough to singe her skin.

"Oh," she breathed, feeling her heart kick, hard.

"I can't look at you?" he repeated in low disbelief. "Are you kidding me? Kenzie, I can't do anything *but* look at you."

CHAPTER FOUR

At Aidan's words, Kenzie's breath caught and held. She didn't know how to take him, especially the way he was looking at her, as if maybe he could see all the way through her, to her heart and soul, right to the very center of her being, where all the hurt was so carefully bottled up.

She'd gotten over him. Years ago. She really had. She'd gotten over how he'd once made her laugh, made her think, made her happy…

Made her come…

No way could he possibly reach her now. Not with that hard body, not with the look in his eyes and definitely not with the memories.

Okay, maybe the memories got to her, just a little bit. For one glorious summer, he'd been the best part of her life—before he'd walked away without so much as a glance back, that is.

Good. There was her anger, which would hopefully negate the fact that he was standing right here in the flesh looking good enough to…well… That thought made her want to sweat. But apparently she could be both over him and turned on by him at the same time, which confused her to say the least. She had no idea what that was about. No idea at all.

None.

She'd moved on years ago from that young, sweet, innocent girl. Now she was a woman with a backbone of sheer steel that had gotten her through some tough times.

She knew people tended to look at her carefully cultivated outer package—thank you, stylist to the stars—an outer package that was petite and willowy, even fragile-looking, and completely underestimate her.

But on the inside she was one-hundred-percent survivor, thank you very much. She'd lived through losing her parents early, through a happy-as-it-could-be teen-age-hood with just Blake. She'd lived through being in the public eye, through the ups and downs of TV fame and most recently, through the death of her brother. All of that would have cracked most women, but she wasn't easily cracked.

She would get to the bottom of this mess, no matter what she had to do in order to get there. *No matter what.* Even if she had to use her beauty, her checking account, her damn body.

She would do it.

Whatever it took.

For Blake.

"I heard you talking to the investigator," she said softly.

Aidan's eyes met hers, and she wished like hell she could read his mind. But she couldn't, and he didn't say another word to help.

"I think he's wondering if I'm guilty of something."

He just looked at her some more.

"The only thing I'm guilty of is knowing that he hasn't done his job if he thinks Blake did those things."

At that, his face softened, and regret filled his eyes,

along with a grimness that had her shaking her head before he even spoke.

"Don't say it," she warned, not willing to hear it, not from him. Not from anyone. Not when she was this close to a breakdown. A grief breakdown. "Don't." She *knew* Blake, goddammit. She did. She didn't remember much about her parents before they'd died in a car crash, but she remembered Blake. Every bit of him. He was the boy who'd held her hand every time they'd had to move to a new foster home. He was the teenager who'd punched a boy in the face when he'd hurt her, he was the man who'd believed in her enough to work double shifts to pay for her publicity shots so she could pursue her acting dream.

He could *never* have committed arson. She'd have sworn Aidan would have known that as well, but apparently she was wrong.

"There's evidence——" he began, but she shook her head.

"Circumstantial." She swallowed hard but a lump of emotion, the one that had been there since Blake's death, remained. "I see that you're no better a friend than you were a boyfriend."

He opened his mouth, but before he could respond, the nurse pulled aside the curtain and entered the cubicle, followed by a doctor. "Everyone out," the nurse ordered.

"I'm the only one here," Aidan said.

"So get out," the nurse responded sweetly.

Kenzie closed her eyes and lay back. She didn't look at Aidan again; in fact, she didn't open her eyes until she heard the rustling of the curtain, signaling he'd left.

Which was fine. Perfect, really. Because she'd sure

as hell rather be alone than look into his eyes and see things she didn't want to see.

A<small>IDAN</small> EXITED THE emergency room, feeling like a class-A jerk. Though how that was possible, what with his saving her life and all, he had no idea....

Okay, he knew.

She'd seen the look in his eyes; she'd understood something she hadn't wanted to understand—that he knew Blake was involved with those arson fires.

Aidan felt torn up about it, sick over it, but facts were facts. Blake had been placed at the scene of each arson by various witnesses. He had been depressed since losing Lynn, his partner before Cristina, in a fire the year before. His home had been seized and searched, and in his garage they'd found a stack of wire mesh trash cans, similar to the ones identified as the point of origin in each of the arsons.

Most damning, Aidan's partner, Zach, had also seen him holding a blowtorch just moments after Zach's house had been set on fire, with Zach and Brooke inside. Zach had almost died there.

And Blake *had* died there, perhaps deliberately. He'd died, leaving all of them, Zach, Aidan and the other firefighters, even Tracy, the woman he'd had such a crush on, everyone, destroyed.

Kenzie was in denial. He got that. She was angry. He got that, too. She needed someone to vent that anger at, to place it on, and he'd been handy enough.

I see that you're no better a friend than you were a boyfriend.

Yeah, that had been a direct hit. Having her look at him as if *he* was the bad guy had really gotten to him, especially considering he still had the scrapes and bruises from saving her.

The late afternoon sun was sinking fast, cooling off the day. Having been up for two straight days now, he desperately needed sleep. He could close his eyes standing up right there in the hospital lot, and not wake up if a cyclone hit. He was so tired that he'd probably sleep completely dreamless. Well, except for maybe dreaming about Kenzie's bare ass. Yeah, now that he'd seen that again, he'd most likely dream about it for a good many hours.

Days.

Years.

"Aidan."

Hell. Tommy was leaning up against Aidan's truck, a file in his hands, mouth pinched tight, looking as if he had plenty of things to say, and all fantasies about Kenzie's ass vanished. "What now?"

"I wasn't aware that you knew her personally."

"Who?"

"Come on, Aidan. Don't play with me. Mackenzie Stafford. You didn't say that you knew her."

He sighed. "So?"

"So it felt to me like maybe you knew her...*well*."

"Yeah. Once upon a time."

"Okay, and so once upon a time, did you know she was Blake's sister?"

Getting into tricky territory here. No one had known he and Kenzie had dated in the past. It'd been a quick, hot thing, *very* hot, and he certainly hadn't been in any hurry to tell Blake he'd gotten his sister in bed. Kenzie hadn't told Blake, either, for her own reasons, and then when Kenzie had gone off to Los Angeles, it hadn't mattered anymore.

Did it matter now, with Blake dead? He couldn't see how it did. "Yeah, I knew she was Blake's sister."

"Did you know that boat was Blake's?"

"Where are we going with this, Tommy?"

"Did you?"

Aidan let out a breath. "Not until we were in the water and she told me."

Tommy nodded. "Because you always sit around with someone you're rescuing and chat about property ownership."

"I asked her why she was there, on that boat. I was under the impression that she was in Los Angeles."

"Yeah?" Tommy's eyes studied him, considering. "So just how well do you know her?"

"Irrelevant."

"I wonder if Blake would have thought so."

Aidan fished his keys out of his pocket. "I'm going home to sleep. For many, many hours. When I'm back on duty you can drill me all you want. Maybe I'll be able to think more clearly."

"Maybe I don't want you thinking more clearly."

"And what the hell does that mean?"

"It means I need answers now. Did you know she was staying on the boat? Did you maybe visit with her there before the fire?"

"I told you. No. And no."

"Ms. Stafford thinks Blake is innocent. That he was not only framed but possibly murdered, and she intends to prove it."

Sounded right. Kenzie might look like a pretty ball of fluff, but she had sharp wits and was loyal to a fault.

She also had the tenacity of a bulldog. Once she got her brain wrapped around an idea, there was nothing anyone could do to change her mind. Not about falling in love with him, not about being an actress and most definitely not about believing that Blake couldn't be guilty of arson.

"So the question stands," Tommy said quietly. "How well do you know her?"

"Did." Well enough that when he'd looked into her eyes, he'd felt an odd stirring, a sensation almost like coming home. Yeah, once upon a time he'd known her well. As well as he'd known anyone. "Past tense."

"Good enough."

"For what?"

"To get you to tell her to stay the hell out of this investigation and not interfere."

"People don't tell Kenzie what to do."

"You're going to. Because the chief has put out the word. If anyone hinders this investigation, we'll have them arrested, Blake's sister or not."

Great. Perfect. If Aidan told her that, she'd jump in with both feet, because one thing he remembered and remembered well—nothing scared her. Nothing. "Seriously. It's not a good idea for me to tell her anything."

"Well, then, I hope she has bail money."

Shit. Aidan watched Tommy walk away, then he turned to his truck. Needing sustenance before he passed out cold for at least the next twelve hours straight, he stopped at Sunrise, the café that was the perpetual hangout for everyone at the station. The two-story building was right on the beach. Downstairs was food central, while the second floor was the living quarters for Sheila, the owner. The rooftop was the place to go to view the mountains, the ocean, the entire world it seemed, and to think.

Stepping inside, his sense of smell immediately filled with all the aromas he associated with comfort: coffee, burgers, pies... Sheila smiled at him, and as the sixty-two-year-old always did, fawned over him as he imagined a mother would.

His own mother wasn't too into fawning, at least not over him. She'd divorced his father when Aidan had been two, and he'd spent most of his childhood years being shuffled from family member to family member while she'd relived her wild youth. Granted, he'd been more than a handful of trouble, purposely going after it in a pathetic bid for attention, so in hindsight he didn't blame anyone for not keeping him around for long.

Eventually, he'd ended back up at his dad's, where the two of them had spent a few years doing their best to tolerate each other until, when Aidan had been fifteen, his dad had remarried and promptly given his new wife three babies in a row.

Aidan had landed at his mom's once again, a little bit rebellious and a lot angry, but by then his mother had settled down some, remarrying as well.

Now Aidan had five half brothers and sisters, and didn't quite belong on either side of the family.

Not that he'd had it as rough as Blake and Kenzie had. He knew exactly why the brother and sister had been as close as they had, and exactly why Kenzie would fight tooth and nail to prove her brother's innocence.

What he didn't know was how to convince her to let the law handle things, or if he even had a right to ask such a thing of her.

Between a rock and a hard place.

He ate his fill, and by the time he set down his fork, he felt halfway human. He still needed his bed, badly, but with Tommy's words echoing in his head, he knew he had to try to talk to Kenzie again first. He needed to warn her to let Tommy do his job. For old times' sake.

Or so he told himself.

He pulled out his cell phone and called the hospital, but was told she'd been released.

Where would she go? Back to Los Angeles? No, she wouldn't leave Santa Rey, not until she did what she'd come to do, which was prove Blake's innocence, so he asked Sheila for the local phone book and a slice of key lime pie, both of which he took up to the roof. Sitting facing the ocean, he began calling. But as it turned out, Kenzie wasn't registered at any of the three hotels in the area, probably because there were two conventions in town and everything was fully booked. He looked at the remaining list of several dozen motels and B and Bs, and sighed. He'd made his way through the most likely candidates when Sheila came out on the roof with a fresh mug of coffee.

"What's up for you tonight?" Even with her bouffant hair, she barely came up to his shoulder. "You planning on saving any more damsels in distress?"

He didn't bother asking her how she knew about last night's fire—the gossip train in Santa Rey was infamous. "No damsels, distressed or otherwise. I have a bed in my immediate future."

"You sleeping alone these days?"

Unfortunately, yeah. The last woman he'd gone out with had found someone else, someone with more money and more time, and he'd gotten over her fairly quickly but hadn't yet moved on. He couldn't tell that to Sheila, though, or she'd set him up with her niece, as she'd been trying to do all year....

"My niece would be perfect for you, Mr. 2008."

He winced. "You saw the calendar."

"Honey, I saw, I bought, we all drooled. Now about my niece..."

Her niece was divorced with four kids, and while she was a very lovely woman, a waitress at Sunrise, in fact, he wasn't anxious to help create yet another fractured family. "I'm sorry, Sheila. But at the moment, I'm—"

"Enjoying being alone," Sheila finished for him with a sigh. "Yeah, yeah, I've heard it before."

Standing, he handed her back the phone book, then gave her a hug. "How about you? You could marry me."

She cackled good and long over that one, and walked to the roof door. "If I was thirty years younger, you'd be sorry you said that...."

He laughed, but his smile faded fast enough. With no idea how to track down Kenzie, he left and drove home, thinking he'd just go horizontal for a little while and then figure it out, but as he drove up to his house, he saw a red convertible Mercedes Cabriolet in his driveway.

And the outline of a woman sitting on his porch, lit from behind by the setting sun.

She was wearing two hospital gowns layered over each other and a pair of hospital booties, reminding him that her clothes had gotten sliced and diced pretty good and probably any luggage she'd had on the boat was long gone.

Her hair, wild on the best of days, had completely rioted around her face in an explosion of soft waves, the long side bangs poking her in one eye and resting against her cheek and jaw, where she had a darkening bruise that matched the one above her other eye, accompanied by a two-inch-long butterfly-bandaged cut. She was cradling her splinted left wrist in her lap. Her good hand was cut up as well, and so were both her arms—nothing that appeared too deep or serious, but enough to make him wince for her. Her legs were more of the same.

She was alone and beat up, and hell if that didn't grab him by the throat and squeeze. Then there were those melt-me eyes that lifted to his and filled.

Jesus. He thought he was so damn tough but one soft sigh from those naked lips and he was a bowl of freaking jelly.

She had a plastic bag beside her, and one peek at it tugged at him harder than he could have imagined given what he did for a living and how often he'd seen this very thing.

Her clothes from the fire.

Probably all that she had left here in Santa Rey. In her unsplinted hand she clutched a small prescription bottle, most likely pain meds. *Hell.* He was such a goner.

"I haven't taken any yet," she whispered, shaking the bottle. "Couldn't, because I took a cab from the hospital to the docks where I had my car, which I drove here."

"Kenzie—"

"You had a package. It was torn, so I looked in." She lifted one of a stack of firefighter calendars, with his own mug and half-naked body on the cover.

"Nice," she said, a ghost of a smile crossing her lips. "Mr. 2008."

He bit back a sigh. "It's for charity."

"And you definitely contributed." She waggled her

eyebrows, then winced. "*Ouch.* I'm not allowed in Blake's house—evidence. And the hotels are all booked up, just my luck. Did you know you have a convention of dog trainers in town? Why are there five hundred dog trainers in Santa Rey?"

"Because we let dogs on our beaches."

"Oh." She sighed. "So we let dogs on our beaches, but not me into a hotel. Kinda makes sense when you think about it."

How that made sense, he had no idea.

"Because my karma sucks."

"Okay, come on." Gently, he pulled her up, taking the bag. Letting her hold onto the medication, he led her inside, telling himself he was going to give her Tommy's warning and that was it.

Other than that, he was going to stay out of it entirely.

But holding onto her, he realized she was trembling, and as he took her into his living room, she went directly for his couch, which she sank onto with a grateful little sigh. "I think she went on vacation."

"Who?"

"My karma." She gave him an exasperated look, like he wasn't listening to her, and then very carefully leaned her head back and closed her eyes.

"Hey." Squatting down before her, he put his hands on her thighs, looking into her eyes when she opened them. "You okay?"

She let out a sound that might have been a laugh, or a sob.

He hoped to God it was the first. "Rough twenty-four hours," he murmured.

Another nod, carefully slow and precise, giving her away. She definitely wasn't laughing. In fact, she was in pain, lots of it; rising, he went into the kitchen for a glass of water. Bringing it back to her, he pried the prescription drugs from her fingers, read the label—yep, painkillers—and shook one out.

"I'm okay."

"You don't look it. You look like hell."

"You say the nicest things."

With another sigh, he once again hunkered down at her side. "Look, you've been through a lot. I know you're alone and…"

"If you say helpless, I'll slug you with my good fist."

Once upon a time she'd been the most amazing thing in his life.

The. Most. Amazing. Thing.

On the outside she'd been so mind-blowingly, adorably, effortlessly sexy. Inside, she'd been pure warmth and sweetness, loyal to a fault, always believing the best in everyone, willing to defend what she believed in to the death if necessary.

From their very first moment together, she'd wreaked havoc with his common sense. Before her, nothing in his world had been warm or sweet or particularly loyal. She'd brought lightness into the dark.

Until he'd sent her away. "Not helpless," he said a little thickly. "Never helpless."

"Okay, then." She hugged herself and shivered.

With a frown, he moved to the fireplace. For late summer, the evening did have a chill to it, and she probably was still in some shock. He set up kindling and held a lit match to it until it flamed with a low *whoosh*.

With a startled cry, Kenzie shrank back from the small flames, covering her face.

Yeah, still in shock. He should have thought about

how she'd feel about a flame of any kind, and cursing himself, he rose and went to her.

"I'm okay," she whispered, peeking out from between her fingers, very carefully not looking at the flickering fire. "It's the crackling." She grimaced. "And, okay, the sight. I don't know what's wrong with me."

"It's normal."

"I don't feel normal."

He didn't feed the small fire, letting it burn out. "I'm sorry. Let's go with the heater instead, okay?"

Once again she leaned her head back, carefully not moving a single inch more than she absolutely had to. "Thanks."

She was killing him. "Kenzie—"

"Could we not talk? It's threatening my head's precarious perch on my shoulders."

"Take the pill."

"I guess I could use a little oblivion. Okay, I could use a lot of oblivion...." Turning her head, she eyed the fireplace as if it were a spitting cobra. "You know, they don't call me Kenzie in Los Angeles."

"Or in the gossip rags."

Without moving another muscle, she arched an eyebrow, appearing to be genuinely surprised. He'd given himself away.

"You read them?"

"Hard to miss when you're going through the grocery store," he said defensively. "They're right next to the candy bars."

The smallest smile crossed her lips.

"You dated that underwear model. The one who danced naked on all the commercials. Chad."

"Chase. And he wasn't naked. He was wearing the

underwear he was marketing. Which isn't that much less than what you're wearing in that calendar, Mr. 2008." She gave him a long look.

"Last year you went out with a European prince."

"Now that was just publicity."

He didn't know if he believed her, or cared.

Strike that. He cared. "Take the pill." He watched her chase it with the glass of water he offered.

Yeah, he cared.

Dammit.

"Problem," she said, and licked a drop of water off her bottom lip.

He dragged his gaze up to hers. "What?"

"Even if there were no dogs. I still couldn't get a room. I have no money—my purse either burned up or is below several yards of water, probably both." Kenzie winced. "The hospital had to give me an emergency taxi voucher to get to my car. I'd be really screwed right now if my keys hadn't been in my pocket. Luckily, I also left my cell in the car, so I called my financial manager and he's overnighting emergency funds. But your address was the only one I could think to give him, and I have no place to go until it arrives. And now I can't drive." She shook the bottle of pills. "It's not recommended."

Their eyes met as the implications of her little speech sank in.

"Apparently, I still trust you," she whispered. "At least a little."

Damn if that didn't cut right through everything to the heart of the matter. For better or worse, she trusted him, and he had to admit, that meant something to him. Plus, there was the other truth—there was no other place she could go. Like it or not, he was her only contact in town. Which meant...

She was staying here.

With him.

CHAPTER FIVE

KENZIE SAT ON Aidan's couch absorbing the awkward silence. Her eyes were closed but she could feel him close. Thinking. Probably panicking. "Or if you loan me a few bucks, I'll call a cab."

"And go where?"

Right. Well, dammit, if he'd just give her some room, she could just sit and try to ignore him—*try* being the key word.

It wasn't his good looks that held her interest. She'd had her fill of good-looking guys on a daily basis at work and she would have said Aidan wasn't that pretty, at least not soap-star pretty. Until she'd seen the calendar. Because holy cow, he'd looked pretty damn fine in eight-and-a-half-by-eleven color glossy, there was no doubt. But he was also tough, and far more rugged than that. There was just something about his eyes and mouth, and the laugh lines lining both that suggested he could be dangerous or outrageous, sweet or maybe not so much so, sheer trouble or the boy next door....

She knew all to be true.

What she didn't know was why she'd come *here,* to his house.

Okay, she knew. He was the only familiar thing in her entire world. She'd gotten his address easily enough by calling his station, where some friendly firefighter

had recognized her and cheerfully offered up direction.
She'd driven here on auto-pilot, having no trouble remembering her way around Santa Rey, getting spooked
only when she'd thought she was being followed by a
gray sedan.

Which was ridiculous and paranoid. God, she needed
a nap.

Aidan's house was tiny, and definitely old, but cozy.
From the looks of things, he'd been remodeling it. The
living room had lovely hardwood floors and gorgeous
wood trim on all the windows, which looked out to the
ocean and the rolling hills surrounding it.

He'd always been handy—with tools, with his mind,
his words.

His body...

Yeah, he'd been really good in that department. In
fact, it was fair to say he'd been her willing tutor, and
she a most apt pupil.

But that thought led to others, including the fact that
she'd once been young and stupid enough to believe
in fairy tales. Aidan had been her prince, her happily-
ever-after.

Until he hadn't been.

Luckily she was no longer young or stupid. She no
longer dated men while dreaming of that white picket
fence and two point four kids. Nope, she dated simply to have fun, and once in a while, to have good sex.

Easy come, easy go.

Too bad she and Aidan weren't having a go at things
now, because she was finally with the program, she
finally got the rules. They'd probably have a hell of a
time.

An evening breeze came through an open window

and she drew in a fresh breath. Her pain pill had begun to kick in, and she sank a little deeper into the very comfortable couch. The last time she'd been in Aidan's place, which back then had been an apartment, he'd owned a bed, a TV, a stereo and a box of condoms.

That'd been all they'd needed.

She hadn't been the only one to change. His needs had apparently upgraded. His couch was extra large, and double extra comfortable. There was a TV, triple extra large, and the perennial stereo. But he also had a desk with a computer on it, and some beautiful prints on the walls, which were painted in muted beachy colors.

No condoms in sight. That was undoubtedly for the best. But she liked the house. Low maintenance, calm, even warm and clean. Her place wasn't so different, which meant she felt far more at home here than she would have ever admitted out loud.

How ironic that she'd come back into town to handle Blake's affairs, and to raise hell on the arson charges, intending to stay as far out of Aidan's path as possible, only to end up here in his house, with nowhere else to go.

High on meds…

From the windows she could hear the waves slapping against the shore. Next to her, he was still, just sitting there breathing, soft and even, but she didn't look at him. Wasn't ready to look at him. Yet apparently her nose didn't get that memo because her nostrils quivered, trying to catch a quick whiff of the man—except all she could smell was herself and the smoke and soot stuck to her skin. "I stink."

"It's stress."

"No, not like that." She rolled her eyes, which hurt like a son-of-a-bitch. "Like smoke."

"You could take a shower." His voice was low, a little gritty, and a whole lot suggestive, although she knew that last was all her own imagination.

She couldn't help it, the guy had a voice that brought to mind slow, hot sex. Seriously, if he could bottle the sound, he'd have been rich.

"Kenzie? Do you want to take a shower?"

Yes, please. In her own place with her own things and her own thick, cozy, warm bathroom and fuzzy bunny slippers. And then she'd like a good DVD and a bag of popcorn, something to give her mind a mini-vacation from its current hell. "That would be nice, thanks."

He offered her a hand. She stared at it, and then into his face, which was solemnly watching her. "Just a hand," he murmured.

Knowing she was a bit wobbly, she put her hand in his bigger, warmer one and let him pull her up. She staggered into him, and for a moment he held her, and caving in to her own yearning, she pressed her face to his throat and was immediately overcome with memories.

But she didn't do memories, at least not anymore, so she forced herself to step free of him.

He led her down the hall and into what must have been his bedroom. The walls were a soft cream, which went beautifully with the cedar ceilings. But what caught her eye was the biggest bed she'd ever seen, piled high with a thick navy-blue comforter and a mountain of pillows. It was made, sort of. It was *boy*-made, which meant the covers had been tugged up. His hamper appeared to be a pile of clothes in the corner, but other than that, the room was as warm and clean and welcoming as the rest of the house.

She shouldn't have been surprised. The Aidan she'd known had been rough-and-tumble tough, always cool and calm and impenetrable no matter the circumstances, which she imagined served him well in his field. She'd seen that in action on the boat and in the water.

But much like his house, he had a warm, soft, welcoming center. It was what had made him so damn likeable.

Now, with the dubious honor of a few years and some maturing, that likeability had turned into an undeniable sex appeal she discovered while standing there staring at his bed, feeling a rather inexplicable stirring deep in her belly.

"Here." With a hand to the small of her back, he gently nudged her all the way into the room, then passed by her, his arm brushing hers as he moved into the bathroom, which was all cool, white tile and more wood trim. He flipped on the shower, which was nearly as big as his entire kitchen.

"Wow," she said, staring at it.

He shrugged. "I like showers."

"I remember." The words slipped out of her mouth before she could stop them. *Damn,* she really needed a script writer for this real-life thing.

His gaze slid to hers. Very slowly, he arched an eyebrow.

She turned away to blush in peace, but he turned her back toward him with a careful hand on her arm. "Kenzie?"

She stared at his chest, her vision a little compromised by the nice little pill she'd taken, but not so much so that she couldn't appreciate the view. "Yeah?"

"Do we need to talk?"

Absolutely not. "No."

She didn't want to discuss her carnal knowledge of his love of showering. Not when she remembered, in vivid Technicolor, taking more than a few with him. She remembered, for instance, the time he'd backed her up to the shower wall in his apartment, lifting her legs around his waist, thrusting into her until she couldn't have told him her own name. She remembered the feel of him, hot and thick inside her, remembered how it felt to be pressed between the hard wall and his harder body, the water pounding down over the top of them until she'd cried out so loudly his roommate had pounded on the bathroom door to make sure she was okay.... They'd laughed so hard they'd barely been able to finish, but they'd managed.

They'd always managed.

The humbling truth was, once upon a time, he'd been able to make her come in less than three minutes, using nothing more than his mouth and his portable showerhead.

God.

Just the reminder had her beginning to sweat and her knees wobbling. And if she was being honest, there were some other even more base reactions going on. She firmly ignored them all and lifted her chin. "No. We don't need to talk."

He nodded very solemnly, but she would have sworn his eyes had heated, and along with that heat was a sort of wry humor.

Oh, perfect. Now *he* was remembering, too.

But what really cooked her goose was while she was squirming, nipples hard, thighs trembling, he was amused.

She ought to slug him. She thought about it, but just then, from the plastic hospital bag came the muffled sound of her cell ringing. Since it could only be someone she didn't want to talk to, like her agent wanting her to get in line for auditions before everyone else from her show snatched up all the jobs, she ignored it.

He gestured toward the steaming shower. "It was the first thing I redid in the house."

Thinking about his shower was infinitely more appealing than thinking about being unemployed. Thinking about him *in* the shower? Priceless. But he was still looking just amused enough at her interest that she shrugged lightly. *Look at me not caring...*

But on the inside she was caring big-time, wondering how the hell to get him *un*-amused and hot, because dammit she wanted him hot.

Why the hell she wanted it made no sense to her, none whatsoever, but she couldn't stop thinking about it. *She* was hot, so *he* needed to be the same. Call it petty revenge on the guy who'd once walked away from her. Call it desperation for a diversion from her real reason for being here. But she wanted him to want her. *Needed* him to want her. She wanted that more than her next breath, and she wanted him to suffer for it.

Around them the steam started to rise, but instead of declaring his undying lust for her, he turned and walked back into his bedroom, vanishing from view.

Kenzie let out a breath. Weary, tired of her own smoky stench, she removed her splint and reached for the tie on her hospital gowns, then went still in surprise when Aidan reappeared.

His broad shoulders filling the doorway, his dark eyes met hers as he held out two folded towels. "You still like to use two?"

She blinked as he set them on the counter by the sink. "Yeah." She cleared her throat. "Thanks."

Jaw a little tight, he nodded, and very carefully didn't come any closer.

Huh. He didn't look that amused now. He looked, dared she think it, a little...hot.

Interesting.

He was going to give her some privacy. Privacy that, shock of all shocks, she didn't actually want. But there he went, turning away again.

"I'll be in the other room if you need anything," he said. "Just call for me."

Wow. He was being considerate, sweet and sensitive, none of the traits she would have associated with him. "You know, this would probably be a lot easier on me if you could continue to be the asshole that you once were."

"Yeah, there's a problem with that."

"Which is?"

"I'm not the same guy I was then."

She opened her mouth, not sure what she planned on saying, but it didn't matter because he walked away, shutting the door quietly behind him.

Kenzie stared at the closed door before stripping and then getting into the shower. Once there, she hissed when the water hit her various cuts but she stood beneath the spray anyway, for a very long time, before finally soaping up. It took five shampoos to get out the smoke smell and even then she wasn't sure she managed completely. By the time the hot water was gone, her skin was wrinkled like a prune and she smelled like Aidan. It was ridiculous but she kept lifting her arm to her nose so she could inhale the scent of him.

When she'd wrapped herself up in the towels, one on her head, one around her body, she opened the bathroom door and found Aidan sitting on the bed, his legs spread, his hands clasped between them, his face pensive. "Better?" he asked, looking for himself.

"Almost human."

A brief smile curved his lips as he held out bandages and antiseptic cream for her injuries. "I was wondering if you planned on drowning yourself in there."

"I'm angry and frustrated and devastated, but not stupid."

He let out a slow nod, his gaze dropping from her face to her body, studying the towel covering her from just beneath her armpits to mid-thigh. She was gratified to see an absolute lack of humor now.

Slowly he stood up, and something surged within her. Lust, which she beat back. Triumph, which she let take over. *Want me*... Yeah, that worked for her, him wanting her. Because when he admitted that out loud, she was going to lift her chin, flat-out reject him and maybe feel just the tiniest bit better.

She hoped. God, she hoped. Because *something* had to ease this knot in her chest. *Knot, hell*. It was a ball, a huge ball, and it was suffocating her. If she gave too much thought to it, it swelled even bigger and threatened to overcome her.

Then he walked toward her, and she shivered in anticipation because here it came, the him wanting her portion of the evening.

But he simply held out her cell phone. "It went off again when you were in the shower. Local cell number."

"Oh." She flipped it open and looked at it, having no idea who would be calling her locally. Blake had been her last tie to Santa Rey. In any case, whoever it was hadn't left a message so she set the phone down.

Aidan strode right past her, going to his dresser.

Okay, she could work with this. Maybe he was going for a condom. Which of course he wasn't going to need—

He held up a shirt. "You still like to sleep in just a T-shirt?"

She stared at the shirt in his hand, at the hand that had once been able to make her purr. She lifted her head, met his gaze, and smiled.

He gave her a little smile in return, and it was all the more sexy because it was a little baffled, a little bowled over, as if he was surprised, pleasantly so, to find her finally smiling at him.

But she wanted more than that. Needed more than that, and she thought maybe she knew what to do.

If she dared…

But she'd always been bold, especially in front of a camera. And if she closed her eyes, she could be bold here as well.

Doing just that, she then reached up, pulling out the end of the towel from between her breasts, and let the thing drop.

It hit the floor with a soft thud.

Naked as a jay bird, she opened her eyes.

Aidan, unflappable, cool, calm as the eye-of-a-storm

Aidan, had gone still as stone, his only movement his Adam's apple when he swallowed hard.

She held out a hand for the proffered T-shirt.

He didn't let go of it, seemingly frozen into place, as he looked her over from head to toes and back again.

She'd never thought of herself as particularly vengeful, and especially didn't wish him harm after he'd saved her life, but he'd once been able to walk away from her without a backward glance, and that had not only broken her heart, but destroyed her confidence.

The look on his face took a good part of that remembered pain away. "Thank you," she said, tugging on the T-shirt, practically having to pry it out of his fingers.

He didn't say a word, he didn't have to. The bulge behind the button fly of his jeans said it all, and with a little shimmying movement, she pulled the shirt over her head, letting it cover her body, before turning and walking out of the room, a real smile on her face for the first time since she'd heard about Blake's death.

CHAPTER SIX

THE MOMENT HE was alone in his bedroom, Aidan let out a long, slow breath. He needed to go after Kenzie to tell her she could have his bed to sleep in, but after the past sixty seconds, he needed a moment.

Or ten.

Or maybe a cold shower.

Bending for the towel she'd dropped, he winced. Still hard as a rock, but who wouldn't be? She had the body that most red-blooded males fantasized about—all soft, warm curves, and then there'd been her tan lines, outlining what looked like a string bikini.

God bless tan lines.

Yeah, he was going to need another moment. He calculated a few multiplication problems in his head, and then went after her. She stood in his living room with her back to him, facing the large picture window that looked out on a darkening sky. She wore the T-shirt he'd lent her, which thanks to the show she'd given him a moment ago, he now knew she had nothing on beneath it. Her shoulders were ramrod straight, her hands at her sides.

And he had no idea what she was thinking.

"I wanted to spread Blake's ashes into the ocean," she said softly to the window. "Off the bluffs. He would have liked that."

He let out a low breath, knowing what was coming next, hating what was coming next.

"Only there are no ashes."

The pain reverberated in her voice, and somehow bounced off his own chest, rolling over his heart. *Dammit*. He headed toward her.

"All I can do is put a marker next to our parents' graves." Her voice wobbled at this, but she didn't lose it, just stared out at the night. "He's innocent, Aidan."

The Kenzie he'd known had always believed the best of everyone, to a fault. Seemed that hadn't changed, only this time it was going to bite her on the ass.

"And I would have thought you'd think so, too," she said with more than a little accusation in her voice. She sighed, the sound soft and heart-breaking as it shuddered out of her.

"Look," he said. "Why don't you go to bed and get some sleep. You'll feel better if you do."

"I doubt that." But she finally turned from the window. The last of the day's light slanted in through the glass behind her, casting her in its soft glow, rendering the T-shirt just sheer enough to stop his heart.

Not sure how much more of her glorious body he could take without dropping to his knees and begging for mercy, he stayed right where he was instead of getting any closer to her.

Closer would be a mistake, especially with those hugely expressive eyes on his, and that look of grief all over her face.

"Sleep won't change anything that I'm feeling," she whispered. "He'll still be innocent."

"Kenzie, they found a scrapbook of all the fires in Blake's house. He was keeping track of them."

"That doesn't mean he's guilty."

"What *does* it mean?"

"Something else." She hugged herself, looking miserable and alone, and hurting. "I wish we were friends," she said very quietly. "I wish that you hadn't hurt me, and that I didn't have the urge to hurt you back."

Feeling bad, feeling a whole host of things he shouldn't be feeling at all, he took her hand. "I'm sorry I hurt you back then. I'm sorry I let you go. But I was young and stupid, Kenz. I was a complete ass."

She lifted a shoulder, tacitly agreeing with him.

"I'd like to think that if we were seeing each other now," he said softly, "and one of us wanted out, that we'd do better. That we'd make the friendship work."

Another lift of her shoulder, with slightly less temper in it this time.

Okay, that was something, a step at least. Pulling her toward him, he turned to lead her back to his bed, where he was going to tuck her in and then walk away.

Be the good guy.

Only she tugged him back, and suddenly he was holding onto her and she was pressing her face into his throat and breathing in deep, and...and *hell*. He was in trouble, sinking fast. "I showered at the station," he murmured into her hair. "But I need another. I still smell like smoke, Kenz, and—"

"Right." Pulling free, she turned away. "Sorry."

And now she thought he didn't want to hold her, when that was *all* he wanted. "Kenzie—"

"No, you're right. Absolutely right. Let's not go there." She smiled, and anyone who'd ever seen her smile for real would have recognized it as a first-class fake, but he didn't dare say a word about it because he had the feeling she was barely hanging on.

As was he.

She turned away. "You're right. Sleep might be best. But I'll take the couch—"

"No, don't be ridiculous. I—"

"Make no mistake, Aidan. I still want to hurt you. It's immature and extremely juvenile of me, but it's fact. So, no. I'm not sleeping in your bed." She walked back to the couch.

"Kenzie—"

"Please," she said, sinking down to the cushions and closing her eyes. "Could I have a blanket?"

"Of course." He went and got several, came back and spread them over her.

She didn't speak, or for that matter, move.

"Call me if you need anything," he finally said.

She gave no response to that, either, and he nodded even though she wasn't looking at him. "Okay then… night." He paused, but she still didn't say anything to release him from the strange torment he felt. In the end, he did as she seemed to want, and left her alone.

A FEW MINUTES LATER, Kenzie heard the shower go on, and in spite of herself, pictured Aidan stripping off his clothes and climbing in.

Soaping himself up…

Standing there beneath the steamy hot water all naked.

And unintentionally sexy.

Behind her, from somewhere else in the house, a phone rang. A machine clicked on and she heard Aidan's voice saying, "You know what to do at the beep."

Then came a "Hey, you" in a low, Marilyn Monroe–like purr. "It's Lori. You didn't call me back. I've been lonely for you, baby. Come over sometime soon, okay? I'll be waiting…"

Kenzie listened to the click as the machine went off and silence filled the house.

Seemed Aidan was still the guy who left women feeling lonely for him. She should return the favor. She should go…somewhere.

But as she listened to the shower running, she let out a long breath and admitted to herself—as silly as it seemed—there was something undeniably consoling about being here with him. She'd told him she trusted him a little, and that was as truthful as it was unsettling. Yes, she had nowhere else to go, but it was far more than that. At the moment, he was the only familiar, comforting presence in her life. At the moment, she wanted to be there, she really did, even knowing that the longer they spent together, the more they would grow closer, whether she liked it or not.

Only, she was afraid she would like it. A lot more than was wise.

AIDAN SURFACED FROM a deep, deep sleep, aware that something had woken him, but not sure what. He opened his eyes and saw his dark bedroom lit up in black and white by the faint glow of the moon slanting in through his horizontal blinds.

There, by his bed, stood an angel.

An angel in his T-shirt, in the same white swaths of moonlight as his room.

She was hurting, sad, scared…and why the hell hadn't he given her a suit of armor instead of just a

T-shirt? Had he been looking for punishment? Because there it was, in flesh and blood and glorious curves and wild hair, and a face so hauntingly beautiful she took his breath. He was in trouble, deep trouble, because although he'd managed to resist opening his heart to her that first time, he wasn't quite sure he would be able to manage it this time.

Without a single word, she lifted his covers and scooted into the bed.

With him.

He was exhausted, beyond exhausted, and was afraid he didn't have the self-control to deal with this. *"Jesus,"* he gasped as she pressed her icy feet to his.

"Sorry."

But she didn't pull them back. Nope, she tucked them beneath his, sucking the warmth out of him.

"Don't look at me like that," she whispered.

He had no idea what she was talking about. There was no way she could clearly see his expression, she couldn't see any more than he could in the strips of moonlight. He could see her eyes, not her nose. He could see her mouth, not her chin...

"I'm not sleepwalking, or pain-pill walking." She pressed a little closer, so that her legs entangled in his.

Now would probably be as good a time as any to remind her that he slept naked, but as he opened his mouth, she spoke first.

"And I'm not here for another broken heart like I got the last time." She poked a finger into his chest. "In fact, if anyone's going to have a broken heart this time, it's going to be you. So you can just wipe that look of pity off your face."

"Pity is the last thing I've got going on," he assured

her. He lay there achingly close, freezing his ass off thanks to her feet. "So you're going to break my heart?"

"Going to do my damnedest."

"I never meant to break yours."

"At least let me think I'm getting my revenge, okay?"

Her toes were killing him. So were her legs, the ones all caught up in his. And somehow he had a thigh between hers...

She propped her head up with her good hand, staring at him in the oddly lit room. Now he could see her forehead and her nose, but not her eyes or her mouth.

"It really is going to be you nursing the heart this time," she whispered.

That could very well be. But honestly, he wasn't sure his bruised heart functioned enough to break. Hell, it was probably dried up from misuse. And yet...and yet lying there with her in his arms seemed to jump-start the organ. It ached, and not just because of their past, it ached for the here and now, for the woman she'd become.

"You," she repeated softly, even a little smugly, and for some reason, some sick reason, it was a turn-on.

And because he was weak and maybe just a little bit stupid, he put his hand on her hip and leaned in to see her better, which he couldn't. She was still in slatted black and white. "I meant what I said, Kenz. I'm sorry you got hurt."

"Good. I *want* you sorry. Very, very sorry."

Yes, but did she want him aroused? Because he was. Her T-shirt had risen up enough to remind him she wasn't wearing panties.

Yeah, colossally stupid.

By now it had to be crystal clear to her that he was

butt-ass naked. In the name of fair warning, he pulled her in a little closer.

"What are you doing?"

What was he doing? No idea. Bending his head, he rubbed his jaw to hers, bumped the tip of his nose to her earlobe.

With a shiver, she clutched at him and arched her neck, giving him better access.

Which he took.

"I can't remember what I was saying," she murmured.

He let out a breath in her ear and she shivered again, which he liked. He liked that a lot. "You were telling me how you're going to break my heart."

"That's right." Her fingers dug into the small of his back as she moved, the black and white shadows shifting over her. "I am. Aidan?"

"Yeah?"

"You're naked."

He'd been wondering when that would come up. Seeing as he was already quite "up"...

She gulped, and then did something he didn't expect. She rolled to her back and pulled him on top of her, allowing him to settle between her thighs, which were not cold like her feet, but warm and cushy and very, very welcoming.

"You should know," she whispered in his ear, making sure her lips brushed his flesh, causing a series of shivers of his own. "I plan to make you beg for mercy this time."

God. "I'm close to begging right now," he admitted.

"Really?"

She sounded breathless as hell, which was another big turn-on. So many... "Really."

He was hard. She was soft, so soft, and pressing all that softness up against him. "If you're not sleep-walking, or having a bad dream," he wondered, "why are you in here?"

"No hotels, remember?"

"Why are you in bed with me?" he clarified.

Her hands glided up and down his back, going lower on each pass. "My feet were cold."

He pressed his feet to hers, and then his mouth to her throat. "Is that all?"

"Absolutely. That and the begging."

He let out a huff of low laughter against her skin, and then because his mouth was right there against her neck, and because she was touching his butt, and because she smelled good, he took a little nibble.

Her fingers dug into him, telling him how much she liked it but she shook her head. "No more touching until you beg."

"I wasn't touching, I was kissing."

"No kissing until you beg. No anything until you beg."

"I've never begged for this before."

"No? Well, it's good for your character to try new things."

He laughed again. Laughed while trying to get laid. That was new. "Okay." Lifting his head, he cupped her face between his hands and looked into her eyes. She was smiling, too, and it was good to see her doing so. It was good to see her period; his smile slowly faded. "Can I kiss you, Kenzie?"

"Is that the best you got?"

"Can I pretty-please kiss you?"

"Well, I *suppose*..."

That was all he let her get out before he lowered his mouth to hers and kissed her. She let out a little murmur of surprise and what he sincerely hoped was pleasure, because *holy shit,* it was like taking a time machine back in time, back to that sweet, hot, most amazing summer he'd once spent in her arms.

She made the sound again, the one that drove him crazy with wanting, and then she entwined her arms up around his neck, gliding her fingers into his short hair and tightening them, as if she didn't want him going anywhere.

Fat chance.

When he slid his tongue to hers, it was another home-coming, and this time her shuddery sigh was pure, hungry delight with a sprinkle of unadulterated lust on top.

Oh, yeah. Pulling back just enough to look into her eyes, he found the same sense of bewildered wonderment across her face that he imagined was across his. Because, yes, they were attracted to each other because of their past, but suddenly it was much, much more than that. Then the next thing he knew, they'd lunged for each other again, trying to climb into each other's body, just like old times.

Only it was new, all so damn new, and all the more heart-wrenching and gripping for it. They were no longer young and stupid. They were old enough to know better, old enough to know exactly what they were doing, old enough that he knew that this time, there would be no escaping unscathed.

It didn't stop him.

CHAPTER SEVEN

OH. MY. GOD.

Kenzie struggled to think, but Aidan had taken her breath away And, as he surged up to his knees between her spread thighs, his hands fisted in the hem of his own shirt, his intention perfectly clear, he nearly stole her sanity—but she held on by a thread. "Wait," she gasped, putting a hand to his chest. "Hold it."

Still kneeling between her sprawled legs, his hands on the big T-shirt, about to strip her as naked as he was, he looked into her eyes. "Wait?"

She could have drowned in his gaze. Happily drowned. "You stopped begging."

He arched an eyebrow, which was highlighted by the slants of moonlight across his face. Stripes of light and dark, and in them, he was beautiful. "I mean it," she managed. "Absolutely nothing else happens here without some serious begging."

He stared at her, then lowered his head for a moment. When he lifted it again, she expected him to tell her he never begged for anything. That this—she—wasn't worth it. After all, she hadn't been once.

But he surprised her. "When we were together," he said quietly, "I dreamed about your body on the nights we didn't sleep in the same bed. Did you know that?"

"No." She shook her head. "You never said." He'd never said a lot of things. He'd held back so much.

And to be honest, so did I....

"I'd get off on it," he said, not holding back this time. Which did exactly what she hadn't wanted—it opened her heart to him.

"On you," he murmured. "For years afterward, I'd get off thinking about you."

She stared up at him. "You mean you..."

"Uh-huh. I jerked off." Leaning over her, he was nothing but a shadow until he bent even closer. Through the shutters, rectangles of light slashed over him as he let her look into his eyes, which were dark and scorching. "So much I'm lucky I'm not blind."

She laughed but also swallowed hard, surprisingly aroused at the thought of his touching himself while picturing her. "Oh."

"Yeah, oh." His eyes glittered with heat and memories and suddenly both the heat and memories were making her feel awfully warm from the inside out.

Actually, they were making her hot.

Very hot.

"Tonight, just looking at you..." He let out a long breath and shook his head. "It brings it all back, but it's even stronger."

His mouth was in the shadows. She couldn't see his lips moving but his voice washed over her, as did the images he evoked. He was bringing it all back for her, too.

"You were beautiful then," he said. "But you're even more beautiful now. I want to take this shirt off of you, Kenz. Please let me."

At his words, she nearly turned the tables and begged *him*. She could feel the T-shirt caught high on her thighs. His hips were holding her legs open to him, and with just a little nudge of the shirt, he'd be able to see all her god-given goodies, along with the fact that she was already wet.

"Please," he murmured. "Please let me."

Oh, God. "Yes."

He shifted, and then she could see his mouth, which rewarded her with a smile as he made his move, his fingers closing around the hem of the shirt, slowly tugging it up, revealing her body.

She'd wanted this, sought it out under the guise of getting her long-needed revenge, but that was really just a lie, and her first flicker of doubt hit.

Just who was going to get hurt here...?

The night air brushed over her breasts as he pulled the shirt all the way off and over her head. Her nipples hardened. Goose bumps spread over her flesh, and it wasn't because she was cold. There were five stripes of moonlight across her body, one across her eyes, her throat, another highlighting her breasts, her belly and her crotch. He couldn't have lined her up more perfectly for his perusal, and he definitely perused.

"Aidan—"

His hand stroked over her hip, and her breath backed up into her throat. She opened her mouth to say maybe she'd been hasty about this whole breaking his heart thing, but before she could, he'd put a hand on her inner thigh and pushed, further opening her to him.

The slants of shadows hampered his view, but he didn't seem bothered, not with his front row seat.

The only sound in the room came from him as he let out a groan. "God, Kenzie. You're so pretty." He lowered his head, then paused, his mouth a hairsbreadth

away from her trembling belly. "I want to kiss. I want
to taste. I want that more than I want my next breath.
Please let me…"

As far as begging went, it was pretty good. "O-okay,"
she managed, and almost before the word was out, he'd
nudged her legs open even wider, wedging them there
with his broad shoulders. He slowly lowered his head.
"Pretty please," he whispered across her flesh.

Her wet flesh.

"Yes." Her heels dug into the mattress as he "pretty
pleased" his tongue over her, and then his teeth, and
then his warm lips, over and over again leaving her
a panting, gasping, quivery mass of sensitized nerve
endings, and when she exploded for him, he surged
up, produced a condom and slid into her with one sure,
powerful thrust.

"Oh," she gasped, reaching up to hold onto him because her world had just spun on its axis. The feel of
him deep inside her—and he was deep, as deep as he
could get—had her spiraling. Gone were all thoughts
of hurting him, or revenge. She could think of nothing
but this, but him. Not that she would admit such a thing.
"You…you didn't beg for that."

Cupping her face, he tilted it up to his. "Pretty-please
may I drive you out of your living mind?"

Oh, God.

"Kenzie? May I?" His voice was thick with the same
hunger and need that was driving her.

"Yes."

"Good. May I also pretty-please make you scream
my name?"

In answer, she arched up, her breasts pressing into his
hard, warm chest, her legs wrapping around his waist.

He groaned, a low, rough sound that scraped at all her good spots but he didn't move. "Can I?"

"I don't usually do much screaming."

He just smiled, and then took her mouth as he took her body, indeed driving her out of her mind with all too disturbing ease, and when she exploded again, she cried out his name.

Loudly.

She might have even screamed it.

As the blood finally slowed in her veins, as the roar of it lowered to a trickle in her head, she became aware of the fact that she was gripping him tight, holding him close with her arms and her legs, not letting him escape.

He didn't say a word, just nuzzled lazily at her neck as his breathing slowed.

Hers wasn't slowing. Embarrassed at how tightly she was holding him, she forced herself to let him go, certain he'd roll away.

But in perhaps the loveliest thing he'd done all night, he didn't. Instead, he remained right where he was, turning just his head to press his lips to her jaw, murmuring her name on a sigh.

It was one of those defining moments, where she suddenly knew the truth—she'd not exacted a single ounce of revenge. In fact, she'd made things worse.

She'd risked her own heart.

But for that one moment at least, she didn't care, because maybe he'd changed. Maybe things could be different this time, and—

"You screamed my name." He lifted his head, revealing a strong smile. "You begged." He out-and-out grinned then, not broken, not even a little bit. "We still work hard."

"There's no *we*." She pushed him off her, suddenly and irrationally irritated. "No we at all."

Completely oblivious to the picture he made sprawled out on the bed, buck naked, he put his hands behind his head and continued to smile like an idiot. "Are you telling me you have no desire to do that again?"

"None."

"Ah, Kenzie. You're such a pretty liar."

Yeah. Yeah, she was. A pretty liar, and a good liar. But she had no idea how else to hide the fact that she still had feelings for him in spite of their past—or maybe because of it. *God.* She needed to get out for a while, needed to clear her head. Get some answers. *Alone.*

"Stay," he murmured.

"Okay." She looked at him. "I'll stay if you tell me this. Why did you really dump me?"

At that, his amusement faded. "I told you I was an idiot back then."

"Granted. Why else?"

He looked at her and she nearly backed down; she certainly held her breath, but he touched her face. "Because I didn't know what I had."

AIDAN SLEPT LIKE the dead. Or like a man who'd been far too close to serious exhaustion. When he opened his eyes, he felt the various aches and pains from the fire, and from the mattress gymnastics he and Kenzie had executed, and was grateful to know he had two days off, because more sleep was on his To Do list. Much more.

So was more mattress gymnastics.

Considering that Kenzie was wrapped around him like a pretzel, that shouldn't be too difficult to manage. As he looked into her face, taking in each of the cuts and the bruises there in the light of day, he felt a tug in his belly.

He wished like hell he could say he was just hungry, but he knew the truth.

He was a goner.

She was as cut up and bruised as he was, more so, and if *he* hurt like hell, he could only imagine how she felt. He was used to such injuries. She wasn't.

"I realize I've spent my days on a television set, where my worst injury was a paper cut from that day's script," she whispered, eyes still closed. "But I'm not feeling as bad as I probably look."

Her face was relaxed now; and he realized it hadn't been before—not on Blake's boat, not when she'd crawled in bed with him, not even when he'd stripped her out of his shirt and proceeded to make her scream.

That he'd undone her so easily didn't stroke his ego. She'd undone him just the same. It'd always been like that for them, a virtual explosion of need and lust and hunger.

But he'd attributed much of that to being young and horny. He hadn't anticipated a resurgence of those feelings, and he doubted she had either. But that's exactly what they'd gotten.

With a sigh, she slid out of his arms and off the bed. He enjoyed the view as she walked to the bathroom, but when she shut the door, his smile faded. She needed sustenance, and a bandage change. Getting up, he pulled on his jeans and went into the kitchen, where he grabbed a pan and eggs and went to work getting them both some protein so that they could go back to bed and burn it all off again.

His doorbell rang and Aidan stopped dicing peppers long enough to sign the clipboard of a pudgy guy in brown shorts, who handed him a slim package.

When he heard the shower go off, he finished the eggs and then grabbed his first-aid bag and knocked on the door. "Bandages, aspirin and breakfast. And your package from L.A. is here."

"Perfect timing—I've got to run."

"You mean back to Los Angeles?"

The door opened and steam came out. As did Kenzie wrapped in another of his towels. "Not back. Not yet."

The towel was tucked between her breasts, which pushed them up and nearly out, a fact he'd have taken the time to thoroughly enjoy except for the nasty bruise arcing along her left collar bone. "You need rest."

"I need clothes." She moved past him and into his bedroom. "Can I borrow a pair of sweats?"

"Sure." He opened his dresser and handed the clothes over.

"Thanks. I've really got to go."

She was going to go snoop. Get in Tommy's way. Get herself arrested. "Kenzie, listen to me. You need to stay out of the investigation. The chief doesn't want you digging—"

"I don't work for him. He can't tell me what to do."

"If you stay—"

"No. Thank you, but, no."

Usually in the light of day, with a woman in his bedroom, *he* was the one who had to go. Usually.

Okay, always.

It felt odd to have the shoe on the other foot. Especially given the magnitude of what they'd shared last night, and he wasn't alone in feeling it, dammit. He knew he wasn't.

But Kenzie moved carefully away from him, slowly, as if still in pain, but with conviction. She was set on going, leaving him with a disconcerted feeling in his gut.

Was this how he'd made women feel? Like they'd already been forgotten? "Let's change your bandages—"

"I can do it on my own."

Seemed she was used to doing stuff on her own. That was new.

So was his unsettledness over the way this was going down.

"Yeah," she said at his quiet surprise. "I'm not the same helpless little thing I used to be."

"I never thought you were helpless."

"Well, I was. But I've grown up. I've changed. In many ways. And I don't need anyone's help. For anything."

He arched an eyebrow. "You needed me when we—"

"No. Well, yes, *yes,* I needed you to save me from the fire, but—"

"That's not what I was talking about." He pointed to his bed.

"Oh, no. That was just me, breaking your heart. I warned you, remember."

Bullshit. That hadn't been just revenge. "Kenzie."

"Sorry. Got to go. Have to go." Once again she dropped her towel, which had the same magical effect on him as it had last night. While he stood there taking in the glorious sight of her naked body, she pulled on the sweats, kissed him on the cheek, then walked out of the room.

And, given the sound of the front door opening and then closing, out of his house.

And, most likely, out of his life.

Fitting justice really, as he'd once done the same to her. Moving to the living room, he looked out the window in time to catch her taillights as they vanished down his driveway.

I've changed, she'd said, and she had.

But as the blood once again began a northward flow from behind the zipper of his pants back up to his brain, another thought managed to get his attention.

He'd changed as well. And he was going to prove it.

CHAPTER EIGHT

SOMEONE WAS KNOCKING on Aidan's door when he turned off the shower. *She'd come back.* With his pulse kicking, he grabbed a towel and wrapped it around his waist, heading for the door at a speed far faster than his usual get-there-when-I-get-there saunter.

Only it wasn't Kenzie at all. "Dammit."

His best friend and partner Zach just looked at him. "Nice to see you, too." Without waiting for an invitation, he pushed past Aidan and walked in.

Fair enough. Aidan had let himself into Zach's house plenty of times. Aidan shut the door behind Zach and shoved his fingers through his wet hair. "Sorry. Thought you were someone else."

Zach took in Aidan standing there dripping wet, wearing only a towel. "Clearly. Who is she?"

"How do you know it's a she?"

"Because if you're meeting a guy dressed like that, we have a whole different issue to talk about."

Aidan rolled his eyes and left Zach to go get some clothes. In his bedroom, he looked at his bed as he pulled on a clean shirt. The covers were tossed half on the floor, and on his nightstand were two empty condom wrappers.

And though it was crazy given that Kenzie had used his shampoo, his clothes and his soap, he'd have sworn he could smell her scent, some complicated mix of soft, determined, sexy woman. He stared at the bed, remembering how he'd felt when she'd crawled in with him, remembering how natural it'd been to kiss and touch her, to sink into her body and go to a place he hadn't been in a long time.

Then they'd slept together, and that had felt good, too, being all tangled up in each other again. Familiar, but new. Even better, if that was possible. Things hadn't been complicated in the dark.

Things had been amazing.

But she'd left.

When he walked back into the kitchen, he found Zach staring at the breakfast he'd made for Kenzie.

"You made breakfast," Zach said. "As in got out a pan and cooked something."

"Yeah. So?"

"You put out napkins."

"Let me repeat myself. So?"

"So you never put out napkins. Not when it's me or the other guys."

"Do you want to split the food with me or not?"

"You didn't cook this for me."

"You're right."

Zach raised an eyebrow.

"You're going to question a plate of food?" Aidan said. "Really?"

Zach didn't have to be asked twice. He grabbed a plate and pulled up a chair.

"I thought you and Brooke were going away for a few days since you haven't been cleared to go back to work yet."

"We are. We're leaving tomorrow morning. Wanted to see you first."

"Ah, that's so sweet. You're going to miss me."

"Actually, I'm not." Zach shoveled in some food, and looked at him. "I heard about the explosion. I should have been there."

Aidan looked at the cast on Zach's left wrist, remembered how close he'd come to losing him along with Blake, and felt the food get caught in his throat. "You're not healed yet."

"It's coming along though." He squeezed his fingers into a fist, then stretched them straight out. "I could be back at work, dammit. I have no idea why the chief's being so hard-assed about this. I'm willing and able."

"Enjoy your few days off. You and Brooke deserve it."

"Yeah." Zach sighed. "So is the boat a complete loss?"

"Unfortunately."

"Kenzie all right?"

"Heard about that, too, huh?"

"Yeah." Zach paused. "Was it awkward, considering your past with her?"

"To be the one rescuing her?"

"What else?"

Yeah, genius, what else. Maybe sleeping with her... But that hadn't been awkward. Not one little bit.

Zach was looking at him. "What am I missing?"

Aidan shook his head. "Nothing."

"Come on."

"Okay, nothing I want to talk about."

"That I buy," Zach said, and like the good friend he was, changed the subject. "I heard that Blake must have kept his accelerants on the boat, which is why it blew like it did."

That was one theory, Aidan was sure.

But he had another. "Well…"

"What?" Zach asked.

"You're going to tell me I'm crazy."

Zach stood up and went to the refrigerator for the milk. "All those times I thought those fires were arson, you were the only one who believed me. I'll be the last one to tell you that you're crazy."

"Yeah, but now we know that Tommy was behind you the entire time, he was just in the middle of his investigation. Still is, with the chief riding his ass to put an end to this."

"Yeah." Zach pushed away his plate. "So I wonder what they'd say now."

"About…?"

"About your not buying that boat fire was any more accidental than the other fires. Or me not buying it, either."

Aidan looked into his best friend's eyes and let out a breath. "That boat was blown up for a reason and I think that reason was to hide something. Something that someone didn't want found."

"What?"

"I don't know. And I'm betting Tommy and the Chief don't know either but they want to."

"It doesn't make sense," Zach said. "Blake's dead."

Aidan pushed away his plate. "Yeah." Goddamn, but he wasn't going to get used to that any time soon, the fact that Blake, a friend, *one of them* for Christ's sake, was not only gone, but accused of arson. "Which means that he wasn't working alone and whoever the other person is, they're running scared of something."

"Or someone," Zach said. "Kenzie shows up out of the blue after what, six years? Seems kind of odd, doesn't it?"

Aidan's gut tightened. "Her brother's dead, Zach."

"Yes. Her arsonist brother. They were close, right?"

"What are you saying, that she's his co-felon?"

"Look, I don't want to think about Blake doing the things they've accused him of, either. And I really don't want to think about the fact that if he was still alive, he'd be in jail. But those are the facts."

Aidan scrubbed his hands over his face. "She *just* got into town."

"You know that for sure?"

Actually, no, he didn't.

"Why was she on his boat?"

"Going through his things." Listen to him defend her. "Missing him."

Zach closed his eyes and rubbed them hard. "If that were true, wouldn't she have come sooner?"

"I don't know. I don't know anything except that Blake was all she had." Aidan got to his feet because he had to move, had to pace the length of the kitchen. "She's...devastated. Horrified. And pissed off that we all believe that Blake's guilty. I think she's going to go digging on her own and find out what she can."

"Which should make Tommy oh-so-happy."

"He's going to have her arrested if she hinders the investigation," Aidan admitted. "And she's going to hinder. It's in her nature. She intends to prove Blake innocent."

Zach raised a brow. "You got all that from pulling her out of the water?"

Well, shit. Aidan picked up his fork and shoveled some food in.

"You saw her after the fire. At the hospital."

"Yeah."

Zach paused. "And after that as well, I'm thinking."

"Yeah."

Zach peered around Aidan and into the living room, pointedly looking down the hallway.

"She's not still here."

"But she *was* here? Jesus, Aidan. What would Tommy say?"

"Since when does that matter?"

"Since we both now know that he was on our side about the arsons all along. He'll be on this, too, you can guarantee it."

Yeah. In hindsight, sleeping with Kenzie been a pretty stupid thing to do. And yet, what else could he have done but given her a place to stay?

Except for that using up two condoms part. He probably could have not done that.

"We've got to let Tommy do his thing here," Zach said quietly.

"I can't believe you're suggesting I stay out of it, when you did the very opposite."

"And paid for it," Zach reminded him, lifting his casted wrist.

"She was hurting, Zach. And alone. Her purse had burned in the fire and she had nowhere else to go so I let her stay here. End of story."

"You could have lent her money. She's a famous soap diva—I think she'd have been good for it."

"The hotels were all booked up."

When Zach just looked at him, Aidan lifted a shoulder. "It was just bad luck on her part."

"Just bad luck, huh? Funny, you don't look so put out."

"Don't you have a fiancée to go home to?"

Zach grinned dopily. "Yeah."

"So go already."

Zach got up, then paused. "Look, Aidan, I know she meant something to you once, but—"

"She's Blake's sister."

"And *your* ex. I'd think that'd be reason enough to stay away from her."

Yeah. One would think...

OPENING THE SLIM envelope she'd scooped from Aidan's kitchen table on her way out the door, Kenzie practically kissed the credit card she found inside. She needed some personal items, like clothes of her own, not to mention underwear. Not that she didn't love Aidan's sweats, because she did. They smelled like him. They felt like him.

Which was exactly why she had to get *out* of them.

She did her best not to pout over the loss of her Choos, which she wasn't going to find at Wal-Mart, but the store was still one of God's greatest creations. When she'd bought and put on a peasant skirt, two layered tank tops and a pair of sandals, she got back into her car. She'd missed two calls on her cell, both from that same local number as before, but no messages, so she put it out of her head and drove to the docks. Then she sat in the parking lot nursing a hot chocolate and a blessed box of donuts, staring at the charred remains of Blake's boat.

She was alone except for the occasional car. One was a light-gray sedan that slowed as it passed her, the windows so dark that she couldn't see in. Probably another looky-loo like herself, except...except she'd seen a car like it before, somewhere...

She ate a donut.

Until a couple of weeks ago, before Blake's death, she hadn't had chocolate or donuts in months. Maybe years. She'd been on a strict eighteen-hundred-calorie diet, combined with a workout every single day, without fail. All to look good.

That's what TV stars did. They looked good. She was paid to.

Except she no longer had a TV show to look good for. Back in L.A., she knew the job-finding frenzy had already begun. All her co-stars were busy auditioning, and what was she doing? Eating donuts instead of facing the fact that she was unemployed.

Her cushy, easy, comfortable, fun job had come to an end.

Life over.

She looked at *Blake's Girl* and felt the last donut congeal in her throat. No. Her job was over, not her life.

Blake's life was over.

God. Brushing the sugar from her fingers, she got out of the car. She wasn't looking her best, but then again, there were no paparazzi in Santa Rey. And thanks to no one in the press making the connection between her and *Blake's Girl,* there were no reporters to take pics of her pale, makeup-free face, or all of the bruises and cuts she'd sustained in the fire. Her wrist wasn't bothering her, but the splint was a pain in the butt. She hadn't been able to corral her hair into a ponytail, which meant it was flying wild around her face and in her eyes.

She could have asked Aidan for help but she'd rather have the wild hair than have his hands on her again.

Okay, that wasn't true, wasn't anywhere close to true, but she could pretend it was.

Dammit.

For those few hours last night in his arms, she'd not been alone and lost and hurting. She'd been transported, taken out of herself.

And along the way, she'd forgotten to make him regret dumping her. *Nicely done.* Rolling her eyes at herself, she moved closer to the docks. The charred remains of *Blake's Girl* were taped off with yellow crime scene tape.

She didn't know what that was about.

They thought Blake was a criminal? Fine. But they couldn't pin this one on him, he was already gone.

Gone...

Chest tight, she walked along the yellow tape, getting as close as she could, which wasn't close enough. No one was around, on the dock or otherwise, and she couldn't stop the thought—what if she ducked under the tape? Surely, as Blake's only living relative, she deserved to have a look.

The two boats on either side of *Blake's Girl* were still there. Barely. One was nearly burned black, and in fact looked as if it might still be steaming. The other was half gone, and half untouched.

And between them? A shell of a boat, blackened and charred beyond recognition.

Blake's boat was completely destroyed.

Looking at it, she could see it as it'd been two nights ago, when she could stand on it and still feel her brother's presence, when his things had still been okay. She wished she'd gotten something of his, something, anything...

Maybe she could crawl beneath the tape and get onboard to comb through the torched remains, and thinking it, she bent down, but at the sound of an engine, stopped and turned.

It was the gray sedan again, making another pass of the parking lot.

Goose bumps rose on her arms as she got that same sensation of being watched she'd had at the hospital.

Who was following her?

It wasn't Aidan. No way. He'd make himself known, that was for damn sure. He had a way of making himself known...

Someone else then.

Tommy?

No. Tommy didn't have the resources to have her followed. She doubted anyone in Santa Rey did.

Then she remembered her earlier missed calls, and pulled out her phone, hitting the number.

No one answered.

She ran her hand along the yellow police tape, but the truth was, she didn't quite have the nerve to boldly defy the law.

At least not during the daylight hours.

But tonight...

Yeah, tonight.

Under the cover of darkness.

Turning away, she squeaked as she accidentally bumped into a hard wall.

A hard wall that was really a warm, hard chest she recognized all too well, along with the big, warm hands that settled on her arms.

CHAPTER NINE

THE COLLISION SET Kenzie back a step, but Aidan held her upright.

She tilted her head up, up, up…and looked into his face, which was unfortunately indecipherable.

"You okay?" he asked, his voice low and calm, and concerned.

Okay, concern was good. Concern implied that he hadn't noticed what she'd been about to do. But was she okay? *Hell, no.*

Not even close.

"Are you?" His gaze swept down her body, then up again, as if categorizing her injuries, which reminded her of last night, when he'd also been categorized her body.

With his tongue.

"Yes," she managed. "I'm fine."

"Good. What the hell are you doing here?"

"Funny, I was going to ask you the same thing. Are you following me?"

"No."

"You're not driving a gray sedan and going everywhere I go?"

"I drive a truck, a blue one and I didn't follow you here. I got lucky on the first try. I figured you'd come here and try to do something stupid."

"I did nothing of the kind."

"You don't consider ducking beneath that yellow tape stupid?"

"Only if I'd gotten caught."

"Hello," he said, still holding on to her. His fingers tightened. *"Caught."*

"Yes, but you don't count."

He looked both boggled *and* irritated. "And why is that?"

"Because what are you going to do, arrest me? Last night you were kissing me, touching me, fu—"

"Okay," he said with a low laugh. "Now just hold on a second—"

"I'm just saying." She narrowed her eyes and went for bravado, even though she could hardly breathe while looking at the big blackened sailboat that less than two days ago had been *Blake's Girl*.

Aidan had saved her.

He'd saved her and she was poking at him because she was all twisted up inside. So she let out a breath and looked into his face, where she found a surprising blend of sympathy and old affection mixed in with the frustration and fear.

"I came here to talk," he said. "Not arrest you. Jesus. Now what the hell is this about a gray sedan?"

"Nothing."

He just looked at her for a long moment. "What aren't you telling me?"

"Nothing."

"More like everything." He let out a breath. "Tommy expects you to let him do his job."

"I'm not going to get in his way. I'm going to help him."

"Now see, I don't think he likes help."

"Too bad for him."

"It's going to be too bad for you if you piss him off. He can and will have you arrested if you don't stay out of his way."

"Believe me, I plan to stay out of his way."

"Okay." He nodded. "New subject then."

Uh-oh.

"Last night…"

Kenzie didn't know how she felt about last night. And because she didn't, she absolutely didn't want to talk about it. "Yeah. Now's not a good time for me."

"You don't think so?"

She shook her head.

His eyes lit with something that might have been wry humor. He'd been just as beat up as her yesterday, but unlike her, today he did not look like something the cat dragged in. No, he looked tall and fit, and in his loose cargoes and T-shirt, he seemed very in charge of himself and his world.

She, on the other hand, was in charge of exactly nothing at the moment. "Maybe later." And maybe not.

He hadn't taken his hands off of her arms, and if asked she'd have said she wasn't sure how she felt about that, but that would be a lie. At the moment, his support felt like a lifeline.

Her only lifeline. "Tell me something," she said very quietly, her eyes on his so she didn't miss any little nuance, because this was very, very important to her. "Arson. It's a well studied crime, right? The people who do it, most of them belong to a particular character type. Aggressive. Violent. Repeat offenders."

"Yes," he agreed. "How do you know this?"

"We did a whole plotline about an arsonist last year. Would you characterize Blake as aggressive or violent?"

"Not even close."

"Exactly," she said.

"Which doesn't prove anything. There's physical evidence—"

"Okay," she agreed. She knew about the evidence. "But most arsonists *want* their work admired. Isn't that correct?"

"Yes, but—"

"*But* Blake maintained his innocence. Tommy told me that much."

"Yes," Aidan agreed, his expression reflecting his worry for her, whether he wanted it to or not.

Which she didn't want to face. She meant to do two things when it came to Aidan, especially after last night. First: keep her distance. And second: leave *him* pining for *her*.

It was going to be nearly impossible to handle the second while doing the first but she would give it her best shot. "So can't you concede that it's possible that you're wrong about Blake?"

"I'm not the one accusing him of anything."

She looked at him, really looked at him, and understood something she'd missed before. He didn't want to believe the worst of Blake any more than she did, and that was so much more than she expected from him, from anyone, that it was like a balm to all her fear and grief.

He wasn't against her or Blake. She wasn't completely alone, at least not in that moment, and she found herself closing the gap between them to wrap her arms around his broad shoulders, hugging him hard, so damn relieved to have him there with her.

With a rough sound, his arms came around her, too, and he pulled her in, letting her lean on him. "Kenzie," he whispered, bowing his head over hers. "It's okay. It's going to be okay."

Yeah. Keeping her distance from him was going to be damned tough.

So would be breaking his heart, but she was still going to do it. It was that, or see hers crushed again, and that was simply not going to happen.

AIDAN HAD NEVER been a hugging sort of guy. He loved physical contact, especially the naked kind, with the fairer sex, but touching just out of sheer affection and nothing else? That hadn't really been a part of his life. Having been the sort of child who'd made it difficult for others to like him, much less love him, he hadn't inspired a lot of affection growing up. And working with mostly guys all the time...well, they tended to shove and wrestle rather than hug.

So this, with Kenzie, should have felt awkward. Alien. At the very least it was an intrusion of his personal space that he would have thought would make him squirm to be free.

But it didn't. Even though a piece of her hair was poking him in the eye and she was stepping on his toe, and her nose—pressed against his throat—was icy enough to make him wince, he didn't move.

In fact, he tightened his arms on her, pressing his face into her hair, inhaling her as if he didn't want to let go.

Because he really didn't.

She was warm and soft and sweet, and when her fingers slid into his hair he nearly purred. His hand skimmed down her spine, pressing low on her back, urging her even closer as he just continued to breathe her in.

Just down the dock, two seagulls argued over some found treasure. Water slapped at the wood pylons. Beyond that, the devastation of the fire sat right before their eyes. Aidan didn't want her looking at it. "You need to get out of here."

"Yeah." She stepped back. "I know. I'm going."

He caught her hand, and when she looked at him questioningly, he saw the truth in her eyes. Wherever she was headed, it was to make trouble.

"I'm a big girl now."

Yes. She was a woman who could more than take care of herself. Which in no way eradicated the need within him to protect her. "Have you eaten?"

She stared at him, then let out a low breath. "I tell you I can take care of myself and you want to feed me? Even after I also told you that I only wanted to be with you in order to break your heart?"

"Yeah, see, about that..." He stroked a loose strand of hair off her face, letting his finger trace the rim of her ear, absorbing her little shiver. "I don't really believe you."

"Oh, it's true," she said with utter conviction. "I'm going to break your heart."

"That wasn't the only reason you stayed with me last night. Slept with me."

"Okay, true. You saved my life. I owed you."

He shook his head. "That wasn't it, either."

"What was it then, smart guy?"

"You like being with me."

A helpless laugh escaped her at that.

"I like being with you, too, Kenz."

She shook her head. "You're off your rocker."

"Already established. So. Food?"

She stared at him, then caved. "I guess I could eat."

She followed him in her car to Sunrise Café. Aidan had no idea why he took her there, other than that taking her back to his place, where they'd be alone, seemed like a really bad idea.

Sheila was thrilled to see him and gave him a huge hug, smiling with some speculation at Kenzie. Even though it was afternoon by then, Aidan ordered a large breakfast. When Kenzie tried to get just coffee, he merely doubled his order, and then took her up to the roof.

There was a long bench against the far wall, where they sat to watch the surf. It was rough, which didn't stop the surfers from enjoying it.

Kenzie stared out at the waves. "It's nice up here. A good place to think. You come here a lot?"

"I do."

"Sheila's fond of you."

"Very," he agreed.

She smiled at him, and just like that, melted his heart. "You've made some good ties," she said softly.

He got a little lost in her eyes, and leaned in with some half-baked idea of kissing her, and—

"Come and get it!" Sheila yelled up from the bottom of the stairwell.

Sighing—what else could he do—Aidan led the way down to the crowded dining room. Sheila seated them, then brought them their plates, winking at Aidan before leaving.

Kenzie looked down at her loaded plate. "I'm not that hungry."

"Uh-huh." He nudged her fork closer to her fingers. "That's what you always used to say. You'd tell me you weren't hungry and then you'd eat everything off my plate, remember?"

Humor lit her eyes. "What I remember is that you were my boyfriend. You were supposed to share."

"So, what are you saying? That you wouldn't, say, eat off Chad's plate?"

"Chase. And he's vegan and doesn't eat anything that isn't completely raw, so, no, I wouldn't."

Aidan leaned over and stroked another stray strand of hair off her cheek. He had no idea why he kept finding excuses to touch her, other than she looked sad and just a little lost. She wore no makeup, and all those gorgeous blond waves had rioted around her face, a few long strands curling around her jaw. It was just Kenzie. No smoke and mirrors, no pomp or celebrity. Just the woman who'd once touched his heart.

And, apparently, still did.

So he did what he'd wanted to do on the roof—he leaned over their food and kissed her, just once, softly on the lips. When he pulled back, she gave a baffled little smile and touched her fingers to her mouth. "What was that for?"

Before he could answer, Zach walked up to their table. "Hey."

"Hey," Aidan said in surprise. "Kenzie, this is Zach. Zach, Kenzie is—"

"Blake's sister." Zach's eyes softened as he looked at her. "I miss your brother."

"Thank you," she murmured. "Me, too."

Zach turned to Aidan and handed him a file.

"What's this?"

"I wanted you to have it while I was gone. In case you need it for anything."

Aidan opened the file and instantly knew what he held. All the evidence Zach had gathered over the past few months on the mysterious arsons. Zach had been the first one to suspect something was going on and the first to go to Tommy for answers. Closing the file he met Zach's steady gaze. "Thanks. Want to join us?"

"Can't. Brooke's waiting for me. I just talked to Eddie and Sam. Did you know there was another explosion last night? The hardware store on Sixth."

"Injuries?"

"Several, and one death. Tracy Gibson."

Aidan's stomach dropped. The woman Blake had had a crush on for months before his death.

Kenzie divided her gaze between them. "Who's Tracy?"

"She was an employee at the hardware store," Zach told her. "Same setup as *Blake's Girl,*" he said to Aidan, tapping the file with meaning. "So keep this."

Aidan understood. Zach thought he might need the info in the file when he was gone.

"Nice meeting you," Zach said to Kenzie. With a squeeze to Aidan's shoulder, he left.

"So what does that mean?" Kenzie asked. "If there was a similar explosion, maybe Blake's boat wasn't an accident."

"Maybe."

"A new serial arsonist?" she scoffed. "What are the chances of that in a small town like this?"

"I don't know."

"I know," she said. "Next to nil."

She was watching him with sadness still in her eyes, along with a sense of sharp intelligence that said she wasn't going to let this go. The brash tilt of her chin alluded to a strength of will, of passion, he knew first-hand, and suddenly he was afraid for her.

For her, *of her,* and of the feelings she invoked inside him. Damn, not again... Not falling for her again, he told himself. But it didn't matter that he was seated across from her in a crowded café, surrounded by people.

She was all he saw.

He watched her push her food around the plate for a few minutes, then wrapped his fingers around her wrist, guiding her fork to a large bite of eggs and bringing it to her mouth.

She took it into her mouth, chewed and swallowed, all with her gaze never leaving his. "You keep looking at me like you care."

"I do."

"You shouldn't."

"Why not?"

"Because I'm not going to care about you back." At that, she broke eye contact and stared down at the food. "At least not like I did before."

"So you've mentioned."

"I mean it."

"I believe you." He also believed that she just might get her big wish, because looking at her sitting there, knowing *she'd* be walking away from *him* this time, caused a strange sensation deep inside him. He'd have sworn it was his heart rolling over and exposing its underbelly.

Kenzie took another bite of food as his cell phone buzzed. It was Dispatch. "Sorry," he said, standing. "I have to take this."

"No problem." She was suddenly engrossed in her food, not even looking up when he went outside to get good enough reception to hear that two firefighters had come down with the flu. They needed replacements for the next shift. So much for a day off—he was going back on duty, starting now.

He turned to go back inside the café and nearly bumped into Kenzie. "Sorry," she said, flashing a smile that didn't quite meet her eyes. "I've got to go."

Huh. That had been *his* line.

"I paid the bill—"

He reached for his wallet. "Let me—"

But she put her hand over his and shook her head. "It's on me. Consider it a very small down payment."

"For what?"

"For what I owe you for saving my life."

"Kenzie—"

"Thank you," she said softly, looking into his eyes, making his head spin. "I'm not sure I said that enough. I am extremely grateful."

Wait. That sounded like a goodbye. "Okay, hold on a second. Are you—"

Going up on tiptoes, she put a hand to his chest, leaned in and kissed him on the jaw. She added a smile to the mix, one that went all the way to her eyes this time as she touched her fingers to her lips and then blew him another kiss.

Then she turned and walked away.

As he'd once done to her. "Kenzie."

But she'd already gotten into her car. Where the hell was she going? She revved the engine and was gone, out of the lot, perhaps out of his world. He stood there a moment, absorbing a barrage of emotions, starting with regret and ending with a surprising hurt, and then he shrugged it off and walked inside to say goodbye to Sheila. That's when his head stopped spinning and it hit him.

Kenzie had stolen his file.

CHAPTER TEN

UNFORTUNATELY FOR KENZIE, the doggie convention was still in town. She tried a couple of B and Bs and got excited when a cute front desk clerk recognized her and said he'd stir up a room. But then he picked up his phone and yelled, "Ma! Get out of the room, I've got a girl!"

Kenzie shouldn't have been surprised, since her karma was clearly still on vacation. She made the clerk leave his mother in the room and escaped. Back in her car, she sighed, feeling very alone.

She missed Blake.

And dammit, she already missed Aidan, too. Missed his voice, his smile, his touch.

How was that even possible? She'd just left him. She'd stolen his file for God's sake. No doubt he was cursing her right this minute.

And definitely *not* missing her.

She pulled into the library and made herself comfortable on a large chair in a far corner, then opened the file. Almost immediately she felt an odd prickle of awareness, and then the hair on the back of her neck stood up.

She was being watched again.

She craned her neck left and then right, but no one in her immediate area was so much as looking at her. Behind her was a set of shelves, and she shifted, trying to see through a gap to the aisle on the other side.

Nothing.

Clearly she was still in the process of losing her mind. Determined, she went back to the file. Zach and Aidan had been thorough. There was a list of fire calls from Firehouse Thirty-Four over the past six months, five of them highlighted. The questionable fires, she realized.

The arsons Blake had ultimately been accused of starting.

Attached were details of those five properties: architectural plans, permits, a history of ownership, purchases and sales. Each had been plotted out on a map, and scrutinized up one side and down the other, including everything that had been found on-site after the fire.

Zach had noted finding a metal mesh trash can at each site, and even had a picture of one, from the fire just before the one at Zach's own house. As she was looking at it, her cell phone vibrated. She nearly ignored it until she saw it was the same local cell phone number as before, and she grabbed it. "Hello?" she said breathlessly.

When several people in chairs nearby glared at her, especially one older woman going through a stack of history books, Kenzie hunched her shoulders, mouthed a "sorry" and whispered "hello" much more softly.

An equally soft voice spoke in return. "Forget about it, forget about *all* of it, and go back to Los Angeles."

Kenzie clutched the phone. She couldn't tell if she recognized the speaker because the voice was purposely being disguised. "Is that a threat?"

"You're going to be stubborn. Goddammit."

"Who is this?" she demanded.

"It doesn't matter. Just get the hell out of Santa Rey."

"So you *are* threatening me."

"If I said yes, would you go?"

"No."

"Shit." There was a beat of silence. "Okay, listen to me. There's only one way out of this."

"What?" she said, forgetting to whisper, receiving more glares for that. With effort, she lowered her voice. "What do you mean?"

"Your laptop was destroyed in the boat fire?"

"How do you know that?"

"You have backup."

"What does that have to do with—" She went still as it hit her. She and Blake had shared files. Music files, movie files…they'd emailed and IM'd each other regularly. And once a week he'd send her a large backup file from his laptop so that if it ever crashed, she could just send him back what he needed. She'd done the same. She'd saved all her stuff, *and* Blake's, in her Yahoo account. All she had to do was get to another computer. *"Who are you?"*

"Check the demos. That's the key."

"What?" Kenzie clutched the phone. "What does that mean? Who are—"

But she knew before she even finished her sentence that he was gone. But who was he? A friend of Blake's? *"Dammit."*

"Shh!" everyone around her hissed.

Yeah, yeah, fine. But the prickle in the back of her neck hadn't gone away. She got to her feet and moved to the end of the aisle, peeking around the corner just in time to catch sight of the back of a guy running away. No red shirt this time but she knew it was the same guy she'd seen at the hospital. She hightailed it after him, but when she got to the other end of the aisle, she plowed directly into the librarian.

"No running in the library!"

"Sorry." Kenzie stepped around her, but it was too late. Her helpful mysterious caller was gone. She turned back to the librarian. "Can I use an online computer?"

"You have to sign up."

"Okay, where?"

"We're closing in half an hour, and the computers are in use until then. How about the morning?"

"Fine." She'd spend tonight going through the boat and Blake's place for anything that could help her. Then she'd borrow Aidan's computer—if he let her—or come back here to prove that Blake had been set up. Because that was the only answer she was willing to accept.

Someone had framed him, was *still* framing him.

And she was going to find out who.

AT THE STATION, Aidan was run ragged by one call after another. Near the end of the shift, his unit was called out to a secondary fire at the hardware store, where the explosion from two days ago had killed Tracy. Looking at the scene woke Aidan right up. The new fire wasn't from any smoldering spark left over from the explosion. No way. This fire had been set.

Purposely.

In a wire mesh trash can.

Tommy was already there, and at the look on Aidan's face, shook his head. "Don't start."

"Arson."

"I said don't start."

"Let me guess. We're not going to have this conversation."

"Bingo." Tommy sounded extremely tense. "And this time I'll tell you why." He got up in Aidan's face. "Because I'm close, okay? I'm very, *very* close to finishing this. So you need to let me do just that. Got it?"

Aidan didn't see that he had a choice. Later, back at the station, he stretched out on the station couch, closing his bleary eyes, needing to think.

Somehow it was all connected, he just knew it... He fell asleep trying to piece it all together, and then dreamed of a certain hot, curvy, sweet woman. A hot, curvy, sexy woman who happened to also be a *thief*.

He woke up when someone sat on him.

And then bounced on him.

Opening his eyes, he met Cristina's frowning ones. "Trying to sleep here."

"No, you're not. Your eyes are open."

"Watch this." He closed them again.

She bounced again, a maneuver that threatened to break his legs. "How's Blake's sister?"

"Why are you asking me?"

"Because you're sleeping with her. Is she okay?"

He shook his head. "How? How do you know what I barely know?"

"Rumor mill." Her derisive humor hid her misery. Cristina was hurting. Hurting over losing Blake, her partner. Hurting over somehow blowing it with Dustin. She was so hard on the outside that they all forgot how soft and sensitive she was deep inside. She'd loved Blake like a brother, and cared about Kenzie by default.

"How is she, Aidan?"

"I don't know," he answered honestly.

"What do you mean you don't know?"

"She hasn't returned my phone calls."

"So you're losing your touch, too." She broke off, momentarily distracted when Dustin walked into the room.

The tall, tough-bodied, soft-hearted EMT pushed up his glasses, glanced at Cristina and a muscle jumped in his jaw.

Cristina didn't appear to breathe. Five agonizing seconds passed, and finally, she looked away first.

Dustin merely sighed.

The two of them had been doing some kind of emotional tap dance for weeks now. Dustin said he wanted more. Cristina said she didn't.

Now the tension in the room was so thick Aidan could hardly even see them anymore. "Hey, here's an idea. You two could lust after each other in secret and then ignore each other in person. Because it's not awkward at all."

"Shut up, Aidan." Cristina sent a glare in Dustin's direction, one that said *you're an idiot*.

Without a word, Dustin walked away, into the kitchen.

Cristina expelled a low breath.

"Looks like I'm not the only one losing my touch," Aidan noted. "What did you do?"

"How do you know I did something?"

"Please."

Cristina sighed. "He's got his panties all unraveled because I went out with an ex."

"Ouch."

"No. No ouch. It was just dinner for God's sake. No biggee."

"Yeah. But it was dinner with a guy you've gotten naked with."

She shrugged, but dejection had settled over her pretty features. "Whatever."

"Cristina."

"I told you, it was just dinner." She got off of his legs, making sure to get an elbow in his gut. "And if he can't see that then screw him."

"Why don't you just talk to him? Tell him the truth?"

"Talking isn't what I want." She headed outside, slamming the door as she went.

Aidan's cell rang and he leaped for it, hoping for Kenzie, but he got Tommy instead.

"Might want to get down to county," the inspector said in an undecipherable tone.

"Why?"

"Because I had your girlfriend arrested."

"You arrested Kenzie?"

"You have another girlfriend I don't know about?"

"She's not my—" He pinched the bridge of his nose. "What the hell happened?"

"She's in for trespassing and interfering with a crime scene, so you figure it out. You don't control your women very well."

"She's not my woman!"

"Either way, I'd hurry. Oh, and get your checkbook. This date's going to cost you big."

CHAPTER ELEVEN

JAIL WASN'T NEARLY as adventurous as it'd been that time Kenzie had been arrested on her soap. Then she'd had a costume director and a makeup artist. Oh, and nice, soft, flattering lights. Plus she'd been able to walk off the set when the director had yelled "cut", and had sipped her iced tea and laughed it all off.

No such luxuries today.

Real life sucked.

She was given her phone call—which went to her attorney, who promised to work on getting her out. With Kenzie's own checkbook, of course.

After several hours in a holding cell, during which she contemplated the odd and unwelcome turn her life had taken, and also chewed on a few nails, she was handed her see-through baggie of personal belongings—that was twice in two days—and shown the door.

Standing in front of it wasn't her attorney, but her own gorgeous, personal savior.

Aidan was dressed in his firefighter uniform, which told her he'd come right from the job. He still wore his firefighter badass expression, too, and was looking more than a little bit temperamental as well.

Yeah. Not exactly thrilled to see her.

Nor was she thrilled to see him.

Okay, so a little part of her was. The bad girl part of

her, which reared its horny head and begged *Oh, please can we have him just one more time?*

She ignored that and her quivery belly, and tried to brush past him.

"What, no thank you?" He shifted so that she was forced to bump into him.

Backing up, she put her hands on her hips and sent him a glare as mean as she could conjure up after a few hours spent in jail. "I didn't call you."

"Yeah. I noticed."

There were several people milling around, all from a different part of society than she was used to. The guy closest to her might have been fifty, or a hundred and fifty, it was hard to tell with the multitude of hats and coats he was wearing, despite it being summer. He pulled out a cigarette and a match, and even though she saw it coming, when he struck the match to the match-box and the little *whoosh* hit her ears, she cringed.

Aidan was there in a second, holding her steady, which only further embarrassed her. "Easy."

"Damn." She let out a shaky breath. "What *is* that?"

"Post traumatic—"

She waggled a finger in his face. "Don't say it."

"—stress. Why didn't you call me, Kenzie?"

"Who did?"

"Tommy."

"Rat-fink bastard." It was coming back to her, her childhood here—the small town mentality, the utter lack of secrets, the way everyone stuck their nose in everyone else's business. She'd had enough of that from her early years to last her a lifetime.

She and Blake had been kept together as they'd gone into the child care protective services, where they'd landed in a total of three foster homes, each as kind and as warm as they could possibly be, and for that she was more than grateful, she was also lucky—but she'd never really settled into any of them. She didn't tend to settle, didn't tend to get comfortable; it was what had made her so certain Aidan was the one.

Look how that had blown up in her face.

When she'd gone off to Los Angeles and begun acting, she'd found heaven. Pretending to live someone else's life, already all scripted out? Perfect. She'd loved it. *Still* loved it.

But a small part of her knew that she couldn't always rely on a script. That at some point she would have to wing it. She'd eventually need a life, a *real* one, and she'd always figured that life would somehow be entwined with her brother's, maybe even right here in Santa Rey....

But now there was nothing for her here, nothing except proving Blake's innocence.

Aidan caught her arm as she stepped outside. She yanked free and he put up his hands, letting her step away from him as they walked outside. He leaned a hip against a tree, looking big and tall and attitude-ridden as he eyed her like she was a lit fuse.

His hair had been finger-combed at best. She could smell soap and man, and the potent mix of testosterone and pheromones boggled her mind. If she lived to be two hundred years old, she'd never understand her attraction to him. Back in her L.A. world, she had access to dozens of gorgeous men. Hundreds.

But while some had been nice dalliances, none of them had ever really gotten anywhere. Probably because a good number of the men she met were like her.

Pretend.

Not Aidan. He lived life with his eyes wide open, no script needed. His job demanded a lot of him, and he was tough because of it, but he hadn't ever shied away from something just because it was hard. Except for her.

"Thanks for bailing me out," she conceded.

"Need a ride to your car? Or are you going to manage that on your own, too?"

The sun was warm and bright, and she stood still in it for a moment, tilting her head up to it, inhaling deeply. Then she turned to the man who had once been her everything. Whether she liked it or not—and for the record, she didn't—he could still stop her heart, make her pulse race, and worst of all, make her hormones stand up and shimmy. "Yeah. A ride would be great, if you don't mind."

He let out a sound that told her what he thought of that, and took her to his truck.

"About that ride…" She slowed, dragging her feet. "Everything's still booked. Maybe there's something—"

"You know where there's something." He turned on the engine and pulled out of the lot. "At my place."

"Yeah." She shook her head. "No."

"Yeah no?"

She sighed. "It's just that staying with you seems like a whole lot of trouble I don't want to face."

"Why?"

"Because I don't want to lead you on."

"I thought you enjoyed exacting your revenge on my body."

With more than a slight twinge of regret and, *dammit,* guilt, she avoided his gaze.

"Come on, Kenz, be honest. You're not afraid of hurting me. You're afraid *you'll* get hurt."

Wasn't that the plain ugly truth.

"You made sure I understood that you'd changed," he said softly, looking over at her for a beat before returning his attention to the road. "Now you have to understand something. I've changed as well."

Yes. Yes, he had.

"Look, you wanted to know what happened all those years ago?" he asked. "I got scared, that's what the hell happened. I'd always lived my life without letting people inside my heart, where they could hurt me. But you got in, and, yeah, that terrified me. You're doing it again, by the way, getting in, and I'm not any more thrilled about it now than I was then."

Something warm slid through her at his words, and the low, rough tone in which they were spoken. Warm, and dangerously seductive.

He pulled into his driveway and shut off the engine, turning in his seat to face her. "You'll have to make do without the five-star rating." He paused a beat. "Although there are certain five-star services I *do* offer."

When she met his gaze she saw the sparkle of pure wicked trouble in his eyes. *Oh, boy.* "Aidan—"

"I'm talking about my breakfasts, which you happened to miss out on. And then there's my massage specialty." He didn't add any obvious eyebrow waggle or other suggestive gesture, but his eyes crinkled and she knew he was *thinking* suggestively.

Yup. Dangerously seductive. She already knew how erotic his touch could be, just how earthy, how naughty, and she wasn't ready to go back there. Not if she intended to be the one to walk away this time.

And there would be walking away when this was over...

Even while she was thinking it, he took her hand and led her to his door. Her instinct was to make a smart-ass comment to piss him off, chase him away, and yet she didn't do anything but allow him to open the door for her. Once she started to step inside, he stopped her. When she met his gaze, he asked, "You planning anything else I should know about?"

"Like?"

"Shit. Anything. It could be anything."

The sun was bright. The surf behind them loud and choppy. She loved the scent of the ocean. She'd missed that, working long, long days on set in the middle of Los Angeles. Now that she'd been cancelled, she could see taking a laptop out on the beach and just writing to her heart's content if she wanted. "My immediate plans involve a shower."

"That's all?" he asked so warily that she smiled.

"Yeah. That's all."

He touched the corner of her smiling mouth. "That's a good look for you."

"What are you talking about, I smile all the time."

"On TV, maybe. But I haven't seen much of it here."

"Well, maybe that's because I was in a fire, then facing the fact that my brother's dead, and then..." And then she'd been in his bed, naked, panting, sobbing his name, holding onto his head as his mouth and then his body had taken her to heaven—

"*That* look," he said, pointing at her. "I want to know what you were thinking just then to put *that* look on your face."

She crossed her arms over her suddenly aching breasts. "Nothing."

"You are such a liar," he chided softly.

He gestured her inside his place, and she took a better look around than she had when she'd been fresh out of the hospital, and then fresh out of his bed. She saw the pretty windows, the wood floors he'd done himself, and felt another ache, this one in her chest.

She knew that growing up, Aidan hadn't had much of a stable home life, either. He'd been shuffled around as much as she had. Going into the fire academy had changed his life, given him a team, but more than that, his first *real* friendships. The kind of friendships that would last, the kind of friend that had his back no matter what. He still hadn't had any real understanding of what that meant when she'd gone off to Los Angeles, but she could tell it had come to him in the years since. There was an easy confidence about him, an air that said he'd been well liked, well taken care of...

Well loved.

Her heart did a little flop at that because she hadn't given herself the same. Oh, sure, she was liked. She'd been taken care of. But loved by someone other than Blake?

No.

And if she took away the fame, leaving just small-town girl Kenzie Stafford, what would actually be left?

The answer was as unsettling as the thought, especially given that now she really was without that fancy job. "Aidan?"

He'd headed for the kitchen, but stopped and turned to her. "Yeah?"

"Thanks."

"For?"

"For bailing me out. For waiting to make sure I was okay."

He leaned back against the wall and studied her. "So why did you do it, Kenz? Why did you go back after I'd warned you not to—" He broke off and shook his head. "Never mind. I just heard my own words and realized *exactly* why you did it. *Because* I warned you not to."

"Am I that stubborn?"

"Hell, yeah, you're that stubborn."

She rolled her eyes, then caught the flash of humor in his. He was laughing at her, and not with her, which should have made her defensive and possibly bitchy, but in spite of herself, she let out a laugh, too. "Okay, so it wasn't the smartest thing I've done. But it was the right thing."

"How about stealing my file, was that the right thing, too?"

She let out a low breath. "I was wondering when we were going to get to that."

He just looked at her, big and bad and…patient. So damn patient. She pulled the file from her bag and handed it over. "Thanks."

"I'd say you're welcome, if I'd given it to you."

"You'd have done the same thing in my position."

"You think so?"

She looked into his compelling eyes and felt her breath catch. "Okay, no. You would have asked. But maybe you're a better person than I am."

His eyes expressed his surprise at that statement. They both knew she hadn't always considered him such a great guy. "People change," she whispered, mirroring his words back to her. "Right?"

"That's right." The smile hit his eyes before his lips slowly curved, and there was an answering quiver that began in her belly. *Oh, boy.* Not good. He was standing too close, and not being annoying or antagonistic, and suddenly it all seemed too intimate.

She started to turn away but that was cowardice, and if she was going to learn anything while being back here in Santa Rey, it was not going to be that, so she faced him again. "I really am sorry for dragging you into this. For getting arrested and you having to bail me out. For driving you crazy. Pick any of the above."

"You didn't drag me into anything."

"Maybe not, but I'm about to." She let out a breath. "I need to tell you something."

"Okay." When she didn't go on, he raised an eyebrow. "Is it something that's going to get you arrested again?"

"No. I'm kind of hoping to avoid repeating that experience."

"Good."

"But there are things you should know. Things you're not going to like."

"Try me."

"Okay. I've been getting calls from someone I think is trying to help me."

He stared at her. "Your local cell caller?"

"Yes. He told me the key, whatever that means, is in Blake's computer files."

"He?"

"I think so. But I can't place the voice, he's disguised it."

"How the hell does he know the key's in Blake's computer files?" Aidan asked her.

"I don't know."

"Blake's laptop was never found. I'm betting it went up in *Blake's Girl*."

"As did mine. But with a computer, I could access my backup files, which would include Blake's backup files."

"I have a computer." He was close enough that she could see the green swirling in his light brown eyes. The scar bisecting his left eyebrow, the lines on his face, only added character, and a sexiness she couldn't have explained to save her life.

His mouth was slightly curved and she knew if she leaned in and touched hers to it, his lips would be warm and skilled, and most of all, giving.

"I didn't think I'd be happy to see you," she murmured, stepping closer. "But I've been proven wrong on two accounts now. When you saved me from the fire, and when I came out of jail and saw you standing there."

"Just the two?"

"Well, *maybe* one other time…"

Leaning close, he let his mouth brush her ear. "Try a couple."

At the reminder of how he'd made her come *several* times, easily she might add, as if he knew her body better than she did, a little shiver of awareness went down her spine, chased by another one, this one pure anticipation.

He could do it again. He could take her there again, to heaven, to oblivion… Only this time it wouldn't be adrenaline. This time she'd go in with her eyes wide open. His needed to be as well.

"I was worried about you," he murmured. "You've

got to stay out of this one, Kenzie. Stay out of Tommy's way."

Somehow her face was nuzzling his throat, and she was trying to breathe him in. "I'm going to prove Blake's innocence in all this," she told him, liking the feel of her lips against his skin. "No matter the cost."

"Even if the price is my friendship?"

Her throat actually tightened at the thought and she pulled back to look into his eyes. "Is it going to cost me that?"

"Depends." He took her hand, put it on his chest and offered her a smile. "You still intending on stomping all over my tender heart?"

At that, and the crinkles at the corners of his eyes, the ones telling her he was teasing her, she out and out laughed, feeling much of her tension drain away. "Yes."

His hands went to her hips, pulling her closer, and she stared into his face, feeling so at home in his house that she found herself hesitating, not for the first time that day, and wishing she had a script for what came next.

"You're thinking again," he murmured.

"Yeah."

He leaned back against the front door, unexpectedly giving her space. Space she thought she'd wanted, but found she didn't want at all. "I really did intend to stomp all over your heart, you know. When I first saw you again, I wanted to hurt you the way you'd hurt me. But then we kissed."

"We did a lot more than kiss."

She flashed back to that night, when she'd climbed into bed with him, pressing her icy feet to his, then her body. She remembered realizing he was naked and warm and strong and hard...*God*. He'd been so utterly irresistible, she'd lost her head. And, yeah, they'd done a lot more than kiss. "Fine. We kissed, and then I decided I should sleep with you and then walk away. Perfect, neat revenge."

"Neat, maybe. But not perfect." His eyes were glittering with knowledge, hard won. "Because it wasn't as easy as you thought, was it?"

No, it hadn't been. Because it'd been amazing between them. So damned amazing. "Maybe I've been looking at this wrong."

He didn't move from the door, just kept looking at her, his eyes warm, his mouth curved, his body big and bad and so gorgeous she could hardly stand it.

She wanted him.

Again.

Still.

"Maybe it's not about sleeping with you once and walking away," she heard herself say. "Maybe it's about letting this thing take its own lead for as long as I'm here."

"'This thing'? You mean the way we apparently can't stay out of each other's pants?"

At the huskiness in his voice, her nipples hardened. "Yes."

CHAPTER TWELVE

AIDAN PUSHED AWAY from the door and came toward Kenzie, all easy, loose-limbed confidence, yet radiating an intensity that made her breath catch. He didn't stop until they were toe-to-toe, and she slowly tipped up her head to look into his inscrutable eyes.

"You want to have sex," he said silkily. "Here. Tonight. Now."

Her breath caught at his bluntness. "And then maybe again later."

"Later," he repeated, as if trying to process this.

"Maybe even until I leave Santa Rey. At which time we both walk away, eyes wide open."

He just stared at her for the longest moment. "What happened to trouncing on my heart?"

"It seems you were right. I don't really want to hurt you."

When he shot her a not-buying-it look, she caved. "Okay, so I want to hurt you less than I want to sleep with you again."

"You know, you'd think I'd be tough enough to walk away from such an overwhelmingly romantic offer," he said drily, sounding both intrigued and baffled. "But apparently..." He put his hands on her hips. "I'm not."

She offered a smile that was sheer nerve. "So...yes?"

His eyes never wavered, holding hers, leveling her

as he pulled her in. "I don't know, Kenzie. I'm a little afraid…"

"Be serious."

His smile was crooked and impossibly endearing. "I am. This time you could really do it, whether you're trying to or not. This time, you just might take out my heart."

"Come on," she quipped, even as a part of her was afraid he was right, for both of them. "If we're just having a physical relationship and nothing else, how can we get hurt?"

With a soft laugh, he slid his hands up her spine, and then back again, low enough now to cup her butt and squeeze.

He was hard.

Bending his head, he put his mouth to her ear and let out a breath that made her shiver in longing. "Just a physical relationship, Kenzie? Is that all this is? Really?" He sank his teeth into her lobe and she shivered again.

"It—it's all it *should* be," she managed.

Another soft, deprecating laugh rumbled through his chest, this one aimed at the both of them. "Okay, well as long as we're being honest, you should know…" His hands glided up her spine again, this time beneath her shirt to touch bare skin. "Even though you *are* going to hurt me, it's not enough to make me say no. Truth is, nothing could…"

She opened her mouth to say something, but then he kissed the spot he'd just nipped at, soothing the ache as his fingers stroked over her skin. Her eyes drifted shut, and she slid her arms around his neck, pressing close. "No pain, no gain," she whispered, and he let out another low laugh as he lifted her up and carried her to his bedroom.

To his bed.

He settled over her, looking down into her face for a beat before lowering his head and taking her mouth with his demanding one.

If simply walking into his house had felt like a homecoming, then this, here, now, felt even more so. He felt like home, he smelled like home, and he tasted even better; she hesitated, thinking, *uh-oh*.

His hands came up to hold her face. "What?"

She stared up into his eyes and saw herself reflected there, as if they were one, and although it was deeply unsettling to realize that this time she could fall even harder for him—if she let herself—she also couldn't imagine walking away, without being in his arms again.

"Kenz?"

"Nothing, it's nothing." And she pulled him down for another kiss as the heat of him seeped into her bones, warming her with a sensual promise of what was to come. Those big, warm hands slid along her arms, lifting them up over her head, entwining their fingers as his mouth continued to plunder hers, delivering on that promise.

It was familiar, and it was comforting, and yet it was so, so much more as well. Not since being with Aidan six years ago had she given any thought to what it would be like to be with a guy long enough that he felt...like home. She was a woman who liked change, who liked the new and exciting, who lived off the lines someone else wrote for her each day.

But with Aidan, she knew what he felt like, what he tasted like, exactly how crazy he could drive her with a touch of a single finger, and yet being with him felt almost unbearably *right,* and far more arousing than she could have ever imagined.

Still kissing her, he pulled off her top, then her skirt. Her new bra was a front hook, which didn't slow him down at all, and when he had her naked except her panties, he hooked his fingers in the thin strip of cotton on her hips and let his gaze meet hers. Then he tugged, slipping the underwear down her legs and off, sailing them over one shoulder. Towering over her, fully dressed while she was as naked as she could get, he let out a low breath. "You're so beautiful."

"And you're overdressed." Still in his fire gear, in fact...

"In a minute." He was kneeling between her legs. He spread his, which in turn spread hers, and his gaze took her in, in one fell swoop, heating her skin everywhere he looked. He traced his fingers over her breasts, her belly, her thighs.

Between.

When he bent his head with fierce intent, she sucked in a breath, a breath that clogged her throat when he replaced his fingers with his mouth.

"Aidan," she managed, hardly recognizing her own voice. "I—"

His tongue encircled her tender, sensitized flesh, making her quiver from the inside out, and she promptly forgot what she'd meant to say. While his tongue and fingers circled and teased and stroked, she gripped the sheets and stared down at him. His hair stood up, from her fingers, she realized. His eyes were closed, his expression dreamy as he brought her such bliss she could hardly even see, much less think.

But she didn't close her eyes. She watched him concentrate on her pleasure as if it were his own, took in his moves, the moves that were driving her right out of her ever-loving mind.

It was as if he knew what made her tick, inside and out. That was a terrifying thought, really. Because the girl he'd once known no longer existed, and since then... well, she hadn't really let anyone know her.

An ever-changing script.

That was her life.

A life she was no longer sure about. But having him take her apart the way he was, *that* she was sure about.

He opened his eyes, so molten hot that they were nearly black, and looked up at her. He was sure, too, which should have stopped her cold, and she stirred. "Aidan—"

"Shh."

Then he swirled his tongue in a precise rhythm over ground zero, and she lost it.

Completely.

Lost.

It.

Panting for breath, arching up off the mattress and into his mouth, she dug her fingers into the sheets, throwing her head back at the peak, sobbing out his name.

Slowly he brought her back to planet earth. She closed her eyes, savoring the pleasure, still quivering and pulsing as he kissed his way back up her body, his tongue stroking a rib, a nipple, her throat...and then he cupped her face and smiled at her.

"You shushed me," she said, her voice sounding weak and raspy.

"It was for a good cause." He rocked his hips into hers.

"I'm going to get you back for that."

He smiled wickedly. "Should I be scared?"

"Terrified." Rolling him over, she sat on him and tugged his uniform shirt off. She could have spent a year lapping him up with nothing but her tongue. He had a tight body, toned from years of physical labor. His chest was broad, hard, his belly rippled with sinew and rising and falling in a way that assured her she was in no way alone in this almost chemical-like attraction they shared, which transcended both time and logic.

His hands went to the button on his pants to help speed up the process, and she ran her fingers up the taut, corded muscles of his abs. He unzipped, she tugged, and then nearly drooled at the sight of the part of him so happy to see her.

She licked her lips.

He groaned.

She kissed him, on the very tip.

"Kenz—" he choked out, tunneling his fingers through her hair.

Since her mouth was now full, she couldn't answer, and he said something completely unintelligible anyway, which, she had to admit, only egged her on. God, she loved rendering this big, bad, tough man completely incapable of speech. Loved the power that surged through her at the way he was breathing, saying her name.

Loved so much about it that it scared her. Scared her into being even more bold and brazen so that she didn't have to think about how much being with him meant to her.

How much he meant to her.

Using her hands and mouth, she drew him to the edge. "Two-minute warning," he groaned out, his hands fisted in the sheets at his sides as she ran her tongue up his length. "Okay, thirty seconds. *Maybe*."

She kept going until he swore and grabbed a condom, nudging her to her back, his hands running up the undersides of her arms until they were over her head. His knee spread her legs, his thigh rubbing against the core of her.

"In," she gasped, arching into him. "In me now."

Lowering his body to hers, he nipped at her lower lip, then kissed her, hard and deep, his tongue slipping into her mouth at the very moment he slipped into her body. "Like that?"

She couldn't answer. Hell, she could hardly breathe.

"Kenzie?"

"Yes," she managed, then shuddered as he withdrew, only to thrust into her again. And again. *"Like that."*

The feel of him, thick and hot and filling her to the brink, had her gasping his name, wrapping her legs around his hips, leaving her unable to remember exactly what she was supposedly paying him back for. Her toes were curling, her skin feeling too tight for her body, which seemed to swell from the inside out. "Aidan—"

"Come," he demanded, grinding his teeth in what looked like agony. "I want to feel you come before I—"

She burst in mindless, blind sensation, and barely heard his strangled answering groan as he exploded.

For long moments afterward, they lay there entwined, panting and damp, and powerless to move, their breathing echoing loudly through the bedroom.

"Is it just me," she finally managed, "or does that get better and better?"

"Oh, yeah."

She fell quiet a moment, but then couldn't resist. "You think it'll keep happening? You know, until I leave?"

"If it does, it's likely to kill me."

"Yes." She sighed dreamily. "But what a way to go."

His soft huff of laughter was the last thing she remembered before she drifted off to sleep.

AIDAN WOKE UP sometime later with a smile, his body ready for another round. In the pitch-dark, he rolled over for Kenzie.

And got nothing.

With a very bad feeling in his gut, he sat up. "You're gone, aren't you?" he said into the night.

When he got no answer, he tossed back the covers and got out of bed, but it was too late. She had left. He told himself he wasn't her keeper, and she could go wherever she wanted, but he'd been lulled into the impression that she hadn't been done with him yet.

She *wasn't* done with him, not yet. Which meant she was probably out there looking to poke her nose into the arsons. Aidan hurriedly got dressed. He had no idea where she was but he needed to find out, because with whatever information she'd get, she'd go snooping into things that were guaranteed to piss off Tommy.

Hell. They'd just spent hours in his bed. And in his shower. And then his bed again. Hadn't he tired her out?

His stomach was grumbling and his head starting to pound when he picked up his cell phone and called hers; he was shocked when she answered.

"Hi," she said in that soft, breathless voice that had only a few hours before made him come.

Just hearing it stirred him halfway to life. He was little better than Pavlov's dogs. "Where are you?"

"Oh, out and about." She still sounded breathless.

"Kenzie, what are you doing?"

"Um…exercising?"

"That's a bad word to you."

"Not anymore. Do you have any idea how much work it takes to stay in TV shape?"

And then he heard it, the unmistakable sound of a sliding door either opening or closing. "Where are you?"

"Whoops, bad connection," she said.

He gnashed his teeth together. "We have a great connection. What are you up to?"

"Wow, I can hardly hear you…"

"Kenz—"

"Gotta go."

He didn't have to hear the click to know she'd shut her phone. Nor did he bother with swearing. Instead, he grabbed his keys and went after her, figuring her options were severely limited. She wouldn't have gone back to the docks because there were no sliding doors there. So she was probably at Blake's house. He supposed she could also be at any one of the arsons Blake had been accused of, but most of them had been demo'd, and plus it seemed likely that if she was butting her nose in, she'd start at the top.

So would he.

He hit the jackpot on his first try. Pulling into the small house Blake had claimed as his own, he parked right next to Kenzie's flashy Mercedes. He got out of his truck and felt the hood of her car.

Still warm.

So she hadn't been there long. She was just damn lucky she hadn't gotten herself arrested again, considering the yellow tape surrounding the house. Just thinking about what Tommy would say, and how long he'd jail her this time, had him sweating. The front door was shut and, as he discovered, locked.

Aidan moved around the side of the house. His plan was simple. He was going to scare the hell out of her. And then he was going to kiss the hell out of her.

And then…and then he had no idea. Spanking her seemed like a good option.

The sliding back door on Blake's deck was unlocked and opened an inch. This was where she'd entered, and following suit, he slipped inside. The place was dark, but there was a light on upstairs, and he headed in that direction. At a sound behind him, he whipped around just as two hands smacked him in the chest and shoved. As he fell back, he reached out and hauled his assailant with him. He hit his ass on the bottom step and Kenzie landed on him.

"What are you doing?" she demanded.

The stairs biting into his back, her full weight over the top of him, he hissed out a breath of pain. "What am *I* doing? What are *you* doing?"

"I'm—" She bit back whatever she'd been about to say, crawled backward off of him and stood up.

"No, it's okay, I'm fine, thanks," he muttered, getting up on his own and brushing himself off. "How did you get in here?"

"Blake gave me his spare key a long time ago."

"Okay, so back to my first question. Why are you here?"

"Looking for clues to Blake's innocence." She glared at him, then pointed to the door. "You need to leave."

"So do you."

"Oh, no. This is my brother's place. I'm his beneficiary. I get to be here."

"Not with the caution tape still blocking the front door, you don't."

She was breathing fast, her voice thick and husky as if she'd been crying. Or maybe she still was. He couldn't see her clearly enough to decide. "Ah, Kenzie. Don't—"

"Go," she said, crossing her arms over her chest.

"Fine. But you're coming with me."

"No, I'm not."

"Yeah, you are." Wrapping his fingers around her arm, he headed toward the sliding door, toting her with him, until she yanked free. Then, lifting her nose, she stalked out in front of him, going willingly but not happily. "Kenzie," he said as she got into her car.

"I don't want to talk right now." She tried to shut the driver's door on him but he stepped closer, holding it open.

"Isn't that convenient."

"Dammit, Aidan. Get out of my way."

"Just tell me where you're going."

For the first time, she hesitated.

"You could try my house," he suggested. "My computer."

She paused another beat. "I wouldn't want to impose."

"Imposing would be getting your pretty ass arrested again, goddammit. Meet me there."

"Fine." Putting the car into gear, she peeled out, leaving him little choice but to hope that she would.

CHAPTER THIRTEEN

WITH LITTLE TO no traffic in the middle of the night, it took only five minutes to get home. Aidan pulled into his driveway next to the little red sports car, watching Kenzie storm up the walk to his front door, looking irritated and frustrated.

Just as irritated and frustrated, he followed. Did she have no clue what she was doing to him?

How could she not?

"Wait," she said, stopping so fast he plowed into her, staring back at the street. "Did you see that car?"

"No."

"It was gray." She chewed on her thumbnail. "Look, I'm not trying to change the subject here, because trust me, I'm pissed and enjoying being pissed, but I think someone's following me."

Reaching past her, he unlocked the door and gestured her in ahead of him, keeping his body in front of her back as he turned to eye the street.

He didn't see the car—at the moment, there were *no* cars—but he didn't doubt her. "You've seen it before?"

"Yes. Truthfully, I'm beginning to feel sort of stalked." She whirled to face him. "Okay, so back to being pissed off."

Oh, no. Not yet. He'd anticipated her, and was standing so close she bumped into him, squeaking in surprise, but when she tried to take a step back, he held her still. Christ, she smelled good and the way her hair framed her face... "How long have you suspected someone's been following you?"

"Since the boat fire, I guess."

"Have you told anyone? Tommy? The police?"

"I wasn't really sure. I'm still not sure. It's just a feeling."

He let go of her to pull out his cell phone.

"What are you doing?"

"Calling the police."

Kenzie stepped close and shut the phone, stuffing it back into his pocket. "Aidan, listen to me. We both know that you and I don't do *real* relationships, especially not with each other. Now sex, we do that just fine. And in case you're confused, the biggest difference between the two is that with just sex, there's no sharing of personal information."

He was not liking where this was going. At all. "Meaning?"

"Meaning I don't have to account to you, and you're not responsible for me."

He stared at her, more stung than he'd like to admit. "Well, shit."

"I mean it, Aidan."

"You don't want me to call the police."

"And scare off the guy? No, I don't."

"Fine."

"*Fine.* Now where the hell is your computer? We have some files to access."

"My bedroom."

They were nose-to-nose, now. Breathing in each other's air. He could feel the heat of her radiating into him,

and for whatever reason, his hands ran down her arms
and then back up again, squeezing a little, more moved
by the close proximity than he'd like to admit.

The very tips of her breasts brushed against his shirt.
Her thighs bumped into his. Sparks were flying from
her eyes, her mouth grim.

A mouth that suddenly he couldn't stop looking at.

Her hands had come up to his chest and she dug her
fingers into his pecs, hard enough to have him hissing
out a breath. Her eyes were on his, but then they lowered to his mouth.

She was thinking about kissing him.

Leaning in, he took care of that little piece of business for her. Covering her mouth with his, he swallowed
her little moan of pleasure and promptly lost himself in
her when she melted against him, entwining her arms
around his neck so tightly he couldn't breathe. Since
breathing was overrated anyway, especially when kissing her, he just hauled her up tighter against him and
kept at it. Her hands were in his hair, his molded the
length of her body to him, until suddenly, she shoved
him clear, turned and stalked off, heading down the
hallway and into his bedroom. He stared after her,
breathing like a misused race horse, warring with himself. He could go after her. Or *he* could walk out on *her*
for a change of pace.

Yeah, right. He went after her.

WHEN AIDAN OPENED the door of his bedroom, Kenzie
held her breath. She hadn't turned on the light, so he
was silhouetted from behind by the lamp in the living
room, looking tall, dark, and so sexy she could hardly
stand it.

And attitude-ridden. Don't forget that. Stalking past her, he opened his laptop and hit the power button. While it booted up, she just stared through the dim room at him, wishing…hell.

Wishing things were different. That's all. If only she could call the writers and complain about this particular plotline, and maybe get it adjusted. Or get a new script delivered. Yeah, that would be best. One with a happy ending, please. With a sigh, she moved to the laptop. "Should I download it to your desktop?"

"Yes."

She accessed her mail, and the files she'd saved, clicking on the first of Blake's. "It's going to take a while. It's a big file. And it'll take even longer to flip through it all and see if there's even anything in it that we can use."

"Your caller suggested there was."

"Yes, but how did he know? *What* did he know?"

"Let's find out. Kenzie—"

"I'm not ready to talk."

He stepped closer, a big, tall, badass outline. "What *are* you ready for?"

"How about the only thing we're good at?"

With a low sound that might have been an agreeing groan, he came even closer. "Kenzie—"

"No. I mean it." He was hard. She could feel him. Could feel, too, the tension shimmering throughout his entire body. It matched hers. "No talking."

"Fine." With a rough tug, he hauled her up against him. His body was warm and corded with strength, his hands hard and hot on her. And his mouth…

God, his mouth.

He was the most amazing kisser, his lips warm and

soft and firm all at the same time, his tongue both talented and greedy and generous.

So generous that she moaned into his mouth and
held on for the ride until she couldn't stand it anymore.
"Clothes," she muttered, and yanked off her own top,
gratified to see him doing the same. She stared through
the dark at his bared torso as she worked the buttons on
her jeans while simultaneously kicking off her shoes.
God, he was gorgeous. Sleek, toned and so damned
yummy she wanted to gobble him up on the spot. She
shoved down her jeans, watching him do the same, but
unlike her, his underwear went bye-bye with his jeans,
and her mouth actually went dry.

Riveted by the sight, she stood there in her bra and
panties and socks. Staring.

He stood there in nothing. In glorious, mouth-drop-
ping, heart-stopping nothing. Yeah, she'd seen it before,
all of it and more—*but, damn.*

"You cheated," he said, reaching for her bra.

His erection nudged her belly, and forgetting to finish stripping, she wrapped her fingers around him.

He hissed out a breath.

"Too tight?" she asked as she stroked.

"No, your fingers are frozen."

For some reason that made her laugh. How the hell
that was even possible with all the sensations crowding and pushing for space in her brain was beyond her
but she stood there, her fingers wrapped around a very
impressive erection and laughed.

"Yeah, see, you're not really supposed to hold onto
a guy's favorite body part and laugh."

Which, of course, made her laugh harder.

With a shake of his head, he just smiled, clearly not

too worried because he remained hard as a rock in her hand...

As his fingers worked their magic and her bra fell to the floor at their feet.

When he stepped even closer, her nipples brushed his chest, and it was her turn to hiss in a breath as they hardened.

And then she couldn't breathe at all because he dropped to his knees, hooked his thumbs in the edge of her panties and tugged.

At the sight he revealed, he gave a low, ragged groan and slid his hands up the backs of her thighs, cupping her bottom in his big palms. "God, look at you."

"Aidan—"

"You're so pretty here." He ran a finger over her. "All wet and glistening. For me." There was a deep, husky satisfaction to his voice that made her thighs quiver.

"Spread your legs," he murmured, skimming hot, wet, openmouthed kisses up an inner thigh. "Yeah, like that." He pulled her forward, and right into his mouth.

At the first unerring stroke of his tongue her knees nearly buckled but he had a grip on her, one hand on her hip, holding her upright, the other exploring between her legs, working with his tongue to drive her out of her mind. "Aidan—"

"You taste like heaven," he whispered against her. *"Heaven."*

And he felt like it. She strained against him, her fingers tunneled into his hair, her head thrown back as he took her exactly where he wanted to her to go, which was to the very edge of a cliff, so high she couldn't see all the way to the bottom, couldn't speak, couldn't do anything but feel.

And she was feeling plenty. Mostly a need for speed at this point, but he purposely slowed her down, dancing his tongue over her as light as a feather. She tightened her fingers in his hair, silently threatening to make him bald if he didn't get back to business. Her business. "Aidan, dammit."

"I could look at you all day."

"Look later. Do now."

"Always in a hurry." He tsked, but obliged.

Oh, God, how he obliged, skimming his hands up the front of her thighs, gently opening her. For a moment he pulled back, admiring the sight before him, wet from his tongue, wet from her own arousal.

Standing there so open and vulnerable, she let out a growl of frustration and need, and he leaned in, this time sucking her into his mouth hard, giving her the rhythm she needed to completely lose it.

When her knees gave out, he let her fall, catching her, rising to his feet, spinning toward the bed, his mouth fastened to hers. His hands moved over her body, thoroughly, ruthlessly, ravenously kissing her as they went, until from somewhere behind them, from the pocket of her pants, her cell phone went off. She couldn't even think about getting it. Hell, the entire place could have gone up in flames right then and there and she doubted she would have thought about it. "In me, in me."

He let out a rough laugh.

"Now."

Because now was the only thing that mattered, and this was the only thing that registered, the feel of his hands on her body, molding, sculpting, flaming the wildfire flickering to life inside her.

Aidan crawled up her body. He'd found a condom,

and made himself at home between her thighs. Then he stared down into her eyes, his unwavering and fierce. "This is not just sex." His voice was low and rough. "It's not. Not for me."

She blinked, trying to clear her fuzzy head.

"And if that's all it is for you, I want to know it now." He lifted her hips, his strong callused fingers gliding over her flesh, making sure she was ready for him.

She was.

Beyond ready.

"Tell me," he demanded, holding still, waiting on her word. She stared up at him, her heart swelling at the truth. "It's more," she admitted, which—*ding, ding, ding*—was the right answer because then he spread her thighs wider and drove himself into her, hard and fast, the way she'd wanted, and took her right where she needed to go.

Halfway there, with her breath sobbing in her throat, with their bodies straining with each other, she cupped his jaw and looked into his face.

He was damp with sweat, hard with tension, and so damned sexy she could scarcely speak. "Aidan."

"Don't stop me."

She shook her head at his rough plea. Stop him? Was he kidding? She wanted him to never stop.

Never…a terrifying thought. "Aidan…"

His mouth nuzzled at her ear. "Yeah?"

"I missed you," she whispered, letting him in on her biggest secret, giving it to him without reserve, letting him look deeply into her eyes.

She absorbed both his surprise and his next thrust, and then that was it.

She burst.

And so did he.

CHAPTER FOURTEEN

AIDAN LAY ON his back, a hot, naked, still quivering Kenzie in his arms, and let her words soak in.

She'd missed him. "Kenz?"

"Mmm." Her face was pressed against his throat, her mouth sending shivers of delight down his spine even now, when his bones had turned into overcooked noodles and he couldn't have moved to save his life.

Well, except a certain part of his anatomy, which appeared to have segregated from his brain. That part moved. That part wanted round two.

And possibly round three, please.

Kenzie lifted her head and looked at him, all sleepy-eyed and still glowing. Waiting for him to speak.

He found himself cupping her face, and bringing it in for a kiss that lingered.

And deepened.

"I missed you, too," he whispered against her lips.

She pulled back and closed her eyes.

Staring down at her, he let out a breath. Okay. So she hadn't meant it. It'd just been the heat of the moment talking. He supposed he could understand that. Had to understand that. After all, the moment had gotten pretty damn heated. "It's all right." God, listen to him lie. "I get it."

Across the room sat his laptop, with answers. Or so

he hoped. "We'd better get up." He was relieved to note that his voice seemed to sound normal, that he was still breathing and that the heart she'd just stabbed was apparently still in working order.

Even if it was bleeding all over the place. Internal carnage...

But he had no one to blame but himself for opening it up to her in the first place. She'd warned him, hadn't she? She'd warned him and he'd been cocky enough not to believe it possible.

"Aidan?"

He managed to look at her.

"I *did* miss you. I missed this. But..."

"But life intrudes. I get that, too."

She looked into his eyes, sighed, then slipped from the bed. Gloriously naked, she walked to his computer. Lit only by the glow of the screen, she afforded him a particularly fine view. "Huh," she said, and bent over a little so that her fingers could move over the keyboard.

She was absolutely clueless about the picture she made in green glowing profile, with her hair wild around her head, a whisker burn from his face across a breast and her ribs, and her very sweet ass looking good enough to bite.

"That's odd," she muttered, her fingers moving faster, the furrow between her eyebrows deepening as she frowned.

He opened his mouth to ask what was odd, but she bent a little farther and he couldn't gather enough working brain cells to do anything but stare. Her spine was narrow and pretty, and his gaze followed it down past the indention of her waist and the gentle flare of her hips to one of his favorite parts of a woman's anatomy.

Her legs were spread slightly, her thighs taut, allowing him a peek of the treasure between—

"Aidan?"

At the tone, he managed to squelch the lust. *Barely.* Rising, he walked up behind her. Also naked. Curling his body around hers from behind, a good amount of that lust came barreling back, hitting him like a freight train. He couldn't help it. His chest was against her back, her world-class ass pressed into his crotch. His hands went to her hips, one slipping around to her ribs, his fingers just brushing the underside of her breast. Pressing his lips to the side of her neck, he let his hand skim up, gliding over her nipple, which hardened gratifyingly in his fingers.

Oh, yeah.

His other hand slid to her belly and began a southward descent—

"Look." Catching his hand, she pointed to an opened Excel worksheet. She had brought up an interesting list. "My mysterious caller said to look at the demos," she told him. "I didn't know what he meant, but all the burned buildings have been razed to the ground. I saw the photos in Zach's file—not all of those buildings were severely damaged."

With great difficulty, he frowned at the computer and not at her nude body, his hands still full with warm, sweet, sexy-as-hell woman. "It's true," he said. "But the properties were demolished anyway. Except for the last two."

"On whose orders?"

"The records have been sealed."

"Why?"

"That's the question. Zach tried to get the answer to that and it cost him."

Forcing his concentration from her body, he took in the worksheet in front of him. "Pretty impressive information here." Blake had been busy.

So had he been keeping track of his own handiwork, along with what happened to each property after the fires?

"Who has the power to order a demolition of a burned property?" Kenzie asked him.

"The owner, anyone acting on the behalf of an owner or the fire department, if the property is deemed unstable or unsafe for any reason."

She pulled free and went for her clothes, which were strewn across the room. He watched with great regret as she found the pieces one by one and covered up that gorgeous bod.

With a sigh, he reached for his jeans and slid them on. Back to the grown-up world apparently... "How is it you've never looked through Blake's files before?"

"I never thought to. We regularly sent each other files, just in case. It was our backup system."

"What did you send him?"

She lifted a shoulder. "Rough drafts of stuff."

"Stuff?"

"I've been writing. Scripts." Another lift of her shoulder. "For the day I finally ate too many donuts and didn't get asked to audition anymore."

"I bet you're a great writer."

"Really?"

He thought about how deeply she felt things, how good she was with words, and nodded.

Looking touched, she smiled. "Thanks."

"How long ago did he send you this file?"

"He sent me a backup file every week. We were supposed to keep only the latest version for each other, but I was always too lazy to go back and delete the week before, so I should have them all—" She stared at him for a beat before whipping back to the computer. Her fingers raced over the keys as he bent his head close to hers, looking at what she brought up.

An entire list of arson-related backup files from Blake, starting shortly after the first suspicious fires, until the day before he died.

"So," she said slowly. "Either he was a damned stupid felon, or he was investigating the arsons himself."

Her tone made it clear which she believed.

"Or," he said softly, knowing she was going to hate him. "He's keeping track of the arsons for a partner."

She looked at him again, her eyes cooling to, oh, about thirty-five degrees below zero.

"Open the first file."

Without a word, she clicked on it. It was a Word document, a diary of notes with a running commentary. The first read:

Hill Street fire:
Second point of origin mysteriously vanished on day of cleanup. Wire metal trash can, unique enough in design that it should be traceable. When I mentioned this to the chief, he said I should stick to fighting fires.

Kenzie read the entry out loud, twice, then scrolled down to the next entry, several weeks later.

Blood is thicker than water. I was told that today and apparently need to remember it. If I want to live.

Kenzie whipped her gaze to Aidan. "What the hell does that mean?"

"Sounds like a threat," he said grimly.

"Blood is thicker than water," she repeated. "Who is he talking about? We have no family. At least no family who cares about us, anyway."

He hated the look on her face, the faraway, distant, self-protective look she got whenever she had to talk about her past. There was no doubt, she and Blake had had it rough growing up, being shuffled from one foster home to another. The saving grace was that they'd been kept together. It was what had made their bond so strong—they'd been all each other had had. "Is there possibly a blood relative somewhere?"

"A few, scattered here and there across the country. A great-aunt in Florida, an uncle in Chicago, a cousin in Dallas…" She crossed her arms, closing him out mentally and physically. "Just no one who wanted us."

Gently he turned her to face him. "Could he be talking about you, then?"

"Definitely not. We were in touch all during that time, but we never had a conversation about any of this."

Aidan went back to reading the entries, one of which mentioned employee hours. Copies of the schedules were attached. So was Blake keeping track of *his* alibi, or someone's whereabouts?

Blake had somehow gotten Tommy's first official reports on the arsons as well. Aidan and Kenzie discovered that he hadn't been on duty at any of the suspicious fires, a fact that Tommy had apparently considered evidence since it left Blake without an alibi for when the fires had been lit. Aidan scrolled down the list.

"Whoa, stop." Kenzie pointed to the second fire. "There. That one can't be right. He had an alibi for that one, he was with me. He'd come to Los Angeles that week. I remember because he was my date for the Emmys. He flew home immediately after, catching a red-eye because he said he had to be back at work for an early shift."

"Okay." Aidan pulled up the employee schedule for that day. "But he's not listed as on duty."

Kenzie stared at the screen, shaking her head. "He wouldn't have lied to me."

She said this with utter sincerity, and Aidan was inclined to absolutely believe because *she* believed. But if Blake *hadn't* lied to Kenzie, then there was only one other explanation.

"The schedule got changed?" she asked.

"It could have happened. Someone traded. Or—"

"Or something physically changed the schedule after the fact," she said flatly. "And Blake isn't here to defend himself."

"No, but we are." He was looking at the screen, until he realized that she wasn't. She was staring at him. "What?"

Her eyes were shimmering brilliantly with anger and something else, a deep, gut-wrenching emotion. "I didn't think it was possible." Her voice sounded thick. "I didn't want it to be possible. Oh, God." She covered her face. "This is so stupid."

"What?" He looked at the screen again, trying to figure out what she was talking about. *"What's stupid?"*

"That I could like you more than last time."

The words reached him as little had in all these years. "Kenz." Melting, he pulled down her hands. "I—"

She put a finger in his face. "Don't get excited. I don't want to feel this way, and I'm telling you right now I *am* going to fight feeling this way."

His heart was squeezed tighter than a bow. "We were just kids, Kenz."

"And now we're not. It doesn't change anything except we're older, and *actually,* it's going to hurt more." Jaw tight, she shook her head again and looked at the screen. "This first. Blake first. He's far more important than rehashing old emotions that I don't really want to have." She worked the keyboard. "There. He's not on the schedule there, either, but he called me from the station. I know because it was my birthday, see? And he called me at 6:00 a.m. to catch me before work, but I didn't have an early morning shoot that day, and I was irritated that he woke me up. I'd been up late the night before celebrating."

"With Chad?"

She swiveled her eyes in his direction. "Actually, Teddy. Teddy White."

"Wasn't he on *People's* Most Beautiful list?"

"How do you know that?"

He knew it only because someone had stolen the porn out of the station bathroom, and Cristina had left her *People* magazine in there in its place, and— And Christ. He was crazy. "Never mind."

"It was just a one-night thing."

Oh, great. Even better. Now he could picture them having one-night sex, and—

"He's a friend."

A friend, as in someone who'd pulled her out of a fire? Someone who'd bail her out of jail?

"Yeah," she said softly. "I realize the word *friend* is a loose term, especially in Hollywood. Not like here."

"Do you miss it? Hollywood?"

She opened her mouth, then closed it and sighed. "I almost said yes, out of habit. The job is fun and the pay is amazing, but..." She lifted a shoulder. "It's empty. And I didn't really get that until I was here, either."

He tried to sort out his feelings regarding this revealing fact.

"And, anyway, it no longer matters." She turned back to the screen. "It's over."

"What do you mean?"

"My soap got cancelled."

"It did?"

"Yeah, and there are auditions for new parts but I've been eating too many donuts, so..."

"So...what?"

"So I'm going to get fat."

He let out a low laugh. "You look great, Kenzie. So great I haven't been able to keep my hands off you, as you might have noticed. But I'm very sorry about your job." He couldn't believe he was going to say this. "You could always stay in Santa Rey."

"I thought about it." She sighed and faced him again. "But staying seems like a comfort thing. You know, like going back to the last place where I was happy. It's a cop-out. And I was only happy here because of Blake."

He held his breath. He'd made her happy, too. Until he hadn't. "Maybe it was more than that."

"I don't know." She sighed without giving away her exact feelings on the matter, although he suspected she didn't know her exact feelings. "I wouldn't be able to get a job here."

"I know they don't film TV or movies anywhere close, but you could do something other than act."

She scoffed, then looked at him with heart-breaking hope. "Like what?"

"You know what. You could write. And eat all the damn donuts you want."

She just looked at him for a long moment, until he nearly squirmed. "What?"

"I'd have thought you'd be holding open the door for me to get the hell out of Dodge."

"Yeah, well, that was the old me."

"Well the new me is here to get Blake's name cleared. That's it."

"And also to stomp on my heart. Don't forget that part."

"I won't." She sighed. "Except I'd really rather get out of here without hurting you at all." With no idea that she'd just stunned him to his core, she leaned in close to see the screen better. A strand of her hair got stuck to the stubble on his jaw. It smelled good.

She smelled good.

It was all he could do not to bury his face in the rest of her hair and say things that would lead her back to his bed but not really get them anywhere. In fact, he'd opened his mouth to do just that when she spoke.

"Look." She pointed to where Blake had entered another note:

Not noted in any of the official investigation reports is the fact that the source for the wire mesh trash cans is the hardware store where Tracy works.

Kenzie frowned and turned her head to look at Aidan, who had gone still in sudden shock. "The Tracy who…"

"Died." Aidan managed to find his vocal cords. "Yeah. They dated a couple of times. He really liked her."

"Really? He told me he'd gone out with Tracy, but he never said how much he liked her."

"Maybe he didn't tell you everything."

"He did," she insisted. "We told each other everything."

"Kenzie, you didn't tell him when *we* were going out. Maybe—"

"No." She shook her head. "You're going to say he kept secrets. That he kept the arsons a secret, but he wouldn't have— He wouldn't have done this, Aidan. Tracy being killed, well that's got to be a terrible coincidence."

"I'm beginning to believe that nothing's a coincidence. Look at the next entry."

Tracy's going to get me a list of people who've purchased the trash cans, but she has to wait until the weekend when her boss isn't in.

The next entry didn't clear anything up, but made it all worse.

Got the list, and holy shit. Blood is thicker than water. Got to remember that…

Kenzie's fingers dug into Aidan's arm. "What does that mean, 'blood *is* thicker than water'? He's written that twice now."

Aidan frowned and shook his head. "I wish I knew."

He's onto me. Need to be damn careful now.

"*Who's* onto him?" Kenzie stood up and paced the length of the bedroom. "God. Whoever he's talking about, do you think…?"

Yeah. Yeah, he did. Blake had gotten himself into hot water with someone. And that someone had either been his partner in crime, or, as Aidan was coming to believe, it was the person whom Blake had been privately, quietly, investigating on his own.

And if *that* was true, and Blake had been a victim, then this other person had not only been an arsonist, but also a murderer.

Aidan's cell phone chirped with a message that he was needed at work, ASAP.

"Go," she murmured. "It's okay. I'm just going to go through all of this and see what else I can find."

"Stay here."

Her gaze slid to his.

"Kenzie…" How to say this without sounding like a complete idiot? There was no way to sugarcoat it, so he decided to just let it out. "I have a bad feeling."

She arched an eyebrow. "You, the most pragmatic, logical, cool person I know, have a bad *feeling?*"

"Go with me on this."

"You think I'm in danger," she said flatly.

He didn't just think it, he knew it. Only he couldn't explain how or why, and that was going to drive him crazy, along with worrying and wondering where she was and if she was okay.

And safe.

And alive.

"Aidan, I'm not going to hole up here. That's ridiculous. Besides, no one knows what I'm doing."

"You were arrested, Kenzie. Everyone knows what you're doing."

"I'll be fine."

Short of tying her up, which had a *most* interesting vision popping into his head, what could he do? "Promise me you'll be careful."

She looked at him for a long moment, her hair still crazy from his fingers, her shirt crooked, her feet bare, looking like a hot mess.

A hot mess he wanted in his life.

"I thought we weren't going to do the promise thing," she said. "Not ever again."

"Promise me," he said again.

"Don't worry." She backed away from him, her face so carefully blank. "I intend to be careful and smart, and I intend to get out of here unscathed, on all counts."

What the hell did that mean?

"See you, Aidan."

Okay, that was no simple *"I'll see you later."* It seemed like a we're-done-doing-the-naked-happy-dance see-you. The get-over-me because I'm-over-you see-you.

Which didn't bode well for his heart, the one that in spite of himself, had gotten attached. Again. More attached, if that was even possible. "I'll be back."

"Okay."

"I will." He paused. "Will you be here?"

She met his gaze. "I don't know."

Well, hell. That didn't bode well.

CHAPTER FIFTEEN

IN BETWEEN CALLS, Aidan slipped into the office of the fire station. He'd never spent much time in there, always preferring to be outside or working, or just about anywhere else.

But he made himself comfortable now. He told whoever gave him a strange look that he was working on his taxes, and given the sympathetic grimaces that got him, it was a genius excuse. Left alone, he went through the daily fire reports and employee schedules, pulling the dates that matched the arsons.

Which is where he discovered that those schedules did not match the ones Blake had saved on his computer.

In fact, according to the office reports, Blake *had* been scheduled on each of the days of the arsons, whether by coincidence or design, Aidan had no idea. Dispatch didn't always need all available units to go out on the calls. On two of the fires, Blake's unit hadn't been called to respond at all and yet he'd been placed on scene by witnesses.

Had he been the arsonist, or simply trying to stop him?

The door to the office opened and Aidan turned around, the excuse already on his lips about being late getting his receipts together—

"Save it," Tommy said, and dropped a disk on the table.

"What's that?"

"A copy of the surveillance tape I got out of the camera I had at Blake's place."

"You had Blake's place under surveillance?"

"I'm an investigator. It's what I do, investigate."

"What were you looking for?"

"There's a bigger, better question. What was *Kenzie* looking for?"

"I couldn't tell you."

"Couldn't, or won't?"

Aidan didn't respond to that.

"You're doing a shitty job of keeping her out of my hair."

Yeah. He was doing a shitty job keeping Kenzie out of *his* hair as well.

"Okay, here's how this is going to work," Tommy decided. "You're going to tell me everything you've discovered about these arsons and Blake, and in return, I'm not going to charge you with interfering with my investigation."

Aidan didn't care about the underlying threat in Tommy's voice. What he cared about was discovering the truth. For Blake. For Kenzie. And as big a pain in his ass as Tommy was, Aidan believed them to be on the same side.

"Yes?"

"Yes."

With a nod, Tommy locked the door and pulled up a chair.

KENZIE HAD NO problem keeping herself occupied. She spent the day reading Blake's files, poring over them, analyzing each of her brother's entries.

She slept in Aidan's big, wonderful bed all by herself, which wasn't nearly as much fun as sleeping next to the big, wonderful man usually in it. Her dreams were wild, vacillating between nightmares about being trapped in a fire and hearing Blake scream for her, and another type of dream entirely. A dream where Aidan slowly stripped her naked and used his tongue on every inch of her body, a dream she woke up from damp with sweat, panting for air, her own hand between her thighs.

Damn, the man was potent.

In the morning, she went back to *Blake's Girl*. She couldn't help herself. She stood on the end of the dock staring at the shell that used to be Blake's sailboat, a huge lump inside her throat, wondering what the hell she was supposed to do next when her cell phone rang. Her local caller.

"Did you get the backups?"

"Who is this?"

"You need to stay away from the boat. There's nothing there for you."

With a gasp, she whirled, searching her immediate area but seeing no one. *"Where are you?* Are you watching me?"

"Don't be scared."

The parking lot had only three cars in it, no people. No one was on the docks, and the neighboring boats seemed deserted. "Don't be scared? Are you crazy?"

"Listen to me," he said urgently. "It's time for you to back off. Time for you to go home, Kenzie."

The hair at the back of her neck prickled and she once again turned slowly. Behind one of the three cars was another.

Gray. Tinted windows.

Eyes narrowed, she headed toward it, needing to know who the hell she was talking to and why his voice made the hair on her arms stand up, as if she could almost recognize him, but not quite.

"Don't come any closer," he warned.

She kept walking. "Do I know you?"

The car's engine started up.

"No," she cried, breaking into a run. *"Wait—"*

The gray sedan squealed forward and to the right, giving her only the briefest glimpse of the driver behind the wheel. But it was enough to have her gasp in shock as her chest tightened beyond all bearing.

The car ripped out of the lot. She hardly even noticed as she hit her knees on the concrete, her hands fanned over her chest to hold her heart in because she'd have sworn, she'd have laid her life on the line, that the driver of that car had been none other than her dead brother.

Blake.

SHE SPED ALL the way back to Aidan's house before remembering he was at work. Still shaken, she turned around and headed to the station. Zach was there, standing in the middle of the main room. He wore jeans and a T-shirt and a rueful smile as he stuck a pencil down the cast on his arm.

"This thing is driving me crazy." He tossed the pencil to a small desk against a wall. "You looking for Aidan?"

"Yes." Because she wanted to tell him her brother wasn't dead. Or that she was losing her mind. One or the other.

"He's on a call." Zach took a closer look at her and frowned. "Are you okay?"

No. "I saw the file you put together on the arsons." The fires had cost Zach his house, which in itself would have given him a good reason to hate her brother. "When Blake died, there wasn't a body."

A shadow crossed his face. "The fire was hot. Nothing survived it."

She begged to differ. "Anything survive? Anything at all?"

"A portion of the shell of the blow torch Blake had been holding, and his hard hat."

"But no physical evidence of *him?*"

He paused a long moment. "Why?"

Oh, because maybe he hadn't really died... "Do you know when Aidan'll be back?"

"No, but I can have him call you. He was worried about you."

"I'm fine." She smiled to prove it, but truthfully, she was worried, too. She left the station, got into her car and pulled out her cell. Taking a deep breath, she dialed her mysterious caller's number.

"Hello."

Kenzie went utterly still at that voice, still disguised, but it didn't matter. She now knew who she was talking to. "Blake?"

Click.

Oh, God. Heart pounding, she drove straight to Tommy Ramirez's office. He opened his door at her knock, raising a single eyebrow at the sight of her, then simply sighed when she pushed past him and let herself in.

He had three unopened Red Bulls on his desk. She grabbed one, cracked it open and drank deeply. Eyes closed, she stood there until the caffeine kicked in. "God, I needed that."

He shut the door, leaned back against it and just looked at her. "That was my Red Bull."

"Thanks for sharing."

"You know, most people are afraid of me."

"Yes, but most people don't know that once upon a time you paid for my dancing lessons."

"Keep it down, will you? I don't want that to get out."

She shook her head. "Always the tough guy." Back when Blake had been in the academy, she and her brother had made some financial mistakes. Lots of financial mistakes. Tommy had known Blake's situation and had lent him some money to see him through fire school, and Kenzie enough to cover her dance lessons.

Not many knew the investigator had such a soft side; he didn't like to show it. He hadn't shown it to Kenzie since, but she'd never forgotten. Nor had she ever even briefly considered that it could be Tommy framing Blake. Blake had trusted Tommy, and she did, too.

Tommy tossed the files in his hands to his desk and grabbed one of the remaining Red Bulls. "I put you in jail to keep you safe. I didn't intend for you to bail yourself out. I wanted to keep you there until this was over, but it's taking longer than I thought."

"You put me in jail to keep me safe?"

"Trust me, it made sense to me. Look, I know this has been hard on you."

"Yes," she agreed blandly. "It's been hard on me having my brother blamed for something he didn't do. It's been hard on me knowing that all his friends, his coworkers, *everyone,* believes he committed arson. It's hard on me knowing that he can't defend himself. But it's even harder knowing that you're not."

"You don't understand."

"Then help me to."

He opened his mouth, and then shut it. "I can't."

"Would you like to know what the hardest thing of all is?" she whispered, her throat tight with a sudden need to cry. "I know he's innocent and I know that you believe it, too."

"Kenzie—"

"You can't talk about it, I get it. But I think I saw Blake alive. Can you talk about that?"

He stared at her. *"What?"*

"I think I saw him at the docks, in the parking lot."

Tommy sank to his chair. "What were you doing at the docks?"

"Blake. *Alive*. Did you hear that part?"

His eyes filled with sympathy. "Kenzie—"

"No." She let out a low laugh. "Listen to me. *I saw him.* Plus someone's been calling me, giving me clues. It's him, he—"

"What kind of clues?"

"I don't know, that the key is in the demos, which I don't get. And that blood is thicker than water. I don't get that either, honestly."

Tommy went pale. He came to her, taking her arm and leading her to the door. "I need you to listen to me, okay? Listen very carefully. Go back to Los Angeles. I'll call you—"

"No." She pulled free. "I'm not leaving."

"Yes, you are. If I have to have you arrested again—"

"On what charges?"

"I'll find something."

She looked into his face, where his emotions were clear. "Okay, you're scared for me. I get that. I'll stay back, I'll stay clear."

"Promise me."

She took a long look at him. "What did I say? Was it the blood is thicker than water thing?"

"Promise me."

"I promise," she said very quietly. "Now you promise me this. You'll come to me as soon as you can with answers."

"Deal."

DURING THE SUMMER MONTHS, Santa Rey swelled to upwards of three times its normal population, which was reflected in the increased volume of calls the fire station received. In the past twenty-four hours alone, Aidan had fought a restaurant fire, a storefront fire, a car fire and two house fires, each caused by human stupidity. Then, it happened.

Another explosion.

It thankfully occurred in an empty warehouse this time. No one was injured, except Cristina, who fell off a ladder and hurt her ankle.

Dustin wanted to take her to the E.R. for an X-ray, but in typical Cristina fashion, she wanted to tough it out.

Aidan left them alone to their silent battle of wills, and let himself inside the burned shell of a warehouse.

Tommy was there, with his bag of equipment, his camera out. When he saw Aidan, he jaw ticked. "I've got it from here."

Aidan's eyes went to the wall in front of Tommy, where the burn marks on the wall indicated a hot flash, and most likely, the point of origin. "I never did get onto *Blake's Girl* after the explosion. But I'm going to take a wild guess that you found something like this there, and also at the hardware explosion that killed Tracy."

Tommy clearly fought with himself, and then finally sighed. "Look, I'm not going to insult your intelligence the way I insulted Zach's, okay? That was a mistake, shutting him out, because it only made him all the more determined to prove he was right—"

"He *was* right—"

"Yeah, but I was on it. I told him that, but he didn't listen, and then he dug harder and got himself targeted by the arsonist."

"The arsonist? I thought you were so sure it was Blake."

"I'm not going to insult your intelligence," he repeated tightly, "by letting you think what we want the general public to think. So know this. I'm going to nail this guy. So when I say back off, *do it*. Don't pull a Zach and get yourself hurt."

Aidan stared at him. "You know there's someone else."

"I'm close."

"You've always known."

Tommy acknowledged this with a slight nod. "So now all you have to do is stay out of my way. And keep Kenzie out of the way as well. No one else dies."

"Blake's innocent."

"That's one theory."

"Is it the right theory?"

"Jesus, Aidan." Tommy scrubbed a hand over his face. "Are you just playing with that girl?"

"No. And how is this any of your business, anyway? A few days ago you were arresting her."

"Just don't hurt her. You hear me? Don't even think about it."

Aidan let out a low, mirthless laugh. "Trust me, if someone's getting hurt, it's going to be me."

THE MINUTE AIDAN got off work, he went straight home, hoping Kenzie would be there waiting for him. It was with great relief that he pulled in next to her car. Letting himself in, he called out her name.

No response. Dropping his keys on the small desk in the living room, he moved through the house and heard the shower running. Things were looking up if he had a naked, wet, hot woman in his shower. And at that realization, all the myriad things he'd wanted to say to her flew out the window, replaced by memories of how she looked standing under a stream of water.

She hadn't left...

Weak with relief, he knocked on the bathroom door. "Kenz?"

When she still didn't respond, he cracked open the door and found her sitting in his shower, face to her knees, arms wrapped around herself.

"Kenzie?"

"I'm fine."

Yeah. She was fine, he was fine, so they could just all be fine together.

She lifted her head when he opened the shower door but didn't say a word as he stepped into it with her.

"You're dressed," she finally said, inanely.

Yeah, which sucked. "Tell me what's wrong."

"You're not going to like it."

He already didn't like it, or the clothes now sticking to him like a second skin. "Try me."

"I saw Blake."

He blinked away the water in his eyes. "You…saw Blake." He crouched before her. "In a dream?"

"No."

"You saw Blake," he repeated, trying to understand, and failing. "Not in a dream. What does that mean?"

"It means he's alive."

CHAPTER SIXTEEN

KENZIE WATCHED AIDAN try to absorb her news while the shower rained down over top of him, soaking into his hair, his clothes. "I know, it's a shock," she said.

The water ran in rivulets down his face. His shirt was plastered to his broad shoulders and arms, his pants suctioned to his legs. There was something about the way he'd rushed in there to save her from her own demons that got to her. More than got to her. He devastated her.

She wasn't sure how it'd happened, especially when she'd set out to keep her heart safe, but she'd fallen for him all over again.

"You saw Blake," he repeated.

"He's alive. He's the one who's been calling me." She stood up. "He's been alive and didn't tell. The men I love suck."

Aidan hissed out a breath and straightened to his feet as well, towering over her, his broad shoulders taking the beating of the water. "The men you love?"

"Go away."

"The men you love?" he asked, staring down at her. "Kenz—"

"No." She shook her head. "Not doing this." She put her hands on his chest to shove him away but somehow ended up fisting her hands in his drenched shirt and yanking. Surprised, he lost his balance as he came toward her, slapping his hands on the tile on either side of her to hold himself upright. "Kenz—"

She stopped whatever he might have said with her mouth. It made no sense, none at all, but she wanted to have him, needed to have him, right there, right then, if only for this one last time before all hell broke loose.

"God," he managed on a roughly expelled breath as she kissed her way over his jaw while she fumbled with the buttons on his Levi's.

His hands left the tile and squeezed her arms. Water was running down his face. "I thought you'd said good-bye to me."

She'd tried. After all, she had a life to get back to. Too bad she had no idea what that life would entail—but that was a worry for tomorrow. After she figured out the Blake being alive thing. "So I said goodbye. Now I'm saying hello." Still squished between the wall and Aidan, she slid her hands up his chest, her fingers entwining in his hair as she arched back, her breasts sliding along the material of his wet shirt.

Her nipples hardened and she felt the rough grumble of the groan in his chest. Almost as if acting of their own accord, his hands moved down her sides, to her hips, her bottom, which he roughly squeezed while letting out another of those incredibly arousing groans. "Is there another goodbye coming my way after this shower?"

"Maybe not right after," she panted because something was happening to her, something that had nothing to do with lust or hormones or getting an orgasm, but far deeper. Far more dangerous. Tightening her fingers in his hair, she lifted his head from her breast and stared into his eyes. There, she could see the reflection of her own. And in that reflection was her heart and soul, her very life.

She loved him. And if they did this, if she let him inside her body again, she'd never recover. She knew it, but like last time, it wasn't going to stop her. Small wonder when he was against her like a second skin, holding her to the wall. Closing her eyes, she hugged him close, pressing her face to his throat.

Her name tumbled from his lips in a harsh whisper, and then their hands were fighting to get his clothes off, pushing off his shirt, shoving down his jeans. Then he was reaching for those jeans, and the condom in his pocket. He pressed her back against the wall, freeing his hands to skim down her bare, trembling thighs, which opened and wrapped around his waist, bringing him flush to her. In one thrust he was deep inside, and she was…lost?

Not lost.

No, when she was with him, she was found.

AIDAN'S HEART WAS still thundering in his ears in tune to the water pounding his back when Kenzie slid free of him. Drained, he watched her lean past him and turn off the water. She tossed him a towel, grabbed one for herself and left him alone in the bathroom.

He had no idea what had just happened.

When he managed to dry himself off and walk out of the bathroom, on legs that still quivered, he found her dressing in his bedroom. "Did you get the license of that truck that just hit me?"

She didn't smile. "I really saw him."

When he just looked at her, she slipped into her shoes. "And I'm going to go find him."

"Kenzie," he said gently. "Blake is—"

"Dead. I know. But he's not." She left the room.

With a sigh, he headed to his dresser for clothes. He'd gotten into a dry pair of jeans when he heard her keys jangling. "Kenzie," he called out. *Dammit.* "Wait." He grabbed a shirt and headed down the hallway just as she opened the front door. She hesitated when her cell phone beeped an incoming text message.

"Is it…him?" he asked.

"Yes, it's him. Texting me from the dead." She opened her phone and let him read over her shoulder.

Go home. I'll find you there when this is over, when you're safe.

As they stood there in his open doorway looking down at the screen, a huge trash truck lumbered down the street, making the earth shudder as it went past—

Boom.

Kenzie's bright red sports car vanished in a cloud of smoke and flames and flying metal as it exploded.

KENZIE SAT ON Aidan's curb looking out at the street, which was littered with cops and various other official personnel, including Tommy and the chief. And lots of red car parts.

Everyone was trying to figure out what the hell had happened.

Her car had gone boom, just like *Blake's Girl,* that was what had happened.

"Kenzie." Aidan's athletic shoes appeared in her peripheral vision, and then the rest of him as he sat at her side.

"My insurance company isn't going to be happy," she said. "I blame the trash truck."

"The trash truck saved your life. You car had been rigged to blow when you got into it, but the truck vibrated the street so much it went up early."

"Oh." She winced. "I wish I didn't know that."

"Give me your cell phone."

"Why?"

"So I can call whoever's been calling you."

"Blake. Blake's been calling me."

"Whoever it is." His mouth was grim as some of his clear frustration and fear for her filtered into his words. "I just want him to stay the hell away from you."

"This wasn't him."

"Then who?"

"I'm working on that."

He looked down at her. "By yourself."

"It's how I work best, apparently." She stood up. During the time she'd been gone from Santa Rey, she'd closed herself off, both her heart and soul. It was a hell of a time to realize that. But no matter what happened here—whether she left and went back to Los Angeles, or whether she stayed—whatever she settled on for herself, she couldn't go back to closing herself off.

"Kenzie."

"I didn't mean to get so good at being alone. I didn't realize, living in L.A., the land of pretend, that I'd never built myself any real relationships." She let out a long breath and met his gaze. "But that changed when I got here. When I was with you. I love you, Aidan. Again. Still. I love you."

And while that shocking statement hung in the air,

someone called for Aidan. But he just stared at Kenzie. "You—"

"Aidan!"

With a grimace, he looked over his shoulder. "Shit, it's the chief."

"Go."

"Kenzie—"

"Go."

A muscle ticked in his jaw. "Don't move, I'll be right back."

Nodding, she watched him walk toward a tall man whose back was to her, stretching out a dark blue shirt that said Chief across the shoulders.

Then she walked away. She didn't have a car, so she had no idea where she thought she was going, but she had to leave.

In her pocket, her cell phone buzzed with an incoming text.

Another half block. Gray car.

I love you. Aidan muttered the three little words that Kenzie had said to him. She'd said them, and then she'd vanished, and he had no idea where she'd gone. One moment he'd been talking to the chief, and the next... She'd been gone. It'd been hours, and not a word.

He was at the station now, and she still hadn't answered her damn cell phone, and he was starting to lose it. He shouldn't have walked away to talk to the chief, he should have dragged her with him.

"Hey, Mr. 2008." Cristina came into the station kitchen and went straight for the refrigerator. "What are you pouting about?" She helped herself to someone else's lunch.

"You could bring your own."

"I could." Cristina pulled out a thick turkey sandwich. "But I don't."

"Hey, that's mine," Dustin said, joining them from the garage. "What did I tell you about stealing my sandwich?"

Cristina spoke around a huge mouthful. "If I was still sleeping with you, I'd bet you'd *give* me your sandwich."

Dustin's eyes darkened. "You slept with me once."

"Your point?"

"My point is that if we were *still* sleeping together, I'd *make* you your own damn sandwich."

She took another bite, chewing with a moan. "You know, I should give that some thought, because you do make the best sandwiches."

Dustin tossed up his hands and walked back out of the room.

When he was gone, Cristina dropped her tough girl pose, watching him go with a naked look of longing.

"You could just tell him the truth," Aidan said.

"What, that he makes crappy sandwiches?"

"No, that you're scared. He'd understand fear." Hell, he understood it all too well.

"Are you kidding me? I'm not scared." Cristina tossed the sandwich back in the fridge. "I'm not scared of anything." But as she shut the fridge, she pressed her forehead to the door. "Ah, hell. I'm scared. Everything's messed up. Dustin's mad at me. Blake's gone. There's no good food. Blake's gone."

"You still miss him."

"Hell, yeah, I still miss him. He was a great partner. And now even the chief, his own flesh and blood, wants to make him out to be a monster that we know he wasn't."

"Wait." Aidan grabbed her arm. "What?"

"He wasn't a monster."

"The flesh and blood part. What did you mean about that?"

Cristina's lips tightened. "Blake asked me never to tell."

"He asked you never to tell what?"

She sighed. "That the chief's his uncle. They were estranged, though. Blake's parents were—"

"Dead. They died years ago."

"Yeah. But his father was the chief's half brother."

Blood is thicker than water... Good God. "If that's true," he asked hoarsely, "why did Blake and Kenzie spend their childhood in foster care?"

"Because the chief didn't want kids. Or something like that." She shrugged. "Not sure on the details."

Neither was he. Except that somehow...*Christ.* Somehow the chief—

His cell phone rang. When he looked down at the screen, his heart skipped a beat. "Thank God," he said to Kenzie in lieu of a greeting. "Listen to me. I just realized—"

"Aidan, I need you. I'm sorry, I know I don't really have the right to say that to you, but I do. Can you come meet me? Now? Please?"

"Just tell me where."

AIDAN BURST INSIDE the Sunrise Café and looked around the tables.

No Kenzie.

"She's on the roof," Sheila told him, standing behind the bar, drying glasses.

"Thanks."

"Something about Tommy being on his way, and having all the answers you need…"

Aidan had the answers. He just didn't have the girl, which he intended to rectify. He headed for the stairs as Sheila turned her attention to someone else. "Hey, there, good-looking," she called out with a smile of greeting. Aidan took the stairs without looking back, coming to a relieved halt on the roof at the sight of Kenzie sitting on the bench.

"Tommy's on his way," she said, standing up. Someone stepped out from the shadows behind her and Aidan's heart stopped.

It was Blake, who by all logical accounts should be dead.

Only there was nothing logical about any of this. Not the arsons, and not the way Aidan knew he loved the woman standing in front of him like he'd never loved anyone before.

"Listen to him," Kenzie said quietly. "Listen to your heart."

He *was* listening to his heart, which had kicked back to life and was screaming, demanding that he pull Kenzie close and tell her he loved her, too. That he was sorry it'd taken him so long, but like Cristina, he'd been afraid, was in fact *still* afraid but would no longer run from how he felt.

He'd never again run from her.

But that would have to wait. He looked at Blake, who was thinner than ever. And he walked with a cane. "I know, it's crazy," his old friend said, his voice low and urgent. "You thought I was dead and I'm not. I...faked my own death."

"I'm getting that."

"When I found out who the real arsonist was, I realized no one was safe." Blake's face was twisted in tortured misery. "He killed Tracy right after he blew up my boat."

"I know. I know all of it. I even know *who* we're talking about. I just don't know why."

"Oh, I can tell you why," said the man who came through the roof door to stand in front of them. The chief nodded in Aidan's direction. "If you really want to know."

Shit. Aidan pulled out his cell, hit Tommy's number and put the phone to his ear.

"Nearly there," Tommy said tensely.

"Hurry. Bring backup."

"Oh, it'll be too late," the chief said conversationally.

"Uncle Allan?" Kenzie breathed, staring at the chief. She looked at Aidan. "He's the fire chief? I thought..." She turned back to her uncle. "I thought you were in Chicago."

"I was. I came back here a year ago. A shame we lost touch or you'd have known."

"We lost touch—" Kenzie took a step toward him, or tried to, but Blake grabbed her hand and held her back "—because you didn't want us."

"Now, now. That's not entirely true. I just didn't want to be responsible for raising kids. I never wanted kids."

"But it's okay to be responsible for *killing people?*"

"*One* person," he corrected. "Not people. And that was an accident."

"You killed Tracy and that was no accident," Blake ground out. "You murdered her."

"Ah, now, see *murder* implies intent, and I don't have intent. I have an addiction." He smiled sadly. "It means I can't help it."

Kenzie again tried to charge him, but this time it was Aidan who held her back, not trusting that asshole with her.

"If I was an alcoholic," the chief asked, "would you still be looking at me like that? If I had a drug problem? No, you'd be trying to get me help."

"I *tried* to get you help," Blake told him. "When I figured out you had started that second fire all those months ago, you begged me to understand. You lied and said it was your first time, and that you'd stop, that you'd get help. Instead a child died and when I tried to turn you in you threatened me."

The chief slowly shook his head. "Tommy was getting close. You wouldn't leave me alone. I had to do something. I had to keep you quiet."

Blake gave Aidan an agonized look, as though pleading for forgiveness. "By then he had implicated me. He'd changed the schedules, he'd planted evidence. He discredited me so that even if I did tell, *I'd* be the first one they'd lock up. And once I was in jail, he threatened to hurt Kenzie.

"Then Zach started asking questions and the chief tried to kill him by burning down his house. I had followed him, Zach saw me, and I didn't know what to do. I panicked and faked my death. If I was gone, he had no reason to harm Kenzie."

"And I didn't."

"You killed Tracy!"

"But not Kenzie," the chief said calmly. "Look, Tracy was going to put together a list of people who'd purchased those metal trash cans. I would have been on that list."

"You didn't have to kill her," Blake shouted.

"He had to set more fires," Aidan said grimly.

"That's true." The chief nodded emphatically. "I can't help myself. I tried like hell. I couldn't stop, but at least I went for old and dilapidated properties, or overly insured buildings." He paused. "Like this one."

Aidan stared at him. "What?"

"Sheila is getting ready to renovate," the chief said.

"She has to," Aidan said. "The building has structural problems."

"Yes, and now she's over insured to protect it. It's a situation that cries out to an arsonist. It needs to burn."

"Ohmigod," Kenzie breathed, looking horrified. "You're a very sick man."

"Agreed." Her uncle smiled without any mirth. He clapped his hands together. "Well, it's been nice clearing all this up but I've got to end this now."

"You're not walking away," Aidan said. "Not from this. You have to pay for your crimes."

"I'm not paying for anything. You didn't get hurt. None of you died."

"Are you kidding?" Aidan asked incredulously. "Blake nearly died trying to stop you. You nearly killed Kenzie on *Blake's Girl,* and then again when you blew up her car."

"*Nearly* won't hold up in a court of law. I was just trying to scare her out of town, anyway. The car was supposed to blow an hour earlier, but a fuse failed me. And the boat was an accident. I was just trying to get rid of Blake's laptop. I didn't know she was there that night."

"There's something else you don't know," Aidan told him. "Blake emailed Kenzie backup files."

The chief's mouth tightened. "I'm not going down for this, for any of it. I'm the chief."

"Not for long you're not," Blake said. "You're going to be stripped of that title and put in jail."

"Not happening," the Chief declared. "I won't go to jail—I've made sure of it. I've risked my life to save people for almost thirty years. I *won't* be remembered as an arsonist."

Aidan's gut clenched. There was only one reason the chief would come out in the open like this and confess his crimes. And that was if he didn't intend for them to live to tell the tale. "Whatever you've planned, *no*."

"You're too late." The chief looked first to Kenzie, then to Blake. "I'm sorry. Truly sorry."

"What did you do?" Blake demanded. "Oh, Christ, you didn't—" Without finishing that thought, he whirled and limped to the roof door, yelling as he took the stairs, "Evacuate! Everyone out—"

Which was all he got out before a thundering explosion hit. The entire building shook, throwing Aidan and Kenzie to the ground.

CHAPTER SEVENTEEN

AT THE EXPLOSION, the world seemed to stop, or at least go into slow motion. Kenzie managed to lift her head just as Aidan rolled toward her, his face a mask of concern. Her uncle, ten feet away, wasn't moving at all. Pushing to her knees, she stared at the doorway where her brother had just disappeared. "Blake!" she screamed.

He didn't reappear, no one did, nothing except a plume of smoke that struck terror in her heart. "Ohmigod. *Aidan*—"

"Are you okay?" He was on his knees before her, running his hands down her sides, pushing her hair from her face, looking her over, his expression calm, only his eyes showing his fear. "Are you okay?" he demanded again hoarsely.

Shaken, but all in one piece, she nodded and pointed to the doorway. "Blake—"

His eyes and mouth were grim. "I know. He's down with the others. We'll get to him." He glanced at the chief.

"Is he—"

Aidan checked for a pulse. "Just out cold." He pulled her to her feet, yanking his cell phone out of his pocket. From far below, they could hear screams and yelling over the whooping sound of smoke and car alarms going off.

All of it brought Kenzie back to the night on *Blake's Girl,* back to that irrational terror. Then they'd been able to jump into the water. Now there was nothing down there except concrete.

Three floors down.

"Call 9-1-1," Aidan said to her, shoving the phone into her hands as he ran past the very still chief to the edge of the building and looked over the side. "Dammit, I can't see if people are getting out of here."

The café hadn't been full to capacity, but there had been at least twenty people inside when they'd entered, and then there was Sheila and her staff.

And Blake. God, Blake. Could she really have found him only to lose him again, for real this time? "Aidan—"

"Listen to me. There's no way off of here except for the stairwell. No outside fire escape or ladder."

They both looked at the dark doorway, emitting smoke now. "Ohmigod." She felt frozen. Logically she knew she had to go down to get to Blake, not to mention to safety. But there was nothing logical about the fear blocking her windpipe. She'd thought Blake had died in a fire. *She'd* nearly died in the boat fire. Instead of seeing the roof's doorway, she kept flashing back to *Blake's Girl,* the black night and blacker water. She could feel the heat from that fire prickling her skin even as she could feel the iciness of the water closing around her body—

"Kenzie."

She blinked Aidan into view. He had his hands on her arms and he was frowning into her face.

"I can't go in there," she said, unable to catch her breath. "I just can't."

"Okay." They both looked at the chief, who still wasn't moving. Again Aidan went to the edge of the roof and looked over. Whatever he saw made his jaw go tight and his eyes, grim. Then he backed Kenzie to a corner and gently pushed her down until she was sitting there, her back to the wall, facing the opened door to the only exit. "I'm going—"

"No." She gripped his arms, digging her fingers into the muscles there.

"Kenzie—"

"No!" Icy, terrifying fear overcame her as she stared at the smoke now pouring out through the opened door. "There's a fire down there!"

He didn't say it, he didn't have to.

"I already hear sirens. They're coming to put out the fire. It's going to be okay. But I have to go help. This roof won't be safe to be on for long."

"I know."

With his eyes reflecting the torment he felt at leaving her, he pried her fingers from his arms.

"Come right back," she ordered.

"Okay."

"And stay safe, you hear me?"

"I will."

"And Blake. Bring me Blake."

"I promise." He held her gaze for one beat, letting her see into his heart and soul. He never made promises, never, and yet he did now, to her, which meant more than anything he'd ever done. Pretending to be brave, she nodded and then sagged back, covering her face with her hands so she couldn't see the smoke pouring out of the doorway as he vanished into it.

Dammit, she really needed a new script. Aidan was probably worrying about her instead of completely focusing on the fire—and that was dangerous. She forced her eyes open, glued her gaze to the black doorway. He had saved her life on Blake's boat, and that had been amazing, but she could have saved herself. She knew how to swim.

And she could save herself this time.

All she had to do was get past her fear. Any second now...

The sirens were louder now, and that reached her somehow. Tommy was probably nearly here, too. She got to her feet, wiped the sweat from her eyes and headed to her uncle. He'd hit his head on the A/C vent. Turning her back on him, she headed toward the door. "You're a coward," she told herself. "You're fine, you're fine..." She kept up the mantra as she entered the dark doorway. Unable to breathe through the smoke, she pulled her shirt up over her mouth and took another step.

And then it happened. The floor beneath her rumbled, the walls shimmied and shook, and she froze as a second explosion hit, flinging her against a wall. Then the power flickered and went off, leaving her in complete darkness.

Oh, God.

Sitting up, she felt for the railing and pushed herself upright. She was okay. Relatively speaking, anyway.

Just as she began heading down again, the stairs beneath her began rumbling, but not with yet another explosion. This time it was pounding footsteps as someone ran up the stairs, and then reached out toward her. "Kenzie?"

"*Blake?* Ohmigod, Blake, you're okay—"

"Where is he? The chief?" he demanded.

"On the roof."

"Stay here," he commanded. "Stay right here!" And then he rushed up and out.

Like hell. She was going to be proactive this time, dammit. She was rewriting this script her way. And when it was over, she was going to write scripts all damn day long to her heart's content. And eat donuts. Yeah, lots of donuts. Heart pounding, she stumbled after her brother. Bursting back out on the roof, she was horrified to see that part of it had begun to cave in, with flames flickering out from underneath. And standing far too close to that area was Blake, facing off with the chief.

"No," she cried, just as Aidan came out the doorway behind her, looking as if he'd been in a car wreck, all torn and bloody, calling her name hoarsely.

"You're hurt," she cried, rushing to his side.

"The explosion kicked me down the stairs." He hugged her tight, not taking his eyes off the chief and Blake. "I'm okay."

It was like a bad movie, playing in slow motion as the chief leaped for the edge of the roof, and Blake leaped for him the best he could, wrestling him to the ground.

Flames shot up through the floor at all of them and Kenzie screamed, trying to get close to her brother, but Aidan had a hold of her, even though *he* was the one with torn clothing and blood seeping from his various injuries, all covered in soot.

On the ground now, Blake rolled with the chief, the two of them still throwing punches.

"Stay back," Aidan told her, holding onto her. "The flames—"

They were licking at them from all angles now, but suddenly, from below, they were hit with water. Streams of it, coming up from the street.

The fire trucks had arrived, and none too soon as the flames forced Kenzie and Aidan back from yet another cave-in.

"Hold still, you son of a bitch," Blake growled out to the chief, who was trying to crawl free and get to the edge of the roof.

Aidan tried to move around the flames to help Blake with the chief, but suddenly he wavered, then sank to his knees.

"Aidan!"

"Yeah. Think maybe I hit my head before." He blinked at her face as she dropped to her knees in front of him. "There's three of you."

"Oh, God." She touched the gash along his temple, which was bleeding freely. "Hold still!"

"Not a problem."

A ladder and bucket came into view over the roofline, lifted by a crane from below. It held two firefighters, who took one look at Blake and staggered to a shocked halt.

"Later," Blake yelled at them. "I'll explain later! Aidan's down and we need Tommy and some cuffs. Tell me someone has some cuffs!"

IT ACTUALLY WASN'T that easy, nothing ever was, Kenzie thought. Hours later, they were all sitting around Aidan's hospital bed, where he was being held overnight, thanks to a concussion.

The chief had been taken to jail, which was such a huge town scandal that Tommy had left to prepare for a press conference. Sheila was sitting in a chair, her wrist in a sling. It was her only injury, but the café was a complete loss. Dustin was next to her, his arm around her shoulders. Cristina was there, too, holding a bucket full of money from emergency personnel on the scene who'd already poured some of their support into it for Sheila.

"I could go to Hawaii with all that." Tears were thick in Sheila's voice.

"Or you could rebuild," Aidan said from flat on his back.

At the sound of his voice, Kenzie's heart squeezed. He'd been so damn quiet, and she'd been so damn worried.

On the other side of Aidan's bed, Blake stirred. "The chief's in custody," he told Aidan. "And he's not going to get off easy."

Aidan's gaze tracked to Kenzie. "I don't want to get off easy, either." He reached for her hand. "Not tonight, or any night."

She gripped his fingers tightly and pressed them to her aching heart. He was talking, but not making any sense. She hadn't taken a full breath since they'd taken him for X-rays and she didn't take one now. "I'll go get your nurse—"

"No." His grip was like iron. "I'm not crazy."

"I know—"

"Listen to me. You pulled it off, you broke my damn heart. We're even."

Oh, God, and now he was delirious. "Aidan—"

"Maybe we should give them a moment," Dustin said, guiding Sheila out of the room. Cristina followed.

Blake did not leave. "What's going on?"

"I love you back, Kenzie." Aidan managed a smile, although it was crooked. "But I think you already knew that."

"No." She shook her head, finding herself both laughing and crying. "I didn't. I hoped…"

Blake was staring at the two of them, mouth grim. "Wait. Love?"

Aidan, who still hadn't stopped looking into Kenzie's eyes, nodded. "Definitely love."

And just like that, Kenzie took a full breath. God, it felt good to breathe. Breathe and live and love.

"Okay, somebody talk to me," Blake said.

"Well you've been dead, or I'd have told you before now," Kenzie reminded him. "I've been busy trying to make Aidan pay for breaking my heart all those years ago."

At this, Blake blinked, then sent a glacial stare at Aidan. "You broke my sister's heart?"

Aidan winced. "Yeah, but if it helps, I was an idiot."

"He really was," Kenzie agreed.

"And trust me, she got me back," Aidan said. "Her evil plan worked. I fell hard. I love her, Blake." He broke eye contact with Kenzie and looked right at Blake, his smile gone, eyes dead serious. "I love her with everything I've got."

Blake looked as if a good wind could knock him over. "You put your heart out there? *You?*"

Bringing his and Kenzie's still joined hands to his chest, Aidan nodded. "Yeah."

"And then she stomped on it?"

"In boots, with spikes on the soles," Aidan assured him.

Blake took this in and considered, then relaxed. "Okay, then. As long as you're even."

"Not even," Kenzie whispered. "Not yet."

Uncertainty twisted Aidan's features. "Kenzie—"

"We're not even until I get my happily-ever-after." Her throat was so tight she could barely speak. "But since I'm going to be writing, I'm pretty sure I can plot it out for myself."

Aidan's eyes registered both surprise and pride. "You're going to be great at writing. But about that ending... Am I in it?"

"I can guarantee it."

He smiled, and right then, Kenzie knew. She didn't need a script for this, her life, not anymore. The real thing was so much better. Taking the first step, she cupped Aidan's gorgeous face and kissed him.

* * * * *

We hope you enjoyed reading this
special collection from Harlequin® books.

If you liked reading these stories,
then you will love
Harlequin® Blaze® books!

You like it hot!
Harlequin Blaze stories sizzle with strong
heroines and irresistible heroes playing the
game of modern love and lust. They're fun,
sexy and always steamy.

Enjoy four *new* stories from
Harlequin Blaze every month!

Available wherever books and
ebooks are sold.

Red-Hot Reads

www.Harlequin.com

STEPHB

SPECIAL EXCERPT FROM

HARLEQUIN®

Blaze

A wounded Marine returns home and
rekindles a sizzling affair with his first love.
But will their passion be enough to keep him
from returning to a war zone?

Find out next month in

Seducing the Marine

by Kate Hoffmann!

Olivia pressed her hand against Will's chest. She could feel his heart beating, strong and sure, beneath her palm. "We can't do this."

"I know," he said. "But when I touch you, it all makes sense. All of the dark places are filled with light."

She'd made a vow to help him, and now she had to make a choice. If growing closer, more intimate, was what he needed, was she really prepared to refuse him? Especially when she didn't want to? Olivia smoothed her fingers over his naked chest. "We should probably talk about this," she said.

"I don't want to talk," Will murmured. "I want you, Liv. I need you."

Will spun her around and grabbed her waist, then lifted her up to sit on the edge of the kitchen counter. He pressed her back, standing between her legs and deepening his kiss.

HBEXP79831

He was hungry, desperate, and Olivia surrendered to the overwhelming assault. Will pulled her close and then, as if he were uncertain, held her away. But their lips never broke contact. Frustrated by his indecision, she furrowed her fingers through his tousled hair and tightened her grip, refusing to let him go.

"Tell me what you want," he whispered, his lips pressed against the curve of her neck.

Olivia knew exactly what she wanted. She wanted to tear her clothes off, finish undressing Will, then drag him to the nearest bed. She wanted to spend the day discovering all the things she didn't know about him and all the things she'd forgotten. Most of all, she wanted to lose herself in sexual desire.

This wasn't love, she told herself. It was just pure, raw desire…

**Look for SEDUCING THE MARINE
by Kate Hoffmann,
available January 2015 wherever
Harlequin® Blaze® books and ebooks are sold.**

Copyright © 2015 by Peggy A. Hoffmann

HBEXP79831

When it snows, things get really steamy...

Wild Holiday Nights
from Harlequin Blaze offers something sweet, something unexpected and something naughty!

Holiday Rush by *Samantha Hunter*

Cake guru Calla Michaels is canceling Christmas to deal with fondant, batter and an attempted robbery. Then Gideon Stone shows up at her door. Apparently, Calla's kitchen isn't hot enough without having her longtime crush in her bakery...*and* in her bed!

Playing Games by *Meg Maguire*

When her plane is grounded on Christmas eve, Carrie Baxter is desperate enough to share a rental car with her secret high-school crush. Sure, Daniel Barber is much, *much* hotter, but he's still just as prickly as ever. It's gonna be one *looong* drive...and an unforgettably X-rated night!

All Night Long by *Debbi Rawlins*

The only way overworked paralegal Carly Watts gets her Christmas vacation is by flying to Chicago to get Jack Carrington's signature. But Jack's in no rush to sell his grandfather's company. In fact, he'll do whatever it takes to buy more time. Even if it takes one naughty night before Christmas...

Available December 2014 wherever you buy
Harlequin Blaze books.

Red-Hot Reads
www.Harlequin.com

HTHMS1014-5

HARLEQUIN®

A Romance FOR EVERY MOOD™

**Stay up-to-date on all your
romance-reading news with the
Harlequin Shopping Guide,
featuring bestselling authors, exciting new
miniseries, books to watch and more!**

The newest issue will be delivered right to you
with our compliments! There are 4 each year.

Signing up is easy.

EMAIL

ShoppingGuide@Harlequin.ca

WRITE TO US

HARLEQUIN BOOKS
Attention: Customer Service Department
P.O. Box 9057, Buffalo, NY 14269-9057

OR PHONE

1-800-873-8635 in the United States
1-888-343-9777 in Canada

Please allow 4-6 weeks for delivery of the first issue by mail.